Of Air and Fire

The Mora Chronicles, Book One

E. S. Portman

Author's Note

This book contains elements that may be unsettling to some readers, such as violence, violence against children/young adults, anxious thoughts/panic attacks, and mild, near sexual scenes.
Also, this book mentions the word 'nipple' three times. Readers should expect more references, along with several other body parts, in later books within this series. Choice and explicit language is also used prolifically throughout the book.

For all the people who helped me along this journey,
and for all the people who never believed they were good enough
to be everything they never imagined they could be.

This one's for you.

SAANA
FIREBORNE TERRITORIES
NORLANA
FOSCARA
LAKE VIARTA
VIZNA
HYDRASEL
AE
TER
Isles of Avicante
BELANDOR
Hollow Woods
PRYDIA
Shreeve Port
Lake Kree
High
WATERBORNE TERRITORIES
Costa
Highland Mounta
SAPPHIRE SEA
Prynn Springs
SORDUR
Amaliro M
LYSTOS

BOSTE
AELLETHIA
SENTRA
FORGA MARKET
Triad Arena
DAYUK
EARTHBORNE TERRITORIES
IRAMIS
Field of Bones
Torren Valley
Tilvey Mines
Starmere Falls
BURYON
Araros Peaks
Fields of Araros
Krulen Mts
EASRICH
STARMERE

ONE

PAIGE

There she was, appearing more helpless than I ever thought she could be. Though truly, that wasn't saying much. The ever-revolving door of her conditions turned out to be more perturbing for me with each passing year.

But there she was.

My mother was hooked up to what seemed like a million machines, all coercing her to bring her back to her normal self, or hopefully, a better self.

My mother never knew when to quit. She was so headstrong and resilient. What qualities could have made her superwoman turned her cold and dark a long time ago. She chose to close herself off from the world, myself included, and only allowed herself the company of alcohol and the occasional pill or two. She drank all day and all night, frequently attempting to hide the fact by drinking clear alcohol that she could pass off as water. I discovered at an early age that it most certainly was not water.

The thought alone singed my throat.

"Hey, honey." The usual nurse, whose name I couldn't focus long enough on to remember, strode into the room towing a beeping machine behind her. "We need to check her vitals now." I remained in the chair next to her bed, my foot tapping on the tile as I watched as the nurse moved in closer toward my mother.

"Okay ma'am," I rasped, the thought of vodka quenching my mother's thirst for so many years burning in the back of my throat. My eyes landed on the bag of saline that dripped continuously into her veins, and I released a sigh.

Saline, not alcohol. If she gets through this, she will technically be clean. She could start new.

"Why don't you go on home and get you some rest? You've 'bout been here all of two days, haven't you got school or somewhere else to be?" The nurse's words rolled on into the distant corner of the room, my ears only perking up as she mumbled about how sad it was that I had no one to go back home to. She was right in that aspect—I never knew my father, nor did I care to meet the man who left us both before I was born.

But she was also partially wrong. I did have someone, and he was picking me up shortly. "My friend is coming to get me soon," was all I said. I didn't feel like elaborating to Nurse No Name about how I'd graduated the year before, and if anything, I was missing out on work that I couldn't afford to miss. I shifted in my seat, waiting for the nurse to finish her routine and stifling my foot as it seemed to enhance the silence that filled the small room. If only our town were more populated, then maybe there would've been a different nurse on staff, someone who wouldn't remind me of everything I was failing to do. Things that I neglected because I couldn't just leave my mother alone in the hospital all day long.

"You be safe now, hear?" Her forehead crinkled as she gave me the look of agonizing pity, the one I was oh so familiar with. I nodded, although being *safe* was the last thing I needed to work on in my life, and she left the room.

A knuckle tapped against the door a few minutes later. "Coffee?" Aeden asked as he leaned against the door frame, waiting for me to give him the 'okay' to enter. He'd been here to pick me up before, yet he waited by the door each and every time before continuing into the room, a move that was just so...*him*.

I inclined my head and held my arm out to accept one of the paper cups he held onto. "Yes, please. Thank you, for this...and for coming to pick me up. I really appreciate it."

"You're always welcome, you know." He slid into the seat next to mine and took a sip of his coffee. His free hand went up, slicking back medium-length, dark brown locks that fell around his forehead and almost covered his eyes. "I can wait here longer if you need more time." His brows furrowed with worry through the few remaining wavy tendrils of hair, but I shook my head and took a sip from my cup.

"No, I could use a shower." I stood up from the chair and walked over to my mother, placing my cup on the table before bending down to kiss her lightly on her cheek as the intubation tube pumped more air into her lungs. "I'll be back, Mom," I whispered into her ear, then turned abruptly and took a step right into Aeden, who'd just gotten up from his chair. His arms shot out to either side of me, his muscles flexing as I knocked into one of them. He held me there for a moment and my heart skipped a beat as I peered up at him, the golden flecks in his dark brown eyes shining against the harsh fluorescent lighting until he flicked his gaze away and dropped his arms.

He cleared his throat and raked his fingers through his hair again. "Have you eaten anything today?" he asked, looking me over first before swinging backward to pick up his coffee from the side table he'd left it on.

I bit down on my bottom lip, thinking of what I'd managed to eat, but it wasn't much. The nurse had forced me into ordering something from the hospital's menu, but when it came, my stomach turned sour. Not that I wasn't hungry, or that I didn't appreciate that I was being fed. But I couldn't shut off my thoughts, and watching my mother next to me as I was able to eat freely made me feel almost *guilty*. I knew I shouldn't, but I did.

As if my thoughts were written on my face, Aeden dropped his shoulders and let out a sigh. "I'll get you something from my house, I still have a lot of leftovers from last night." I nodded my head once, not wanting to turn down more food. It would be unhealthy to continue turning down food and my stomach started twisting at the thought, demanding I accept the offer.

Aeden took one final sip of his coffee, then tossed the empty cup into the trash can. Just as I picked up my cup again before walking out of the room, the door flew open and I turned to see an old man standing in the doorway, holding a bouquet of lilies and roses. His eyes grew wide while he fumbled his grip on the handle, his obsidian black eyes roaming over us in an almost predacious way.

"Can I help you?" I asked as his eyes continued to search over me thoroughly, making the hairs rise on my arms as the black pools stroked up and down the length of them.

Aeden took a step closer to me. "I'm sorry, I must have the wrong room," he clarified, then he turned and walked away.

"The way he was looking at you was...odd," Aeden whispered as his eyes lingered on the abandoned doorway. I had to agree with him, but he could have just as easily been an elderly person who was genuinely confused.

"Those were my mom's favorites, the flowers he was holding. I thought maybe they were for her, from someone in town who...well, never mind. They weren't," I said as the last bit of hope I had that someone else may have cared about my mom sank into the cold tile beneath my feet. I'd frequently suggested moving away from here, getting a fresh start for her. Maybe then she'd be able to make friends who weren't swayed by town gossip, people who would support her in her sobriety that I imagined came with new beginnings. A chance at happiness. It was a dream of mine. A big one. But it was something my mother was adamant against doing and forcing her to do something she didn't want, well, there was no chance in hell it would happen if she didn't agree. And then I met Aeden and the desire to move started to shrink into the background.

"Wait right here," Aeden said, but before I could tell him to stop, he was out the door and down the hall. Moments later he came running right back, almost bumping into me as I neared the door. "I couldn't find the guy anywhere. Figured he might not mind parting with a few of the flowers from his giant bouquet, and with the way he was looking at you, it would be the *least* he could do."

"You didn't have to do that. Besides, she wouldn't know about it until the doctors decide to wake her up." I shuffled my feet, feeling the hole in the sole of my shoe. "They'd probably be wilted by then." I doubted she would be awake within a week or two like they'd suggested. I hadn't seen my mom recover from something in a long time, and never from something like this. Even if she did wake up, I had to wonder if she would keep her sobriety and turn her life around after it was all over with.

Probably not.

Aeden pressed his lips into a thin line, choosing silence as he fell into step beside me down the hall toward the exit. As we turned to go down the last corridor, an elderly man stepped out in front of us in a hospital gown, clutching onto a walker complete with tennis balls on the bottom. "Sorry, I didn't mean—" I stopped in place and my words froze on my tongue as I looked up to see the same man from before.

"Isn't that...the same guy?" Aeden whispered behind his hand as he leaned toward me. It did look *exactly* like him, only this man's eyes were a pale blue color, and the man before had nearly black eyes. Of that, I was certain. A prickle went down my spine just thinking about those eyes.

"Maybe it's his brother? It explains the flowers and his confusion when he saw me," I suggested. "I mean, I don't look anything like *him*." I swooped my arm down over the length of me, and Aeden cocked his eyebrow and the corner of his mouth went up with it.

"Right...yeah, okay." Aeden drew a thumb over his bottom lip as we watched the man walk away slowly, using every ounce of strength he had to hold onto the walker to support his frail body.

The ride home was only twenty minutes or so from the hospital and Aeden and I had opted for a bit of silence. I rolled the window down as I sat in the passenger seat and relished in the calming atmosphere as Aeden's older sedan hummed each time he shifted gears. As I gazed beyond the rolled-down car window, the pine trees swayed in the approaching dusk wind. There was something about the breeze whipping through my long hair and the sun setting just over the tops of the lowest trees that made even the darkest of days seem like a faint memory. I took it all in, acknowledging how freeing it felt. The serene ambiance calmed my thoughts and helped me push down all the feelings of being lost, alone, and afraid. All the darkest parts of my life were tossed to the wind.

Aeden broke the silence just a few blocks before we made it to our street. "There is a party going on at one of the frat houses, a few of the guys on the team will be there." I flicked my eyes to him, his knuckles turning white as he flexed his hands on the steering wheel. I thought for a moment, and then he continued, "If you don't want to go, that's fine. You know how I feel about parties anyways."

"Yeah, let's go," I said, trying my best to plaster on a smile but the tugging on my cheeks felt strained and my smile fell flat.

"Are you sure? I can stay at your house with you instead if you'd rather just..."

I bobbed my head. "No, yeah. I'm sure." A party was a distraction, and if alcohol was involved—which knowing frat guys, it definitely was—then that would only double the distraction. It was something I probably shouldn't indulge in but I felt the desperate need to get out of my head for a while.

His brows furrowed together. "I just wish I could have been home that day, you know, to help your mom. I was working later than usual, and—"

"You can't possibly blame yourself for not being there to help my mom not get hit by a car, Aeden. That's insane," I blurted out, slightly frustrated that he felt even a modicum of guilt over my mother and her antics. Sure, it wasn't her fault, but she could have waited for me to get the mail. It wasn't like she paid the bills when they came in, and she didn't have any friends left that gave a damn, to my knowledge. What on Earth could've been so important for her to leave the house, let alone do it so sloppily that she hadn't checked the road before crossing, was a mindfuck. It was a big part of what'd made me toss and turn these past few nights, unable to make it make any sense.

Nothing about her made sense though, and I had to remind myself, and apparently Aeden as well, of that fact.

"I can, and I do. If I was there, then—"

"Then what, Aeden? You can't be everyone's knight in shining armor. She did what she did, and that's not on anyone else but herself and the driver of that car. Now please, stop worrying so much about me," I begged.

"Okay, then." Aeden ran his fingers through his hair with one hand while he pulled into my driveway. "I'm going to grab a few things and heat up a plate for you and then I'll be back. Take your time." He stepped out of the car and I followed suit, each of us walking up to our respective porches.

The doorknob clicked open without the use of a key because I rarely locked up my house, something Aeden scolded me for on more than one occasion. I didn't feel like anyone would bother to rob us, being there was nothing of value to take to begin with. I heard him laugh as he stood on his porch, watching me as I stood in the doorway. "Really?" he huffed out, then shook his head and walked inside. I grinned to myself a bit, knowing I would get more shit from him for that, but we didn't own anything that would be worthwhile to steal, and I'd already pawned anything that was as I tried to make ends meet for my mother and me. There really was no reason to bar anyone from coming in, especially when the only person who did was him.

And I wasn't about to stop that from happening.

The only thing of value in our small home was a photo I kept up in the hallway, not that anyone would value it but me and maybe my mother when she was in between drinks and pills. As I walked past the living room and into the kitchen, I saw that photo—my mom and I on my eighth birthday. She was so beautiful that day—her blonde hair melting over her vibrant emerald eyes that resembled my own, her glowing sun-kissed skin perfectly complemented by a white knee-length sundress. I hadn't seen her like that in ages. That was one of the happiest days of my life, or maybe it *was* the happiest day of my life. What I would *give* to have her be that radiant again. The way she smiled at the camera was breathtaking, the rewards of successfully committing to a rehab program for more than a single month. I tried my best not to linger any more than I was on that photo and quickly shifted my focus to the shower.

Setting the heat on full blast while I undressed caused the windows to fog in mere minutes. I considered myself in the mirror through the few patches that had yet to fog over completely, and I couldn't look away. I looked so much like her that it was almost eerie at times, and catching myself with my hair down only made the resemblance stand out. Thinking of her pulled out feelings that had started to consume me, pointing out how lonely I had grown to be and the sadness lingering within the deepest parts of me. I was all by myself, and in a way, I had always been that way. I turned away as the last bit of fog rolled over the mirror, pushing those thoughts down, and climbed into the shower, trying to leave the pain behind while soaking in the hot steam.

As I climbed in, I remembered the man with near-black eyes at the hospital and touched my arm, thinking of how his eyes fixated there.

What the hell was he looking at?

There was nothing on my arm but I felt like I was going crazy racking my brain for what that encounter even was. Was he looking me over because he thought one of us was supposed to be the man we saw in the hallway? And if he were at the hospital for that man, where was he while the other man was walking around with his walker? I shook my head, knowing it was dumb to reminisce on such a minute moment, and pushed it out of my thoughts.

As I was pulling on a pair of jean shorts and a tank top, I heard the clicking of the door as it opened and shut again, a few footfalls following after. "I'll be right out!" I shouted while I brushed through my hair, making the waves scrunch up in my palms. The freckles that usually dotted my cheeks were faint due to the lack of sun from being in the hospital for days on end, but I let them shine through. I didn't bother with makeup most of the time anyway, and tonight was no exception.

I came out of the room to see a plate of leftovers laid out on the kitchen counter, complete with a fork and napkin, while Aeden sat on the couch. He was waiting for me, his long athletic legs bent over the edge of the dingy couch. I swallowed thickly as I took note of his swelling veins which formed ridges like rippling waves as they pressed up against the suntanned skin of his arms, stretching to either side of the back of the couch. His attractiveness was so effortless, almost god-like but in a rugged, grungy way. His hair was never brushed, save for what his fingers did, and his skin was worn from working in the sun and playing football for hours at a time, which also made him broad and muscular. It also, notoriously, drove many girls wild. He jerked his stubbled chin, guiding my sight back to the plate of food as my stomach started to knot—over the food or Aeden, I wasn't sure.

"You should eat, I put the rest in the fridge if you want more," Aeden said, his eyes lingering between me and the plate of spaghetti and meatballs he'd left out for me.

I gathered up the warm plate and walked up to the couch, sliding down next to him. His muscles tensed slightly before I began eating, trying hard not to eat it as fast as my stomach demanded but ended up failing at that miserably. I distracted myself, thinking about how the years of football training certainly paid off for him in more ways than one as I glanced at the way he tossed his head back against the couch.

He was granted a full-ride scholarship for four years to play football at Bunnell University, one of the top schools in the country. Yet, why Aeden decided to live off-campus, nearly half an hour away from Bunnell in the smallest town possible was a complete mystery to me. He was much deeper, more down-to-earth, and genuine than the average person would have assumed, and it was something that drew me to him time and time again.

I finished my plate and put it down on the coffee table, sinking myself back into the couch. Aeden shifted his head to face me, his hair falling over his forehead and framing his eyes that caught a small glint of light from the sconce above, catching the flecks of gold that floated there. "You don't deserve this," he breathed out while his eyes made slow movements around every bit of my face. I didn't know if he meant the lack of food that he must have seen in the fridge, yet again, or my mother and all the issues that came with that. Or maybe, it was everything. I caught my breath when his eyes stopped briefly on my lips, but then he cleared his throat and looked away, sending my hopes to the ground. He was here to comfort me like the amazing friend he was, and I was here admiring his beauty, not that it would get me far. He definitely wasn't into me like I was into him.

"I don't know, Aeden." I sighed. "Sometimes I feel like I must have done something really wrong to land me here. Maybe I drove her to start drinking. Maybe it was all my fault—"

"No. It was never and will never be your fault." He drew a finger under my chin and spoke softly, "I'll always be right next door if you need anything, or just want to talk." He flicked his finger from my chin and smiled solemnly. "I'm right here for you." He always knew what to say, how to make me forget about how distraught I was.

How was he so perfect?

Aeden stood and took up my empty plate, walked it to the sink, and began washing it. It took every ounce of willpower that I had to not stand up and tell him to stop, make him see that he was catering to me and my crap way too much. But instead, I let the mindset of having a friend who cared try to take over while I put my head in my hands, my elbows propped against my thighs. I'd lose that fight anyway.

"The people in town are already talking, I'm sure." I started chewing on my bottom lip, thinking of all the things I would hear around town once the night was over and I had to go back out again. It was inevitable.

Aeden turned the sink off, drying his hands on an old rag he fished out from a drawer. I didn't even know where we kept the towels in the kitchen, but he did. Turning his head just over his shoulder, he lowered his tone as he grumbled, "If I hear anyone talk about you or your mom, I will waste them."

We pulled up to a secluded two-story home, frat letters leaning on the lawn and navy-blue streamers wrapped around the columns by the front door. There were several guys I'd recognized from going to Aeden's games as his teammates, running around shirtless on the long front porch, beer bottles taped to their fists with duct tape. Aeden parked and I looked at the time. It was almost nine p.m.

We got out of the car and rounded the side of the house, going to the backyard where three keg stands were taking place. Someone was shouting a count of twelve seconds as we approached and I glanced back at Aeden right away, our eyes meeting as he lit up with the prospect of a challenge. The girl doing the keg stand was the first to go down at fifteen seconds, followed by the two large football players wearing their Bunnell jerseys falling in unison at twenty-four seconds.

"Hey Flynn, get your ass up here!" slurred one of the two football guys who had just finished their stand as he gestured for Aeden. His jersey read

'Little' in bold white letters and I laughed at the irony. He threw a wink my way as Aeden bent down to grab hold of the keg with both hands.

"You too, doll face," Little cooed, and Aeden jerked his head in the direction of his teammate, eyes darkening as he glowered at him. I took hold of the keg next to him as Aeden was lifted into the air by his ankles, unable to interject as I followed with Little holding my legs up for me. Little gave me a smirk when I tossed my head over my shoulders, then I turned back around and put the spout into my mouth. My skin prickled as he rubbed his thumb along my ankle, making me feel almost dirty before he shouted, "Chug!"

And the count began.

I lasted a whole sixteen seconds before I tapped out and Aeden tapped out at twenty-six seconds in, eyeing me for the last ten seconds as I stood and watched him. The party whooped Aeden's last name as he won and I joined in, pumping my fist in the air. Little was behind me toasting his beer up to Aeden, landing his other hand on my shoulder. I turned my head to glance up at him, my eyes following the trail of tribal tattoos up a foot or more above me to where it felt like I was looking toward the heavens for divine intervention. There was no denying that Little was hot, in a way that he would be on the cover of a magazine covered in only whipped cream and it would sell millions of copies. But I forced that thought from my mind.

"Let me get you a drink, beautiful." Little rasped into my ear and dragged his finger up along my neck. Aeden was being greeted by the shirtless football guys, each one slapping their hand to his before going in for that 'bro-hug' embrace.

"No thanks, Little," I refused and turned my head to the side, choosing not to face him directly. I didn't like hooking up just for the hell of it, especially not at parties that Aeden took me to. But when alcohol was involved, it was inevitable not to consider. Aeden usually got the attention of several women very quickly, leaving me to my own devices.

"The name is Richard, or Dick if you like." His breath was coated in a thick fog of alcohol and orange Tic-Tacs, all rolling out of his mouth at once. I couldn't hold myself back from the immediate roar of laughter that left my lungs.

His name was Dick Little.

"Are you normally successful in picking up women by telling them your name is Dick Little?" I deadpanned.

"Sweetheart, there is nothing *little* about me," he purred. The alcohol was beginning to kick in and it became obvious that I didn't normally drink that much in such a short time. Little placed his hand on my lower back to steady me, and it was either the alcohol or the fact that Dick was hot that made heat spread across my stomach.

I glanced to check on Aeden, who was now surrounded by three walking pairs of boobs holding shots up to him through the sliding glass door, his face practically glowing against the cheesy neon lights that hung on the wall inside as each one of them vied for his attention. It was hard to remind myself that we were only friends, but he looked well enough occupied and there was no need for me to keep waiting for him to make a move that was never coming.

"Lead the way, Dick." I let out a heavy sigh, giving Dick my hand as I spun around to face him, knowing it was probably a bad thing to do but also knowing I just needed to get out of my head tonight. I needed to forget about everything.

If Dick was going to help me do that, then I'd let him.

Two

AEDEN

Twenty-six seconds. I chugged for twenty-six seconds straight, leaving my head in the clouds and my body desirable to girls just as trashed as I was going to be once the alcohol took its full effect on me.

A few more drinks couldn't hurt.

I didn't come here to hook up with any girls—especially not since I brought the only girl I wanted. I wanted to make sure she was going to have a good time, let loose, and forget her problems. And bringing her to this boozy party full of frat guys was the first thing that came to my mind.

What a complete idiot.

Her mom was an alcoholic and I brought her here to get sloshed with me, a whole lot of sense that fucking made. I should have just pushed the offer to stay at her house with her, comfort her, and listen to her talk about whatever she wanted to talk about. Hell, she could talk about all the books she read for all I cared and I would think it was the most enthralling conversation because anything that came out of her mouth pulled me right in. But every time I thought about Paige, I couldn't keep my mind straight. My thoughts swam, leaving me completely at her mercy.

I had to catch myself every time I found that I was looking at her for too long—at the way she smiled so genuinely when she saw me or how she twirled her honey-brown hair around her fingers when she was reading. Saying she was pretty was an insult. She was beyond stunning, beyond a measurable quality that others would use to define how pretty a woman is. No, she was absolute perfection personified. And yet, she never seemed to notice how my breath hitched when she came near me, or how I couldn't keep away from her. To me, she was everything—to her, I was a decent neighbor and friend. And it sucked.

I knew her life was complicated. Her mother's health was constantly in decline the more and more she drank away her existence. How a mother could be so callous to such an extraordinary person I had yet to understand. Paige wasn't just beautiful, she was also brilliant in the nerdiest, hottest way I'd ever seen. She was well-read, top of her class by the time she graduated, and learned about random topics whenever she could. She even asked to borrow my college textbooks which I happily lent to her, seeing as she couldn't go to college with everything her mother needed from her. She could probably tutor me in my classes if I needed the help, but I got by enough to keep my place at Bunnell.

Anytime I wanted to show Paige a little more of my true intentions, she seemed to have another issue arise and it took precedence over my own feelings. Her recent trauma with her mom getting hit by a car out of nowhere was just another large stone added to the pot of overwhelming shit she had to deal with. She was also constantly taking care of their house because her mother was unable to do much for them. The girl lived off of freezer food and rarely had a home-cooked meal unless I made something and brought it over whenever I wasn't out working, training, or being in classes that droned on and on. She loved when I cooked for her and I loved taking care of her in that way. It gave me goosebumps seeing her happy, and I tried to make it a habit to bring about that happiness for her as much as I could.

If it wasn't football practice or classes that pulled me from being with her every day, it was working whatever job I picked up to earn enough to rent the house next to her. No one was helping me, which was something I was used to. My last foster family seemed to have a burden lifted the second I turned eighteen. They may have fed, clothed me, and put a roof over my head but they took no interest in me and rarely acknowledged my existence. I could have been much worse off, but finding the one house for rent in the tiniest town I could was the best escape into my adulthood that I could've ever dreamed of. Throw in the football scholarship, and I was set.

My hazy eyes darted around the now-crowded living room of the frat house until they finally settled on Paige. She was standing against the kitchen island with my teammate, Dick Little, who negated his name at any chance he got, boasting an exuberant confidence about his size and making it a point to anyone who could hear him to note that his dick was huge. Didn't matter if we were half fucking naked in the locker room, he always made big dick jokes.

This can't be good.

I knew exactly where his mind was at, and judging by his lingering proximity and his occasional groping at her waist, I knew I couldn't let her be near *him*. His hands were getting dangerously close to areas that no other man should be taking his liberties with.

I tilted my beer back, the act of lifting it more and more giving my eyes a better vantage point beyond the girls who were throwing themselves at me. And every time I took a swig, the girls in front of me disappeared from view as well, leaving only Paige.

Bonus.

"Bottoms up, beautiful." Dick Little's voice carried over the thudding music as he caressed Paige's waist from behind her, holding her too fucking close to him as she grabbed the shot from the island and took it in one swift movement. Seeing her with someone else sent a jolt through my body and made my hand clench around my bottle.

I was never great at keeping my emotions at bay, much less controlling the urge to punch someone once I learned just how strong I was after the first fight I'd ever been in ended with the guy on the floor, begging me to stop. It wasn't something I boasted about, not like Dick would if the question ever came up, though I'm sure many could prove him wrong there as well. He may have been a big dude but he was all talk, and I heard his dick was fucking tiny. Paige would end up thoroughly disappointed and I would be livid if I didn't end this shit now.

I set the beer bottle down on the nearest table and moved away from the three blondes too suddenly for them to speak against it as I stalked toward the kitchen island. Paige turned to face Little who looked down at her, heedless to my oncoming approach. Her body swayed slowly against his to the thumping rhythm of the house music as he started to bend down to kiss her, reaching his hands down to cup her ass.

Hell no.

"Paige, let's go," I ordered and reached out to tug her shoulder back, stopping Dick's advancements on her face and any further attempts at groping her. My eyes darted down at him, burning with an intensity that told him to back the fuck off.

"I'm having fun with Dick Little," she slurred and giggled, pointing up at Dick and emphasizing his name as she glanced down at his crotch. *Shit,* how many shots could he have possibly given to her? A few other people around the island seemed to freeze in their tracks, their eyes landing on the ensuing altercation.

"Hey Flynn, what's the problem?" Dick piped up and threw on an apologetic face, removing his hands from Paige's ass and snapping his head away from her as he noticed my fists clenching. I stood a few inches taller than him, and he saw the training that I went through to be the best quarterback Bunnell University had seen in decades. He knew he would lose a fight quickly if this escalated. He was the second-string linebacker on my team, and we both knew the differences between us were vast when it came down to sheer force and power. It would be a sign of pure idiocy if he didn't relent.

Paige folded her arms in revolt and eyed me up and down, almost daring me to do something about the man who was two seconds away from taking her on the kitchen island just seconds before.

"We are leaving, *now*," I raised my voice in retort, standing my ground firmly, fists ready to fly the minute he tried to continue even thinking about hooking up with Paige tonight, or any other night for that matter.

She let out a drunken sigh and shrugged as she looked up at Little and put up a sloppy hand to guide him backward and away from her, the movement like she was flicking away a pesky fly, not a guy a foot taller than her. She turned to me and pouted as she held out her other hand for me. I unfurled my fists, my arms still pulsing with the readiness to fight off the fondling tool looking at me with terror in his eyes as an understanding set in. She was *mine*, and no one else had the right to touch her. Something she was still so infuriatingly oblivious to, though the alcohol was making it worse. I closed my fingers gently around hers, leading her away from the party and out through the front door.

THREE

PAIGE

Aeden led me back out from the frat house and down the long driveway to his car, his growls of disapproval audible just over the thudding bass echoing from inside. He tried to let me into the passenger side door but I rushed in front of him and leaned against it with my back on the door to face him instead. He stood there glaring down at me, the heat of his anger radiating down my spine making goosebumps prickle on my skin.

His deep brown eyes were locked on mine, his jaw tight with rage. I put my arms down and pressed my palms against his car to stabilize myself, the weight of the alcohol becoming overwhelming under the weight of his silence and the way he stared at me like I was the one who did something wrong. Aeden wasn't acting like my friend at all, and I needed to know what his problem was before I set foot in his car.

"How much did that asshole give you to drink?" He stepped closer to me and pressed his hands to the top of the car on either side of me, his fingers sprawled out as he consumed more of my space, caging me in. He left only a few inches between his chest and my face until his chin dipped down, taking that allowance as well. The intensity of his anger was beyond anything I had ever seen from him, sobering me up slightly but not enough to wipe away my own anger from the situation. What did it matter to him if I was with Dick? He was with women at the party too, having a good time. Or that's what it looked like when I went to take shots with Dick.

He kept his gaze fixed on my eyes, his muscles flexing with tension visible through his white t-shirt. I didn't know whether I should be apologizing for making him so upset or pushing his question back into his face, even if the look he gave to Dick and me inside promised to burn down anything, and anyone, in his path. He had no reason to demand an answer about my sobriety with a guy while he was off doing the same thing.

"Probably as much as you drank with those blondes," I goaded. "We were drinking, and having fun, just like you were. Did *I* do something *wrong*?" The words came exploding out of me as I snapped at him, unable to hold his intensity for much longer as his lips hovered just above me and pursed in contemplation, making it hard to think—to *breathe*.

He let out a massive exhale and lowered his head to the ground, his pushed-back hair falling and brushing against my forehead. His anger visibly dropped several notches which finally brought him back down to Earth. The veins in his arms stopped pulsing furiously at me, and he rolled his head and shoulders back, so they no longer stayed up by his ears.

With his arms still on either side of me, he lifted his head. "I just don't want you getting mixed up with...*him*. I've been drinking too, Paige, but do you see me trying to take advantage of you?" His eyes darkened and his jaw tensed as the thought must have sent him over the edge again. Was he *jealous* of Dick Little?

"Why does it matter to you? You're my friend Aeden, not my boyfriend." I remained firm like a fortress that wouldn't give, unwavering to his sudden jealousy over me being with his friend.

He winced noticeably and his eyebrows furrowed together, not at all trying to hide how he felt at that moment. I hurt him. And truthfully, it hurt me too. But dammit if I didn't have the right to be mad at him. He never said we were anything more than friends, and I knew he hooked up with random girls, or at least it appeared that way. Why should that stop me from doing the same?

If I couldn't have fun with his friend, he needed to give me a damn good reason why. Now my only prospects of forgetting all of my problems tonight were my couch and my books, and eventually, inevitably, crying myself to sleep. Option one with Dick Little sounded much more appealing. *Tonight was going to suck and it would be his fault.*

"Friend, huh." He scratched at his stubbled cheek, rubbing at the sweet muscle that kept ticking as if he were contemplating his next move. He threw his hand back against the car and leaned in closer, brushing his nose against mine and sending heat to my cheeks. "Is that what you *want* me to be? A *friend?*"

My mind needed no time to confirm what my mouth refused to say out loud. Of course, I wanted more from him. But we were drunk, and I was pissed at him, though it was hard to say which emotion was more overpowering. Just as I put my hands up to push him away or tug him in closer, I wasn't sure which, his mouth crashed into mine.

Decision made.

I pulled him in closer, my hands roaming over his thin t-shirt, tracing over the hard lines of his stomach. I'd never felt so unhinged before. His hands broke the cage he built around us as he wrapped one hand around my neck, sending shivers down my thighs. His thumb dug into my jaw as his lips pressed into me harder, wilder, matching my ferocity with his own. But it wasn't enough and I could hear his groan as if he needed more. Aeden's fingers moved to cup the back of my neck, reaching his fingers up into my hair and tugging, making my head tilt up further and I moaned against his lips. *Perfect. He was so—*

My phone started to ring and after the third one, I let out a breathy laugh, easing our pace with small pecks along his cheek before stopping entirely. His head hung over my neck, rubbing his nose along my throbbing pulse as I fumbled for the phone in my pocket. I answered, sliding a sloppy finger over the cracked screen before fully acknowledging who was calling.

It was the hospital.

"Hello, may I please speak to Ms. Paige Johnson?" The soothing voice sobered me immediately as I turned away from Aeden's caress and pressed my side into the car.

No, no, no.

"This is sh—she, is everything...alright?" I stuttered, slowing my words down, unable to grasp what I already knew in my heart. The hospital never called if someone was doing well. Aeden's hand squeezed my shoulder as it tensed, letting me know he wasn't going anywhere.

"No dear, I'm sorry to inform you that your mother passed away a few minutes ago. We need you to come in as soon as you can. I am deeply sorry for your loss—" My fingers fell slack and the phone dropped to the grass by my feet.

Everything around me blurred and my ears began to ring. My legs buckled beneath me like the ground had given way and was taking no prisoners. Aeden caught me as I fell backward into him, and he steadied me as we sank to the ground together, our bodies dragging down the side of the car together. I didn't need to turn to feel his eyes burrowing deep holes over my shoulder with worry, searching for an answer before he edged back into the grass and moved my head into his lap. His lips were moving above me but I couldn't concentrate on a single word he said. The ringing, the pain. The emptiness. It was all too much.

When it finally died, Aeden's words faded in. He was saying my name, over and over, waving his hand in front of my face. *Blink.*

"My mom's dead," I let out through ragged breaths as if the air in my lungs was taken from me as well. He immediately lifted me and wrapped my body into his arms as he pulled me close. I buried my head into his neck as I sat with my legs wrapped around his torso, letting sobs escape and tear their way through my throat. I wanted to scream, and he was ready to let me hurl every emotion his way as he held me firmly against him.

"I'm here, I'm...fuck, I'm here," he whispered softly, ceaselessly, reminding me as I continued my onslaught of sadness and utter grief. I felt my heart ripping apart and my stomach sinking to my feet as I grappled with the fact that my mother was no longer with me. Aeden gripped me tighter in his embrace and I crumbled further into him.

We remained there for what must have been close to an hour before I finally attempted to move from Aedens' warmth and security. I needed to be strong, but it was so damn hard to settle on the thought that plagued me for years becoming a reality. I knew she wouldn't live long with the way that she lived, but I was always hopeful she could change. Now she wouldn't have that chance ever again and it ripped me apart. Part of me felt responsible. I didn't do enough, didn't say enough to change her and right her wrongs. I was working on getting a second job, somewhere out of town that would pay more, and I was going to get her the help she needed desperately. I was going to fix everything for us, for *her*. Now it was only me. And I didn't know where to go from here.

I quieted myself, still sitting on Aeden's lap, the throbbing in my head and weakness in my body settling into a hollow feeling. He helped to ease me from the bend of his neck, cradling my face delicately with both of his hands. He knelt his head down and swept his lips across the top of my head.

"I'm not going anywhere," he whispered as his lips pressed down against my hair, his thumbs making soothing circles on my cheeks lined with tears. "Let's get you home."

He lifted me in his arms and didn't put me down until I was settled in the passenger seat, even reaching over me to buckle me in as I sat numbly in the seat. The alcohol seemed to have faded from Aeden faster than it did from me as he slid into the driver seat and expertly maneuvered the car backward from the frat house, dodging several parked cars in the dark. He rolled the windows down, glancing at me several times while I leaned against the door panel, unable to speak or think clearly.

"I'll take you to the hospital when you're ready, just tell me when." He didn't push any further conversation or put any music on to drown out the dark. We just sat in silence the rest of the drive home while my thoughts waged on. Between the death of my mother and the burn I still felt on my lips as we drove on, I didn't know what to think or how to feel.

Pulling up to my house, where we'd left from hours before, felt like I was returning to nothingness. Bleak and utter darkness spread through me as the thought that my life's purpose and drive hindered so much on helping my mother—everything meticulously thought out and planned for to keep our house, keep us fed, and keep her from getting worse before I could try to make her better. And now, where was I supposed to go from here? Was I supposed to make a new life for myself here?

And what about that *kiss*?

I rubbed at my temples as I fought against the alcohol that tore at my mind. The sound of the passenger door whooshed open before I realized Aeden had left his seat to come open my door, his forehead creasing as I looked up at him.

"Let me help you," he commanded as he leaned down to unbuckle me and tugged me up by my arms. The weight of my body became foreign as gravity took hold of my legs. Aeden caught me before I fell to the ground and I let out a groan.

"Fuck, Paige." He hesitated, glancing between me and the door, my head throbbing more as I looked up at him through slitted, swollen eyes as the tears threatened to come back again. "I'm going to carry you inside. Did you leave it unlocked again?"

I nodded and his lips curled in as he refrained from scolding me about it while he carried me up the stairs and into the house, then walked me into my bedroom, laying me down on the bed. "Stay right here," he instructed, and I fell against the pillow and groaned more, holding back the urge to throw up and cry at the same time. I felt hollow and woozy all in one. Aeden came back with a glass of water and urged me to sit up and finish the entire glass, tipping it back by the base as he held it up to my mouth and mumbled things about Dick that weren't very pleasant. I couldn't tell if my nausea was from drinking so many shots or from crying so damn hard but it didn't matter as the water rushed down my throat.

I grabbed the glass from his hands, taking it shakily into my own. "Thanks. I'm sorry for all of this. You can go back to the party if you want, I'll be okay here," I said as I finished the last sip and placed the empty glass down on the nightstand.

"There isn't anywhere else I'd rather be than by your side right now," he said gently, reaching his hand up to rub a thumb along my cheek as he took my face in his hand and I wondered how the hell he managed to go from drunk to caretaker so fast and how he looked so good doing both of those things.

"I don't want you to go, but, I can't—" I stopped myself, not wanting to insinuate whatever that kiss meant for him or if I could fully grasp what it meant to me. All I knew was that I felt empty and my heart ached in ways I could've never imagined before. I desperately wanted there to be nothing else in my heart than what our kiss should have done to me, but it waged a heavy war inside of me with the conflicting pain of losing my mother. And I was losing that battle tonight.

He took a seat next to me on the bed, looking down at me with heavy eyes. "I don't expect anything from you, you know that, right?" He paused, his thumb moving to the edge of my mouth before he withdrew his hand and dropped it on the bed beside me. "The last thing I want is to make things harder for you," he whispered, unable to meet my eyes this time. My heart tore at the pain that I might've been causing my best friend to go through before it settled on ripping apart again and again as thoughts of my mother burst through the seams.

"I know," I said as I shook my head. "Stay. Please," I breathed out as I tried to compel more words to come to me that could explain how I was feeling about everything, give him some sort of validation that I wanted him, but I just couldn't muster up anything more than those two words.

His shoulders sagged and his head dipped low as he stared at his feet, taking in my request. He stood up slowly from the bed and turned, giving me a faint smile as his eyes finally found mine then grabbed the blanket from the foot of the bed and pulled it up as I laid down.

"I'll take the couch. If you need anything, anything at all, I'll be here." His hand reached to the back of his neck just below where his unkempt hair fell as he sighed while I nodded my head. His feet shuffled toward the door and part of me wanted to stand up and run to him, grab his hands, and pull him back into the bed with me, to lay next to me all night while I tried to feel something more than the agony that tore through me. But that would be selfish, and Aeden didn't deserve that.

He froze by the door, looking me over once more before my mind stopped racing and for a moment we just stared at each other, the softness in his gaze steadying my heart as it tried to piece itself together. He broke our matched gaze as he dipped his head and then turned again, shutting the door softly and leaving me alone to process the many thoughts that I knew I couldn't keep pushing down. Sobs rolled through me the moment the door clicked shut and I cried myself to sleep, the rawness of every emotion of the night taking its bitter hold over me.

FOUR

AEDEN

Her cries and whimpers echoed through the hall and into the living room as I paced helplessly in front of the couch. I should be in there, holding her, or doing something more than just being in the next room waiting for her to let me back in. But since I had to go and fucking kiss her tonight I doubted she wanted even more to worry about. And I didn't want to be the asshole who kept her from crying and feeling everything that she needed to feel. Even though she'd just used me as her own personal pillow *slash* punching bag after she got the news, I knew she needed this time on her own. If I dared to go back into her room, to take this time away from her, I'd only feel more guilty than I already did.

But it fucking killed me.

I could almost feel her troubles coursing through her as the sounds of her tossing in her bed set me more on edge. I wanted to protect her, to keep her from ever feeling alone and let down. *But isn't that what I was doing by staying out in the living room and not going to her?* Or would I be causing more stress and more pain by laying next to her, taking her into my arms as I'd dreamed of so many times? Only, this isn't how I pictured us being together. I couldn't save her from the pain she was going through, that was something I was told only time could do.

I'd never lost anyone close to me because I never had anyone close to me to lose. I was too young to remember anyone caring about me the way that a parent only could before going into foster care, and the people who fostered me over the years never cared about me. I'd seen Paige go through times where it was almost like she had already lost her mother, when her mother would dive even deeper into the alcohol and pills and she would neglect Paige and her existence so much that I could tell she'd been crying the nights before. Her suffering pulled at my chest, and those mornings I'd seen her like that, with her eyes puffy and her face pale when I'd bring her breakfast, made me want to storm into her mother's room and demand that she fix her shitty life for the sake of her daughter. But I knew that anger would be misplaced and that at her mother's core, someone must've fucked her up pretty badly for her to act the way she did, and nothing I could say or do would ever fix her. I'd kept trying to remind Paige that it shouldn't be her duty to turn her mother's life around, but the girl was so stubborn and set into thinking she could fix her that I didn't have the heart to continue that argument for long.

She was a fighter, and if she set her mind to doing something, you could be sure that her efforts wouldn't run dry.

I moved from pacing in front of the couch to pacing down the hallway by her bedroom door while my chest broke apart as the sounds of her crying became deafening, carving out parts of me that I didn't know existed. My head hurt from the mix of beer and liquor that was supposed to ease the tensions of the night as I made the move that I'd thought through hundreds of times. Only I didn't think I would actually do it, and now it seems to have made things more complicated than I wanted. In truth, it was the main reason why I hadn't made a move before. From the first time I saw Paige, I knew I wanted her. Even if the way that I wanted her wasn't as pure as it was now, my lust and jealousy eventually settled into protectiveness and the closest thing I'd ever felt to love—so much so that it scared the shit out of me. How could I possibly love someone when I'd never been loved by anyone myself? Yet the way my heart was ripping apart as I continued to pace her small home solidified that thought.

I finally sat on the couch, my bent legs moving up and down as my feet nervously tapped on the floor. *I should be doing something* I thought as my eyes darted between her near-empty house, trying to find anything I could do to help Paige, but the lack of furnishings and the near-empty fridge meant I couldn't do much other than sit here and wait. Wait for her cries to stop, for her torment to end, and for her sleep to take her.

An hour passed and the sounds of her sheets shifting ceased, causing me to dart up from the couch and push my ear against her door. Silence fell over the hallway and through the door I could hear her faint breaths as they changed from ragged to steady. She'd finally fallen asleep and I let loose a heavy sigh as I pushed my hand against the door, turning the knob slowly and then pulling my hand abruptly back and pushing away from the closed door.

What the fuck am I doing? I shouldn't be checking on her, and she all but told me that she can't, meaning she doesn't want me in there with her, comforting her. And if I woke her up right when she'd finally fallen asleep, then I would be the asshole for staying here and making sure she wouldn't get any respite from her life-changing night. That was *not* what I wanted for her, for *us*. If there was a fucking *us* to begin with, and the mindfuck *that* sent me on was another cataclysm in my chest that made even more guilt take over my thoughts.

I groaned as I slouched against the wall and slid down against it, letting the rough texture grate against my back in a way that reminded me of the unease that I'd felt growing up, not knowing where I belonged or to whom. Suddenly, my phone vibrated in my pocket and I pulled it out, clutching it so tight that a crack grew along the front of it as I read the name of the sender. It was Dick, writing out a drunken apology filled with misspellings and multiple spaces where he'd erased part of a word and typed a new one in front of it that even my diluted brain could spot. It wasn't like I enjoyed being feared by the people who'd overstepped and rubbed me the wrong way, but saying I didn't enjoy it wasn't accurate either. It was something that took time to adjust to since I'd grown into my body, but in that moment it made me fucking furious as I remembered his hands touching Paige in all the places I'd only been able to dream of. And the fact that that asshole did that to nearly every girl who gave him an ounce of attention sent another wave of anger through me.

If I hadn't been so set on staying here tonight, watching over Paige through her bedroom door to make sure she was alright, then I'd have half a mind to drive my car back to that frat house and beat him until he couldn't walk or see straight. For someone who thought that's what he did for women after displeasing them so thoroughly in the sack, it was only fitting that someone do it back to him.

My head fell to the side as my eyes fixed on Paige's door, the tension in my shoulders relaxing as the victory of not giving Dick that satisfaction of having her, much less getting a reply from me, washed over me and I drifted off to sleep.

FIVE

PAIGE

A wave of nausea rolled over me as I sat up in my bed, the sunlight creeping in through my window, causing me to wince back like a damn vampire as I realized just how late into the day it must've been. I rubbed at my eyes which were swollen and sore, noticing as I tried to clear my throat that it was dry from crying so much last night. I looked over at the time and saw it was just before noon, but I wasn't in a hurry to get to the hospital. Part of me would rather put it off as long as I could, and I wasn't going to fight that part.

And then I remembered that Aeden was supposed to be here, claiming he didn't want to leave my side. I wished last night had played out differently, that for once in my life something good could come of all the bullshit I went through. The fact that I wanted to blame my mother for dying on a night that finally felt like it was about me instead of her had my hands digging into the sheets as I fisted at them.

What the hell is wrong with me?

I knew it wasn't her fault, but I was so mad at her that I couldn't think straight. What grief I started going through last night had settled on anger this morning as I thought back to all the times she'd damn near abandoned me. Yet the man waiting for me in my own home felt more obligation to be there for me than she ever did, and for him, I was forever thankful. More than thankful. I was damn lucky that he moved in next door and chose to take a leap one day and introduce himself, quickly becoming the only person who I could trust, lean on as a friend. Maybe even be more than friends if he'd ever think of me like that.

The way he kissed me last night could have been a fluke, maybe he was just drunk or maybe he was going through something on his own. But I shoved the thought of him ever being selfish away because that was not Aeden. He didn't do things for himself like that, and always thought of others before himself. Not at all like the selfishness I felt last night when I wanted him to stay next to me, to make the anguish that burned in me cool into passion that I only wanted from him and him alone. Not some fucking frat guy at a party, or anyone else.

I could only hope he could see the desperation I was in last night, getting drunk and letting Dick put his hands all over me as if I'd actually wanted him. But I only wanted the distraction, knowing the person I really wanted wasn't pining for me the same way I was for him. I dipped my head between my knees as I sat on the edge of my bed, wondering how to approach Aeden this morning. I knew I should be focusing on my mother and going back to the hospital, but she was dead. And I couldn't fix that, no matter how much I wanted to.

I forced myself out of bed, shooting over to the small mirror that hung in my bedroom, taking in the pathetic face of a girl who spent all night crying over a mother who was hardly there for her to begin with. I straightened up my back, pushing the coolness of my fingertips into my cheeks and eyelids to calm the puffiness that resided there. But it was no use. I croaked out a groan, realizing my voice was rigid and borderline gone. I recited my name in the mirror to myself until my voice regained some composure as my vocal cords fought the torment I'd put them through. I'd only hoped Aeden didn't hear anything last night, but the knowledge that my home was so small and the fact that I may have used a pillow once or twice to try to dull the sounds knowing I was being loud made heat rise to my cheeks as I finished attempting to soothe my swollen features unsuccessfully.

Fuck, I look rough.

I reached for the handle, pulled it open, and let out a shriek in surprise as I found Aeden slumped against the wall outside my bedroom door. The sound that escaped me caused his eyes to widen as he startled awake. His eyes darted to me and he stood up abruptly, pushing a hand through his wild hair as he looked me over. His eyebrows furrowed as he took a step closer, cupping my face in his warm hands as thoughts of last night raced to the surface. I tried to school my features but it was no use as evidence of the torment I went through plastered across my face and a tear escaped my eye as he held me there, his thumb sweeping across my cheek to wipe it away before I said, "I didn't mean to wake you up, I'm sorry, I thought—" I bit my lip, drawing his eyes down for a moment before they shot back up again.

"Are you okay?" His eyes grew heavy with worry as they moved slowly over the puffiness, the bloodshot eyes, and the complete mess I knew I looked. Suddenly becoming more aware of the pity he was aiming at me, I inclined my head in the direction of the bathroom door, feet from where we stood, and blinked away more tears as they arose. He released me, running his fingers through his hair once more as he stepped to the side, letting me through. I closed the door of the bathroom, putting my back against the wall to support my body as it became weak, sliding down until I was crouched on the floor.

Minutes went by and I could see the shadow of Aeden's feet from the thin crack just under the door. He knocked and his feet shuffled back and forth. "Paige?" His voice came out soft, and delicate, and I hugged my knees in, clasping my arms over them even though I wanted nothing more than for him to save me, for him to take away all the pain and suffering. He creaked the door open when I didn't answer, moving to sit opposite me in the tiny bathroom.

"I don't want you to feel alone, and I know it's stupid of me to ask if you're okay knowing damn well you aren't." His head rested back against the wall as he let out a heavy sigh. "How about I go get you some breakfast, and we can head out?" His foot reached out to brush mine, being gentle as he still wore his shoes and at some point last night he managed to remove mine, something I hadn't noticed until now. I gave him a faint smile as he stood up, reaching into the shower to turn it on for me. "I'll, um, go now. Take your time. Eggs sound okay?"

I nodded, letting out a noise of approval as he left the bathroom door. I wondered how I came out of my bedroom so conflicted and somehow became even more conflicted and torn. This pain was unlike the hunger I'd grown used to, or the stress of not having enough or being enough. It tore through me in waves, making me want to scream and cry one minute, and then the next I wanted to punch a hole through the wall. None of that would help, and I wished I knew how to cope with things better.

We ate mostly in silence, Aeden twirling his fork nervously between his fingers and making small glances at me that let me know he was worried. I cried even more in the shower, but the steam helped to soothe my face so it didn't look nearly as puffy and wild as it had when I'd woken up. Yet I still looked pitiful and I still carried the weight of the world on my shoulders as I sagged down into my chair. When I was done eating, miraculous in its own way because even though Aeden was a great cook, all the food sounded just like it had tasted—like cardboard—he took my plate from me to wash it in the sink. I pushed against the chair to stand up and noticed Aeden stepping forward to come help me, but then he seemed to think better of it and stopped as he saw I was more than capable of walking.

"I'm not drunk anymore, you don't need to carry me," I let out, my voice bitter and annoyed but I didn't intend to be so cruel to him as I stood up and walked over to the kitchen counter, leaning against it as I felt the weight crashing in again.

"I liked carrying you," he said, chuckling and trying to ease the tension or direct the mood of the room into something more cheerful while he finished washing dishes. A distraction, I told myself, that I should've leaned into, but it was so damn hard to make any emotion that wasn't negative rise to the surface. He dried his hands, looking dejected as I didn't laugh back. A part of me wanted badly to wrap my arms around his waist, kiss him frantically, and forget everything, and for a brief moment, my eyes couldn't leave his lips until he cleared his throat, taking notice of where my gaze had fallen.

He reached his hand up to cup the back of his neck. "About last night, Paige, I—" he began, but I cut him off.

"You don't need to apologize. I get it Aeden, you were drunk," I said, feeling every bit as unsettled on that being the reality of it all as I spoke.

He cocked a brow at me. "You think I wouldn't kiss you unless I was drunk?" His question sent my jaw slack as I parted my lips in response. Aeden didn't play games, not ones that would risk our friendship anyway, yet his eyes were glinting like the spark of a bet had just been placed.

I corrected my mouth and shrugged my shoulders, acting indifferent even though I finally felt something other than grief and despair and pain. I felt longing, my heart beating uncontrollably as he took a step closer to me. Then another. And a final one until my face had to look up into the dreamy pools of his eyes as they stared down at me, unfaltering. His chest moved in and out, the muscles pressing against the same shirt he'd worn at the party. He didn't bother to change out of his clothes even though he'd given me the time to get ready and the evidence of my crying fit where I pulled on his shirt was still starkly visible by the nape of his neck.

His eyes fell to where I'd been looking, and he reached down to my hand, pulling it up to his chest and planting it firmly there. "Does this feel like I don't want to kiss you?" he questioned, and I bit down on my lip as his heart beat to a rhythm in tune with my own.

He wanted me, and I wanted him. I was a mess, a fucking disaster and I could hardly find it inside of myself to push out thoughts of my mother but just then, he was all I could see, could feel, could connect to.

"No," I said, my acknowledgment coming out too breathy. He released my hand but I kept it planted there, his lips curving as he put a hand against my cheek, edging the roughness of his palm along my jaw until his fingers reached for a bit of my hair, tucking it gently in place behind my ear.

"Tell me to stop," he dared.

I shook my head, leaning into the warmth of his hand as my eyes dared him to move, to make me feel, to take away this hollow fucking feeling that continued to tear into me and tried to consume every ounce of emotion I had left to give.

His thumb sent shivers down my spine as it moved across my bottom lip, tugging it from my teeth effortlessly. He leaned in, dipping his head low and our foreheads almost touched as he leaned in slower, closer.

"If we start this, I don't know how I'll ever stop." His hand slid to the back of my neck as I sucked in a breath, his thumb edging under my jaw to tilt my head up while his fingers laced into my hair.

"Then don't," I said, and before I could overanalyze which part I was edging him toward in saying *don't*, his mouth crashed into mine, solidifying his need to never stop as he moved to push me against the counter.

I reached my arms around his neck as he claimed my mouth hungrily, his hand tilting my head back more while he moved down to kiss along my jaw and I swear for a moment I saw stars as the waves of the night's torture had somewhere to rest for a moment. With him, the world stilled. And I needed that more and more with every kiss he planted as he moved down my neck.

His mouth moved back to mine, and he bent lower to lift me in his arms, his fingers digging into the backs of my thighs as he planted me firmly onto the countertop. My legs reached around his hips, tugging him in closer as I felt his desire press against my inner thigh, releasing a moan from my lips just as he parted them, his tongue sliding in expertly with mine.

Our bodies hungered for each other unlike anything I'd experienced before as I started to move my hips, shifting to edge him more firmly against me, and he let out a deep groan of satisfaction as his length pressed harder against me. I heard something clatter and fall behind me as he pushed me further onto the cabinet until the back of my head thumped against the upper cabinet, but I didn't care. The house could crumble around us and I wouldn't move from this very spot, from being in his arms and feeling the warmth of his skin as his hands explored my stomach, pushing my shirt up slowly while I clawed desperately at his.

His kisses grew more tender, slowing his pace as he continued his search above my ribs, sliding his hand smoothly over my lace bra and I let out another moan against his lips as he cupped my breast in his hand. I could feel a smile tugging at his mouth as he continued pressing his lips against mine in kisses that could destroy us both. Our bodies moved with desire, ebbing and flowing together until all that was left was him and I. My hands trailed down his shirt, reaching for the hem, but he pulled back, breaking our kiss but keeping his eyes fixed on me as he tugged up on the collar and removed the fabric that kept me from clawing at him. Which I did. He pushed back into me immediately, my fingers digging into his chest, his back, and the taut muscle of his shoulder blades that moved with every flex of his hand as he found my breast again, this time tugging the lace down and exposing my nipple to his fingers.

"Fuck," he breathed the words against my mouth and I let another moan escape me before pushing back into his lips, needing to feel the warmth of him everywhere, to erase the darkness and free me from every burden that ever took hold over me. My hands moved from his back, tracing my fingers lightly down the muscles of his chest and down further along the wall of muscle that stacked on top of one another, following the thin line of hair until I found the waistband of his jeans. My fingers dug into the top edge of them, tugging him in as close as I could so that his towering frame was slanted against the counter.

His hand fell still under my shirt and he pulled back slightly, his forehead creasing and eyes softening as if he didn't expect me to want to push this any further. But how could I not want to get lost in him, in us, when the alternative was feeling outright misery?

"Please," I begged, desperation coming out heavy like the world would end if we didn't continue. And for me, maybe it would. The sadness and aching were already taking over in every spot his body wasn't pressed into, and it was becoming too much to bear.

Aeden slid his hand down slowly from my breast, the places his fingers moved across forming goosebumps in their wake before he settled them on my waist, his fingers flexing as he wrapped them around me.

"Paige, I—"

Just then, a loud crash sounded against the door, followed by tapping and the sounds of something whooshing. Aeden frantically threw his shirt back on, racing for the door and I pushed off the counter to follow behind him. Aeden swung the door open in a fury and an owl swooped inside, heading straight for me. It scraped the back of my head with its beak as it flew around me, its wings beating feverishly as it continued its attack. I swatted and flailed my arms above my head, ducking as Aeden tried to catch the damn bird, waving his arms around it to get it out of the door again.

Finally, Aeden caught hold of the bird's wing then he flung it forcefully out through the door and chased it beyond the porch. I lifted my head, wincing at the few scratches that were on my arm and trying to still my beating heart to focus on the bird. I blinked as Aeden stood frozen on the porch as I approached, my eyes unable to blink away the light I saw trailing behind the bird as it flew into the trees across from my house. A translucent light—bright, purple, and glowing—followed behind the bird in thick waves, moving up and down like a living thing as it writhed in the air.

SIX

AEDEN

"What the hell is that?" Paige asked as she stood still beside me. Purple waves rolled like a tide in the ocean, flowing from the owl as it flew toward the woods and my jaw went slack as I gawked at the white owl leaving the magnificent trail. Paige could see it too as she stared off at the purple light, the glow of it reflecting in her emerald eyes even with the light of the sun overhead. It was beautiful and terrifying and incredible and I found I was unable to move my body as the astonishment took hold over me, and clearly over her as well as she reached down to grab for my hand.

The desire to turn back and go inside the house was waning in my mind, knowing I was just about to put a pause on the rapidity of my arousal by telling Paige we should stop, and slow down. My body certainly didn't give a fuck as my dick was still coming down from the high that was all of her, but I didn't want to take advantage of her or make her regret doing things with me when she was hurting.

Leading her on wasn't like trying to hook up with the girls who threw themselves at me. I felt no remorse for those girls, but with Paige, it meant everything to me. I wanted it to be special, wanted to make her scream my name with a goddamn smile on her face and we could fucking cuddle afterward. *Not* the day after her mom's death, when I knew she was suffering in ways that I couldn't permanently end with my skills in the bedroom. But fuck. She had no idea how good she felt. How perfectly she fit against me. How mad she drove me with her soft moans as I tried to claim her.

I pushed myself off the railing of the porch and rushed to walk in front of Paige, who started moving from the porch and was halfway down the driveway while I was sitting here thinking with my dick again at the thought of her screaming my name. I wanted—no, needed to protect her, and an aggressive owl with waves of light stemming from it didn't give me much hope for what we were walking into.

What the hell are we doing?

I should have felt panicked but instead, a swell of calm poured over me as we were prodded across the street and into the depths of the woods, the waves begging us to follow, coaxing us along.

We both glanced at each other as I reached out for her hand. She must've been feeling the same strange pull that I was, like a deep desire under my flesh that I was heading to where I belonged. It pulsed longingly inside of me, a weird sensation that I couldn't grasp as we continued weaving in and around the trees. The owl was carving a smooth path from one tree to the next, leaving dense waves of light that ushered us as we wandered on through. The purple light made the sensation inside of me grow more and more with each step. I looked down at Paige's arm where scratches from the damn owl resonated and I flexed my fingers against the top of her hand, suddenly wanting to chase after the bird and beat it down. But the light we were walking into didn't allow for anything more than the need to find out where it was leading us.

"Do you feel something weird? I mean beyond us following a fucking owl with a crazy purple path, there is some—" I started but Paige was nodding her head vehemently as she cut in.

"Yeah, I do. Like a strange urge in my bones but I think…" She paused for a moment, looking back toward where we'd entered the woods with narrow eyes. "We have to follow the light." She held out her other arm, observing it closer. I gripped her hand tighter and tugged her a bit closer to me, unsure of what was happening.

"I'm starting to feel hot, almost like I'm on fire." I lifted my shirt and glanced down at my stomach, searching for literal flames but found nothing other than the lingering redness from Paige's nails on my chest as we continued to follow the bird. The burning sensation came in waves just like the path we were on, and the heat swelled more and more like a fever blooming throughout my body.

Where is this bird leading us? We must have walked a half mile as my body continued to heat up.

"Aeden, look." Paige pointed ahead and I pulled my face from the heat that now seemed to caress my arms and legs to see the owl perched on a large branch, cocking its head toward us. Underneath the owl was a swirling oval that was glowing in the same purple hue the bird was trailing behind it. The swirl shined so bright I had to lift my arm to shield my eyes, having grown used to the darkness of the woods that blotted out the sunlight as we walked on.

"What the…" I breathed out, my gaze fixed on the torrent of purple.

Paige guided us closer, her soft hand still in mine as she tugged me to follow her lead. She led us to the other side of the huge swirling mass, surveying it—a purple, never-ending vortex shown on both sides of the mass. She turned to me, pressing her lips together as she reached out and grabbed my arm with her free hand, rubbing soothing circles on my bicep. She lifted her chin and I lowered my head as she spoke.

"Something, or someone, is calling out to me in there. I know this sounds bizarre and it sounds even more crazy as I'm saying it...but—I have to go in there."

Bizarre was an understatement. This whole thing was bizarre. We were supposed to be heading to the hospital, or making out like animals back at her house, not walking a mile into the woods about to walk into some glowing purple shit. But, undeniably, I felt the pull of it too. I didn't hear a voice but I believed her, her eyes growing wide as she watched me in contemplation.

"We should turn back, go to the hospital, your mom—" I stopped and shook my head, unable to finish that sentence. I didn't want to send her over the edge in bringing her mother up or make her look as crushed as she did when she first woke up and I know she hadn't forgotten where we needed to be instead of here.

"I know." She looked down and shuffled her feet in the dirt below us. "Something inside of me is telling me I *have* to do this." She began biting her lip and glanced at the vortex and then at me, still holding onto my arms in reassurance. If she said she heard a voice calling her, and she needed to step into it then hell if I wasn't going to go in with her. I would bend heaven and hell to protect her, and I was not going to leave her.

"If you go in there, I'm coming too. I'm not leaving you. Ever." And I meant every word while I tucked a knuckle under her chin to lift her eyes, meeting my own. I was never going to leave her side, and I was always going to try to protect her, and now more than ever I wanted her to know that. It was more than a desire inside of me, it was like a personality trait. I couldn't quite explain it, but I just had to make sure she was okay and that she was safe.

It had always been that way from the moment I met her. It wasn't like I felt a familial bond to her but I did feel something that made me very protective of her, almost like I existed for that purpose alone. As I learned more about her mother and her history of being neglected, the protective instinct in me grew for her. She never had anyone around who seemed to give a consistent shit about her. Even her dad left them both before she was born. All she knew was her mother and me, and now her mother was dead.

"I'm sorry," she said softly and rolled her lips in. I could tell she was fighting back the barge of tears that she wanted to let loose again, yet she had no reason to be sorry for anything. She was always apologizing and trying to fix things but I knew that was just her way of coping.

A tear rolled down her cheek and I reached my thumb up to brush it away. Her damp emerald eyes glistened back at me, wells of tears waiting to fall.

"You should never feel like you need to apologize to me, okay?" I demanded

I pressed my forehead to hers before our lips melted together one last time, the roaring fire inside of me burning more profoundly as I fought hard against the urge to run through the fucking light that was calling to both of us, demanding that we move steadfastly.

Seven

PAIGE

Aeden's heat flushed through me as he held me in a firm embrace, crushing against my mouth hard.

How have I lived without this for so long?

I felt light, almost like my body was filling with air, the strange feeling in my gut growing tenfold as he wrapped his arms around me. We should've run back to the house, fought off the pull from the light, and neglected the hospital visit that would surely end me even further. But this feeling inside of me kept pulling me to the swirl that hovered only a few feet from us.

I put a hand against his cheek to stop him softly, grazing the stubble of his facial hair along his jaw with my fingers. He stopped kissing me and picked his head up to look into my eyes, then flicked his gaze back to the vortex, now making a *whooshing* sound like a vacuum.

He felt the pull too.

As he let out a quivering sigh, I reached my arms around his neck and linked my hands together. His pulse thrummed under my linked arms as I planted a final few soft kisses on his cheek, and he picked me up into his arms.

"Paige…" He hesitated and drew his brows together.

"I know, we have to go." I inclined my head towards the vortex, urging him to get closer. It was pure insanity, yet I couldn't get the need to enter the light out of my mind as it consumed every fiber of my being.

He walked us to the edge, holding onto me and pressing me hard against him as if the light would rip us apart, its purple waves flowing all around as it pulsed in a welcome to us. But it was growing smaller now, disappearing with every passing minute. He looked down as he held me there and grabbed me tighter, placing a slow kiss on my forehead.

"Don't you dare let go of me," he whispered and, as one, we stepped through.

EIGHT

AEDEN

My head was throbbing like I'd smashed into a ton of bricks. Thick mounds of sand slid under my fingers, a thick coat of dust all around me. I peered through narrowed eyes to find myself in some kind of bar, the floor made of sand and dirt and the smell of liquor and puke filled the room. Wooden barrels with the words "Costa Whiskey Imports" in thick black letters stamped across the middle lined the rotting wall next to me. The wood on the walls crumbled in some places like an old sunken pirate ship straight out of National Geographic, revealing the starry night sky through one of the holes.

Shit. It was undoubtedly daytime when we walked into the woods.

Candles lit the walls and cast heavy shadows of the surrounding people to the ground. The sound of laughter ripped through the bar as the inhabitants took notice of the struggle I was in, just as the realization that I must've been out for some time clicked into place. I heaved my body slowly from the ground and shook my head to clear the sand from my face.

"Aye Boyo, havin' a tough day there are ye?" A man sitting at a long wooden table lifted his beer in greeting to me. He tipped it back and guzzled the full glass in three seconds flat. He had fiery orange hair, drunken blue eyes, and a beard that went down to his collarbone. He threw the cup down on the table that resembled the same torn wood the walls were made of.

"Are ye lookin' for someone there Boyo?" He cocked an eyebrow up, his voice stern like he was a teacher that had caught me skipping class.

"Show 'im the door, Seamus!" A girl wearing a long blue dress with a lot of cleavage spilling over shouted, cupping her hands around her mouth to project her shrill voice. The noise sent a piercing blow to my throbbing head—threatening to crack it in half.

Where the hell was I, and where was Paige?

Maybe she'd gotten here before me, wherever *here* was. I ignored the cleavage bearer and the drunkard with an oversized leprechaun appearance and glanced through narrowed eyes around the small bar for Paige.

"Oy, I think he could use a clean-up, Seamus!" another drunk bastard shouted from the other side of the bar. A cold flood of water rushed over me, having appeared out of nowhere. Seamus released a husky laugh and flicked his wrist as another blast of water shoved me to the side.

Where the fuck is this water coming from?

Seamus stood and sloppily pushed his sleeves up, revealing an elaborate tattoo of waves crashing in a circle covering his forearm. The rest of the bar burst with laughter, sloshing their beers and cheering jovially. He came up to me, his fist ready to meet my face. I caught his arm as he swung it up, throwing my fist straight into his gut. The force sent him backward a few steps as he clenched his stomach and grunted. He lifted his head and smirked up at me, enjoying the challenge I posed. He bent slightly more and rushed into me, looking to throw me off balance by ramming into my side. Bad move, because that was something I was trained to fend off. I darted to the opposite side faster than he could blink. He turned around to find me as I reared up to meet his chin with an uppercut, angling his head back and putting him on the floor on one knee.

He leaned over and spat blood on the floor and chuckled as he lurched back up. His wrist noticeably jerked again and more water hurled into me, sending me into the barrels of whiskey.

Rage coiled in my veins and lit a searing burn throughout my body like a match lighting a canister of kerosene—and I was ready to explode. I stood right back up, releasing an audible growl, and bared my teeth. Just as I moved to raise my fists, the bar top behind Seamus lit up in a fiery blaze, matching the heat blazing throughout my body. The fire died down rapidly when I shook my head in confusion. Black marks scorched deep crevices on the bar top, and flecks of ash and smoke rose into the air.

The bar fell eerily silent.

I felt a raging fire burning on my arm and stared down in horror. A tattoo began to form on my forearm, slicing into my skin with a fire so hot it burned white. I felt no pain but a sweet release as the strange feeling that had been building within me began to soften and settle like a satisfied lion after killing its prey. The tattoo finished unfurling around and up to the top of my left shoulder, the burning flames reaching the base of my neck. The mark pulsed bright red, the image of a fire circling in large plumes now burned into my flesh.

The woman showing her tits to the world jumped up from her seat and bolted through the swinging front door. The rest of the bar stood frozen in place.

The man who shouted for Seamus earlier fell to his knees, appearing to pray or plead for forgiveness as tears rolled down his plump red cheeks. Seamus walked up to me, the fight in his bright blue eyes gone.

"So yer a fire-wielder, eh?" He approached me cautiously, holding his arm out as if he were taming a wild beast.

"A...what?"

"Aye Boyo, where pray tell are ye from?"

My jaw tensed as I held my tongue from answering any questions. I still needed to find Paige, yet all the people in this shithole were too desperate to see a fight. They wanted me to fight—and to lose. Why the hell would I tell them anything?

But the fire swarming up my arm in a tattoo that formed from beneath my skin had a lot of eyes glaring my way. Uncomfortably, glaring.

"Tom, give this lad yer shirt." A man at another table stood shakily and unlaced the top of his long-sleeved shirt without question and pulled it over his head, revealing a tattoo similar to Seamus' on his left arm. *A cult. This is definitely a fucking cult.* He balled it up and threw it at me as I caught it from across the room.

"Put it on Boyo, that mark on yer arm can get ye killed. The Mora of Prydia will have ye gutted."

"Mora of Prydia? What the fu—"

"Put it on will ye, and come with me." His eyes darted around the bar as he curled his arm, gesturing between me and the door.

"The hell I will, I—"

He interrupted me again and I curled my heated fists in as he said, "Look, I could ask ye again nicely, but I have a reputation to uphold. So come with me now, and I'll answer ye questions. If ye say no, I'll just use more water to push ye through those doors." He inclined his head toward the swinging door that the woman had run through.

I had no choice as the bar remained quiet, fear spewing from them like a busted pipe. There was nothing in the bar for me anyway—Paige was clearly not in it.

I scoffed and tugged on the shirt, letting the long blue sleeves fall to cover my arms. Thankfully, shaky Tom was about my size. I jutted my chin toward the door gesturing for Seamus to lead the way. At least if he tried anything again I knew I could take him on. He was still sopping drunk, and we just proved in the bar who the better fighter was. The people in the bar were afraid of me, and the fire tattooed on my arm, so I had to assume Seamus also held some of that same trepidation.

As we walked outside, we were met with a light breeze that wafted in the sultry smell of salt and ocean air. We were on a beach where the tide was low, exposing a long stretch of wet sand as the waves rolled idly in under the moonlight.

There was no beach anywhere near Jessup Falls.

"Let's start with where we are. What is Pry—"

"No, no Boyo, let's start with where *yer* from."

I gritted my teeth as I spat out my answer, "Jessup Falls, which I can see is *not* where I am." I gestured at the sea. "Your turn, fire crotch."

"The only *fire* I see is you, Lad. You're in Aellethia, more specifically the town of Costa."

"Aellethia...right..." I smacked my teeth and rolled my eyes knowing I was getting nowhere. He wasn't going to tell me where I was, and he didn't want to help me beyond leading me out of the bar. Finding Paige on my own was probably going to be my best bet. Getting more from the drunken, bar-fighting asshole didn't seem promising.

I turned from Seamus and started walking away from the lapping ocean water and moving toward drier ground. Suddenly, I heard someone stumble through the door of the bar as they exited. I kept walking, trying to pay no mind to the cult members as I narrowed my focus on finding Paige.

"Seamus! Don't help the boy, the Mora of Prydia—"

"For fucks sake, what is the Mora of Prydia?" I turned and shouted back, huffing out an angry growl, making both men halt. Seamus was motioning for the man to stop talking and I felt anger begin to rise and burn inside of me again. This time, the fiery feeling formed a large ball in the palm of my hand. My jaw fell slack as I stared down in awe, the heat licking at my flexing fingers while an orb made of fire floated above my stretched-out palm. The drunk man waited all of two seconds before running back inside, screaming like a petrified child.

Seamus' wrist moved at his side and a rush of cool water streamed over my burning palm. I didn't understand what was happening but I knew that when Seamus made that motion, water was going to come flooding.

"Ye need to calm down Lad," he said as he put a hand to his forehead and shook his head. "That fire inside ye will burn everything down." He approached me slowly until he was standing in front of me and pushed my fiery arm down to my side. He looked me over and let out a sigh. "Okay, 'ere it is. Ye landed in our bar with a portal over yer head. Only a Mora can make a portal, so either ye traveled with one, was sent 'ere because of one, *or* one of them made a portal hopin' to catch a mortal from the mortal world. Seein' as how yer arm proves yer a fae, like one of us, I'm thinkin' ye traveled here with a purpose. So tell me Boyo, who sent ye here?"

Fae? One of them? I glanced again at Seamus' tattoo. It was a wave. *Water.* This cult was obsessed with water, and they somehow made it appear out of thin air. I thought back to the people inside the bar and realized they all had a water tattoo, some smaller and others a little larger. It had to be a cult.

"You are telling me that I am in *another world* and that I belong here because of some *tattoo*?" My fists clenched at my sides as the fire on my arm pulsed in recognition.

"That's right Lad," he said flatly. "I can cast water and bend it to me will. All the fae here can be expected to cast an element. *Yers*, however, has not been seen in these parts in a long time."

My *element.* This guy was a whack job and a drunk. And apparently a fanatic cult worshiper.

I paused, considering everything around me. I was nowhere near a wooded area anymore, the lapping sounds of the tide confirmed I was not in Jessup or near Bunnell University. Dingy cottage-type homes made of dilapidated wood—much like the bar I was just in—lined the shore. Several homes were lit by candles against their jagged windows, which were just holes cut into the homes. No glass. A path made of compacted sand curved its way onward toward slightly larger buildings marked with signs hanging by posts that jutted out over each door frame. It was primitive and so unlike anything I'd ever seen before.

My eyes glazed over the dark water where a few fishing boats were docked further out to avoid becoming trapped in the lowering tide. They had large cages with seaweed draped over them, a few large harpooning guns dotting the sides. The smell of fish wafted thick through the air on the warm ocean breeze but even that was overpowered by the lack of bright lights that allowed the stars to shine brighter than I believed possible. But there they were.

And here I am.

"One more time Boyo or I'm going to send me waters to ye again. Tell me who sent ye here." This time he wasn't questioning me, and he lifted his arms in preparation for *his waters.*

"Paige—she's my...friend." A shudder rolled down my spine at the thought of us and that kiss and being just friends. There was no way we were just friends anymore, but Seamus didn't need to know any of that. "I was holding her as we walked through a purple fucking vortex and then I came crashing out of it without her," I said, not trying to show how distressed I was over not having her here with me. I silently wondered if she could see the ocean and the stars wherever she'd ended up. I wondered if she was trying to find me, too. Because even in the darkness of the night, her presence would be noticeable. A gnawing sensation spread through my chest—she was nowhere near me.

"Ah." He sighed, nodding his head and tugging on his fiery beard as if he understood everything I'd said about Paige and a purple vortex. It seemed almost normal to him—probably because his cult also dealt with swirling masses that lead to alternate realities. Yet the mark on my arm, and his, was hard to deny. And the feeling inside of me? There was no denying the sensations of the flames enveloping my core.

"What do you mean, *ah*? Did you see her before I got here or not?" I needed more help, more answers, but all I found was a drunkard about to fall asleep, too full from all the booze he must've consumed.

"Tell ye what. I'll help ye find out where yer *Paige* is, and we can have a wee bit of a chat on our way to see me friend in the morn. This lass I know can help ye, and if not, then ye can be on yer way on yer own. But I warn ye, searching around 'ere with no wits 'bout ye on what lies in our land is not for the faint of heart. Best we get back to me cottage up the road and get some rest before our journey."

Great. So now I'm on a fucking quest with a ginger elf from Lord of the Rings. "The name is Aeden, by the way—not *Boyo,* and not *Lad,*" I imitated his accent just to piss him off. Normally, I'd have more patience and reacted with less spite Unless, of course, those times involved Paige. Then all cards were off the fucking table.

I had been in a fight before, even if I didn't particularly want to be in them. I had been a foster kid for the better part of my life and never had a steady family—not one I could remember, anyway. Getting picked on a lot as a kid by other kids in different foster homes led me to fighting anyone in pure defense, and losing a lot of those fights more than I cared to recollect. It was like that until my last year of being in the foster care system came around. When I signed up for football and found out I was fucking great at running and throwing, people began to respect and even fear me. Being on the field granted me a sweet release of my built-up frustrations. I trained hard and my body changed from a lanky, six-foot-four tall boy, to a solid man, stacked muscle and all. The other kids started looking over at me fearfully, waiting for me to take my revenge. Not that I cared enough about them to take out any revenge on grudges I didn't bother to hold onto. I learned to stand my ground, and once that clicked into place, there were fewer fights to be involved in—less escalation meant I won without the need to raise a single fist, just as I had done at the party with Dick.

It was simple.

I didn't lose and I wouldn't lose.

Ever.

I pointed a finger at him. "I'll go with you, only because I have no idea where the *hell* I am. If you try anything, and I mean fucking *anything,* you can guarantee I won't shy from finishing what we started in the bar and beating you senseless." He looked me over and nodded once, taking my word for what it was—a threat—as he turned to lead the way.

NINE

PAIGE

"**Y**ou're late."

A male voice, sharp and precise like claws on metal, reverberated through my skull while I tried to steady the floor underneath me. The room was spinning when I flitted my eyes open, taking in the brightly lit room full of windows that reached the towering ceiling and let in the night sky. The stars shone back at me, so bold and bright I felt I could reach out and touch them and I wondered just how long I'd been on the floor for as the moonlight cast a mocking glow back at me. Spread under the brilliant sky was a lavish garden, with rows upon rows of vines and arches all visible under the moonlight. But through the corner of the window—through the corner, was a sea of hundreds, perhaps thousands, of small, flickering lights that cast shadows of the buildings below.

A city.

And it was nothing like back home.

I was not in Jessup Falls anymore.

I clutched at the posh red rug under my fingertips to steady my mind and body, lifting my head an inch momentarily to find the man who spoke out. My head crashed back down as I groaned and placed my hand on my forehead, wincing.

He was sitting at an extended dining table, embellished with wispy wooden flourishes along the sides. Nearly twenty chairs flanked the perimeter of the table, all empty except for one at the furthest end, where the man sat dressed in clothing fit for a king. He looked middle-aged judging by the soft wrinkles on his forehead and at the corners of his piercing gray eyes which were strikingly bold against his light blonde hair. The edge of a billowing tattoo curled just over the top of the low crisp collar of his jacket that wrapped around his neck.

A massive candelabra made of gold stood in the center of the table and shot straight up several feet toward the coffered ceiling which was also adorned with gold. Orbs containing small lit candles hovered above the tips of the candelabra like something straight out of a fantasy book.

How is that possible?

The man put his fork and knife down on either side of his plate as he paused his dinner to look down at me while I fought off the bout of motion sickness and lay flat on the floor with my head to the side. He was irritated, adjusting his purple coat with golden wisps threaded into it as if my presence had altered his state of being. He didn't look like a man who was used to waiting for anything or anyone, and his patience was wearing thin.

The room was finally done with its torment of rocking my mind back and forth and as that nauseating wave passed, I braced my arms down to the rug and willed myself to stand. My mind ricocheted on thoughts of the man in front of me, the kinglike room I was in, the purple vortex, and Aeden's arms around me as we stepped through it.

Aeden.

"Where is he?" I clenched my teeth and balled my fists, not caring who the asshat was in front of me.

"Sit down Paige, that's an order," he barked and the sheer force of his voice compelled my body to listen. I grabbed a chair and sat at the opposite end of the table, as far away from the ritzy stalker who knew my name.

He knows my name.

My head was splitting with the overwhelming amount of questions and panic that rose within me. I lifted my hand, willing my heart to stop beating out of my chest.

"I said, *where is he*?" I spat back at the man who looked thoroughly unaffected by my tone while he resumed his meal. He motioned with two fingers curling up, beckoning an older woman with short white hair and an apron around her waist. She came out from behind one of the massive doors, carrying a plate of food matching what the man was eating. She set it down in front of me and placed a fabric napkin on my lap before rushing back out, excusing herself as she rushed away.

I looked around more at my surroundings, trying to think of where the hell I could be. There were three sets of brown, solid wood doors leading out of the room, each with carvings of what looked like wind, scrawled in all directions. Several paintings of beautiful landscapes and people lined the wall across from the windows close to the table. One showed a mermaid pulling herself up on the edge of a boat, wind blowing through her wavy violet hair as she directed a smiling young man toward her. The man in the painting looked dazed, in a dream-like state as he stepped gracefully in her direction, his shoulders sagged with relaxation. The mermaid had a devilish grin in the painting as she was about to claim her prize. A few other paintings had more fantastical creatures ranging from a lone centaur in a prairie field to a dragon soaring above a mountain.

Nothing wrong with a little fantasy appreciation, but the dickhead across the table did not scream *nerdy* to me. If anything, he looked like royalty with his squared-back shoulders and tight posture. He even held his fork and knife like it were another appendage as if he took classes on the very thing.

The smell of the food in front of me sent my stomach lurching. I'd never seen such elegant designs made out of food before. Three pieces of fish were sliced with flowers and herbs nestled into each crevice as it laid atop a small bed of sweet-smelling white rice in the shape of a perfectly molded leaf.

Sir Dickhead was still silent, but I knew he expected me to eat. I took one more look at the food and pushed the plate away in defiance, folding my arms together across my chest.

He flicked his wrist, gaze still idly on his food, and the plate went sliding back into its place.

What in the actual fuck?

I sat there gawking at the plate, and then at the man. Surely I was dreaming. I stood up and threw my chair back, bolting toward one of the doors that laid ajar slightly, hoping for an exit. If I was in a dream then there must be a way out.

The door slammed shut, and I was lifted from my stance and thrust across the room through the air, landing back into my chair. With another jolt, the chair scooted up to the edge of the table, leaving no room between myself and my food.

Nope, not a dream. Definitely felt that.

My mouth popped open, my hair frazzled around me from the sudden movements as I peered through some wisps of hair at the mysterious man.

"Try that again and I'll throw you through the windows next," he said flatly, no quiver to his voice whatsoever. He meant every word. He continued taking a bite of the fish on his plate, his perfect posture still intact.

Who does he think he is?

I wasn't going to sit here and let him threaten me, whoever *he* was. Anger boiled inside of me and rushed throughout my body, exhausting any feelings of panic and fear that were there just moments before. I pushed the plate away again with notably more force than the last time and watched with wide eyes as a blast of air shot from my palm. The plate flew across the table, skirting under the legs of the candelabra before it lifted into the air, just grazing the man's perfectly coiffed hair as it took flight toward the wall. Wrists draped in purple cloth rolled haphazardly in the corner of my vision, making me refocus on the man with his fork still in hand and the plate that was stopped in mid-air.

The old woman wearing an apron came rushing out again, grabbed the plate as it floated a few feet behind the man, and ran back out of the room, clutching it firmly in both hands as she evacuated.

Anger took over my body and focused its efforts on my left arm, giving me the same strange feeling that I had in the woods when I was chasing after the owl. Only now, the sensation felt like a release of pleasure and pain all at once. A gust of wind cut through my skin like my blood had turned to air and was desperate to get out. The light shone brightly through my flesh in a vibrant purple hue similar to the vortex that led me here. It continued its path up to the bottom of my neck, then ceased all at once, leaving a tattoo of lavender swirling gusts of wind furling all around like a hurricane coursing on my skin.

The man finally broke from his dinner and set his fork and knife down calmly, raising the cloth napkin momentarily from his lap to dab both sides of his mouth clean, then reached up to push a single strand of hair back into place.

The same woman came rushing out to retrieve his plate and silverware and rushed back out in a matter of seconds, her urgency to leave even more so than previous times. Her cheeks flushed bright red and beads of sweat were coursing down like raindrops from her forehead. He cleared his throat and closed his hands together in front of him, looking up to acknowledge my arm first, and then me. He raked his eyes up to my neck and for a moment he showed a slight hint of surprise, his eyes widening just a millimeter before he blinked it away, relaxing again.

"Good. Now that that is settled, I'll get Hector to show you to your room. Your training begins tomorrow." He left no room for negotiation as a husky man made of pure muscle strode into the room and halted just a few feet from me. He clasped his hands together in front of him, waiting for me to move. He did not look at me but rather remained fixed like a statue, his eyes staring at nothing in particular. He wore a black tunic and black pants with hefty laced-up combat boots that screamed *don't fuck with me or I'll stomp on your head*. He was about the same age as Sir Dickhead, as he was now known in my mind, but was bald and had dark brown, almost familiar black eyes that blended into his dark henchman appearance.

I sat in my chair, not faltering the slightest as I drilled my eyes into his. I had to push down my millions of questions and focus on the one I cared most about. I had to forget about the tattoo, the wind I seemed to have summoned, and the floating plate being thrown across the room by pure magic. All of it. Pushed down into the deepest, darkest pit of my mind that I could find to bury it.

More than anything, I wanted to know where Aeden was. I needed to know. I could still feel his warm hands on me as he held me there before the vortex took us to wherever we were now. Took *us*. He had to be somewhere here, possibly beyond the solid wood doors. But he was not in the same room.

Maybe Hector took him somewhere too? I knew I must be in some grandiose house just by the haughty style of the room and the three opulent doors that lay promise to more rooms, I was sure of that. The old woman stood somewhere beyond those four walls and so did Hector before he came striding in to take me away to... *my* room. The creep said he had a *room.* For *me.* He expected me here and said I was *late* as I was lying startled on the floor, waiting for the room and my mind to still.

I mentally shook the intrusive thoughts away.

Aeden.

I have to focus.

My heart wouldn't stop hammering in my chest, the emotions swirling from the insane day I was having. But Aeden was my constant. The calm to my storm and the ebb to my flow.

"I'm not going anywhere until you tell me where Aeden is." I pressed on as sternly as I could, trying not to show any emotion just as he had done the whole time I'd been here. I held firm, pushing my matted hair away and crossing my arms again, ready to counter any shit that came my way. I struggled a bit to ignore the curving new tattoo on my flesh but managed to keep my gaze on the man.

"Hector. *The boy.* Where did you say he landed?" The man's hands still folded together neatly on the table, acknowledging my stance through his riposte. He was terrifying, but awe-inspiring at the same time. I'd never feared someone as much as I feared him. He could burn the world down and would remain as calm as he was now, I was sure of it.

"Costa, sir." Hector never moved from his stance, a perfect soldier in salute.

"There you have it, Paige. Your mortal plaything is in Costa with the fish. Most likely being thrown into a cage and cast to sea by now. I wouldn't be surprised if he were dead, like your mother." His words were a wrecking ball to my gut, taking every last bit of willpower I still contained to keep the feelings and thoughts at bay.

My mother was dead. Aeden was likely also dead.

How can I possibly survive this?

No.

No no no.

Aeden was not dead.

I believed with every fiber of my being that Aeden was alive. And the man was just trying to get under my skin. Aeden was strong and I had to hold on to any hope I had left that the man in front of me was a liar. The reality of my mom's death would hit me like a tidal wave later but I couldn't let him see me like that. He was the kind of man who could manipulate and torment with ease as if that information were glowing in large neon letters all over his face.

I tried not to shed an ounce of the well of tears that I felt building behind my eyelids and nearly choked out the only question I could think of that would distract my fleeting mind.

"How do you know my name?" My voice came out breathy and broken.

He smirked—an evil, twisted grin taking over his face. "I am your father, Gedeon Aerborne. You, Paige Aerborne, will obey my command and take leave of this room. Now. I have business to attend to and you are occupying too much of my time. Hector."

Father? What—

He motioned his wrist again and I was lifted once more into the air and thrown into Hector's outstretched arms. "Be sure she does not leave the grounds. She must remain focused on the task at hand."

"Get your hands off of me!" I kicked out at him, thrashing my body with all that I could against the wall of a man that was Hector. He didn't even flinch as he held me tightly to his chest, unlike the gentle caress that Aeden held me in prior, and walked me through the doors and out of the room.

The only *task* I was set on was escaping the hellhole I was in and finding Aeden.

TEN

AEDEN

Seamus and I walked in silence along the sandy path near the shore, passing several small homes that more resembled shacks or worn-down sheds. Through one of the carved-out windows, a family of four sat around a table lit by a few candles, their wax dripping slowly onto the wooden tabletop. The two parents smiled as their children giggled and spoke around their small portions. Blue and white rags hung loosely over their unmarked, tanned, skinny frames and their long bleached hair was dreaded and matting. None of that seemed to matter to them, their smiles illuminating the home more so than the candles could attempt to. Both parents had the same tattoo that Seamus bore on the same arm, the woman's a little longer than the man's, the blue waves nearly glowing against their darker skin. Above the woman's forearm tattoo was another—green and brown vines braiding along the inner crease of her elbow and outward with several leaves and flowers blooming as they twisted and turned, wrapping around both sides of her arm. The entirety of the mark was much shorter than the waves below it and her skin was free of markings above her elbow.

I glanced over at Seamus as he walked beside me, wobbling now and then as he resisted dozing off. I got the feeling he was used to drinking himself to sleep, possibly finding himself sleeping on the ground or at the bar if he felt like it.

We reached the area I had spotted before, with hanging signs and taller buildings, and I realized then that I was in a market. The path ahead of us opened into a larger circle surrounded by more buildings as we continued. The buildings only reached about two or three stories but resembled the same construction as the rest of the homes around it. Engravings of animals and plants, clothing, and household items like forks and plates, were carved into the rotted planks that hung by rusted thin chains from the space beside the door frames of each building. A couple of large wagons were full of empty netting and fishing cages, left out in the central part of the expansive market.

Seamus pointed toward one of the buildings as he took a turn, cutting me off from the path I was on as his drunken body hobbled to a door, and then mumbled about a key as he sifted in his pocket. Funny that his home would need a key, I didn't see many locks on the other homes and imagined crawling through the paneless windows would suffice for a thief. Maybe he also had trust issues, something I could relate to. Something I wished Paige also considered every time she dismissed locking up. Seamus grunted a bit as he felt his way through his pockets until finally pulling out a black key and jamming it into the lock. He swung the door open and walked in, leaving me to follow.

His home was immaculate and nothing like what I would have imagined. A small, two-seater tan couch sat propped against the left wall, and to the right was a small yellow dining set complete with four chairs. Not a single item was dirty, sandy, or unkempt. A bare kitchen with a stove complete with a slot for firewood underneath was in the back corner of his home next to a spiraling staircase leading up to the next floor where the bedrooms must have been.

He had several portraits hanging up throughout his home, one of Seamus smiling next to a woman with red hair like his own wearing a long-sleeved white dress, and a little girl no more than 8 years old with the same fiery hair, the brush strokes outlining her unruly curls as they flowed down to her shoulders. They stood close together, carefree as his arm wrapped around the woman's waist. The young girl in front of them stood barefooted, the sandy shoreline full of foam from the crashing waves behind them. He looked less tired and a little younger in the portraits. The same people dotted the walls, framed and placed with love.

Seamus had a family. Somewhere. They weren't home now—it was far too quiet.

"Take yer shoes off over there, I don't like sand on me floors." He pointed to another pair of men's shoes that sat there, directing me to place my own next to them. Seamus took a seat at the dining table and began stripping off his shoes and socks before placing them down on the floor next to him. He flicked his wrist casually and a well of water bubbled around them and then sunk back down below the wooden floorboards, leaving his shoes and the surrounding area spotless and free of sand.

"How do you do that?" I motioned to the floor where the water just came and went, taking any trace of sand with it.

"Aye, water is me element. I was born with it in me but was not graced by its presence until I was a wee bit younger than ye're now." He lifted his arm in recognition of his tattoo, tracing a finger along the curling waves.

"So...fire then, is...mine?" I hesitated, noticing how fucking weird it sounded to be talking about elements and magic spewing from me. But I could feel it. I held my left arm out, dragging my hands along the long sleeves that covered my flames. The fire was coursing through my veins, burning and weaving its way into every fiber of my flesh and bones like it belonged there. I wasn't stuck in some weird dream anymore—this was real and it somehow felt right. Like everything before in my life was meant to lead me here, to this place. Even though I'd been in Aellethia for mere hours, I felt more at home here than in any other place I'd been before. The only thing that was more right than this place and this power was how I felt about Paige and how much I needed to be near her.

Seamus nodded slowly. "Aye. Fire is yers."

"How did I do that? Back there at the bar?" I needed to get as many questions as I could before Seamus was consumed by his drunkenness and passed out.

"Ye got lost in yer feelings." His hand sprawled out on the spot on his chest just above his heart. "When ye first feel the magic there in yer bones it becomes...overwhelmin'." He hiccuped and slouched more into his chair. His eyes lulled but then shot open again as he let on more, stroking his beard. "We learn to control ourselves as youngin's so when the time comes, we don't blast our homes and friends to smithereens. Not that it always works." He shrugged, his shoulders staying up by his ears for a few beats before dropping again.

"Everyone here is like this?" I kept the questions flowing and sank onto the couch, my legs stretching out in exhaustion. It was possibly the longest day of my entire existence. *Running laps around the football field would be a lot less tiring than all the shit I went through today.*

"Water, Earth, and Air. Those three elements are what ye can wield, by law. Those are the anchors to the rest of our powers. Fire is...outlawed." He emphasized the term *law* as if it offended him. He was clearly disgusted by it, even grimacing as he spoke.

"Outlawed? That's why people were afraid? Here I thought it was the portal or my terribly good looks," I said with a sly smile, trying to make light of the situation. If fire-wielding was against the law, then Seamus was harboring a fugitive of the law. I didn't know how serious that was in Aellethia but I got the hint it wasn't a good thing. People looked *terrified* in that bar, grown men screamed bloody murder and ran from me. Everyone except for Seamus, who approached me calmly after our bloody bar fight, shielded my arm from view and took me to his home. He was either a looney or he was a rebellious traitor. My bet was on the first option but I had nowhere else to go and I got the sense, for some odd reason, that I would be safe with him.

Seamus eyed me closely, still fighting back sleep and seemingly unsure of how to respond as he tugged on his beard. A long pause suspended us both, neither of us speaking or moving for several minutes. The silence broke when Seamus sighed deeply, his thoughts finally gathered. "Aye, but people don't fear portals, Boyo. Mora's like bringin' mortals in for fun now and then, or openin' them to move about their guards within their territories, or whoever else they please. The Mora's rule the three kingdoms: Prydia, Buryon, and Hydrasel." He raised four fingers and then pushed one down as he recalled, "Vizna fell years ago, yer fire kingdom. I'm bettin' that's where yer from. Anyone with a fire mark is supposed to be captured and taken to a Mora, or killed. No questions asked." I shifted uncomfortably in my seat as his last remark settled on me like a brick.

Was this him capturing me?

If he was going to kill me, he would have done so before taking me to his home, I would think. Why bring me here and answer my questions when we walked by a fucking ocean, and he had a power that could drown me? Drowning sounded like an easy out if he was going to murder me, just a flick of his wrist and I could've been gone if that was how his power truly worked. Maybe he could just think about it and it would happen?

Shit. Maybe I shouldn't piss him off then.

Suddenly, my threat earlier shrank in the distance as nothing more than childish in comparison to what I could only imagine Seamus was capable of. He took in my discomfort as I shifted around on his couch and said, "No need to worry, Lad. I mean ye no harm. Get some sleep, we'll be headin' out 'fore dawn, 'fore the people in town start to stir." With that, he stood from his chair and headed up the spiral staircase, disappearing from view. The plodding of his footsteps gave way to his location just above where I was on the couch—my bed for the night.

I tried to bend my legs to fit on the small loveseat, but it was futile. There was no way in hell I could ever be comfortable with my legs and arms tucked in so tightly, but at least I wasn't dead in the ocean. Stuffing a pillow into my arms, I repeatedly tried to drown out the burning questions I still had. I just hoped Seamus wouldn't be too hungover to listen to all of them when he woke up.

After shifting and shoving my body into the cushions, I was finally able to relax enough to welcome sleep, the soothing image of Paige settling in my head. I dragged my mind out of the gutter, forcing myself to ignore her soft lips and the way she tugged on my hair and that fucking moan of hers. Man, I wanted her so bad it was mind-numbing in itself. Instead, I focused on a memory that lived rent-free in my mind like a broken record on repeat.

It was a few months after I first introduced myself to her. Paige knocked on my door and Gabbi answered, half naked wearing my football jersey and a thong. I was biding my time with that girl, knowing I wasn't and could never be fully invested, but she was gung-ho for me. Sure, the sex with Gabbi was enough to keep me from lamenting too much about my past, but it never felt real with her. I never lit up inside or found myself thinking about what she was doing or what was on her mind, or her opinions about anything really. Truthfully, she was as interesting as a grain of salt and it didn't help that my mind always wandered to Paige, the girl next door.

Gabbi must've been by the door as I heard Paige raise her voice loud enough for me to hear from my room. "So happy to see you in such formal attire, Gabbi. It only took you about ten minutes to drop your panties, a true record-breaking time, even for you." I could hear the seething hatred leaking from Paige, but all I could do was bust out laughing to myself in my bedroom. Gabbi was a total bitch to people, something I had to overlook just to keep getting laid on the regular because honestly, a man has urges. Paige however, learned to stick up for herself and did not take Gabbi's shit like most people would have, a trait that made me want Paige even more.

"I'm sorry, the bar is that way. Is your mom needing a ride home again? The poor thing just won't stop, will she." Gabbi pressed on, being the true bitch that she was. My smile cut from my lips instantly as I picked up Gabbi's pants and shoes and rushed out from my bedroom toward the front door. Some things I let Paige handle on her own but not when it came to her defending her mother. She needed to know someone was there for her.

"Gabbi, time for you to go. Take my shirt to the dry cleaners, I need the smell of bitch scrubbed out of it for my game tomorrow." I held out her pants and shoes to her and held the door open as Paige stepped to the side and made room for Gabbi to leave, the smuggest grin spreading across her face. Gabbi rolled her eyes and kissed my cheek before grabbing her things from me and walking back to her car. That girl had zero self-respect and it was honestly so sad. I should have felt more shameful for taking advantage of her, but she was a leech that never got the hint no matter how hard I tried.

Paige grinned up at me, wearing her Jessup High track & field hat with her wavy hair cascading down either side. Her smile stole my breath for a moment and made fucking butterflies flutter in my stomach. That was the day I knew she had me. Just a smile on repeat in my mind but that was the day I stopped living just for myself. There wasn't a day that went by that her smile didn't light up every darkness inside of me, holding a promise for a future I never thought I could have—a happy one.

Despite everything that had happened, I fell asleep fast with a smile on my face.

The next morning greeted me with a flood of icy water, making me jump out of the couch and fall onto the floor with a loud thud. Seamus laughed at me from the kitchen, a plate of eggs and toast on the counter next to him.

Asshole.

At least he made breakfast.

"Best to eat up Lad, we've got a long walk ahead of us," he said before pushing a portion of eggs into his mouth.

"You guys have coffee in Aellethia?" I groaned as I got up from the floor and strode over to my plate. I could smell something strong like coffee but it bit through my nostrils like a knife.

"Coffee 'ere is a wee bit stronger than what ye may be used to Boyo, but 'ere ye go." He held out a mug to me and I took it hesitantly. I took a sip and spat it back out into the mug instantly, pulling an uninhibited laugh from Seamus as I put the mug back down on the counter. Aellethian coffee was the nastiest, most sludgy thing I'd ever let slide against my tongue, and that was saying something.

"I think I would rather drink a cup of muddy piss water before I finish that." I shoved my mouth full of eggs to get rid of the taste of what people here considered coffee.

"I told ye it was strong. I'm not the best liar as ye'll come to find." He finished his breakfast and downed the last drop of his coffee before slamming the mug down, then wiped his mouth with the back of his hand.

The man could drink me under the table if he could handle coffee like that with such ease.

He was already dressed in similar clothing, albeit cleaner, than the night before. His sleeves were rolled and pushed up above his forearm, revealing the wavy tattoo with an air of pride. My clothing from the day before, and the day before that as well, had picked up a grungy look that was not as disheveled as the people I'd seen so far, but it would have to do. I removed the white t-shirt I'd had on since the party, my fingers dragging over the dips in the fabric where Paige had tugged me so close to her that I almost lost myself completely, and opted to stick with only Tom's tunic, which he was never getting back. I hoped it would help me fit in with the rest of the town, leaving me a fugitive of sorts in disguise. I rolled up my sleeves, cuffing them out of habit, but Seamus cleared his throat and shook his head. I rolled the sleeves back down and frowned slightly, wondering how long I had to keep it hidden but something in his posture, the way he stiffened at the casual act of my sleeves lifting, told me it would be a long fucking time of being concealed. The marks on my skin signaled me as an outlaw, which was something so incredibly outrageous to consider that it made me feel like a madman to think about it. Telling myself I wasn't in Jessup anymore didn't exactly help the situation, either.

I finished up my meal before Seamus threw a pair of boots onto the floor next to me. "Hope those fit ye, but it's time to go, Lad. Keep yer head down until we clear Costa. There's a big field that stretches a few miles before Lake Kree, where me friend lives. Ye'll be needin' this." He reached into a closet beside the couch and pulled out a sword. A fucking sword—like we were in the Middle Ages. I lifted a brow at him and reached for the hilt reflexively, not quite sure where or how to hold it. He pulled out a long scabbard next and secured it around my waist, then plucked the sword from my hands and tucked it into the scabbard that dropped down beside my leg.

"You have to be fucking kidding me, right? I don't know how to use this. You don't have a gun, or something more user-friendly?" I didn't know how to use a gun either, but hand-to-hand combat with a weapon seemed barbaric. That, and the notion that we had to be prepared to fight, was another thing I added to the mental list of shit that was downright weird as fuck since I'd arrived here. But there I was—armed with a sword and illegal fire I had no idea how to command. I was going to have to lean on Seamus if anyone approached us, which made my stomach sink. Relying on anyone had always been difficult for me, and I didn't trust him. Sure, he hadn't tried to kill me, or fight me again, and I didn't wake up to cops at the door or whatever they had in Aellethia for law enforcement. So, there was that. Yet, he was my only hope of finding Paige. And judging by the terrible reactions of the others at the bar, it would be damn hard to find anyone to help me. Willingly, that is.

"A gun?" His face contorted in confusion. He had no idea what a gun was. "We only use elements and weapons, ye know, swords, maces, axes. Things of that sort, Lad. Don't rightly know what a gun is, but if we don't 'ave it, then ye can bet it's as useless as tits on a hag 'ere." He moved toward the door, leaving it open for me to follow.

There was no one in the market, or anywhere in sight up to the crashing shoreline behind the buildings, not too far off in the distance. The breath of relief that flooded out of me made me feel like a kid again, sneaking around whatever foster parents I had to hide my existence, hoping that I wouldn't find myself in trouble for things I didn't do and be sent somewhere else. Again. At least I wouldn't be subject to hearing Seamus cover up who I was while I said nothing, although sober Seamus seemed admittedly much more capable than the drunken version from the night before.

I wasn't used to staying quiet in the background anymore. Not since I'd left foster care, that is. I was the best quarterback at one of the best schools in the country, and with that came a lot of attention. Unwanted attention, mostly by women, but attention that took time to get used to. Besides the odd pull I felt to live in Jessup Falls, I found I enjoyed the peace and quiet of a small town. Parties and girls hanging all over me got old quickly, and if I lived on campus like the scholarship included an allowance for, there's no telling what kind of person I'd be today. Instead, I took the small stipend to stay off campus, wherever the hell I pleased. And the little house I rented next to Paige was where I was drawn to the most, even if I didn't know her at the time. It kept me grounded in more ways than one. And fuck if waking up to Paige next door didn't comfort me more than any foster home ever had.

We quickened our pace until we reached the outskirts of Costa, its entirety about the size of four football fields. There were still a few houses dotted along our path with the same features as the others in the town itself, but not many. We ascended a steep hill, giving way to a sprawling field to our right with mountains cutting into the sky in the far-off distance, and another endless field to the left with a view of the coastline, the water a bright blue with a sheen that was almost blinding to look at. A small path wound its way from the fork we stood upon up to a parting of trees by the edge of the vast lake and a wooden sign staked to the ground. On it was a big red 'X,' the paint chipped and peeling showing wear and age, along with drawn pictures underneath the symbol. Several animal-type beasts I'd only seen in movies crammed onto the sign, but it was clear as day it was a damn warning sign.

Fuck, I'm going to die here.

"I take it there are unicorns and trolls here too, right?" I laughed, albeit nervously, before glancing up at Seamus. He looked toward the woods and back to me, no hint of a smile as he nodded his head, tensed his shoulders, and continued to the right side of the forked path.

"I told ye, there are things 'ere you won't want to come 'cross." We continued our walk in silence, easing our pace, which gave me more time to marvel at how the hell I'd gotten here to begin with. There were fewer people away from the town, making diversion almost too easy, but the rigidity of Seamus' steps and the way his eyes darted around let me know I should be just as alert as he was. Perhaps he was crazy and saw things that weren't really there, but judging by the sign and the eerie silence, his unease was more than likely justifiable.

At the top of the hill, I could see more of the world I'd dropped into. In the near distance beyond a sea of vibrant flowers and tall grasses was a deep blue, almost black lake that swallowed the beauty of the fields and flowers with its low, ominous fog. I looked back down the path we came from and saw an endless ocean and the small town of Costa just before it. The shoreline stretched out on either side for miles with a few large boats beyond the wave break. Aellethia was absolutely breathtaking.

"What else is there here? What, exactly, am I supposed to be ready to fight? I thought the sword was a scare tactic for the people in your town to not come after me, for the rest of the drunken assholes to leave me alone." I halted my steps, demanding his attention by calling him out for what he did the night before. My hand rested on the hilt of the sword he gave me, fingers twitching and elbow cocked back almost unnaturally. I knew nothing about using the weapon he'd given me, but that wouldn't stop me from trying.

"Aye, ye were right about the unicorns and the trolls, nasty big brutes. Hags and centaurs, a long list Lad. Ye'll see some soon enough and when ye do, for now, let me handle the beasts. I've got years of training under me belt and the last thing I need is to let another fire-wielder die on me watch." He looked sad as he was pulled into a reverie at the mention of another person like me.

Another fire-wielder?

I dropped my arm to my side. "What do you mean *another*?" The sun was beginning to rise, making me shield my eyes and narrow them at Seamus. Or maybe that was my incredulity at the notion that there were others like me. The people at the bar made people like me seem...sparse.

His knuckles turned white as they curled up at his sides while he looked out over the coastline. "Me wife was a fire-wielder." His voice cracked on the words. "She died, along with me little girl, when Costa was ransacked by Prydian soldiers looking for anyone who'd claimed fire." I could hear the sadness in his words as he spoke like his chest was ripping apart at the seams and his throat couldn't handle it. He had lost his wife and daughter, all because of some element. I couldn't imagine losing Paige like that, she was all that I had, all that I really cared about, and it was clear in Seamus' eyes as he spoke that he had lost everything he cared for. The drinking just helped cover up the sorrow that lay underneath the surface. Celine, Paige's mom, had that same look when she was alive. The look of pain dulled down by the loss of her senses. The only way I'd ever seen her unless she was in the hospital.

"Shit man...I'm sorry. I...I didn't mean t—"

His back straightened as he unfurled his fingers. "If ye want to get yer girl back then we need to get to Lake Kree before the hags come out to eat." And with that, he turned and walked on up the hill into the field while I tailed close behind him. I had no idea what the hell a hag was but it's eating time didn't sound like something I wanted to be there for. And if I'd just pissed off Seamus by bringing up the memories of the family he'd lost, then who was to say he wouldn't let the hags have me for their next meal.

I put my elbow back and rested my hand on the hilt, unsure of who or what I'd be using it on, but I had a feeling I was about to find out.

ELEVEN

AEDEN

After wading through the field of flowers in complete silence, Seamus halted on the edge of where the thick rolling fog floated above marshy lands, the spot where there was such a stark change in scenery that it felt like entering another world entirely as I walked deeper and deeper into the fog. It was the edge of Lake Kree that I saw from the crest of the hill we were on earlier, the hill that was barely visible now through the haze. Seamus' hesitation made anxiety prickle up my spine and I wrapped my fingers tighter around the hilt of the sword I had no clue how to use but refused to let go of over the past hour since learning about the hags and their mealtimes.

"Keep yer ears open and yer mouth closed," he whispered. "The hags can smell and hear yards from wherever they are." He stiffened his arm out, directing me back behind him even though that's exactly where I'd been the entire time. I wasn't stupid enough to dive headfirst into somewhere, *something* unknown. "Stay. Right. Behind. Me."

I nodded and kept my head and body low as I crept behind Seamus, following his footsteps and matching them with my own. The fog in the marsh grew so thick that it became difficult to breathe in. Our feet sank into mud which should have made a loud noise each time we lifted our feet to take the next step, but there was no noise. I looked up to find Seamus flicking his wrist, removing the water from the mud and turning it into dried dirt before it had a chance to clap back. I tossed my head over my shoulder, seeing the water return into each impression from our boots, eliminating our trail.

We were silent, but something hidden in the fog was making a ripping, shredding sound that pricked at my ears and had my hand trembling on the hilt. *The hags.* A rancid smell like rotting flesh hit my nose, but the heavy fog made it impossible to see beyond Seamus, who was two steps solidly in front of me.

Seamus paused, having just flicked his wrist again to turn the mud into dried dirt. I would've been more awestruck, more in disbelief, had I not been so focused on whatever remained hidden, waiting for the perfect opportunity to turn us both into the next shredded body of flesh that I envisioned with each tearing sound that emanated around us. He lifted a hand and I started lifting the sword from inside the scabbard that flanked my leg. The ripping sound ceased, replaced by the undeniable smack of mud. Something was running in the marsh.

Shit.

Seamus lifted a hand and a wall of water surrounded us, no longer focusing his abilities on the noise we would cause. A lengthy, bony arm with long fingers tipped with sharp nails and covered in blood ripped through the barrier of water Seamus had made. I swung my sword out from the scabbard, the weight in my hands noticeably off balance as I braced myself. The barrier turned to ice instantly and the hag shrieked as its arm became trapped, fingers reaching down at the ice. I lifted the sword, both arms shaking wildly as I brought it down, severing the arm and making the hag cry out in pain. Blood pooled around the ice and the now vacant hole where its arm had been. The hag was freed without its arm, free to climb the wall of ice and come after its revenge. Claws scraped eagerly against ice as Seamus pulled out a dagger from his back pocket, ready to stab the hag in close combat. The hag emerged at the top of the wall and grinned down at me, completely ignoring Seamus.

"Mmm yessss, you sssssmell of power!" The hag's long pointed tongue darted across its gray lips and snapped its teeth. The creature was hideous and terrifying—its red eyes had no eyelids and long black hair fell around its bony, gray body. Its legs as they stood on the top of the wall were bent like the hindlegs of an animal but it stood on two legs like a human, possibly half my height. The hag jumped up into the air, springing like a kangaroo, and attempted to land on top of me. I lifted my sword swiftly above my head and knelt as the hag came crashing down, its hunger making it rabid and oblivious to the sword lifted below it. The sword pierced through its flesh, skewering its body that continued to slide to the hilt as its face came inches from my face. I let go of the sword immediately, dodging the tongue that slumped out from the hag's opened mouth and watching the mud beneath my feet turn copper with its blood.

Seamus hastily put his dagger away and knelt to yank the sword from the dead hag, its limp body lying in a pool of blood and mud. He summoned water to clean the sword and stuck it back into my scabbard as I stood there, shaking and fucking mortified.

That hag wanted to eat me for my power.

My power.

"The more power ye have, the more the nasty buggers want ye, and Lad, ye would've been the best meal that hag ever had." He smirked at me and patted me on the shoulder.

"Congratulations on ye first kill in Aellethia. Gets easier, I promise." Water splashed across my face. My jaw tightened and my eyes peeled away from the hag's body as I came out of my stupor. But one more glance at the hag sent a shiver down my back and arms. It was a fucking thing of nightmares. A thing that was common enough to have Seamus dust it off his shoulder like nothing had come after us as if we hadn't almost just been eaten. I shook my head, sending droplets of water away from my hair and face as Seamus laughed at me.

I raked my hand through my hair, then dragged it back up again and held my arm out to the gray-skinned creature on the ground. "That thing...the hag...are you not powerful? I've only torched a damn bar top by accident, and yet I've seen you use water more times than I can count." I cleared my throat, trying to push away the slight tremor in my words. "The hag must have been confused."

"No Aeden," he said my name for the first time and spoke in a stern, almost foreboding voice that rumbled out from his chest. "Me mark stops at me forearm." He dragged a finger up the length of his arm, then pointed to where mine hid beneath Tom's tunic. "Yers reaches beyond and up to yer neck. The longer the mark, the more power ye have inside. Ye just have to learn how to use it."

"Fuck," was all I managed to get out, then dragged a thumb across my bottom lip, contemplating. It was outlawed to wield fire, to have it on your body at all. "Can you teach me? You know, instead of splashing my face all the damn time?" I asked, the anxiety in me swelling and making heat flush through my body. I lifted my hands to him. "I promise, I won't use it on you. At least, I won't try to." If he could teach me, show me how to use whatever I had, then maybe I'd have a chance at surviving long enough to find Paige. Fire orbs appeared in my opened palms as I flunked out my arms in surrender, all of my anxiety now hovering in my hands.

Seamus shook his head and slapped a hand to his forehead as I tried to shake the fire away unsuccessfully. "Ye want to learn Lad, then fine." He pinched the bridge of his nose, then walked closer to me. "Imagine that orb in yer hand and ye are one. It exists because of ye, and ye exist because of it. There is no barrier between ye and yer flames."

I shifted my arms, positioning them in front of me slowly. I closed my eyes, focusing on the image of fire consuming me and me taking control of it at the same time. I lifted one lid and released a shaky breath. The orb was still there, and I wasn't on fire yet, so I continued. I lowered my eyelid again and shifted my focus on the feel of the orb—on the size and shape—that hovered and melded it onto my own body like another appendage. Eliminating any barrier between myself and the flames. I peeked again and the orb remained, the flames pulsing in tune with my heartbeats.

"Good job Lad! Now turn to the hag and direct your ball to meet its heart like ye'd direct yer own arm out. A soft touch is all ye need." My eyes glazed over to the hag just as Seamus held a hand up. "Control. Picture it movin' away from ye, but with control."

I turned to face the dead hag and held my palms out toward it, willing the fire to shoot out toward the center of its unmoving chest. A tremble of fear and doubt tore through my focus and before I could separate that from the fire in my hands, my orbs grew tenfold as it shot out from my grasp, encompassing the hag's body as it burst into flames. The hag instantaneously exploded as I felt the fire press in on the lifeless body like the fear that tightened in my core, sending bits of hag flesh all over Seamus and I. Seamus bent his body over, his laughter exploding like the hag's body before a flick from his wrist drenched us with water that washed away the pieces. The mess sank into the mud around us, leaving us clean and dry.

"Try bein' a wee bit less in yer feelin's next time, but a good first go." He grinned at me like a proud father would and slapped a hand across my shoulder. My shoulders pinched together where his hand met my back and I couldn't stop the slight curve of my mouth at the friendly, yet familial act. The fear of walking through the dense fog was almost eviscerated as we continued on our path, side by side. I held an arm out in front of us, wielding a small orb of fire to light our path, and found the tension along my arm ease with the release of using the power that rooted itself within me.

The fog finally cleared, stopping as abruptly as it had started in the fields as we reached the edge of Lake Kree. Its waters were dark and almost as vast as the ocean view from Costa. Trees lined the furthest bank of the lake that I could see to the left, and an expansive mountain range loomed beyond to the far right. Ahead of us, where the lake ebbed sleepily across the dirt, stretched a rickety dock ending with a circular cottage that appeared to float on the water. A steady stream of smoke billowed from the rooftop and a faint light glowed from beyond the small window beside a yellow door.

"Shayanna lives just there," he said, pointing at the wooden home at the end of the dock—no bigger than the shacks we passed by earlier. "Might want to tuck yer flames 'way 'til I introduce ye." I pulled my fire back inside and extinguished the orb, letting it rest there under my flesh but ready to wield it again if I needed to.

The floorboards creaked under our weight as we stepped onto the dock. A splash sounded out in the water, and then another. I looked over to see a glimmering blue tail fin and checked to see if Seamus was ready to fight. Instead, Seamus put his hands in the back pockets of his pants and tapped his foot on the dock, waiting for the tail fin to come closer. He almost looked...eager like a kid waiting for the candy to be refilled in a candy store before diving in and taking a full bag for himself.

Suddenly, the delicate, unmistakable arm of a woman shot up and grabbed hold of the creaky floorboards of the dock, hoisting herself up to where we stood. Her legs shimmered blue, the outline of scales fading quickly into a smoothed tan hue. She had long dark hair that reached down to the base of her spine and she was completely naked. Seamus was already unlacing his shirt and I wondered if this was a thing we had to do naked. I was not about to flap my dick around with Seamus and some woman.

"Oh stop, Seamus. I'm sure your handsome friend has seen a naked woman before." The woman flipped her hair to the side as she wrung the water from it. She then maneuvered her hair into two sections which fell to cover her breasts before she turned to walk inside the cottage at the end of the dock, swaying her thin hips. She glanced back over her shoulder at me with her light blue eyes before throwing a seductive wink my way.

Seamus cleared his throat and motioned for me to follow her. "Aeden, this is Shayanna." His arm spread out toward her, directing me to follow behind her. She turned to smile at me, taking hold of a silky white robe that hung from behind the door and draped it over her frame slowly. Every movement she made oozed seduction, and that seemed to work just fine for Seamus. The near-see-through robe left nothing to the imagination as it hugged every bit of her. With every glance she threw my way, I remained calm. The only thing that intrigued me about her was the iridescent sheen of the scales that were still fading against her legs. She could have been a porcupine with a wig on for the amount of intrigue in fucking her I had, which was absolutely none. I had my girl, and I didn't need anyone else.

"Shay dear, please don't eye fuck the Lad. He has a woman," Seamus spoke with a hint of jealousy to his voice and took a seat at a green chair next to a fireplace in the small living space of her cottage. I strode past Shay, giving her a polite nod so I wouldn't come across as rude, and plopped down in the other matching green chair across from Seamus.

"Well, when you bring a man as cute as him to my home, I have to wonder what your intentions are," she said with a wink at Seamus this time and the corner of her mouth lifted as she dragged her eyes up and down my body once more.

Seamus groaned and rolled his eyes, tossing his head back over the chair. He lifted his head and patted his hands on his lap. Shayanna squealed at him as she sat where his hands had prompted. She twirled her hair and pushed her nose to his which made Seamus blush. I got the feeling these two were more than just friends and thinking back on Seamus' family and how his wife and daughter were both gone, I couldn't help but be a little happy for the guy even if she was flirting with me at the same time. Maybe that didn't bother him as much as it would've bothered me if it had been Paige on my lap and her eyes on Seamus like he was something for her to devour on the side.

The fire flickered dimly as the logs burned black, but the warmth it emitted reminded me of the flames just beneath my skin. "So tell me, Seamus. What brings you, and your new friend, to my home?" Shay got right to the point and didn't bother beating around the bush. Her arms curled around Seamus' neck as she sat on his lap, looking between both of us for an answer.

"We need yer help in finding Aeden's lassie. Her name is—"

"Her name is Paige, she has long brown hair that shines golden in the sun. About yea high, big emerald green eyes, feisty and strong but also gentle and—" I cut in eagerly but stopped myself as the two of them looked at me with big grins slapped across their faces like doting parents. When I didn't continue, Seamus took the reins.

"Aye, Paige. 'ave ye seen or heard of a girl like that?" Seamus continued grinning but looked to Shay for an answer, his fingers tugging gently at the tips of her hair.

"Hmmm. No markings, right?" I straightened my back in the chair.

"That's right, she doesn't. We both came from the...from Jessup...we walked into a purple swirling vortex," I replied, trying but failing to ease the slight tremble of my words. She'd be identifiable in this place because she wasn't marked. It hadn't occurred to me how bad that might be, until now. She was defenseless, and the thought made me sick to my stomach.

"Oh." Shay stood up, grabbing a kettle from a small table beside her and holding it up to Seamus. "Tea?" she asked and as if it were something he'd done for her countless times, he flicked his wrist, summoning a smooth stream of water above the kettle to fill it. She beamed back at him and put it on a rack above the fading flames. She threw a log on top of the ashen pile and poked at it with a long metal rod, her eyes fixed on the spot until it roared back to life.

"You've seen her then?" I pressed on, trying to get an answer. Trying to ease some of the terror that was washing over me. I needed to get to her, needed to be able to protect her in this fucked up place.

"No, but I did hear of a girl who came recently, arriving with no mark like all mortals do. Pixies love to gossip, even about things as small as mortals getting trapped here."

It had to be her. She was here. I just had to figure out what a pixie was, where I could find one, and how to get them to talk more, make them tell me where she was. Hopefully, they didn't also feed on flesh and power.

I examined Shay, noticing she had no markings other than the scales that were so faint, they were nearly invisible.

She wasn't a mortal. But she also wasn't like Seamus, like the people back in Costa. Like *me*. Seamus saw me eyeing her arm with a furrowed brow. "Shay here is a mermaid. She doesn't 'ave an element, but she can—"

"Now, now Seamus. Won't you let me show him? It's so much more fun that way." Shay waltzed over to Seamus and pulled on his arm to tug him from the chair. He rose willingly and swooped her into his arms as she began to sing. She sang a soft, soothing melody as she swayed with Seamus. The roughness in his face softened, becoming lighter and calmer with every breath of song that came from her. A weightlessness took over his entire body while I remained tense in my chair, thumb tugging at my bottom lip as I tried to understand what the fuck was happening to Seamus. He looked stuck in a trance as he moved around with her, his gaze fixed on her eyes as she continued her song. It was in a language I had never heard before but flowed from her lips with a dark undertone to it like she was about to lure him to his death. I reached slowly down to the hilt at my side, fingers flexing intently around it. Seamus stopped dancing and stood idly, like a statue or a soldier ready for a command. Shay stopped her song that echoed around the wooden walls and looked up at him, spinning the strands of his beard around her fingers. He didn't flinch, didn't move an inch and I tugged silently on the hilt, lifting the sword an inch, then two, from the scabbard.

"I release you," she whispered, the hint of the song still upon her lips. He dropped back down to the chair and snapped out of whatever state he was in. His eyes were languid but perked at the sight of my hand on the hilt, which I let go of the moment he gave a slight shake of his head. She manipulated people, putting them in a trance as she sang songs. Or was it the dancing that did it? Something she did had made him a willing puppet.

A fucked up kind of hypnotism.

Seamus smiled back up at Shay, who hadn't noticed that I was ready to fight her, to draw my sword across her throat. He tugged her down again on his lap, letting his fingers slide back into the ends of her damp black hair. How the fuck was I supposed to trust her to find Paige with us when she could just make us do whatever the hell she wanted? I'd barely started trusting Seamus, and now I was expected to trust someone, *something*, like her. Or was all of this part of his plan, needing Shay's help to bend me to her will, *their* will, and turn me in?

The kettle whistled, and Shay jumped from Seamus' lap to pour the tea into three mugs. I took mine from her thin fingers, giving her a word of thanks before setting it down on the armrest of the chair. There was no fucking way I'd be drinking whatever was in that cup. I'd seen girls getting roofied at parties before, the girls I'd end up leading away to my car and driving right back to wherever they lived. Didn't matter if I knew them or not, I'd help anyone in that situation in a heartbeat. Had even fought quite a few guys in the process over it. Bunnell may have been a top school, but the guys there were Grade-A assholes.

The steam rose from the mug beside me, the smell floral like roses coated in honey. It smelled harmless enough, but then again, most drugged mixes seemed innocent until they weren't, especially given by someone who looked like Shay. Her yellow door flashed in the corner of my vision like a warning sign. I'd need to keep my guard up and be cautious around her.

Twelve

PAIGE

Hector didn't falter once, not a single time, while I kicked and screamed for him to put me the hell down. Any task made by the man who said he was my father had for me couldn't have been good. And the fact that his henchman was a gigantic man with unwavering loyalty gave me even less hope that I'd be able to attempt an escape from the *task,* or of the walls of Gedeon's home which went on endlessly.

He moved us through the dark hallways and up several flights of stairs, the candle-lit sconces dimly lit along the path to a room I had no interest in occupying. Hector opened a door and dropped me to the floor, a loud thunking noise echoed in the cavernous room as my body slapped against the hardwood. I grunted and glared up at Hector who stared back down at me, his face set harder than stone.

"No use of your air powers unless commanded to do so. I will be back to get you in the morning to start your training," Hector said, his words sharp and irascible. I sneered back at Hector and spat on his shoes in retaliation. He simply turned and walked back out of the room, slamming the door behind him.

I sat there on the floor, hugging my knees to my chest for a while before I willed myself to get up and move around. The room emanated affluence, from the golden coffered ceiling down to the ornate carvings of gusts of wind on the baseboards similar to the wooden doors both in the dining room and the bedroom I stood in now. A large violet plush rug lay underneath the mahogany four-post bed large enough for six grown people to lay in comfortably, a stark contrast to my bed at home that was only meant to hold one, although I'd thought about squeezing Aeden in there with me on more than one occasion. A lofty fireplace blazed across the room, my only source of light at the moment. Next to it was an opening in the wall that led to an en-suite where the flooring shifted from sleek wooden planks to marble and the edge of a circular porcelain tub peeked through. A dresser with the same carvings was positioned on the other side of the bathroom doorway. On top of the dresser was a small painted portrait, framed in an oval of gold, of my mother.

I ran to the dresser and seized the photo. It was undeniably her—her wide smile and dimpled cheeks, the wind blowing through her wavy hair as she sat on a boulder surrounded by flowers, and the same emerald eyes as my own. She looked younger in the portrait, perhaps a little older than I was now, and she looked outright blissful as her cheeks blushed and pinched her eyes to a squint.

I held the picture to my chest, hugging it as tightly as I could, and began to sob. My mother was gone and would never get the chance to be like she was in the portrait again. I had only ever known her to be that happy once in my life but she was not nearly as young. I spent a lot of my time trying to think up ways to make her happy, to get her help, and to change her. Now, I would never have that chance. My hopes were crushed the moment the nurse had called me. And now no one would come to claim her, not even death granting her the reprieve she deserved. Guilt poured over me as my sobs grew heavier while my fingers clutched the frame so tightly that it left impressions on my skin. I slid down to the floor with my back against the dresser, allowing the weight of it all to bear down on me, coming in waves of regret, guilt, heartache, and even anger. How did anyone survive such grief? I began to choke on my sobs, my body consumed by mourning.

The only comfort I had lay in the hope that Aeden was still alive, somewhere in this messed-up place. I couldn't trust what Gedeon said about Aeden being killed, the thought of him hurting let alone dying sent sharp pains to my already wrecked heart. I wouldn't be able to survive the loss of him too. I'd have to fight my way out of here to find him, or hold on to the bit of hope I had that he would find his way back to me.

I stood up and placed my mother's portrait back down on the dresser, slightly shaking as I steadied myself and the wobbly frame. I walked into the gigantic bathroom and glanced around for a sink. Shortly after I'd turned eight when my mother was coherent and sober, she taught me the value of a hot, steamy towel and what wonders it did for any hurt that lingered on your face. I'd taken a tumble off my new bike and cried fearfully as I checked the bike over for scratches, dents, or any damage. Not even considering the scraped knee and cheek on my own body. She'd rushed me inside and held the warm towel to my scrapes, cleaning me up and easing the stress I'd had over my fall.

But that was so long ago and so distant in my memories it felt like someone else entirely lived through that. Someone else had a mother who cared. Someone else had a mother who could stop drinking long enough to care for them.

That wasn't my life. I could care for myself, I just needed a sink to wash away the pain.

A raised porcelain basin was anchored on the far wall, giving the appearance that it was floating in mid-air. A golden curved spout stemmed out from the wall and bent down over the long basin, golden curling knobs on either side that replicated moving wind. I rolled my eyes. The bathroom did not lack in splendor, similar to the rest of what I had seen so far of the house I now presumed was a castle. Even with a giant circular tub in the center, it had a standing shower along the opposite wall from the basin that spanned the entire wall all covered in marble and golden fixtures. A double luxury. A circular stained-glass window showing flames, ocean waves, vines, and wind gusts all twining together was on the wall in front of the tub between the basin and the shower, letting the moonlight flood into the bathroom in hues of red, blue, green and purple.

I went to the basin and turned the water on, staring into the mirror image of myself. The reflection revealed a face that was red and swollen—from my puffy lips to my bloodshot eyes. I grabbed a white hand towel with a gold threaded 'A' embroidered on it soaked it under the steaming water and lathered it with a lavender bar of soap that was perched on the edge of the sink. I draped the cloth over my face, waiting for the magic to take effect. To wipe away my stresses, the pain—all of it. When that didn't come, I threw the towel into the sink. I reeled back my tears again and buried them down. Purple flashed in my vision, the tattoo moving to the forefront of my mind. I took up the cloth and scrubbed until my arm turned raw and nearly bloody, but just as my emotions hadn't changed, neither did the mark.

As if in a fit of hysteria, I laughed. It wasn't exactly what I would've picked for my first tattoo. Purple was one of my least favorite colors, and now it was as much a part of me as the pain that was trapped in my chest.

I pursed my lips and thought back to Gedeon's tattoo, just the edge of it was visible but surely it was the same. I knew he was the reason I was flung across the room and maneuvered around like a rag doll but *how* was another question. It seemed downright crazy, yet some part of me knew that it was magic. A magic that was inside of me. A lightness hummed under my skin like an old muted tune coming back to life. And the way it felt to release it and throw that plate towards him, towards my abandoning, egotistical father, was more than euphoric on its own. It lit a spark in me that I had never felt before, like an addiction I'd given into.

I put the rag down over the faucet and laid my palm out in front of me, flexing my fingers one by one. My eyes took in the sprawling air current outlined in the mirror, going from my arm and upwards to the base of my neck. I closed my eyes and thought back to throwing the plate at Gedeon, my father, who was never there for me but decided to capture me and throw me into a room. My father, whose darkened gray eyes held no sympathy within them. My father, who made his henchman take me away before I could get another word in. My father, who blatantly showed no remorse that my mother was gone.

Madness grabbed hold of me and the air I'd felt earlier at the table swirled in my stomach and spread throughout my limbs. I opened my eyes and found a perfectly shaped ball the size of my head churning on my open palm. The inside of the orb looked like an aerial view of a hurricane—windy spirals moving rapidly matching the intensity of my anger. I took several deep breaths and refocused my thoughts before the anger became all-consuming as the magic dared it to, threatening to push me over the edge.

Kissing Aeden, his fingertips on the edges of my thighs as he lifted me, claiming my lips with a thrust that sent shivers down to my core. The spiral slowed in the orb, and the churning and frantic wind soothed as if in response to the memory of him. Air rubbed against my bones, making them feel light and hollow like bird's wings. The floor sunk away from me and I found myself hovering above the marble, orb still churning softly in my palm as I floated up towards the coffered ceiling.

A blink of my eyelids as the distance between myself and the floor stretched, a mere blink of concentration and I was sent crashing back down to the marble floor, landing with a loud slap of my ass against the hard surface. If I could float, if I could learn to wield whatever was pulsing under my skin, then maybe I could use it to escape.

I could get out of here and find Aeden myself.

I raised myself and a laugh forced its way through my chest as I took in how fucking insane I must be to think about escaping, possibly even flying, out of here. Yet that feeling inside of me quelled any doubts as swells of power whirled under my flesh, easing the tension of being trapped in this room more than any hot towel would have.

My mother never said anything about this place but surely she must have known if she had me, and had been with Gedeon. Thinking of her with a man like him drew up bile in my throat. He was a monster—nothing like the mother I knew I would have had if she'd stayed sober. She wasn't an angry drunk, but rather a depressed one, sulking and gorging on alcohol daily to forget the pain that I now believed was caused by the man down the hall more than anything. Maybe I wasn't the one at fault for her addiction. She was sweet, compassionate, and caring when she was sober all those years ago. Traits I couldn't picture belonging to Gedeon. Not now, not ever.

I moved back to the bedroom, willing my endless rumination to stop. I didn't bother removing my clothes or shoes as I plopped down on the palatial bed.

Holy shit the mattress. It feels light, airy, almost like it's a...

Cloud. The mattress was a damn cloud and as I wiggled my fingers under the sheet I felt the cool brush of flowing air hidden within. It greeted every curve of my body and held it delicately as my muscles relaxed and my face softened, lulling me into a coma-like sleep.

Thirteen

PAIGE

A deafening bang startled me awake the next morning. Hector barged into the room as my eyelids fluttered open. By no way of greeting, he marched to the elegant purple curtains that hung beside the bed and thrust them to either side, revealing a towering window, beaming through with an early morning sun. The brightness made me wince and recoil back under the sheets.

I rolled over and groaned. "Not you again." I hardened my face, hoping to show little to no signs of the slight fear I still had of the soldier-like man. I laid still, hoping Hector would march back out. All prayers were thrown to the literal wind of my mattress as Hector lifted my legs and flung me over his back. I swore at him and punched his back as hard as I could as he moved me from my bed to the bathroom, unaffected by my fury as if I were a gnat buzzing around him. I braced my arms outwardly the moment he stopped walking, expecting to fall to the floor like a sack of potatoes. He released both my legs as if on cue, my arms aiding my fall as I rolled across the marble. Hector walked right back out as several women rushed through the opening to the bathroom all at once, my sneer turning into a furrowed look of confusion. One woman rushed in with a towel, another holding soap, and the third holding a giant loofah on a stick. They were all slightly older than me, but not by much, and moved with such diligence and zeal that it made my head spin.

What a fucking wake-up call.

The women all moved to lift and undress me so quickly that I had no time to stop them or get a word passed my lips as all thoughts were abandoned. In a matter of seconds I was naked and being guided and eased into the tub, the water milky with soaps that smelled of citrus fields as the steam of the hot water wafted up into the air. I shielded my body the moment their hands left my arms, feeling a swell of self-awareness as the cool air of the room furled across my chest, making my nipples peak uncomfortably. The women smacked their teeth at me and pulled my arms from my chest, holding each arm out to scrub every inch of my body with the coarse loofah. I recoiled my spine against the edge of the tub, dipping inward to cover my breasts. One woman pulled a toothbrush from the pocket of her apron and got to work on my teeth, her mouth twisting in frustration as she cupped my chin and squeezed my cheeks to make them open.

"I can do this myself, you know," I said through gritted teeth, the women not pausing their attack on my body as another moved to start washing my hair. I would have barked out at them and screamed for them to stop, but in place of anger, I dug out sympathy for each of them, all just doing their jobs and obeying the same man I was by staying in this room. This was treatment reserved for royalty, for a princess, which I was not.

I couldn't be.

I grew up with hardly enough food in the fridge, let alone enough money to pay for the water and electricity to stay on. My mother received small checks in the mail for her disability, really just her inability to work—as she claimed. But those checks were stretched to their limits each month, and toward the end of the month it was always a wager—would I have enough food if I cut back a meal or two a day or would I choose to tempt my chances at the power company coming out if I paid a week late. Those were the struggles I dealt with most of my life. Yet, here was my father, with possibly more servants than I could count, evidently no lack of wealth or riches about him.

The women finished their raid on my hair, skin, teeth, and nails and wrapped me in a warmed lavender-scented towel before moving me into a purple fabric chair lined with more gold and air swirls. One woman got to work on my hair, drying it with the magic from her palm and braiding it down my back. She was the one who brushed my teeth earlier, her twisted face still in place as she brushed out the waves that always knotted in water. I grunted as she caught a knot in the brush and continued to yank it down, clearing the knot and making my scalp scream in pain. She had her brown hair pulled back in a tight bun and wore the same outfit as the other two, a long white dress with a white apron over it. I noticed they all had a similar mark in style as my own but were significantly smaller than mine, only making their way from their wrist to the middle of their forearm.

The servant woman with blonde hair moved over to the dresser and pulled out three pieces of clothing—one made of thick brown leather, unlaced strings hanging down from the back of what appeared to be a corset, matching long pants, and a long-sleeved shirt that resembled the one Hector wore in style, with more laces going down the part where my chest would be. The last servant woman with lighter brown hair motioned to remove my towel as I sat, still getting my hair braided. She flicked her wrist and my body hovered above the chair by an inch. I yelped as she yanked the towel from my lifted body, leaving me stark naked once again before I floated back down gently into the chair. The dark-haired woman with a constant resting bitch face completed her work on my hair and the other two flocked to grab my limbs and dress me as I sat like a doll, leaving my body limp for them to finish whatever they were doing to me. All three women released me and stepped back. I stood as the blonde woman shed a tear while she clasped her fists together, admiring her work. I turned toward the full-length mirror that rested on the floor near the bed and my jaw dropped. I looked like part of Robin Hood's crew of bandits in leather straps that formed a corseted vest around my waist and breasts and brown leather pants that gripped every curve of my ass. The white tunic that should have flowed down was instead bunched under the tightness of the thick leather. At least the sleeves gave an ounce of breath to my skin as they billowed down before another set of laces cut them off at my wrists. I turned more, seeing the long braid just meeting the bottom edge of the corset and the laces tied tight in the back, pushing my boobs up so high they could suffocate me if I leaned down too far. I had to admit, I looked hot in it. But the purpose of it was lost to me.

I finally willed myself to speak, directing my question to the woman with blonde hair as she seemed most approachable. Her head shook, clearing the awe from her face.

"Why am I dressed like this?" I asked, my eyes over my shoulder, glued on my perfectly rounded butt that even the tightest yoga pants couldn't make appear as lifted as it did in this leather. The tall thigh-high boots squeaked on the floor as I turned to look back at them.

Her smile widened as if the squeak of the boots was the cherry on top. "Your training begins today for your—" The girl with the bitchy face elbowed her sternly and the blonde cleared her throat. "These are the clothes that will allow you to practice your wielding more...comfortably. Nya will be meeting you on the training deck shortly." No bit of what I was wearing was comfortable.

I tugged on the back of the corset, adjusting the laces that dug into my back. Fighting about my comfort seemed fruitless as the light brown-haired woman eyed my laces through the mirror, making sure I didn't mess up all of their hard work. "Is that my *task*? Then I am free to go?"

"Oh...erm...no." The blonde glanced at the darkest-haired woman who only nodded her head, no jibe of her elbow this time. "No. Not exactly."

"How long am I going to be trapped here? When can I leave? I won't be treated like some kind of prisoner." I folded my arms across the tight leather and raised my eyebrows, waiting for a response.

The light brown-haired one spoke up this time, a small glint of sadness in her eyes as she spoke, "When the Mora of Prydia says you can." And with that, all three turned in unison to leave the room as Hector walked back in. He was still in the same clothes as the night before—a black tunic and pants with black boots—which I realized was probably his uniform seeing as the women and myself all donned our own. His big dark eyes looked me up and down but not suggestively—he was making sure I was ready for whatever waited for me on the training deck. He approached me and began to bend down but I dodged him as I darted to the side and around his back. He turned and grumbled at me as I continued to move out of the bedroom and into the hallway. Hector clasped my shoulders and tugged me back, commanding me to follow his lead and not my own. I scowled at him, but in reality, I had no idea where I was going so following him was the safer bet. There were way too many doors flanking either side of the hallways, the walls covered in ornate wallpaper in between the doors of what appeared to be a battle scene stretching on for the entirety of the corridor. People were drawn with such fine detail that even the marks on their arms were visible, some with twisting vines and others with waves, while the ones with fire were dying throughout, their blood inking into thick pools that leached into the beige background color of the wallpaper. It was like a twisted storybook, not a wall decoration. Wall sconces held fresh candles near every door we passed, yet they weren't needed. The hallway opened up to a large room with a balcony overlooking panes of glass, the same size as the ones from the dining area that I glanced out of the night before. Luminous beams of sunlight reached even the furthest corners of the room from the towering windows, the light stretching down all halls that stemmed off of it and covered any residual shadows. A grand staircase that sloped down to another level gave way to another huge room just below us, visible over the edge of the balcony of the floor we stood on.

The balcony inside the home stood above a room big enough to swallow four or more of my own home back in Jessup. Through the windows beyond the first balcony, I could see another balcony, just beyond a heavy set of glass doors. The outer balcony, staggered well below the one Hector and I stood over now, overlooked a superannuated town of sand-colored buildings that wove tightly together, the only gaps made visible by the people weaving in and out of them hundreds of feet below us. Beyond the town, beyond the stark walls that rose along the edges of the buildings, was an endless sea of green-topped trees that speared toward the sky. To the right was a very faint glimmer, a body of water, perhaps an ocean in the far-off distance, and my heart leaped as I remembered Gedeon's words, that Aeden was probably in a cage at sea. I hoped with every fiber of my being that he was wrong. Aeden was strong, more than just physically, and he would fight to stay alive. If there was someone I believed in without a shadow of a doubt, it was him.

Hector grabbed my wrist and pulled me down the boundless staircase while I held my gaze on the shimmer of water beyond the glass. Hector took a sharp turn and I snapped my head toward the deck we were about to set foot on through the glass doors. It was massive, lined with more concrete and glass along the edge, forming a half-wall that kept us in. The sun beat down on the concrete deck that stretched along the side of the house as we walked onto the deck. Only the dead center was made of planks of wood laid out to form a large rectangle. The walls of the castle loomed well above us. The cement shifted from the ground, creeping up the outer walls seamlessly with only the lines of expansive sheets of glass breaking the transition. Five floors above the deck shone a reflection of the sun as it cast off the silvery metal peaked roof. Several long towers were dotted throughout the enormous castle and were made of more windows, giving the illusion that the spiraling stairs inside were floating on air. It was as if Cinderella's castle had undergone a modern, more drab makeover and was more than three times the size of its predecessor. Gedeon didn't just have wealth. He *was* wealth.

My eyes grew wide as I gulped in astonishment. *If he had this much money, why didn't he take care of us? Why the hell did we live in near poverty?* Hatred grew for the man who said he was my father as I stood on the deck, my eyes glued to the substantial monstrosity while his trained pet Hector stood by the balcony's edge with his arms firmly to his sides, looking toward the doors in anticipation. The hatred weaved through my veins, calling on me to let it all go. I held out my palm toward a large window and screamed, granting me a release, a feeling of pure ecstasy as an orb the size of my body shot from my hand and toward the glass. My body shook as the orb bounced off the window and died quickly down to nothing, dismissing my power like it was an annoyance that held no merit. I seethed more, wanting to break Gedeon's precious house into a million pieces. He didn't deserve this. He left us with nothing and didn't even tell me of his existence. He left my mom to wallow in her sorrow and drink her pain away, which for all I knew, he was the cause of.

I braced myself and stood, legs wide with both palms out, allowing my rage to boil and flow freely until I felt the air taken from my lungs. A moment later I was wrenched to the floor in breathless gasps as I pawed at my throat, pleading for air. A shadow neared me and I managed to steal a glance up as my throat tightened.

Above me stood a woman with long, tightly curled auburn hair, her cheeks dotted with freckles that lifted as she smirked down at me. "You came ready for training, didn't you?" she said, her voice patronizing as I struggled for air. She nodded at Hector, then his hand flicked casually at his side and the breath came rushing back to my lungs at full force, causing me to choke on the sudden fullness in my chest.

She reached her arm out to help me up. I scoffed at her and slapped her arm aside, helping myself up instead. I didn't need anyone's help before and I wouldn't start needing it now. She laughed and raised her hand out to stop Hector, undoubtedly on his way to put me in my place, as if taking the breath from my lungs wasn't enough. He'd have me thrown over his shoulder to take me back to my bedroom before I could steady my breath again. I glowered at Hector before turning to walk carelessly away from the woman.

"I'm Nya, by the way, your instructor." A wall of vines sprouted up from the deck, blocking me from continuing my strides away from her. With my nose pressed to the vine wall, I held up my arm, trying to form another orb to throw back at her but only a small wisp of air formed before fading hastily.

"I don't care who you are," I admitted.

"Right, well, we were going to practice calling on your magic to summon it today, but I can see you won't need too much work with that," she said as she gestured toward where I threw the body-sized orb earlier and smiled back at me. "You know when most people come of age, and they first get their power, they actually *want* to learn more and *don't* try to kill their teachers."

"I'm not most people." I tried an orb again and failed, the flicker of purple and air rolling down my fingertips until it blended with the air around us.

"No, no you're not," she replied, lowering her voice to calm me down. But I didn't want to be calm. I wanted to be the exact opposite of calm. I wanted to be what the inside of a hurricane was like before it wiped out an entire block of a city.

"Why am I here?" The words came out more like a statement than a question. Between everything I had just gone through all within the span of half a day, and the growing hunger inside of me to not only eat but also release my power and destroy things, I was a dynamite stick ready to burst.

"Gedeon, your father, said you were in the mortal world with your mother before coming to Aellethia, is that right?" *Aellethia? That's what this place is called?* She ignored my question and shot one of her own at me. And bringing up my mother? *Not helping.*

"Right where daddy dearest left us. Your turn."

She sighed, her shoulders visibly sagging under an invisible weight. A flicker of sadness pulled her brows down toward her arctic blue eyes as she looked at me. "I know losing your parents is hard. I lost both of mine when I was little." Her brows knitted together, recollection sweeping over her features. "You are here because of the upcoming Triad. As you are High Fae and the daughter of a Mora, you are expected to train the use of your powers, and your strength, as much as you can before entering the trials. I'm going to teach you how to wield the air magic you developed last night, as well as basic combat skills, both hand-to-hand and with weapons."

"So, what you're saying is, and correct me if I'm wrong, that my father kidnapped me and trapped me in Aellethia so I could turn into one of...whatever you all are, High Fae you said?" A series of bubbling, near-hysterical laughs escaped me. "And after I turn into a freak with air shooting from me, you want me to use that in, what was it you called it, a Triad? Am I getting this right?" I felt no clearer in my thoughts than I had before I asked her why I was here. If anything, I was doubly fucking confused.

"*You* are High Fae, not me. And you were born that way. Your father is the Mora of the surrounding parts, essentially a king if you'd rather call him that." I didn't. "I'm the class below you, not strong enough to be a high fae—not of royal blood, or descending from one of the stronger families. But don't think for a second it makes me weak." She rolled back her shoulders and corrected her posture, standing pridefully. She righted her words like she did her shoulders, sounding as if she were reading from a textbook, and said, "You will fight in the Triad to claim your birthright, as is being required of you. If you do not, you will potentially be stripped of your power and banished back to the mortal world, or any other form of punishment as seen fit by Lord Gedeon."

A fucking king. Of course, he was a king—the servants, the ginormous castle, the henchman doing whatever he asked them to do. The pieces all fit together perfectly down to Gedeon's flawlessly coiffed hair. The part that sent me reeling into a spiral steeper than the castle's grand staircase was how I was expected to fight in order to stay here.

I had no desire to be here and would happily go back, renouncing anything I had claim to. I never needed a castle, exorbitant wealth, or a father. Only one thing held me back. I had no idea where Aeden was, if he was safe, or if he was working on finding a way back home, or maybe even back to me. I couldn't just leave without him. As much as I wanted no part in the life I was deprived of, to begin with, I wouldn't rescind any claims until I knew I could get us both out of here. Together. If the alternative meant being sent back with nothing, then I would have to train with the woman who stood in front of me, and fight like my life depended on it.

Nya looked into my eyes as the silent battle I waged with my thoughts came to a halt. Mirroring my determination and flashing a wide grin at me, she moved to the center of the training deck and waved for me to follow along.

"Ready now, are you?" she taunted, but the glimmer in her eyes suggested a friendlier tone than she was letting on. I smirked up at her, hiding the tremble of my hands as I moved to join her in the middle of the training deck.

Training tools lined the outer wall of the castle that surrounded the training deck, catching my attention as the morning sun reflected off the hundreds of metal blades that hung there. The weapons rack was full of swords, maces, and axes of various lengths and widths, a long row of daggers and throwing stars, and tons more that I didn't know the names of, all lined up and organized, ready for use. Next to the rack were different dummies, some resembled people and some animals. One even looked like a mermaid, with a woman's top part and a long tailfin below her torso, but that couldn't be right.

I glanced back at Hector, who was still as a door by the balcony's edge and imagined him being the source behind the mashup of animals and people. It helped ease some of the anxiety that spiked to a dizzying level. But that was short-lived. At the end of the row of weapons and dummies was a table full of glass vials and beakers full of colored liquids and vapors akin to what you'd find in a chemistry classroom. Yet, the gurney at the end sent a shiver down my spine as I realized this fight, this Triad, was not just some game that held a winner and a loser, like some sport. I only ran track & field for one season but I still remembered how it felt to run and win, and how it felt to run and lose. I think the losers of the Triad may lose more than just their pride.

Nya stood a few feet from me and noticed my trail of sight moving between each training item, ending with the gurney, lifting her brow at me as I struggled not to gawk. "Those tonics there will help if you are injured...but I'm a healer, you won't have to worry about getting hurt," she said, her voice aimed to soothe but it came off condescending.

"I'm supposed to feel safe knowing you can shove a green liquid down my throat if my arm gets lobbed off using those giant swords over there?" I pointed at the longswords hanging ominously, the intrusive thoughts of dismemberment popping in and out.

"You will never be safe here until you learn to fight like your life depends on it, because it does," she whispered.

"Teach me then," I countered, not lowering my voice to mimic hers as I straightened my back and held up my fists.

"Right." She shook the worry from her face and walked to the row of dummies. "How about we take out some of that anger on this?" She grabbed one of the dummies that imitated a male and moved it to the center of the wooden planks. She maneuvered her wrist by the crown of the dummy's head and a thick twine of vines grew into a sort of hair, shaped just like Gedeons had been the night before.

It was then that I noticed the tattoo on her arm—green and brown twisting vines with leaves and small flowers dotted along the trailing mark that started at her wrist and reached up to cover her elbow. Above it, waves crashed and turned into swirling currents, leading up to cover the bottom of her bicep. It was a small blip of blue, but the mark was the same as the one on the wallpaper in the hallways, as was the earthy one that twined below it. Both were recognizable even through all the bloodshed.

"That should give you something to direct your anger at, now let's get you a sword." She winked at me and I had to hold back on the smile I aimed at her, the knowledge that it grew so genuinely making me more anxious.

But Nya knew Gedeon was a tool, and it felt like we were sharing a secret between us. Neither of us liked the man. And it was comforting to think I wouldn't be entirely alone like I'd so often been in my life before Aeden showed up.

Fourteen

AEDEN

The waters of Lake Kree were more eerie and mystifying than the foggy bog of hags, its water near black leaving only my imagination to wonder what lay beneath as we walked along its shore. Not even the edge of the sand where the tide met the shoreline was transparent enough, going from sand to stark black nothingness almost like a tarry sludge spread across the top of the water. Only the small current of rippling waves lulling from the occasional breeze convinced me otherwise.

Seamus suggested we take the long path to meet with the pixies in the Highland Woods on the other side of the lake, avoiding Prydia and the hundreds of guards lining the walls of the city. He preferred a low profile, and Shay agreed hastily with him when she caught a glimpse of my arm before we left her shack. I was hesitant to share anything with Shayanna, but Seamus gave me no choice when he doused my tunic with a flood of water and told me to remove it. The fucker. He knew I was skeptical of the mermaid by the way I looked at her, it wasn't like I tried to hide it. Her strange twisted power taking hold of Seamus freaked me the hell out. The moment she looked at me and my arm, her shoulders noticeably tensed and she recoiled slightly, glancing at Seamus with such fear in her eyes I thought she would run like the other woman at the bar had.

I knew her twisted power, and she knew my outlawed one. We were even—in a sense.

It wasn't my choice to have the mark. The red flames swept up and engulfed the edge of my neck, visible in the reflection of the pitch-black lake. I was still holding my damp tunic over my shoulder but Seamus assured me we were safe on the far right side of Lake Kree until we neared the Highland Mountains which would take until the next morning to get to. It was...odd that Seamus knew exactly when and where we'd encounter other fae or guards like he knew the land better than the back of his hand. But maybe that's just how it was here.

We walked in silence for nearly an hour before Shay loosened the tension she still held in her shoulders, allowing them to sag down below her jawline. The hem of her ankle-length dress dropped lower while she laughed at whatever jokes Seamus was whispering to her as I followed distantly behind them. They looked like two kids skipping school, giggling and murmuring to each other, only quieting to steal glances at their surroundings to ensure we were indeed still alone and safe.

The way Seamus and Shay were so ready to help me after their initial trepidation diminished gave me a glimmer of hope that others may be like them, and staying hidden while trying to find Paige wouldn't be so bad if I had a few people to rely on. Although Shay's power confounded me, watching her walk ahead with Seamus gave me a sense of peace. It was almost like being with my team again, with Bunnell's best defensive lineman Richards pushing forward to protect me as I ran and took aim with the ball. We worked well together during games and practices, but I never got to know much about him and how he was off the field. I kept my guard up too much and didn't let many people in, turning down outings with my team or putting up a facade at parties. And any girl I brought home to help me forget about my past, and distract me from the person I wanted most never got close enough to learn anything about me beyond how I looked and fucked. They usually got agitated about the second or third time around that I never asked them to dinner, or took them out, to which I would just shrug and suggest they don't come back again, giving them no hope for anything more. Because there wasn't any hope for them once Paige had come into the picture. It was callous, but it was what I learned to do in the foster system. If you trusted people too openly, you left yourself open to getting hurt. Putting up walls was a safer bet and became second nature to me until Paige broke all those barriers down and turned me into the whimpering fool I am today. Now I was traveling in some magical world with two people I would have never approached back home let alone attempt to trust my life and safety with. I was either heading towards my death or successfully navigating this place which I somehow belonged in.

The sun beat down on us but the cooling breeze gusting in from the lakefront made the sun's rays tickle my skin, the warmth coming in waves each time the wind died down. The mountains grew larger as we approached them with every growing hour. We walked on with still no one or thing in sight except for the occasional tail fin and fish jumping from the lake to our left. Each time a tail fin splashed in the distance, I could see Shay glance over. The fins were similar in shape but not in color to the one she no longer showed. She lifted her dress occasionally to walk in the lapping water, raising the hem above her knees, above the faint blue outline of scales that shimmered in the sun. There were certainly more like her, but I had to wonder if they typically left the water and switched to legs or if it was something only she could do. I didn't see any of the fins come closer to us as we pressed on, completely ignoring our existence, unlike the hags who sought us out for a meal. Whatever mermaids ate, it probably wasn't on the menu for the hags.

We walked on for another hour while the sun began to set and our pace slowed dramatically from the one we started with. We were exhausted and hungry. Some water would probably be good before dehydration set in, but there was no way I'd be drinking from the murky lake. But Seamus, Seamus had all the water we'd need.

"Seamus, you think you could do that water thing? I need a drink." I smacked my tongue to my teeth, feeling how dry my mouth had become. I was still reluctant to fully grasp terms like magic and powers, acting like what he did was some kind of parlor trick.

He stopped walking and Shay stood by him as I approached. "Aye Lad, good thinkin'. Tip-up an' open yer mouth." He licked his cracking lips, evidently needing it just as badly as I did. Either Shay distracted him, or the need to keep moving was more vital. Possibly both. A stream of water emerged out of thin air above my head, flowing until I was done drinking what felt like a gallon's worth. The growling of my stomach and slight dizziness finally eased while Seamus supplied the same streaming water for himself and Shay.

"Thanks. What's the plan when it's dark out?" I motioned towards the sun as it continued its rapid descent behind us, an enlarged moon butting up close by the fading sun.

Shayanna pointed to a huge boulder in the distance. "There's a cave about a half mile up, it's well-known by merpeople but they won't bother us if they see someone is inside. It's safe for the night there." Seamus nodded alongside her. I still wasn't ready to fully trust either of them but the little I did give them they had not yet abused. They had more than several opportunities to lead me astray or kill me by now, and I would have to keep reminding myself of that to push on through.

The cave was decent enough to rest in, but I could see why the others wouldn't try to come so long as we occupied it. There would be no room for anyone else, and unless they were violent and tried to come out for blood, I had to assume Shay was telling the truth—that we would be alone.

Seamus left for firewood before setting foot inside, the sun a few minutes away from being fully submerged beyond the horizon line. I wondered where he could manage to find wood, but he showed up shortly after the night came, holding scraggly pieces of driftwood he pulled from the lake, the wood dripping still as he placed it on the sandy ground of the cave in a pile. He motioned his wrist and the water droplets lifted slowly from the wood as if defying gravity, grouping above the pieces of driftwood and forming a larger puddle. With another flick of his hand, the water flew out from the cave, landing with a splash as it returned to the lake just beyond the cave's entrance.

"Now's your turn, Boyo," he said, garishly smiling at me like he was a boy waiting to play with his shiny new toy. He enjoyed watching me use the power that was building inside of me, an almost paternal pride showing on his face each time I managed to summon it.

I lifted my palm out and willed a small orb to form, then shot it into the largest piece of driftwood with a force that nearly knocked the pile of wood over as it shimmied inside. Shay giggled nervously, trying to hide the fear that stemmed from my power and flinching slightly as the orb burst into a larger flame that ignited the entire stack in seconds.

"Ye'll get better at it, in due time." But I didn't want to be in this place longer than was needed. Surely he knew I wanted to leave here with Paige after finding her. Living in Aellethia was not part of the plan.

"Shay, your pixie friends, are you sure they will be able to help me?" I asked, still unsure what a pixie was but if they liked to talk and spill secrets then I'd be there to hear anything regarding Paige and where she may be.

"Pixies are helpful *if* you know where to find them and *if* you don't piss them off. Many people go out looking for them to collect the dust they give off because it fetches a high price at the Forga Market if you manage to get some." Too many *ifs*. I held my palms out to the fire, feeling the pull it had to the power under my skin. "But there're other things in the woods that stop people from looking. Lucky for you boys, I know my way around the Highland Woods, and I've dealt with the pixies before. I was going to head that way for some dust when you both showed up, although I would have preferred to swim." She stuck her tongue out at Seamus and he laughed back at her, stroking his long beard as her words settled over him. He looked protective, like how I looked at Paige when she was about to do something I didn't approve of.

"I told ye 'fore Shay, if ye need to go to the woods for dust, I will help ye. I don't like ye going there yerself." Seamus lifted a brow at Shay.

She shrugged back. "I'm a big girl, Seamus, and nearly a hundred years old now. I think I know what I'm doing."

My jaw dropped and I craned my neck to stare at the youthful, soft-skinned woman sitting between us as she admitted she was older than most people only dreamed of becoming. *How did she look so young?*

They both let out a laugh that filled the cave's walls, echoing around us. "Aye, mortals don't live that long, do they?" Seamus said mockingly. I didn't need to point out that they indeed did not, not while looking that good at least. She should be full of wrinkles, a bend in her back, missing teeth, or sagging jowls. But she'd just walked at least ten or more miles without complaining in the slightest. Age was but a fucking number, quite literally to her. Maybe there were some perks to being in Aellethia after all.

"How old are you then, Seamus?"

I waited as he stroked his beard. "Erm, maybe a hundred forty—no—fifty...aye, I lost count. The drinkin' isn't helpin'." Seamus drew his brows together, counting on his fingers before throwing up his hands. He was older than Shay and appeared so, but I never would have guessed either of their ages correctly.

"Is it normal to age so...well?"

Shay nodded her head. "We can live for hundreds or thousands of years as long as we can keep our heads on our shoulders and avoid any plague. Most of us die in battle, though." Her head dipped low and her eyes trailed to Seamus. He stood up abruptly, fingers tapping on his thigh, and mumbled something about looking for food before he left the cave.

I looked over to Shayanna who was biting her lip as she stared beyond the cave's entrance. "His family died in a raid...both his..."

I sighed the portraits that hung on the walls of Seamus' house flipping through my mind. "Yeah, he told me. His daughter and wife. I can't imagine...losing the people you love most."

"It's not just them, Aeden." Her voice softened to a whisper as she continued. "More than half of Costa burned down that day. Seamus lost his family, along with his friends and neighbors. He was out boating when he saw the smoke and flames and came back to rubble and death, dozens of bodies lying everywhere. He couldn't even find the bodies of his wife and daughter but found skeletons in his home, flesh still burning off the bones." She shivered and wrapped her long, skinny arms around herself. She shook her head and lowered her voice more. "The Mora of Prydia, Lord Gedeon Aerborne, is an evil man. Many fear him, despise him even, but not many fight back. The ones who do, don't live to tell about it."

"He burned down Costa?" The homes. The shacks with torn pieces and missing windows. They were rebuilding what they'd lost with whatever resources they had. And Seamus' home, the locks, and the cleanliness. He was trying to rebuild his home as if his world hadn't been shattered—as if his girls were still coming home.

"No, he had his guards burn it down for him. Moras don't need to do the dirty work, but they can if they must. In the case of Viz—"

Shay fell silent as Seamus stepped back into the cave, holding two large fish by the tail as they flopped around, struggling for breath.

"Time for a lesson, Lad." I wasn't sure if he overheard Shay, or if he was angry at us for talking about his family. I gritted my teeth in response and stared up at him from the sandy floor, not sure if I was anticipating a fight or not. He cocked his brow down at me. "I just need yer help cooking these up, is all. I thought this would be a good time to teach ye somethin' new. Ease up, would ye?"

"Sorry. Everything is new to me." My power, his reactions, this fucking world. I was excited, yet terrified, to learn more about the fire burning under my skin. It wouldn't serve a purpose back in Jessup, but here, it could potentially mean living long enough to get both Paige and me back home.

"Calm yer thoughts and take deep breaths. Picture yer fire inside settlin' down with ye, formin' into a shape in yer mind. We need a surface. Flat. Movable. Mold softly, then release the image to yer palm."

I did as he said, closing my eyes and envisioning a flame simmering down into a flat, smooth surface. I felt the flames calm with my breaths, bending to my will, smoothing with each inhale and spreading thin with each exhale. The image made of flames stayed in my mind as I held out my palm and opened my eyes.

Before us stood the very surface I built in my mind, but smaller as it floated above my palm. I pinched my brows together, concentrating.

"Fuckin' beautiful job! Now move the surface slowly, very carefully. Place it above the fire. One step at a time."

His arms worked in the corner of my vision, mimicking the movements of the small surface. Shay retreated as far back into the cave as she could, her shadow moving against the wall. If she saw what I did to the hag back in the bog, she probably wouldn't be inside the cave anymore.

I took steady breaths as I finished placing the surface above the fire, legs sprouting to support it on either side like a table. My lips curled up to one side as the structure settled smoothly above the flames.

"Steady now Laddie, grow the table just slightly..." I continued my deep breaths and focused all of my attention on the small table, hot flames licking down to the sand to stretch the legs and dancing across the top to widen it. A jolt of excitement rippled up my spine as the table finally met the dimensions that surrounded the top of the fire, allowing a good space for both fish to cook on.

"Now that, Aeden, is a fine fire table. Ye'll master shape formation in no time." He laid the fish out on top of my work and a warmth filled me that was beyond the heat of the fire I sat in front of. Beyond the flames I felt flickering inside of me. I rubbed my palm down the length of my mark, watching the permanent red flames almost glow under the acknowledgment.

Shay came off the edge of the cave wall slowly, edging back into her spot around the fire, our blended shadows flickering along the back wall of the cave. We sat and ate mostly in silence, and only after we finished did Shay and Seamus begin to share stories of somewhere called the Forga Market. Seamus made a living selling the fish he caught at Forga, and Shay specialized in gathering illegal goods—things like pixie dust and minotaur horns she mentioned as I tried to stop my jaw from dropping. I found it surprising that such a small-framed woman with hardly any muscle definition, and delicate, unscathed skin could poach. This world, and what I had yet to encounter, was becoming easier to swallow. Magic and power, elemental marks, Moras, magical creatures—all of it was making more sense with every passing minute as I sat in a cave talking to a water-wielder and a fucking mermaid.

The pull I felt before I entered the vortex with Paige was more than just a desire to sate my curiosity. It was the pull of home. Of longing. Of the magic that thrummed beneath my flesh. The irresistible pull now floated within every fiber of who I was. To my core, I knew this was where I was from, where I would have grown up and learned everything there was to know about magic and being who I should've been. Not some fucking lost foster child who had to learn to become a man too early. I was a fire-wielder. A part of me ached for the knowledge that I didn't have. The void that kept me mentally trapped in the mortal world, in foster care, with people who didn't give a fuck about me. I needed to know who my parents were. I needed to know how I ended up so far from home. Because that's what this place was, what it felt like with each passing breath and pulse of magic that flowed through my veins.

I was home.

FIFTEEN

AEDEN

Shay woke us up the next morning as she jumped into the lake, black murky water splattering the edges of the cave entrance and a reverberating splash that echoed on the walls, breaking the early morning silence as her tail fin smacked the top of the water. Seamus sat up from the sandy ground and stretched his arms out, the entire left side of his body covered in sand from where he slept. I sat up and ran my hands through my hair, managing to shake out an entire pound of sand as it rained down to the ground.

"The sun isn't even up yet and she's already swimming." I pointed my chin out towards the lake to the spot where her tail fin repeatedly broke the surface of the water. She moved rapidly through the water as if her life depended on it, her whole body breaking the surface as she jumped into the air, revealing her entire form. Her metallic blue scales started just below her belly button and encompassed the totality of her long legs ending in a fanning array of lighter blue scales before coming to several sharp points at the tip of her tail. Her tanned skin glistened in the emerging sunlight, her chest bare with a few long strands of wet dark hair plastered to her skin by the water.

Seamus patted the sand from his skin and ran a hand through his short fiery hair then down through his beard. "She needs to swim. It's in her blood like the fire is in yers and water is in mine. Keeping it in only makes ye go mad." His eyes latched onto her body, clearly riddled with lust as he stood up and exited the cave to join Shay by the water. I questioned whether I should follow behind, but Seamus threw his head over his shoulder and motioned for me to come along, all desire gone from his face like he was used to hiding it around her. The same way I'd hidden it from mine for years.

A pale set of ass cheeks flashed into my vision the moment I left the cave, finding Seamus stripped down with a shower of water above him. I had seen plenty of naked guys before in the shower room but that was to be expected when I played football. I did *not* expect to see Seamus naked, ever. I cleared my throat and looked out over Lake Kree instead. Without pause, I dashed into the lake, taking my chances with the black lake waters rather than standing in my full naked glory. I heard Shay's laughter as I dove my head under the cool water. I opened my eyes and found the water was surprisingly crystal clear, like looking through aquarium glass. The lake quickly steepened and led into an underwater oasis. Sunken boats and boulders like our cave on the shore were turned into homes, lily pads lining the roofs like shingles and algae-covered sand to mimic rugs. There weren't many homes, maybe fifteen or so but the lake took a solid day to get as far as we were. This was only a glimpse into Shay's world. I lifted my head and looked at her in awe, feeling like I just discovered the lost city of Atlantis.

"You like what you see?" she asked, pulling on her dress and giggling from the shoreline while wringing out her hair next to Seamus who continued to shower.

"It's...it's incredible. How does the water look so dark from the top, but clear underneath?"

"Why, magic of course. It's as if the Stars knew we needed to be concealed."

I stood chest-deep in the water and felt a strange pull to it, almost all-consuming like the flames had been when they first rushed through me. I lifted my fingertips, skating them across the top of the water as my eyes stayed transfixed on how the liquid lapped against my opened palm. The coolness of the water was combated by my inner warmth, the flames keeping the cold at bay like my own internal thermostat. I tried welcoming the cool in and pushing the fire aside, and my insides started to surge like a tidal wave trying to break free.

"Um, Seamus?" I called out to him, my voice surprisingly gurgled as if I were drowning, even though my face and chest were above the water. My fingers still laced the water in and out, a fluid worm weaving between each knuckle.

He halted his shower and looked my way. "Are ye good Lad? Ye don't sound so—"

The surge of water drowning me from the inside came out with such force from my hand that I was propelled deeper into the lake, forcing me under. I rushed to swim back up, to guide the same force in the opposite direction but found myself lifted by a foreign force of water not coming from within me. My legs were still kicking as I breached the surface and flung back to the shore on a tidal wave so fast that I cried out in surprise. My jaw was wide open as I collided with the sand face first, filling my mouth with the chalky grains.

"What the fuck!" I shouted, spitting out the sand as I brought myself to my feet.

Shay and Seamus's eyes glazed over each other before they washed over me. "Turn around, Boyo." I did as he asked, not wanting to hear what weird shit was happening but acknowledging the strange tingling sensations on my back like I had before on my arm. Shay gasped so loud I swore the other mermaids below the surface could have heard her.

"What is it?" I hesitated and turned back to them slowly.

Seamus tugged on the tips of his beard as the color of Shay's skin faded around her cheeks. "Yer a water-wielder too..." His fingers now raked through his beard furiously, drawing his eyebrows together like this was uncommon. Like I was a marvel, and he was perplexed by it.

Shit.

I walked back to the water and glanced behind my shoulder to take in my reflection. Sure enough, there was a mark all too familiar as the one that filled Seamus' forearm. A blend of red flames dipped and turned starkly to blue like the hottest part of a flame. Only, it wasn't heat that anchored the blue to my flesh. The cerulean and navy waves edged with foam started at the top back of my left shoulder, going down the left side of my back briefly before curving just under my shoulder blades and on towards the right side of my back, creating a hook of tumbling water that rolled back up and stopped right at my spine. The waves curled and crashed in vibrant swirls, dodging the space along my right side and lower end as well.

I looked back up at them whose eyes widened as they stared right back at me, completely speechless. "Is this...bad?" I reached my hand over my shoulder, shuddering as the touch elicited an awareness under my skin that sent the waves flooding through my system.

Seamus shook his head, clearing his expression of concern. "Oh, fae can 'ave more than one element, although less common...that isn't the problem." He cleared his throat and looked at Shay, a silent question being asked between the two of them. "The size is the problem."

"I've never heard someone tell me my size was a problem," I mumbled under my breath, the water-like blood seeping under my muscles that tensed with the new recognition. They fell quiet. "Are we still good?" I needed assurance as if the power inside of me would be sated by the knowledge that it could grow, that I could learn to use this to my advantage with the help of my allies.

"We are good, but you better put that tunic back on. And if anyone talks or looks at you, you are a water-wielder only. Got it?" Shay commanded, noting that Seamus was in shock, stroking his beard with feral pulls that threatened to make his jaw bare if he continued any longer.

"Good. Now for the love of god Seamus, would you please put on some fucking clothes? We have to go find these pixies and I doubt they want to see your ginger junk on full display." Seamus' attention snapped back to us at the turn of harshness in my voice. But with Seamus clothed, and Shay's soothing notions of being able to wield openly with the newfound element, the inner fear that laced my words sunk slowly into the sand beneath my feet. Fear that I'd lose the only hope of finding Paige, fear that I'd lose the people who were helping more than I'd ever anticipated. Fear of being utterly alone again because of things that were beyond my control. A control I was starting to gain as the power flooded and burned within me.

PAIGE

Letting out the bulk of my anger with a sword on the Gedeon dummy worked wonders for my mood. Holding the sword correctly was difficult for the first hour until Nya grew vines that stemmed from the hilt of the sword and wrapped around my hands, becoming an extension of my own arm. It also prevented me from throwing it toward her as she barked orders at me, killing two birds with one stone for Nya.

We practiced with a sword all morning, slashing at the dummy's arms, legs, and neck over and over until I was able to form smooth motions that would fully disable and kill an opponent. I had to admit, it was rather intoxicating. But the idea of having to kill something, let alone someone, made bile rise in my throat. I wasn't sure I'd ever be comfortable causing death or destruction—something Gedeon seemed to have no issues with as his grand castle of achievement, of a former victory, loomed over the training deck.

The Triad was set in an arena that could disguise itself as anything for those beyond the seats, in center-stage—a battlefield, a desert, a thinly veiling fog that descended into a steep pit of fire. Anything. Nya supplied that much for me before narrowing it down to explaining that the Triad was a set of three different tests of my abilities, all designed by the Stars, as she put it. Whether that was figurative or literal, I had no idea. Each of my questions gathered at the tip of my tongue before being greeted by another, then another. All were rolling into the pit of anxiety in my chest, making it compress in on me.

The Triad would start with the first task in just over a week with the others falling shortly after. There was no way I was going to master anything in a week, yet Nya assured me she would do her best. I could only hope her best was good enough to keep me alive.

Finally, she allowed a break right before noon. My stomach screamed in agony without having anything in it yet. I silently cursed my stubbornness as my mouth watered from remembering the plate of food I sent across the room the night before. I should've at least scarfed down something before flinging the rest at my father.

My eyes trailed over to where Hector had been watching us train all morning, not moving an inch from the balcony's edge like the good little soldier he was. That is, not until Nya called for a recess. He responded vigilantly and walked right up to me, trying to grab me again to haul me away. *This man clearly did not get the hint from this morning or last night and I had no idea where he got the notion that you could just walk up to someone and throw them over your shoulder to get them to move.* He had damn well seen me use my legs, and even though he seemed simple-minded, I assumed he had to have a brain to work for Gedeon as his right-hand man. I bolted to the side yet again as his broad arms swung just over my head, skirting his move.

He gave in after trying and failing only once, allowing me to follow him inside the castle. He guided me into the grand room and led me to the far left where a familiar door made of wood was held open by the woman from last night, wearing the same apron and dress as she was before. Her mark, as I was able to recognize now as an air-wielder mark, was the same length as the other women who dressed me—just a flicker of a mark that faded in and out along their wrist. I made a mental note to find out why theirs was significantly smaller than my own as I walked inside the room behind Hector.

The long table with the gaudy candelabra that I wanted to spit on had two plates on either end—one plate to the left was unclaimed, and a chair lay waiting in front of it. To the right was Gedeon, wearing a purple jacket that had golden buttons going down diagonally from his Adam's apple down to where the jacket ended below the table. There were more air swirls, just like the ones on the doors and trim, etched in with a golden thread, adorning his shoulders and weaving in and out of where each button lay. His cold, gray eyes lifted only a moment to welcome me in, though the slight frown on his face told me he was not pleased. I wondered if maybe he was unloved for so long that his mouth was settled in a permanent grimace. I curled my lips in, wondering if my face would have resembled my father's sternly set features more if Aeden never came into my life.

Gedeon resumed eating his lunch which resembled my own—sliced bloody red steak on top of a bed of raw leafy vegetables, garnished with a type of yellow flower I'd never seen before but it looked good enough to eat. He didn't utter a word and the silence in the room dragged on as I dug into my food. I didn't know how to use the three different forks set out beside my plate or the two knives on the other side of it but I grabbed the two that looked the best to use on steak and just went for it. If Gedeon was going to continue to treat me like a nuisance in his life then I would show him how much I didn't care to be a part of his, starting with throwing all manners out the gargantuan window.

I eventually ditched the knife and just used my fingers to ease the pieces of food onto my fork. Just when I was nearly done with everything on my plate, sucking on my fingers to get the steak juice from them, Gedeon slammed his fists down onto the table and growled at me like an animal, even baring his teeth to show his displeasure. I finished licking my fingers and smiled back at him as sweetly as I possibly could before reaching for the glass of water in front of me.

"Do you ever act appropriately and do as you are told or are you just as bad as your mother?" He spit out the last word, clearly very agitated with me.

Goal achieved.

"Oh no *father*, I'm much worse." I held my smile and even dared a wink at him before taking a sip from the glass.

"I didn't invite you here to talk back to me, girl. You are here because I allow you to be here and I allow you the right to train for the Triad. Don't overstep or I will return you to your pigsty in the mortal world." His jaw ticked and I had to bite my tongue on calling his bluff. He brought me here for a reason, and something told me he couldn't just send me back.

"My name is *Paige,* not *girl.* You can abandon me all you want, but at least give me the decency to call me by the name my mother chose for me." I set my glass down and glared back at him, choosing against telling him to just send me back home already. I wiped my mouth with the cloth that covered my lap before ditching it on top of my empty plate. I scoffed, picking bits of steak out from between my teeth as Gedeon's face flushed red. "It is a funny thing, though. It sounded like you just said you invited me here, yet I remember being sucked into a vortex after following a very rude and anthropomorphic owl before landing flat on my face in the most uninviting way ever." If he wasn't bluffing and did send me home, I would most likely never see Aeden again. But my anger was building to unprecedented levels.

His jaw flexed more and his wrist twitched against the tabletop threateningly. "That *owl* was supposed to be a man helping you at the hospital," he said and I swore he redirected his rage from me to Hector as his eyes snapped momentarily toward him and then back my way. "That man was *supposed* to extend an invitation to my home." His tone now rose two clicks above what I was comfortable with, sending a shudder down my back as I recalled the steely-eyed man holding flowers in my mother's hospital room. The same eyes that now widened in fear as Gedeon's words settled over the room.

Hector's face twisted agonizingly and I couldn't tell if he was about to cry or if he had to use the bathroom. "I'm so-so-sor—" he stuttered and then abruptly recomposed his features and cleared his throat. "The plan failed, sir. I failed you, but I got her here, as requested." He neither looked at me nor Gedeon as he spoke. Gedeon rose to his feet and stalked over to Hector, grabbed his throat with one hand, and jerked him up to meet him at eye level, forcing Hector to stand on his tiptoes as Gedeon stood nearly two inches taller than Hector. Hector choked out another apology, now calling him *lord* instead of *sir* which seemed to ease Gedeon's tension to some degree. He was undoubtedly a sadist, through and through.

Hector fell to the floor, freed from Gedeon's white-knuckled grasp, and began kissing the tops of Gedeon's dark brown leather boots. "Enough. I didn't authorize you to shift twice in the mortal world, don't let it happen again," Gedeon ordered, regaining his composure by adjusting the cuffs of his jacket. Hector rose from the floor and resumed his soldier-like stance by the door like a puppet on tightened strings. Gedeon sat back down and took a slow sip of water as if nothing had happened.

What in the actual fuck? Hector could change into different people, different...things?

Evidently, there was a lot that I had to learn about this world, but one thing I'd hoped to discover was that the man in front of me wasn't my father. There was no way we were of the same blood. I had my moments of anger, but his temper was all-consuming. He demanded to be feared by the people around him and showed no mercy or remorse for anyone. I could only imagine what the city below us was truly like with *him* as their leader.

"Do all Moras act so tyrannically or is it just a character flaw?" I pivoted back to calling him out as he sipped from his glass, causing him to raise a darkened brow at me. I didn't care that I was poking the egotistical bear too much. I wanted to see his anger consume him, again and again. I needed to see that we weren't the same people, that I couldn't be like him. I craved the surety that we couldn't possibly be related.

"What makes you think there are others?" He questioned me earnestly, curiously. It was as if he knew I was trying to find the differences between us, and he was going in the opposite direction, trying to find how we were the same. His lips curved up with what my question gave him—the knowledge that perhaps we were more alike than I desired to know about.

"I saw your atrocious wallpaper outside of the room you put me in. I know there are other elements, and if you only have air, then I imagine there are three others, *just* like you." I folded my arms and creased my forehead, waiting for a response. It was beginning to feel like a never-ending cycle of war between Gedeon and me, but hell if I was ever going to back down. He left us, deserted my mother when she needed someone most, and then ripped me from her when her time came. Even in the face of death, he couldn't prove to have an inkling of a heart.

He set his glass down and curled his finger at Hector, coercing him to come to stand beside him. Hector shuffled immediately beside Gedeon and held out both arms in front of him. Gedeon began moving slowly over each of the golden buttons, undoing them and removing his purple jacket, then removed his white collared tunic, placing each piece neatly over Hector's arms. I felt a twinge of discomfort as I saw the scars and wounds covering his torso, with the deepest ones going from his right shoulder down to the left side of his waist like he was slashed by something sharp, almost like a claw mark from an animal. His tattoo, the mirror image of mine, shone vibrantly in the sunlight that beamed through the window, swooping up the left side of his neck. He turned slowly, revealing what he wanted to show me. It wasn't his scars or the singular, purple mark. It was the continuation of marks that flooded across his back, and I refrained from gasping as I took it in. Purple and white wind swirls turned into sprawling green and brown vines down his left shoulder and mid-back which turned into piercing blue crashing waves over his shoulder blades and right side like a contorted yin and yang symbol, sweeping down to meet his lower back which was engulfed in an array of fiery red flames. Each mark, although distinct, flowed into the next without separation. His entire back lit up against the open windows as he turned like each element was alive, twisting and moving and swirling and blazing all together as one.

He turned back to me and smirked wickedly in response to my gaping mouth, his ego burning just as brightly as each mark did on his flesh. He reached back around for his clothing and put it all back on, flattening any minute fold or wrinkle he could find.

"There are others, *Paige*." He enunciated my name as if rewarding me for my thought processes, rewarding me for being just like him. "Actually, I will be hosting one of them. They will arrive tomorrow to train you beyond what Nya can do. But you must not forget who holds the power in this house. I assure you, *girl*, it is not you." With that, the older servant came rushing to clear his meal from the table, and he and Hector left the room together, leaving me alone in this monstrous house with my jostled mind.

The training deck was luckily right beyond the grand room which was just outside of the dining hall I was in. I don't know who would have helped me if I couldn't find it after I left the room but Gedeon must've taken my snarky remarks as a way of saying I knew what I was doing, which half the time I had to admit I didn't. I just took my chances and stuck to my gut, and my stubbornness led the way from there. It's how I survived all these years and what led me to befriending Aeden so it had to count for something.

I found Nya waiting for me on the deck, ready to go with a new dummy and a new weapon. She held a dagger between her knuckles as I approached her, not in the slightest distraught by the urge I had to hold a weapon of my own. I found myself craving the adrenaline, the coldness of the metal against my fingers as my thumb licked over the sharp edges. It had only been hours since I'd entered the world of weaponry yet I only wished I discovered them sooner. She twirled the dagger between her fingers and took long strides backward, away from the dummy that resembled a centaur with another coif of hair like Gedeons on its manlike head. She turned on her heels away from the dummy before whipping back around swiftly, throwing the dagger and landing it right in between the eyes of the faux centaur.

"You'll be practicing with throwing weapons from now until dusk comes. Your first trial in the Triad is soon and it will test your ability with weaponry and fighting tactics—you won't be allowed to use your powers at all during it. Most future Mora's train day in and day out learning how to fight without magic until they come of age and their original nature forms."

"How old does someone need to be, exactly, to form something like this?" I gestured at my arm.

"Well, first off, only a High Fae—someone of noble birth or descended from a noble—would have anything close to a mark your size. Whatever forms on your flesh is what size you are stuck with—what amount of power you can wield." My fingers brushed over my tunic sleeves before I pushed them up. "But if you were to have lived here before, your mark would have formed around your sixteenth birthday. It isn't necessarily the same for everyone." But Gedeon chose now to bring me here, almost a month shy of twenty. He really did despise me. He wanted me to lose. But why not just leave me in the mortal world, back in Jessup Falls, where no one knew about me or could question his reign?

I swallowed the thick lump in my throat. "What are the other trials, then?" I shook my hands out to ease the slight tremor as I walked to recover the dagger from the centaur. Nya threw with such force that only the hilt jutted out from the poor dummy's head. I tugged it out, releasing a grunt with the force which only made me realize just how weak I was.

"The second trial will be a demonstration of the use of powers *not* of your original nature. Your original nature is air, as is your fathers and all the generations of Aerbornes before you." As she spoke I recalled that Gedeon said a Mora from another place was coming to train me, and I had to wonder who that was or what power they would teach me. The mere thought that I could have more power sent my own into a frenzy beneath my skin like an eager friend waiting to be greeted.

"Gedeon said someone was coming. Another Mora. Do you know who?" I had no reason to ask who they were beyond my own curiosity. I wouldn't know who they were anyway. But I liked talking to Nya, and we bonded over our desire to imagine Gedeon as the dummies we practiced and let out our anger on.

She rubbed her lips inward, then sighed heavily as Hector returned to the deck, taking up his position at the edge of the balcony. "His name is

Eoghan, the Mora of Hydrasel. His original nature is water, so Gedeon must want you to learn that for your trials." She moved to the weapons bench to grab another dagger and walked back toward me and the dummy.

"Why doesn't Gedeon train and test me himself? He abandoned my mother and me and left us with nothing, the least he could—"

"Don't ask questions that you know the answer to. Besides, I wouldn't try pissing him off more than you already are, Paige. You don't know what he's capable of or the lengths he goes to in order to show his power. He doesn't forget, much less forgive." Nya pushed the other dagger into my empty hand and I instinctively curled my fingers around the hilt. It was familiar, yet not. Like I was born to hold such a lethal thing. The lonely girl from Jessup, who had no business holding a dagger, was born for this. Clutching both daggers tightly, I looked up to meet her furrowed brow and piercing blue eyes.

She lowered her voice and glanced toward Hector, assuring he was too far away to hear what she had to say. "The best way to get back at him is to learn to fight the best that you possibly can. You wield and you fight. You beat every trial of the Triad, then the kingdom is yours, by right."

"Why are you telling me this?" I whispered, unsure if it was safe for her to talk like this in front of Hector as my eyes darted between them uncontrollably, yet his complacent stance told me he couldn't hear us. I rolled my shoulders back, making it appear like she was preparing me to use the weapons I was holding, which in a way, she was.

"I'm no auror, but I can tell that you are a better option than he ever was," her voice was low, so low I strained to hear her as she continued, "for Prydia, and the rest of the kingdoms." She laughed and threw her arm on my shoulder, acting like she'd just told a joke instead of confessing her desire to have my father overthrown. I didn't know whether to feel astonished or scared. The heavy burden that if I did survive the Triad and win washed over me. If I won, I would inherit an entire kingdom. But where would that leave my father, and again it begged the question, why even bring me here?

We continued training with daggers and throwing stars, taking aim from various distances until I could finally hit the target. Just once, but it counted for something. Nya even wheeled out an archery target she called a *boss* to throw the weapons at, which was fitting in that our targets were all aimed toward looking like Gedeon to begin with. I wondered if Hector would report back on how we manipulated the dummies, making coifs of hair for each of them. He probably thought we just hated men, not one in particular.

Time slipped away from us as we trained through the hours of the day so much that I hadn't registered when the sun started to set. Hector came up to me to retrieve me, deciding against grabbing me up as he ushered me to the weapons rack to put my daggers and stars away. Nya was busy moving the dummies and boss back to the weapons area, but she found the time to nod toward me—her way of saying goodbye—as we left the training deck. I nodded back before rushing inside, noticing Hector was nearly out of sight which would've left me lost inside the grand palace walls.

Hector led us up the staircase and into a hallway I remembered walking through earlier that morning, the same grim wallpaper now lit by candles showing the hundreds of dying elemental-wielders. I tried not to think about what it meant to Gedeon, what sentimentality he had for it. I couldn't stop rationalizing what kind of man my father must be to portray such a brutal event in his hallways like a threatening trophy that stretched on and on, or what kind of person my mother once trusted with her body, maybe even her heart.

My attention snapped from the walls to Hector, who was holding the door open for me further down the hall, impatiently waiting for me until

I reached the threshold. I ignored the behemoth of a man as I pushed on through into my room and refocused on my stomach that gurgled longingly just as the smell of food smacked me right in the face. On my bed was a wooden tray with a large bowl of beef stew and a chunk of bread resting on top. It was far from the elegance of the previous two meals I'd had since arriving. It felt like home, like the rainy days when Aeden would bring me soup and we'd play board games until the rain let up.

A small note lay beside the bowl of soup and when I glanced back to where Hector had been to ask about it, he was already gone and the door was shut tight. I picked up the note and read:

Paige,

I'm not a fancy eater, and if I'm right about you then this is more to your liking as it is mine. See you tomorrow, bright and early.

P.S. If you are also like me and prefer dressing yourself, I suggest you wake up before the three puppets come to your door, four if you can beat Hector too.

Nya

I smiled to myself and sat on the edge of the bed, hesitatingly only for a moment before my lurching stomach sent my hands to the singular utensil. I wouldn't have to guess what went where, or how to use it, and that kindness in itself made my chest feel lighter. Not that I was complaining about the fancy food. It was honestly delicious but having to eat properly with five different utensils and Gedeon glaring down at me from across an expansive table wasn't exactly how I liked to eat. I preferred the informal, steaming bowl of soup and rigidly ripped-apart bread, and felt absolutely no shame in admitting it.

I took the bowl and spoon up into my hands and strode over to the large windows that let in the fading light from the falling sun. The city surrounded the space below me and dots of people moved about the alleyways and paths, some pushing wagons of what I imagined was produce and small goods while some idly walked on. A woman caught my attention as she pulled on the arms of several small children, urging them to get inside before dark. She visibly gave up and moved to stand behind the children, then with a flick of her wrist they were all lifted into the air and floated beyond the threshold of their small beige bungalow, kicking and screaming the whole way. I giggled at the sight, making the bowl jostle, nearly spilling soup out on the lavish rug.

What a different world this must be to grow up in. Not a car, television, or radio in sight. It was almost like being thrown into the past, yet it wasn't entirely difficult to adjust to since we couldn't afford a lot of luxuries to begin with. My training clothes were getting easier to adjust to as well, the tightness of the leather no longer feeling as foreign as they had before. I never imagined I'd ever be wearing tight leather pants and a matching corset, hurtling weapons, and wielding a power that pulsed along with my heartbeat as the day went on. But low and behold.

I glanced over to the dresser, the portrait of my mother sitting on top of it to my right. She was smiling back at me just over my shoulder, looking into a life that could have been hers. Would she have been happy here? It was hard to imagine Gedeon being the cause of anyone's happiness. It was so far-fetched it was laughable. There was no way a man like him was capable of feeling love, or anything remotely close to it. The only love he showed was of the marks on his body—a love of power and violent authority. His sneer and forcefulness that he threw people around with was a firm reassurance of that. Yet, he kept the portrait up in this room for who knows how long. Perhaps it was only up to serve a more malicious purpose—a sad remembrance of what I no longer had back at home. He was either fucking with my emotions to hinder my training or it was left here as an ever-present reminder of her. I moved to slide the frame facedown and placed it inside a drawer below, blowing a kiss to the woman I missed so much it felt like daggers piercing through my heart to even consider ignoring her like that. Ignoring her like she'd done to me for so many years. Years I spent choosing to blindly accept it. But I had to.

Winning the Triad was not optional—I would have to win to live. I couldn't imagine I would be allowed to simply leave after losing, knowing that losing would be from an injury or possibly death. People didn't just fight with swords and daggers and lose by getting a scratch. It was either forfeit, throwing away all chances of finding Aeden and being stripped of the power that now hummed within me as if it had always belonged, or win.

And I would choose to win, every damn time.

Hector's threats to bar me from using my magic were similar to telling a teen not to go to parties or telling a dog not to eat the food left out on the counter. Chances are, that teen was getting sloshed at that party and that dog was running away with every last bite. The same magic that blocked my air attack on the castle was not inside my room, though whether it was beyond my windows raised another question that I was less confident about. Gedeon most likely did not want me to be able to escape and even if I tried, I had no idea where I would go if I succeeded. I was a rat surrounded by traps with one absurdly small exit beyond a fog of rat poison. Even if I made my way through the traps and poison successfully, I'd probably find that I wouldn't fit through the damn exit.

I knew I could float while thinking about Aeden and I could hurl large orbs of air at full throttle while being pissed off at Gedeon. Elemental magic appeared to feed off of emotions, or at least learning how to use the magic at first was influenced by it. Nya didn't have air magic and acting clueless with it in front of another Mora sounded like a terrible mistake. One I was not going to allow.

I showered hastily, wincing as the soap stung the open blisters lining my hands, and scrubbed the grime and sweat off before the water had a chance to roll down my body. I wanted to get the basics of air-wielding down that I had seen used by Gedeon, his servants, and the woman in the town below the castle. Forming orbs and floating would have to wait for another night. The flicking of the wrist was either all flair or essential. Maybe it was a mix of both. Instead of reaching for a towel, I paused, thinking that needing a towel could be a handy, albeit lazy, excuse to experiment. I closed my eyes and thought about getting the towel to my hands, feeling downright moronic focusing so hard on a towel and its movement. I opened my eyes, staring down the inanimate object, the obsession flooding all of my thoughts, and flicked my wrist.

Thank god I paid attention to detail.

The towel flew into my palm and I squealed in delight. I practiced again with a brush left behind by one of the servants, the thrill making my fingers tingle. I imagined the brush floating slowly into my hand and flicked my wrist hastily, still overjoyed with the success of my first attempt. Within seconds, the brush flipped several times in the air before it smacked me right on my chin, falling to the ground beside my feet.

Shit, that hurt. Softer objects, less enthusiasm.

I practiced using rolled-up clothing I found in the dresser, mostly fine silk slips and white tunics, some pressed pants, long dresses, and the clothing I wore when I arrived, now neatly laundered and folded. A green silk camisole set sat folded inside the first drawer I opened and I decidedly put that on rather than be in a towel the entire night. It draped around my small curves and accentuated my eyes so they popped, seeming more green than ever. The servant girls probably gathered my original clothes and found similar sizes for me to wear while I stayed outside and trained. Maybe I wasn't expected to wear training leathers all the time, although I did find about ten pairs of them in the final drawer I opened. So, predominantly, I would be in leathers, occasionally it would be acceptable to not be in them. It was a stark contrast to the jean shorts and tank tops I was used to wearing at home, then again everything was so different now. Reminiscing on the past was not going to get me any closer to my future—to being with Aeden again and winning the Triad.

Clothing flew in every direction for the next few hours, and with no sign of Hector, I was relieved that I could continue on my own to practice using both hand gestures and guided emotions, calming my restless mind to focus on one emotion or thought at a time. Aeden attempted to teach me how to meditate months ago, but it was rather hard to focus on anything when sitting next to him as he meditated shirtless. I did attempt to focus on my thoughts and being in control of them, letting them flow freely when directed by Aeden, or holding onto one aspect like my breath. Mostly, it was a lot of breathwork in between me checking him out, watching the curves of his pecs and ridges of his abs contract with each breath while I tried to steady my own.

He convinced me it was something he needed to work on, that his coach had recommended the practice, and that he was simply following directions. Looking back on it now, I doubted his coach ever mentioned or advised meditation. He never had problems focusing or becoming anxious. It was like looking through a lens in an entirely different color. A color

I found I really liked. The thought brought a smile to my face as I flung another set of clothing across the room.

Seventeen

AEDEN

Shayanna led the way to the edge of the Highland Woods about a half a day's walk from the cave we slept in. I no longer followed behind Seamus and Shay but instead took up the space between them. I could feel Seamus looking around more fearfully as the day went on and the mountains to our right grew larger with every passing step. I didn't wait for him to ask me to cover up again, I could feel the fear seeping off of Shay as well before I slipped the tunic back on. We must have been close to a town for them to both be scared of having me beside them—a fire-wielder who now possessed two lengthy elemental marks. I could feel them flowing together underneath my flesh like a waterfall steadily crashing into a river beneath it, fueling the flow of the rapids harmoniously. Neither overpowered the other. Both marks now settled on my skin as if they had always existed there, red twisting into blue.

We stopped for several water breaks along the way, Seamus teaching me each time how to form a stream above my head for a quick drink. The first time I nearly drowned under the torrent I'd made, releasing the visual of water too strongly and all at once. Even so, it felt fucking amazing.

Aside from the immense pride that came with using literal fucking magic, being doused by water, by my own power, was a sweet reprieve from the heat of the day. The winds from Lake Kree no longer reached us at the border of the woods, where there were noticeably no signs cautioning us from entering the woods like the Hollow Woods had. No mention of pixies or the other things that lurked inside. Things Shay warned would be there.

"Where are the signs?" I asked as I pointed to the path leading into the woods.

"It's known by mostly everyone that you don't enter the Highland Woods. Prydia has a wall bordering the north of it, while the Highland Mountains border the south. The only way in and out from here safely for us is through this end unless you want to meet up with the trolls that linger within the pass between the mountains," Shay answered.

"Trolls? Now you've got to be fucking with me."

"I do not fuck around about trolls. They are huge, thickheaded, and pound rocks into bits of dust and rubble all day long. They could kill you, an untrained fae, in a second if they wanted to." Shay gave me a once-over and looked to Seamus for more input.

"She's right, Lad. Nasty brutes trolls are. Best to keep on this side of the woods and stay close to Shay and me." Seamus adjusted his pants, then glanced around the line of trees. "I've got to take a piss first. Anyone care to join?" He looked to me and then Shay, and took our silence as a response. He mumbled something and went off to piss behind a tree.

Shay walked closer to me and turned to face away from the trees. "Listen here Aeden. The pixies in the woods know me and they know Seamus is a friend of mine, but they don't trust just anyone and are easily aggravated. If you show them *any* fire magic, they will either run in fear or try to kill us. Either one would mean no more business for me, and no girl for you. Understood?" She may have been trying to warn me but it came off like a snake taking hold of its prey, choking it slowly before killing it.

"Hypnosis would be an easy out then, wouldn't it?" If she wanted to be a snake, I'd be a fucking hawk. No one was going to threaten me or my girl.

Her lips popped open to interject, but I didn't let her. "I saw what you did to Seamus, don't think that because I never lived here before means that I don't understand what you were doing to him. You could be tricking us both right now for all I know." I took a step forward and stared down into her bright blue eyes that darkened in the shadow of my height as I towered over her. Her eyes fell to the ground and then came back up slowly to meet mine. I glanced beyond her shoulder and saw Seamus still standing behind the tree, his elbow jutting out just slightly from the edge of the bark.

"I didn't mean to—I just..." she stumbled over her words and then paused to gather her thoughts. "Yes, I can make *most* fae fall into a trance temporarily, but I would never harm Seamus. He has been there for me when others have not. And as for you, I wouldn't try it on you unless you forced me to." She rolled in her lips and eyed me curiously. "But I don't think I'd be able...you...you didn't..." The sound of rustling grass drew her back a step from me, her eyes going wide with a realization that was lost to me.

She snapped her head around to look at Seamus. "Everything alright there, Shay? Ye look like you've just seen a ghost." Seamus threw glances between her and me, his forehead pinching together with his raised brows. She stood up straighter and corrected her face into a slight smile as I took that opportunity to take several steps back.

"It's nothing, Seamus. I'm just a bit nervous about Aeden's...power in the woods. Just make sure you are ready to douse any fires he may cause. The pixies won't let me back in as easily if we turn their home to ash." She observed me once more, a question still hanging in the air, and then turned to lead us down the path between the parting trees. Because now I was supposed to follow the woman who may or may not give a shit if I died in the woods.

Her momentary lapse of apprehension toward me was concerning, but if she was still going on with the plan then I wasn't going to put much more thought into it. We just didn't agree, and that was that. She didn't threaten Paige outright, it was all a misunderstanding. But I'd be ready to knock her off her high horse if I needed to unless she proved she really didn't mean us any harm.

The sun was beginning to set behind the trees but that didn't matter once we'd entered the woods. It was dark, with low-hanging trees whose branches swayed over us ominously in every direction, their gnarled roots bursting from the ground in tangled webs that broke through the dirt path we could hardly see. *Fire magic would be helpful right about now.* Shay's warning flashed through my mind momentarily. I may have been a bit of a dick to her earlier, but that's what happens when I'm afraid. The fear takes over and turns into anger—to me being more on the offensive rather than defensive. I had to wonder why they even stuck around with me, but I chalked it up to a love of adventure and possibly Shay needing to re-up on more pixie dust for the Forga Market she talked about with Seamus. Money was usually convincing enough to do dumb things like walk into notoriously dangerous woods to find pixies. Money and love. So maybe we were both fucking idiots for coming here in the first place.

"How will we know when we are close?" I kept my voice low, still unsure of what these things looked like, but they sounded like tiny cute angry things, unlike the hags. I really didn't want to see more of those. The fewer hags in my life, the better.

"Ye'll know, Lad," Seamus whispered back, eyeing the treetops with Shay as we continued on the path deeper into the woods that darkened with each passing step.

Anxiety built up in my chest, conflicting with my newfound power that pulsed effortlessly with each breath I took and our steps became staggered.

The trees climbed to practically twice the size of the ones that lined the outside of the woods as if the limbs of each branch were opening up to us in some twisted embrace. Seamus and Shay kept their eyes trained on the tops of the trees, causing my anxiety to spike just enough to send sparks to my fingertips. Tiny flames danced across the top of my palm and laced between each finger, releasing a modicum of the tension I tried so hard to keep at bay. A rush of cool water splashed over my hand as Seamus spread his own magic like a blanket over my hand, quelling the fire and the brightness that would give us away. Give *me* away. Shay narrowed her gaze, electric blue eyes sending shock waves of power to ripple through my veins as they moved frantically between the treetops and my hand.

It was silent, and it was dark. Shay and Seamus were momentarily lost in the abyss of blackness until lighted dots exploded in waves all around us like fireflies, illuminating each of our figures as we stood, frozen in place. Except they weren't fireflies. Fireflies didn't hover, didn't glow bright white like stars. Fireflies didn't cast an ominous feeling of dread as you looked at them.

"Shhh...don't...say...anything..." Shay's lips tightened, unsure of how the lights I now knew were pixies would react to her. A sense of dread, hostility, and being utterly fucking unwelcome washed over me. I shot my eyes over to Shay and Seamus as they stood beside me, keeping my body rigid to mimic the surrounding trees. The pixies came closer and closer until I was able to make out the small frame of arms, legs, and torso. *So human.* They were no more than two inches tall, their height and bright, bat-like wings that stretched outward from either side the only difference between us and them. One pixie came to hover in front of me, taking me in as their wings flapped elegantly, unlike the rapid movements of a bat. A few others flew to my covered arms, perching along the blue tunic like birds along an electrical wire.

A breathy, angelic voice hummed, enhancing their glowing beauty. "We saw your fire boy, you can not hide it."

Fuck.

I tightened my already rigid limbs and looked toward Shay for guidance. She'd warned me they'd either run away in fear or kill us, yet it was hard to imagine the beautiful, tiny humanoid things on my arms could kill. Yet as their black eyes pierced into my own as I raked my gaze over each one of them, all doubt vanished. They were fucking lethal creatures in disguise.

"You need not be afraid of us." Lies. "We already heard of your arrival in Costa." Fuck me sideways. "You must be the boy with flames." *Fucking wonderful.* Lethal *and* observant. The voice was not of any pixie on my arm. It was thrown, omnipresent, echoing around us in a hushed tone, that same angelic tone as before.

I swallowed thickly, holding my arms still and slightly elevated like the tree limbs above us. I cleared my throat, keeping my voice level, even, breathing out any fear and taking in all the hubris I could. "Aeden. My name is Aeden. I came here looking for—"

"The girl. Named...Paige?" Another pixie shot forward, closer to my face, inches from my nose making my eyes narrow and nearly cross. This pixie was a woman. Long white hair floated down and around her green, tightened wings with leaves and branches that formed a knee-length dress ending in sharp, jagged points. Tension sagged out from my body at the mere mention of her. *Paige*—more angelic sounding than any of the other words that came from their mouths. I chanced a look over to where Shay and Seamus stood, rigid and unaffected by their words and appearing more timid than ever before. I shifted my attention back to the pixie just beyond the tip of my nose and nodded my head.

"And what makes you believe we will tell you where she is, boy?" I hadn't noticed the slight curve of hope across my lips until it flattened. They wanted something from me. Nothing in the mortal world came without a price, so why should it be any different in Aellethia? I looked at Shay again and refrained from sighing. Shay wasn't in a position to help, but Seamus still held faith in her as he jabbed her with his elbow gently, urging her to speak. To do something.

Shay blinked twice, her pupils dilating against the bright light emitted by the pixies. Several small toes curled in along my forearm and I fought the urge to shake them off of me. "Hyacinth, I brought him to you hoping for answers. I know how kind and gratuitous you are, and only ask for any lead you can provide to...my friend."

Hyacinth flicked her head over her shoulder, a feline-like hiss ringing out in the thickened air around us. "Our agreement was secrecy, and you have broken that agreement." The light peeled away from my face as she flew over to Shay, her usual glowing skin turning pale against the brightness of the light.

She dipped her head, bowing to the tiny creature. "Hyacinth, I meant no disrespect..."

"Hyacinth, is it? I'm the reason we came here, so if you could kindly come back this way, I want to make a deal with you." Shay was clearly in no position to barter, but perhaps I was. Lights flickered in response as I moved my arm and reached into my back pocket, pulling out a golden chain bracelet. The pixies all shifted their weight but remained in their positions along my arm. "This is valuable where I came from. It's yours if you tell me what you have heard about Paige and where she is." I let their lights sparkle and glow against the gold, catching the sheen of each link as I twisted my hand slowly.

A devilish laugh burst out from the depths of Hyacinth's chest. She flew back, landing on my opened palm to inspect the golden jewelry. "Gold is useless to us," she spat, small feet stepping lightly over my skin. "But this...." She inspected it closer, holding up a link and stroking it with her sword-like tongue.

And that was the moment their beauty died.

"Where did you get this, boy?" Her question rose high, shrieking as if insinuating I was a thief. I didn't like her tone *or* her salacious tonguing of my bracelet. Not one fucking bit. I yanked my arm back, forcing her to fly into the air and hover in front of my face. She grinned back at me, revealing her pointed, yellow teeth.

A shiver ran down my spine and I worked a muscle in my jaw to keep from grimacing. "It's yours *if* you tell me what you have heard about Paige and where she is." I folded my arms over my chest and tiny lights poured away from my arm, floating back into position behind Hyacinth. Red crested the corner of my vision, revealing the flaming mark as it peaked out from the cuff of my sleeve. But I didn't push it back. Instead, I flexed my forearms, making the red pop against the light. She already knew I wielded fire by the show I unknowingly put on earlier. If it was fear she was trying to insight by flashing her teeth, then I'd flash my power in return.

She smirked. "This boy is special, Shay. Keep him close. I like him." Hyacinth observed my arm, trailing her gaze up to my neck as she fluttered in place before me. A small part of me wanted to shift my collar, to acknowledge the stare I was receiving from Seamus as his eyes motioned for me to cover the edge of my mark, to tighten the dangling strings of my tunic and shield myself. But the devil on my shoulder was louder and wanted Hyacinth to see just how much I could fuck with her back. I didn't know exactly what I was revealing beyond how much power I had, but it felt amazing as all hell to level the proverbial playing field as her wide eyes darted back to mine.

The points of her teeth stacked over each other as she smiled. "I tell you what, Aeden. I'm in a fairly good mood today. I'll tell you where Paige is by telling you her proper name. The name she should have received when she was birthed by that mortal woman. You can even keep your bracelet as a sign of good faith between us." She winked. "I only ask you to be indebted to me for a single favor, when the time comes, of course." Her thumb rubbed against the rest of her tiny fingers. "Do we have a deal?"

Her grin was carnal, wicked. The angelic voice and the facade of amiability worked their way below my boots. Shay and Seamus remained tense as more orbs of light fluttered around them like a looming threat. *Accept the deal, or we kill you all.* Whatever favor would come from this, it would be between Hyacinth and I, and no one else. They didn't deserve to die because I needed to find her. I'd been selfishly accepting their help and returning their allegiance with snide comments and little thanks. A trickle of guilt spread through me as my brow furrowed back at them.

"Deal."

Hyacinth flew into the air and twirled back down, her wings brushing my ear as she landed on my shoulder. "You seek Paige Aerborne of Prydia, blood and kin of Lord Gedeon Aerborne," she whispered softly against my ear, her sharp teeth raking over my lower lobe before giggling and taking flight again up to the treetops. "And that bracelet is more precious than gold, boy!" Her voice echoed loudly as the rest of the pixies followed behind her. The lights began to flicker and fade out toward the sky above the trees, and then all at once, they were gone.

"What did she say, Boyo?" Seamus came to me as my jaw worked and my fingers curled around the bracelet. The name was new to me, but not forgotten. My focus shifted around Seamus' worn skin, the creases caused by smiling so often from long ago that now faded, blending into his saddened eyes that only years of torture could produce.

He couldn't even find the bodies of his wife and daughter but found skeletons in his home, flesh still burning off the bones.

Many fear him, despise him even, but not many fight back. The ones who do, don't live to tell about it.

The Mora of Prydia, Lord Gedeon Aerborne, is an evil man.

My legs became weak and my knees sank to the ground. Paige had found her father, a man she never spoke of because she knew nothing about him. Or, rather, he found her. A man of this world, a Mora of this world. *She* had a part in this world, just as I did. If she was in Prydia, just north of where we stood as Shay described, then north was where I was going. Even if that meant traveling alone since the initial agreement between us had always been to help me find out where Paige was. Not help me actually get to her.

I opened my palm that still clutched the bracelet and raised my other hand, producing a small fire orb effortlessly and holding it over the bracelet to examine it closer. I maneuvered the links to fold over my fingers, revealing the spot where my name was etched into the foreign metal at the center of the bracelet. My thumb slid over the letters, as they frequently did, extinguishing the orb in the other palm before sliding it back into my pocket, where it had stayed safe all these years.

"She said her name is Paige Aerborne." I let my head hang, unable to see their responses but feeling the thickness of the air between us like we were back at the bar, or in Shay's home.

"Aerborne? As in Gedeon's daughter?" Shay asked, not at all hiding the inflection in her tone, the way she spat out his name like the venom that it was. "He won't hurt her, not if she's inside the castle."

I raked my fingers through my hair, plastering it back with the cold sweat that was forming on my brow. "I'm not going to ask you to come with me, just know there's nothing you can do or say that will make me turn back. I won't stop. I will find Paige and I will get us back home." I knew Shay would want no part in this, but as for Seamus who lost his family because of Gedeon Aerborne, I held out a sliver of hope. Hope that he may want to help just to get back at the fucker himself. Gedeon had taken Seamus' daughter and wife from him, it would only be fair to steal Gedeon's daughter in return.

"Aye, let's hear from the lad. Aeden, is she worth the fight?"

"She's more than worth it." I stood from the ground to meet Seamus eye-to-eye. "She is my everything. Without her I have nothing—I am nothing. I would burn both worlds to ash to get her back."

Shay chewed on her bottom lip as she and Seamus exchanged looks, coming to a silent agreement with a nod. "Then we'll be there with you."

I didn't deserve their unwavering loyalty if that was what made them agree to come with me. If it was about getting revenge for his family, I'd understand. I'd feel a lot less guilty about it, too. But something told me that it was more than that. We hadn't known each other long, but they deserved whatever trust I'd given them. Possibly even more than that.

I extended my arms outward, slugging my arms over both of them like I'd done so often with my teammates. "Thank you. Both of you." I sighed heavily as relief rushed through me, but their stiffened bodies sent my head jerking backward.

"I'm just messin' with ye, Aeden. Come 'ere." Seamus flung his arms around me in a burly hug, reaching up to rub my hair. Shay landed beside him, getting wrapped up in his arms just as she flung her hand up to pat my shoulder. I was used to camaraderie on the football field, but this was more familial. We weren't a pack of testosterone-driven young men forced together into a team that was expected to win. Quite honestly, the odds were stacked heavily against us.

I reached my hand over my head, rubbing the base of my neck. Shay may have some devastating power of her own, but she wasn't lying about what we'd find in the woods. She didn't leave me, either, which was saying more to me than words ever could.

I held out my hand to her. "Truce?"

She nodded and a small curve spread over her mouth, tucked beneath her hair that blended into the night and billowed around her face. "Truce."

We managed to exit the woods faster than we entered. I no longer had to hide my flames from the pixies of the Highland Woods and produced an orb to light our path. As soon as we breached the last few trees lining the woods, I curled my fingers over the orb, dousing the fire. Fae may be deterred from entering the Highland Woods, but Shay didn't say the same for trekking the outskirts of it.

Just north of where we were, well before the wall that blocked Prydia from the Highland Woods, was a circle of about ten large wagons forming a caravan, a fire blazing in the center that fae were dancing and singing around.

"We can join in the fun, what do you say boys? I think we deserve it." Shay winked at both of us before darting toward the caravan of fae.

"Keep your shirt on, Boyo. Please," Seamus pleaded, sounding more like a father than a friend.

"I know. I'm a water-wielder. I got it." I patted his shoulder, pushed my sleeves down, and lifted my collar fully, hoping it would be enough to get by as I tightened the strings over my chest. I ran after Shay as Seamus laughed behind me. But damn if we didn't deserve to have fun. I was more drained—both emotionally and physically—than I had ever been, and that was saying something for someone who moved in and out of foster care his entire life. Paige was safe within her father's castle. I had to believe that with every fiber of my being until I could get her back into my arms and back home or I'd go insane. Utterly fucking insane.

I approached just as Shay tilted a tall dark bottle back against her mouth. Several other fae were holding similar bottles and danced around the fire pit, singing songs while a guitar strummed upbeat chords. Seamus came up beside me and grabbed from the stash of drinks inside one of the open carriages, throwing one toward me as if this were his home. As if we were just as welcome as anyone else here. The surrounding fae smiled and waved us toward the fire, not asking who we were or what our names were. Just welcoming us with no questions asked.

They wore mostly tunics with sleeves pushed back to combat the warmth of the night or flowy short-sleeved dresses, putting their marks on full display. Vines, waves, and another one I assumed was air that looked like a purple swirling hurricane decorated their forearms. Not one fae here had more than one elemental tattoo, and none of their marks reached as far as my own did.

Another group of fae sat down passing around a jar with a crystalline powder inside, resembling a salt that sparkled in all shades of the rainbow. They giggled and tossed their heads back, eyes hazy and pupils noticeably dilated even from across the fire.

I took a hefty swig of my drink which mimicked the strongest liquor mixed with a sweet lemonade and some flowery taste I couldn't quite place. A few sips in and I found myself tapping my foot to the music. Seamus laced his fingers with Shay's and tugged her toward the dancers, spinning her around and moving like they had no cares in the world. A woman came up to me and offered me some crystalline grains in a jar as I sat back watching, but Shay ran toward me and pulled my arm, urging me to join them.

I downed the rest of my drink and grabbed another. If I was going to dance, I'd need to be damn near hammered. Yet, judging by the lightness I already felt consuming me, it wouldn't take much of whatever alcohol it was that I was drinking. I'd be blissfully gone soon enough. I trailed behind Seamus and Shay as they swung each other around, searching for another fire-wielder but found none.

Seamus took a seat after a few rounds around the fire and pulled Shay into his lap. She curled her arms around his neck, looking genuinely at peace in each other's arms. Like how it was holding Paige in mine.

My body pulsed with the music now, and I wanted to be around the fire again, I wanted to move. But I forced myself to sit down beside the two love birds. They seemed to fit together so well it was too damn cute for my drunken senses. Because I was drunk now, out of nowhere. Two drinks in and it hit me like a tidal wave all at once. It was unheard of for a guy my size to be affected after two drinks, but here we are.

"You two ever...ya know..." I stopped the slurring words and tipped my drink toward them, moving it between them both. *Yep. Drunk.*

Shay planted a kiss on Seamus' cheek and then smiled at me—by no way answering me. She was clearly not as drunk as I was, but definitely tipsy. Maybe a bit. It was fucking hard to tell with the darkness of the night and the fire swirling in my vision, pulling on my power but settling it at the same time. Too consuming. Every sensation was heightened. My wants, my needs, my deepest desires—like they were being thrown into the mix of my growing power and shot out of a canon that just perpetuated it back into the spiral of everything under my flesh.

"Did ye and yer Paige ever...ye know...." Seamus smirked back at me and raised his brows.

A fire lit inside of me at the mention of her name. I added it to the canon and it swirled violently upon its release. "Pfft. I wish." I rubbed at my temple, fingers still wrapped around the bottle, then closed my eyes as I thought about how perfect her lips were on mine. "We kissed. But then we got sucked into"—I gestured to our surroundings and took another swig—"all this." I tried not to show the sadness, the utter fucking pain coming to the surface, but Shay noticed immediately and put her hand on my knee.

"That must have been difficult, Aeden." No slurs. No shaky hands. The alcohol was going to take some time to get used to, just like the damn coffee.

"It was, it is, it...fucking hurts down"—I flexed my spread fingers over my chest, the alcohol taking way too much hold over my words as they kept tumbling out—"down in here, you know? Down in my soul." Word vomit. I don't think I'd ever heard the word 'soul' come from my mouth, and the annunciation of each letter in the word only emphasized that very fact.

I was a mess, but I finished another drink of magical fae alcohol and grabbed yet another.

Like a dumb ass.

"She's just so..." I waved my arms around now looking like the fucking idiot that I felt like.

"She's yer one," Seamus said and his eyes welled with tears. *Ah fuck*. His wife and daughter were dead and here I was going on and on about the woman I was gunning for. He had Shay, but that seemed more platonic now that I was drunk and confessing my own adoration. Or maybe I was too busy being consumed with ordeals of my own heart to notice anything magical between them other than pure lust. A lot of lust. They were definitely fucking.

"Yeah, see, Big Red gets it." I patted Shay's hand that remained on my knee. "He fuckin' gets it." I lifted my drink to Seamus, and he lifted his back before we both threw down the remainder of another drink. I had been drunk before and three beers or liquor or whatever this shit was, was doing me in faster than six shots of tequila.

"Shay?" My voice came out sloshed but it sounded innocent like a choir boy in my head. I should've just stopped talking—but I didn't. I needed a woman's perspective.

"Aeden?" She was way more lucid than us, how the hell did she handle this shit so well? Her voice sounded more angelic than the deceiving devil pixies with demonic teeth.

"Am I going to fuck this all up? I mean, I *should* be looking for Paige, right? You think she wants me as much as I want her?" Because what if she didn't? What if she was just caught up in the moment? She was drunk the first time and heartbroken the times after. What if I was no better than the dicks who took advantage of her?

Was I wasted? Yes. Was I going so far into my emotions that I sounded like I was pussy-whipped? Also, sadly, yes.

"Oh Lad," Seamus spoke up, "even if she did want to see ye, she couldn't leave." Seamus lowered his voice and shuffled Shay to his other knee, so he could scoot in close to me. "The M-O-R-A," he spelled out, cupping a hand over his mouth to conceal our conversation from the fae who probably wouldn't give two fucks about what we were saying anyways. We were all well beyond wasted. "Well, to say he's a dick is a nice way of puttin' it. I'm sure she longs for ye, just as ye do her."

"Yeah, Aeden. You're a hottie with more power than most fae here, what's not to like?" Shay said casually, not worrying about announcing my power as the drunk and high fae around us danced their way around the fire to a guitar and some guy banging a set of bongos. Because there were bongos now. She had more balls than Seamus did, and maybe that was the alcohol giving her more strength or maybe she was used to being unapologetically herself. She may have clammed up around Hyacinth, but something told me that was unusual for her.

I had a hard time hearing I was powerful, let alone it being a reason to want to be with someone. Paige wasn't shallow. She wouldn't *care* if I had power or not. She was beautiful, kind, and humble, and...shit, I needed to stop drinking an hour ago. Time was slipping from us and after another downed drink, the edge of the rising sun began to light up the horizon over the Highland Woods.

I moved to the grass and lay face up, watching the sky shift in hues of orange and purple, the light consuming the starry night sky. "If I die, will you tell her something for me?" The level of alcohol in my blood surpassed drunk and peaked into supreme wisdom. The type of wisdom only other drunk people can appreciate.

Seamus and Shay took up their places on either side of me, folding their arms under their heads to gaze up at the changing sky. Because they, like me, had also reached supremacy.

"Of course," Shay said and Seamus nodded in agreement.

"Tell her—tell her I...damn. Tell her I love her. Tell her she's the only one I ever wanted, the only one that I felt was meant for me. Made, just for me. Tell her I'm sorry for being selfish and wanting her so badly that it ended me."

"Let's keep you alive then, Boyo, so you can tell her yerself. Ye don't keep that in, ye hear? Ye tell her and ye let it be known."

The silence drew out between us as the power of my words settled over me. I loved Paige. Truly, deeply, madly, and all-consuming. Loved her enough to risk my life trying to get back to her. And that terrified me, even while I was completely hammered.

The sky sizzled into hues of yellow and orange and other fae began to join us in the grass, gazing into the few stars that were left as they became engulfed by the rays of the burning sun.

EIGHTEEN

PAIGE

It was easy to dodge the women and Hector the next morning. Easier than I expected, which would have been more unsettling had I not grown used to acting invisible all my life. It helped that I was also used to waking up when it was still dark out back in Jessup when I could run in peace and not have to worry about seeing other people in our town. I hated hearing them whisper about me and my mother—

Do you think the poor thing has eaten today?

I heard her mother collapsed at the grocery store the other day.

Her mother is going to drink herself to death one day.

It never ended.

Even now I was sure that the people in town were gossiping about how I abandoned her after she died and left her in the hospital, thinking I did it out of spite. But truthfully, I wanted to be there with her. Desperately. I didn't blame her for her addiction or how she handled raising me. Seeing the man she had me with validated my feelings about her even more. I could see why she drank. Putting up with Gedeon the few times I had, I was ready to throw back a drink myself. Maybe not as often as she chose to, but I sympathized nonetheless.

I got myself dressed in the leather training gear, although tying the corset was a bitch to do alone. But I managed by using the full-length mirror. As I tugged on the laces my forearms trembled, making me realize just how little I'd used the muscles before. It hurt. A lot. I wondered how training today would go if tying a corset was doing me in. How the heck was I going to lift a sword or throw anything?

By the time I made it out to the training deck, Nya was already there, setting up a few dummies. I hurried over to her, ready to thank her for her note and comfort food. Maybe I trusted too easily, but I got the feeling that I could trust Nya. Especially after what she hinted at—no one liked Gedeon, and I wasn't alone. In fact, I had an ally rooting for me to win.

"Glad you read my note. Hector is probably about to be so thrown off." Nya smirked at me over her shoulder, still maneuvering the dummy into position.

"Yeah, I did. Thank you, for the food and for saving me from that dining hall. And from the servants. And henchman." Each time I paused to include more that I was thankful for, I could feel a small burden lifting from me. I managed to find a friend in this place, and I was grateful for that.

Nya laughed and turned to face me, finally satisfied with how she had placed the dummy. She had four dummies lined up, evenly spaced out and all resembling different things I had only read about before in fantasy books I'd borrowed from the library. A centaur, a minotaur, a shorter one I assumed was dwarven, and a giant one that looked like a ten-foot-tall beefy man. All of them had coiffed hair-like vines that resembled my father's hair, making me grin uncontrollably as I took in the sight.

"Are you ready for today? How are your arms?" She moved in closer to me and touched my bicep which made me flinch back.

She sucked in a breath through her teeth. "Ah. Hold still," she said as she clasped her hands around each arm. A yellow glow came from her gentle palms as she held both of my arms. It felt incredible, like standing in the warm sun after spending days without the heater on during a snowstorm. The pain was gone in seconds.

"How did you..."

"I told you I was a healer, what exactly did you think I meant?"

"Not that. I figured at best you could mix up some medicine for me, you know, like a doctor or a nurse. Maybe make whatever this place calls ibuprofen."

"I'm not sure what ibuprofen is. But a doctor, you mean like an alchemist? No. I can heal because it's my gift. I was born with it." She shrugged and started moving toward the weapons rack. I moved to walk next to her but I had no clue what she was talking about. She could heal people using magic, that much I understood just like we both could wield elements. Totally normal. It was going to become normal. For now, it was still fucking weird how magic existed in this world. The fact that there was even another world still blew my mind.

"What do you mean it's your gift? Is there a book on Aellethian powers or..."

She lifted a fist and coughed into it, her eyes darting around to make sure we were alone. Like books were forbidden, almost. "You have one of the biggest libraries in all of Aellethia inside that castle. I'll show it to you after you train today." I had to hide just how excited that made me. I loved reading, and if I could find the answers to all of my questions in the books inside then I would be better prepared to fight in the Triad. It didn't strike me odd that Gedeon had one of the biggest libraries in his home. He had to fill up his monstrous palace and the absurd amount of rooms somehow. It couldn't be for people he loved—no. I doubted he had many, if any, of those.

Nya passed me two daggers and a set of stars to tuck into the side pockets of my leather pants and then reached for a shorter sword than the one I had trained with the day before. One more in proportion to my height. This sword in particular had faded purple lines that grew from the hilt and curved around to the end of the blade like etched-in veins.

"Here, try this one out. This sword was forged with air magic. Today, we will practice channeling your magic through the sword to guide your moves more accurately and give your attacks more power." She laid the sword across my open palms. "Which means even if you suck with weapons, the strength of your magic can correct it for you."

Holding the sword, I could already feel my magic rise in a frenzy, trying to escape the cell that was my body. It wanted—no, needed to be set free. I released my mental hold on the magic inside of me and felt it surge through my palms and into the hilt of the sword as if I'd let a dam break free in my mind. The dull purple lines came to life, glowing feverishly as my magic bonded to the sword, the weapon now no different from another appendage. I could almost feel how lethal, how deadly a weapon like this could be.

Nya guided me to the line-up of dummies she had created and spread her arms wide. "Pick one to test out your bonded sword on. Dismember, then move on to the next. Try not to feed too much power into it. Centaurs are good at what they do but even their weapons can't always hold the strength that a future Mora can give."

"I'm sorry, did you just say centaurs?" Shit. I really needed to read about this place. I couldn't leave the castle grounds to see Aellethia for myself beyond the balcony's ledge and sounding like a clueless person every second of the day was wearing thin already.

The insane notion that centaurs were the ones who'd made the sword I was holding led me to better understand the odd artwork and fictional dummies. It wasn't fiction in Aellethia—it was all a part of this place as much as I now was. The realization made the world around me spin and

I had to refocus on my power flowing into the sword to steady myself. I could only hope that Aeden was not in any danger and was safe, somewhere out there.

Nya raised a brow as I silently contemplated more on Aellethia and Aeden, the sword hanging in my hands pulsing impatiently with power waiting to be released.

"Right...as I was saying—dismember, and move on to the next. Any questions?" She waved her hands in front of me, drawing me from my thoughts and making me jump. The sword fell to the ground and immediately faded to a dull purple again. "Are you feeling...okay?" Nya looked me up and down with worry on her face.

"I'm fine, just a little overwhelmed, is all." I picked my sword back up, the purple glow flaring back to life the moment I touched the hilt again. In truth, I slept like absolute crap and couldn't stop dreaming about Aeden. The dreams were so vivid, so real...like I could reach out and almost touch him, the *real* him. I had to believe he was okay.

Get. A. Grip. Paige.

"I'm ready. Don't worry. I can do this," I said aloud to myself but Nya nodded in agreement. She stepped back and allowed me the room to choose between the selected dummies. I chose the one on the far right—the huge dummy resembling a very tall man but a little distorted. Shoulders too broad, head too small for the rest of its body, and a very long and broad torso. I refrained from asking what it was and made a mental note to look up each one of the foreign dummies when I got to the library.

Dismembering was alarmingly easy with the bonded sword. Then again, my targets were stationary and my arms were healed over from the day before. The sword glowed brightly in my palm as I finished but inside I was more drained than ever. Nya seemed to notice how sluggish I became and strode back over from where she was waiting against the weapons rack.

"Drained?" she asked, some worry lacing her features. "Normally, High Fae have their entire lives to train with weapons and when their powers emerge, they still have a few years after that before attempting the Triad. *He* expects you to be ready, or at least *appear* ready in just a week for the first trial." She rolled her eyes and placed both hands on my cheeks. "This will help make you feel better about being drained, but I can't regenerate your magic for you. Only rest can do that." A warm glow spread through my head and cleared my fogginess from both my lack of sleep and the magic being drained from me. Having a healer was damn useful. I let out a sigh and smiled wide.

"Thank you, Nya."

"Don't thank me yet. You are meeting the Mora of Hydrasel in about an hour in the dining hall with Lord Gedeon."

"Fuck." I wasn't ready. Not in the slightest. But I would have to be. If he was as big of an asshole as Gedeon was, I was very screwed. Two assholes in one room with vast amounts of power meant I wasn't going to get away with back talking. But I was sure as shit still going to do it. It was inevitable. Biting my tongue was harder to do around arrogant men, and I was never good at keeping my mouth shut.

We finished up by throwing daggers and stars. My aim had improved slightly, but was still way off from hitting the dead center of the target. How I was supposed to hit a live target in combat in just a week was beyond me. But I would have to try.

Hector walked over to retrieve me while Nya stored the weapons away, using her earth magic at the same time to cast vines that lifted the pieces of arms and legs and sewed them back into place. Hector only jerked his head to the side and folded his arms, allowing me to follow without attempting to grab me. He was certainly learning quickly, I had to give him that.

I walked beside him with my head held high, bracing myself mentally for what I was about to walk into. Hector moved ahead to stand by one of the grand wooden doors and erected himself like a statue as two male servants—wearing white pants and tunics and bearing small air marks—flanked either side of the door and pulled it open. There were noticeably more servants around the castle today that weren't out earlier when I'd snuck out onto the training deck. There were now dozens everywhere—one positioned along each entryway unless it was a double door in which case two were positioned, one on either side of each door.

I let out a heavy sigh full of anxiety and shook out my trembling hands. *This is going to suck.* I lifted my chin higher and strolled in as lackadaisically as I could, trying desperately to hide how nervous I really was and keeping my eyes glued to the chair I sat in before. Only this time, someone else was already in it, stealing what little breath I had left in my lungs.

The man, who was somewhere around Aeden's age if not a few years older, slouched comfortably in his chair, his clothing straining against his biceps and broad shoulders. His unlaced tunic dipped low and showed off the deep groove between his pecs, and although he was sitting down I could tell he was very tall, perhaps as tall as Aeden. He looked like a god, making me feel no more than a peasant in this world but I pushed my shoulders back instead of curling them inward like every ounce of my being told me to under the weight of his presence. Gedeon seemed aggravated as his eyes refrained from being trained on the man's poor posture, but he said nothing as his fingers tapped along the tabletop.

His clean-shaven jaw was perfectly squared, the muscles there flexing tightly as I moved to sit at another chair in between the two men in the middle of the table without hesitating. The man was noticeably less abhorrent than my father and seemed overall more approachable, but just as deadly. He could kill you in a second, but *would he do it* was another question entirely. There was no question in my mind that Gedeon killed quite frequently, maybe even just for fun or to show the extent of his power.

Gedeon was the first to speak. "Paige, this is Lord Eoghan Waterborne, the Mora of Hydrasel," he let out as if announcing him was like sipping on a fine wine as he tried to ignore Eoghan's lack of royal composure. Eoghan clearly gave zero fucks and smirked over at me, his unbuttoned blue coat edging open as he laced his fingers through his short golden hair that brought out his dark, ocean-like blue eyes even more against his clothing while he slouched flippantly in his seat. He folded his arms across his chest as Gedeon rolled his eyes. "Lord Eoghan here will be training you, along with Nya. He will introduce you to other powers beyond air." My father's jaw flexed as his eyes raked over my arm and I reflexively rubbed my hand over the length of it, trying to wipe the weight of his gaze away. "The Stars deem it necessary for one of the trials, so you must know more than your original nature to partake. And you *must* partake." He waved his hand in the air and I recoiled, thinking he would fling me across the room again. Instead, several servants came out from another previously closed door with small plates of food for each of us. Eoghan gave me a slight nod before winking at one of the servant girls who'd meandered out from behind me as I took a seat along the middle of the length of the table.

What a complete tool, just like Dick Little.

Eoghan eyed his plate as it was set down, wrinkling his nose slightly. "Thank you for the invitation to your home, Gedeon, but I already ate before coming. I'll see my way to the training deck and wait for your daughter there." No *Lord Gedeon,* no remorse for showing his disdain as he motioned to leave.

Gedeon nodded his head at Eoghan without lifting his gaze from his food, his knuckles white with rage as he clenched his fork. I flicked my head over my shoulder just as Eoghan reached the threshold of the door. "It would be best. Prydia appreciates your loyalty to our great kingdom," Gedeon said, dismissing Eoghan as if it were his idea all along.

Eoghan's steps faltered momentarily, his fists curling inward just before he flexed them out at his sides and left the room, making the dining hall feel almost hollow.

At least I wouldn't be the only disappointment in the castle as long as Eoghan stayed here.

Nineteen

PAIGE

The sun was beating down on the training deck by the time I made my way out of the dining hall with Hector tailing my lead. I practically inhaled my food while my father ushered out deep grunts of disapproval. The thought of pretending to enjoy his company made my stomach twist in frustration. He wasn't inviting me to dine with him out of kindness. He was dissecting my every move each time I lifted a fork or drank from my glass like I was some sick version of a science project.

My eyes peeled around the sharp lines of the balcony and a hollow pit formed in my chest as I realized Nya wasn't there, but Eoghan was. He was examining the weapons rack that held my unbound sword, his sleeves rolled up in preparation revealing a blue mark of cascading waves and foam in a torrent that reached beyond where his sleeves were raised. I walked slowly toward him but froze the minute he turned around, unsure if I should fear him as I did my father.

"Do you always walk so loudly? Anything you fight in the Triad will hear you a mile away." He strode soundlessly over to me, carrying my air sword in his outstretched arms.

"I didn't know I was supposed to be *quiet*." I dug my feet into place and stood tall, defiance seeping from every pore.

He smirked back at me as he closed the distance between us. "Take it, you will need it if you want to survive the trials. Any, and all, arrogance should be left inside the castle walls and far-a-fucking-way from the arena." I ground my teeth and ripped the sword from his hands, igniting the blade in a blaze of purple.

"Careful now, we wouldn't want Hector reporting you being unkind to your guest, would we?" He whistled at Hector and flashed him a wide grin before returning to meet my gaze, his nose tipped down as he robbed the stretch of distance between us, leaving but an inch. Too close.

"I'm not here to play games with you, *Lord* Eoghan." I maneuvered my feet backward away from him with two long strides.

"That footwork certainly had me fooled." He threw two daggers that landed right at the tips of my boots. "Do you want to live past the Triad?"

My breath hitched as I stared down at the twin blades that glinted in the mid-morning sunlight. "Yes." My fingers dug into the hilt of the sword, the purple glow pulsing brightly as my magic released in waves that ebbed against every inch of my skin.

"You're going to need more than a brightly bonded sword to fix...that." He gestured at the entirety of my body. "Let's see what you can do with a live target. Nya's use of dummies is absurd." He shook his head as he looked over his shoulder at the lineup of stitched dummies. "She must not want to hurt Gedeon's lost princess."

Lost? Did he really think I was lost all those years? Is that what the rest of this world thought as I fought to feed myself and my mother, fought to keep her from hating herself more than she already did? Gedeon never lost me, not in the way Eoghan insinuated. It was very damn clear that he never wanted me, never wanted us. He abandoned us. But a part of me questioned if that could be true. Were we lost to him before I came here?

No. I refuse to believe that.

"I'm not his princess," I spat out, anger filling too many spaces inside of me driving my magic wild. *Keep it in, Paige. Do. Not. Lose. Your. Shit.*

But it was too late. I threw the sword down and forced both palms out toward Eoghan, unafraid of the consequences of blasting a Mora over the fucking ledge. He did say I should practice with a live target after all. My air power was released in a flurry in the form of a huge swirling tornado that attempted to suck up Eoghan and fling him over the balcony, just as I'd envisioned in my mind. Eoghan merely sighed, dropped his shoulders theatrically, and lifted his palms. A thick wall of ice encompassed him like a tomb and a wave of water gushed from the edges. My tornado sucked up the water instead and flung it right back in my face before dissipating, effectively drenching me from head to toe.

The ice around Eoghan liquefied and seeped into the stone. "That's a good start. Though I did envision you trying to hurl your blade at me, not a storm." *Trying.* Like he knew I'd fail anyway.

Water droplets fell into my eyes as I bent down to pick up the faded sword. "You're supposed to be teaching me to wield other elements. Nya can train me to use this just fine."

"I passed my Triad, fairly recently if I may add. Gedeon hasn't been in a trial in over a hundred years. Who do you want to listen to?"

My jaw dropped. I did that too often around here but how many times was this place going to astonish the shit out of me. Gedeon was over a hundred years old, and he still acted like a dick.

"I don't want to die, can you help me do that?"

"Lady Aerborne, I can do more than that." His wrist twitched at his side and the water fell from my clothing instantaneously. I refrained from rolling my eyes as he said, "I can help you win."

The next few hours of the day consisted of me getting my ass handed to me, over and over again. *Fix your stance. Elbow higher. Are you trying to poke me with that sword of yours or are you just happy to see me?*

At least Nya would heal me whenever she decided to show up. My body ached and was painfully covered in scrapes and dagger nicks. Eoghan was holding back, but he still let me get the beating he felt I needed. It was way worse than any track conditioning I remembered. I never thought my body was built to be a weapon, but he insisted it was. He just had to beat the mortal out of me first. My power, on the other hand, I knew in my bones to be pure destruction—if only the first trial was a test of my original nature I would feel more comfortable knowing I had a chance of living at least another few days.

Most likely.

"How am I supposed to learn to fight well enough in a week?" I protested, nearly dodging yet another dagger being thrown toward my legs.

"You're not, but at least he can say he tried." The next blade that came right after the last one landed with a gnawing rip into my forearm and I let out a scream. Blood pooled in a line down my arm and dripped steadily onto the floor as I instinctively reached for the hilt.

"Stop! Don't yank it out!" Eoghan ran over to me and jerked his chin toward Hector who transformed into an owl in a matter of seconds and flew above the castle walls—the same owl that had coerced Aeden and I to follow him into the vortex. "If you pull it out now only more blood will come. The blade is the only thing keeping you from bleeding all over the deck." I was convinced I was already bleeding all over the deck. I took in deep, shaky breaths as Eoghan held out my arm, restricting me from moving it entirely. How was I going to fight against anyone if a short dagger made me hyperventilate?

Nya came running out as the sky above me swirled and the stone beneath me wobbled, followed by Hector in owl form who swooped down to land at the balcony's ledge and transformed back into his statuesque, more human self. She lifted my arm from Eoghan and I sucked in a sharp breath through my teeth. My flesh pulsed with the movement as Nya assessed the damage, and then placed both palms firmly around my unmarked forearm. Eoghan ripped the dagger from my arm moments before a warm glow spread from Nya's hands. My fingers tingled, the blood no longer filling into a pool beside me. She pulled her hands away and the glow faded, the only evidence being a thin stain of blood that smeared across my forearm.

Eoghan rubbed at his temples and his cheeks flushed red as my vision settled. "She was panicking, is this how you want her to be for the trials? She will *die* if she can't pull herself together." Eoghan started pacing in front of Nya and me, his boots relentlessly soundless. Nya shook her head and looked down at her hands. *Was I not supposed to panic with a knife in my arm?*

I raised my chin high and curled my hands into fists, although it was useless. There was no way I could fake not being afraid, I was still shaking and the sight of the blood beside me was making me feel woozy again. I released my fists, acknowledging my anger was all because of a man who'd forced me into this situation and didn't bother being there for my training. "So that's it then, I'm screwed. Aren't I?"

Eoghan laughed. Fucking *laughed*. "Yes, and no. You can't fight, you only have days before your first trial, and you still only have one element to wield." He lifted a finger, punctuating each one of the flaws—*my* flaws—he'd seen so far. *I wonder how many he'd lift by tomorrow*. "Being *screwed* is an understatement. You were dead before he brought you here. Your best bet is to go back to where you came from."

I shook my head and I didn't bother stopping the tear that rolled down my cheek. "I can't."

"Sure you can, I can open a portal right now for you. Just say the words and I'll send you on back to whatever hole you came from. Gedeon won't fight me on it, especially when I tell him how pathetic your first practice with me was. How you almost fainted from the sight of your own blood. Honestly, I bet he won't shed a single fucking tear in losing you again." Eoghan motioned his hands and a blue vortex started to rip into the chasm of space in front of me. I searched for Hector, assuming he'd put an end to it, but he'd gone back inside the castle after leading Nya to the training deck. That only left Nya to stand in my defense, but her eyes stayed trained on the ground.

We were alone, the three of us, and I was inches from being back home and getting back to my mother. Surely they kept her body in the hospital morgue until someone could come for her. The thought of the cold box they'd undoubtedly squeezed her into sent a shiver down my spine. She was dead, but Aeden...he was most likely still alive. Out there beyond the walls in Aellethia somewhere. I couldn't just give up on him. I had to find him or at least wait until he could find me. My chest cracked at the thought of running back home without him, and for once I was going to listen to what my heart wanted, or rather, who it wanted.

"I said, I can't. And I won't. I'm going to fight, or die trying." I choked on my words as the reality that that actually may be how this all ends roiled over me. Dead. I could very well be six feet under after all of this, so it better be for something more tangible than a kingdom I had no interest in.

"Good, step one is deciding how badly you want this, no matter the reasoning. Determination can get you further than any amount of magic or bonded blades ever could. Without it, you are a sinking stone heading toward the bottom of an ocean, inevitably drowning as the world continues on around you." The portal closed up and Eoghan clapped his hands together. "It's time to end today's practice. See you dark and early tomorrow morning, Lady Aerborne." He winked and left the training deck.

"What the literal hell is his problem?" I let out the minute he was out of earshot. *Were all the men around here just waiting to test me?*

Nya finished checking over the rest of my cuts and looked toward the door. "He's just...flustered. He had to leave his guard at home, and he doesn't like doing that." She stuck her tongue out in his direction and I added my finger to the mix. "Library time?" Nya raised her brow at me as I put my sword back on the rack.

"Hell yes. I'm ready whenever you are."

The library was phenomenal. Long shelves flanked the three-story high walls, every wide shelf full of thickly bound books and scrolls. The information contained within these walls alone made my mouth water. I was too book-obsessed for my own good sometimes but it might actually prove useful for once. More useful than all the times I'd borrowed college texts from Aeden in the hopes that whatever he was learning, I could be involved in it too. Just one more way I tried to be close to him without being too overbearing. I'd accepted years ago that college wasn't in the cards for me. I wasn't involved enough in school activities before graduation to earn a scholarship and without that, there was no possible way I'd ever be able to afford it. Not that I could have left my mother either. None of that mattered now.

Nya stood by the double door that had servants ready to tug it open and closed, waiting for any potential visitors. We found it barren and soundless and that's just how I was hoping it would be. I didn't need Gedeon knowing I had this at my disposal or that I craved to know more about Aellethia. For all he knew, I hated reading or refused to further advance myself than what was already expected of me. And that's exactly what I wanted him to think.

"You okay if I just..."

"Yeah, have at it. Your father hardly comes in here, and none of the servants can read, so it's all yours. The ones you are looking for about what lives in Aellethia are in the back far right, under the section labeled Beasts and other Non-Fae." Nya leaned on the edge of one of the shelves and slid a dagger out from her waist. She twirled it between her fingers and started to whistle a tune that oddly reminded me of water with its fluidity.

"He's labeled the sections?"

"They've been labeled for centuries I'm sure. Some are written in one of the many dead languages we no longer use. Just look for pictures on the spines if you get lost or confused." Nya was lost to her tune and dagger, leaving me to search for myself.

There was something comforting in being secluded within the depths of the library. Nothing but myself and the words. My hand stopped on a book of maps, the spine etched with what I could only assume was a small portion of the world I was in now. I pulled it from the shelf and picked up my pace along the dustless chasms.

The labels changed from a language that more resembled lines with dots around them to English, starting with the 'History of Moras.' I crooked my finger over the top of one of the books there, removing it and tucking it under my arm. I couldn't count on Gedeon to tell me anything *and* be able to believe him. Books were always more reliable.

Nya thrust her dagger back into her pocket and rushed to help me carry some books I'd taken as I returned to the front of the library. "I guess Eoghan's talk about determination truly hit home, huh?"

I rolled my eyes. "Determination isn't something I've ever needed to work on."

"So you aren't trying to prove a point, then?" She cocked her brow, trying to figure me out as if I were that dense. Maybe to some people, I came off that way.

"I don't need to prove anything to him, or to my father."

The doors opened and I could feel the strain of the guard's unwavering eyes as they glued to the walls behind me.

"If you really can read through all of these in a week, you might end up knowing more than I do about this place." *That's the plan.* She flipped through one of the books I'd given her to hold, and I did the same as we walked back to my room in silence.

Twenty

AEDEN

The walls of Prydia drew closer with each passing minute. Large white stones piled no more than three stories in height, peeping just above the trees of the Highland Woods to our right. We passed a few homes, some made of logs and woven branches for roofs and others made of compacted clay. All homes cowered in the shadow of the castle that lay towering above the city, and we hadn't even entered the city walls yet.

Seamus reminded me to cover my tattoo as much as I could, even stopping several times to check that my strides hadn't shifted the fabric too much, exposing any portion that crept along my neck and curled out from my wrist. Each time he checked, he grew more disheveled.

"I'll be okay, I know how to keep my head down and lie low." And it was true. All my years in foster care taught me just that—how to be as invisible as I possibly could be.

"Shay, be ready to distract anyone who even lifts a brow his way, will ye?" The look of worry lining his eyes pulled at my heartstrings as Shay nodded decisively back. This man was becoming my friend faster than anyone else—except Paige that is. I was still weary about Shay, but she proved herself a few times now, so I had to try to forget the power she had could be used against me. Trust was damn difficult to dish out on my end, but I'd need it to survive this place.

The guards were coming into view and took notice of us with trailing eyes but didn't shift from where they stood. They wore long purple tunics with black pants that peeked out from right above their knees and a weapon sheathed at their waists or backs. Some had their sleeves rolled up to reveal their marks—mostly purple swirling air that extended further than the ones I'd seen the night before at the caravans and swept beyond where rolled sleeves stopped at their forearms. They were powerful, but nowhere near as powerful as me as their exposed necks bore no semblance of a mark.

Shay began clearing her throat in preparation and Seamus shuffled closely in front of me as we came to an arched opening in the wall. At least twenty guards lined the edges of the tunneled entrance, showing just how thick the stone walls of Prydia were. One guard with a mace strapped to his back stepped out from the wall and blocked our entrance.

"Where do you think you're going, water-wielder? What business do you have in Prydia?" He took in Seamus' mark and sniffed the air, glancing between Shay and I. Shay started to hum but I elbowed her arm inconspicuously, urging her to stop. We didn't need to draw the attention of every guard along the walls or in the tunnel. I narrowed my eyes at her and her blue eyes lit up like my flames did when I burst apart the hag—a silent argument between two people who were hardly trusting of each other.

"We're here to discuss trades from Costa. Fishing trades." I only heard the stories from Seamus and Shay while walking but I knew that's what business Seamus had here before, and with the way I'd learned how to bluff from foster care, I was ready to discuss fishing and trades. But in reality, I'd never gone fishing a day in my life. Seamus tensed as the guard inspected us over but I reacted quickly, tossing my arm around him in solidarity. "I apologize for my friend here. He seems to have fried his brain in the heat earlier, and the girl behind us"—I leaned in closer to the guard and lowered my voice—"just couldn't get enough of how good I fucked her last night, so she tagged along."

The guard smirked back at me and moved his hungry eyes to Shay, looking her up and down in the most hedonistic fashion. I swear she would have slapped him if he stood any closer to her, anger flushing her cheeks that could have been mistaken for a lack of modesty. His whistle reverberated off the arched stone above us. "She's a mermaid, no?" His eyes raked her exposed arms and I took in a sharp breath, pulling my fingers into my palm, unsure if I needed to be ready to fight. I didn't know if mermaids needed to be hidden. Hadn't even considered it. "I've heard they can bend in ways no fae can. She any good?"

I raised my brows at him and rolled my eyes over to her, then stepped back behind her, unfurling my fingers, and smacked her ass with one hand. "Yeah, she's alright. Not the best, but enough to let her come." I winked at him, noting the double entendre of my words. He let out a cackle and my jaw tensed under the pressure of touching another woman that wasn't Paige. At treating someone so vulgarly.

"The fish traders are around the back end of the market. Help yourself man, and don't let her take up too much of your time. If she's a problem, send her my way. The boys and I would love a bit of fun around here." He stepped back in formation along the wall, his mace swinging heavily along his back until he turned. That mace could be lodged in my fucking skull right about now if I hadn't lied through my teeth.

I waved toward the guard as we passed through the archways, my hand at the base of Shay's spine. Seamus didn't let his shoulders fall from his ears until the guards were far from sight. The crowd of the open market was a good cover for blending into the background and allowed us to continue unnoticed, easing my tension as well just as I removed my hand from Shay's back. When we were more than clear of the guards, Shay spun around and slapped the back of my head, but when I tried to apologize she pulled me in close, hugging me like her life depended on it.

"You stupid boy, why wouldn't you let us handle that back there? You could have gotten us all killed." She was right. I *could* have. But the guard looked like most of the guys I played ball with, which meant he was a dog. A chauvinist, get-her-to-bed-and-forget-her dog. Not to say I didn't do the same thing to every girl I slept with as well but I had other reasons. Most men were just dicks like that, and I was willing to bet he was no different. I also didn't think Shay's song would go over so well with so many guards, and Seamus...well Seamus just locked up. He wasn't doing a damn thing to help. I had to step in.

"Sorry, Shay, but you two were going to get us killed. Turns out the mortal world isn't that different from this one when it comes to assholes. I knew what he wanted to hear and what he wanted to pay attention to." Shay didn't seem like the type to revel in aggression. She got things done, and didn't take people's crap or hold onto it and it reminded me of Paige. If she was upset enough with me, she typically gave me hell that not only drove me mad, it made me weak. Like at the party when I clearly lost my shit over her and Dick Little when she was just trying to have fun. How she didn't notice all the times I was insanely jealous was pure luck. I didn't want to stand in the way of her doing great things in the future for her and her mom. But now her future would look different, and I wanted her to know more than anything that I would be there for her, that I could be in her future plans—whatever that may look like.

"It's alright, Boyo. I failed ye back there. It's just...hard to see all the Aerborne guards. It brings me back to times I wish to forget." Seamus's eyes fell to the ground. When he lifted his face again, tears were fighting to flood down his cheeks. This man was the biggest, brawniest-looking man who could probably crush people without using his powers, yet he wore his vulnerability like a weapon. I almost envied that his emotions didn't diminish how feared he could be while I had learned to hide the very thing growing up in the system.

Shay reached around to Seamus and squeezed his shoulder. "What's the plan then, Aeden?" Both sets of eyes fell on me, hopeful for the next move, the game plan.

I took in my surroundings, searching for the answer. To our left sat the castle that reached toward the sky at the center of the city and grew out from the white stone that was cut to fit the structure. It was eerily well-kept and a grotesquely sharp contrast to the dirt-laden city below. Each time the dust attempted to settle around us, the foot traffic scattered it back into plumes that shielded our vision beyond twenty feet in front of us.

At best, we could see a few buildings beyond where we stood in the midst of what was undoubtedly the marketplace where we'd promised to discuss trade matters in. It was nothing like Costa's market—open, sea-blown air and fewer buildings. Prydia was crammed full of people, buildings, and wagons set out with things to sell ranging from weapons and food to animals and jewelry. However, it was unclear if the wagons were empty because of a lack of products to sell initially or if they were repeatedly selling out.

"Let's split up and meet back here when the sun goes down. Find out what you can." The sun was a few hours from setting, giving us plenty of time to find out something. Anything. There had to be answers somewhere within the walls if she was brought here by her father, the Mora of Prydia.

"Take this and buy yerself a coat, somethin' to cover…" He scratched at his own neck, deflecting from bringing any attention to my own. I shifted my collar around to fix the spot where my first mark burned along my flesh. Seamus gave me a weary thumbs-up and nodded. "Aye, better. Stay away from the guards." He dropped several coins into my opened hand and wandered out into the dust. I put my hand into my pocket, dropping the coins and rubbing the bracelet I kept there with my thumb in soothing circles.

"Be careful, Aeden. You don't understand what will happen if...if they see what you are." Shay reached up to put her hand on my shoulder, squeezing sympathetically.

I put my hand on top of hers and patted. "I can handle staying hidden. And if I don't show up—"

"You *will* be here at sundown. The big guy won't ever forgive himself if you aren't."

I nodded. "I'll be here. Don't get into trouble, I'd like it if you stayed with us." My fire was illegal to wield, but her gifts could potentially piss the wrong people off. I wasn't sure how much she liked to play with that kind of fire, but something told me she wasn't opposed to weaponizing herself more freely than others.

She winked back at me and turned to leave, fading into the dust in the opposite direction that Seamus had left in.

I found myself moving along the sea of people for a while, analyzing their buildings, shops and wagons, and the fae that swarmed the streets. I stopped and turned as a crowd began clapping. Two men dressed in all black walked onto an elevated surface, like a stage—only it wasn't a stage for theater. On the raised wooden platform stood nearly ten posts, all with nooses hanging from the tops. One of the men dressed in black drew an ax from his back and the crowd let loose a booming roar. The other man opened a hatch from below the platform and eight people wearing worn and tattered clothing stepped up from below, each guided into a position behind a noose.

A public execution.

My jaw tensed as rage and fear and utter shock rose up inside of me. Fire was whipping under my flesh just as eagerly as the crowd cheered on. Thoughts of burning down the platform and setting the people free sprang into my mind. I didn't care what they were accused of. No one deserved this. But my body refused to act, knowing my end would come just as quickly as theirs if I lashed out.

One of the people to the far right was smaller than the rest. It was a boy—a teen but hadn't been one for long. Bile rose up from my stomach. No one deserved to die like that, especially not a fucking child.

The man holding the ax waved the blade high in the air and the crowd grew eerily silent. Still.

"These fae, these rats of our existence, are all sentenced to death by hanging. All have pled guilty to crimes that our great Mora and all of Aellethia have condemned." Murmurs coursed through the crowd and the man shook his ax, silencing them once again. "We all know the crimes that lead to this, and yet these despicable fae"—he spat onto the wooden planks—"go against the very foundation our great Mora is trying to set." He lowered his ax and the crowd grew wild again, booing and spitting toward the platform.

The ax was raised again as the man without a weapon walked around to each fae and placed a sack over each of their heads before positioning the noose loosely around their necks. Not one of them jerked away or fought back. They'd accepted their fates, even the boy, who couldn't have been more than thirteen, hadn't done more than lower his eyelids toward the ground. He was placed on top of a box in order to reach the noose before the black sack was placed on his head, his innocence shielded from the unwavering crowd.

"These fae have broken laws that we, loyal fae to Prydia, can not allow within our walls."

He moved to an older woman first, who stood the furthest to the left, her wrinkled hands firmly to her side—unbound.

"This fae is accused of the ultimate crime—fire-wielding. She has refused the power stripping process and has pleaded guilty to wielding." Her hands trembled, turning her wrists just enough to show a small fire mark burning brightly against her pale, sagging skin.

The crowd booed and hissed until a hatch in the platform gave way, sending her to her fate. She flung violently, her legs kicking and her hands clawing fervently at the rope above her until her body went limp.

The man holding the ax walked over to the taut rope and swung his weapon minutes after her body stopped jerking, and cut her body down. Her frame crumpled into the dirt, billows of dust covering her as she lay there lifelessly.

The dust finally settled and the hatch snapped close. Her arm stretched out along the dirt showing a red mark fading to gray.

The executioner moved on to the next and the next in the same exact way, stating the faes were all accused of fire-wielding and had foregone the procedure to strip their powers. They chose to die rather than lose their power. Even the boy. Only when his body fell past the hatch did a woman wearing a white cloak burst into wailing cries and fell to the floor sobbing, screaming his name. The only named fae from the platforms. *His mother?* Cyprian's mark faded to grey and the crowd cheered, drowning out the cries of the woman on the ground.

Flames licked under my skin, urging to be released on the crowd, to free the woman from her tormentors who clung to the laws of a madman. I wanted to burn them all down. But the fear of never seeing Paige again, never freeing her from her father who set the very law that took so many lives, kept my power contained. It fucking hurt to keep it down and took every ounce of willpower I could force back. Like a coward, I stood by and watched all eight of the fire-wielders fall without trying to help and watched as their lifeless bodies were being put into a wheelbarrow and taken away.

I made my way through the diminishing crowd until I reached Cyprian's mother who knelt on the ground. I fell to the ground in front of her, and she stopped sobbing to glance up at me. She tucked a strand of her brown hair behind her ear, revealing dark brown, bloodshot eyes. I put my hands over hers as they clenched the dirt, grounding herself from the weight of the world crashing in on her.

"I'm sorry. I'm so, so sorry about your son." Not that I was sure it was her son. I'd never felt the loss of a parent or child, or really anyone. But if I had, I could only imagine the pain and suffering I'd go through watching them die in front of me.

"Did you know him?" she choked out, her question full of longing, wanting to hear about her son from someone who didn't see him as just one of the hanged fire-wielders.

"Yes," I lied, wanting to comfort her. "He was a nice kid. He will be greatly missed."

"He was so eager to get his mark, and we...we prayed and prayed from the day he was born that he would not wield fire, like...like his father did. But he got his mark earlier than most, and..." It took every bit of her to continue, her body trembling as she recounted her son's life. I looked down at our fingers, clutching onto the dirt together as my hands blanketed hers, and that's when I saw her mark—an air-wielder. "He only wanted to be loyal to Prydia, show the great Mora he was honorable. He wanted to be a guard one day, even though we'd lived in hiding until...and without a mark..." She took in a few ragged breaths. "So he came to the city and presented himself, hoping they would put him through the process of stripping his power. I don't...I don't understand how...." She lost her grounding and cried out again. No one seemed to take notice of us as if sobbing on the ground in front of the platform was an everyday occurrence.

"Are you...are you saying Cyprian asked to be stripped?"

"Of course. If he kept his mark, he would have been...well...what good did it serve him anyway? They pick your fate."

They pick your fate. He *wanted* to be stripped. The executioner said he *refused* to be stripped. And they hung him. A young boy was killed for having a fire mark. And here I was, alive and with the biggest mark I'd seen since I'd arrived. The horror on the faces of the people of Costa, the ones at the bar—the pure terror radiating through them all as they fled from knowing of my existence, from being near me. They weren't scared of my power hurting them, they were scared of this. Of hanging for knowing. Of being on that platform themselves.

"Thank you for taking the time to talk to me, but I have to get back to my other children. They will want to help bury...bury their brother." She stood up shakily and brushed the dirt off her long dress and cloak, wiping the memories of her son to the ground.

"Is there anyone here to help you?" I rose with her, ready to help her in any way she needed. I'd be there for her.

"The guards will help to carry his body out of the grounds. They wouldn't want to leave them out, not with the Aerborne Ball tomorrow night."

"The Aerborne Ball?" *Fuck.* It was too many questions when she'd just lost her son.

She lifted a swollen eyebrow at me, suspicion growing across her face. "Yes...where did you say you were from, again?"

Shit. I said the first and only place I really knew of that wasn't here. "Costa," I replied firmly.

She looked me up and down, her body shuddering with more tears as she folded herself against me. The movement shifted my collar slightly lower. Too low. I needed to get her away from me but the guilt was overwhelming, so I bent my body against her, using her as a shield from anyone who'd walk by.

"Cyprian loved to go on fishing trips in Costa with his older brother. I'm sorry...I took up so...so much of your time. I'll leave you be now." She gathered her cloak in her hand, preventing it from dragging on the dirt. What a damn cruel way to get your loved one back. My chest ached for her and her family. No one should have to endure that, all over a mark on their arm. I watched on as she stumbled toward the wagon where Cyprian's gray mark jutted out from the edge until the dust and crowds of people blocked her from sight.

Twenty-One

AEDEN

I leaned against the wall of a building, wood pieces crumbling as I adjusted my boot against the surface. A smug grin spread across my face as Seamus and Shay walked up to the waiting spot, both looking less than hopeful. I shifted in the new black frock coat I'd purchased from a shop not far from our meeting place, lifting the tall collar securely over my neck.

"What 'as ye so happy Lad? Did ye find something other than that new coat ye're wearin'?" I pushed off the wall and glanced up at the ominous castle, then back at them both.

"The Aerborne Ball is tomorrow night."

"That's my man! Why didn't you figure that out, Seamus?" Shay smacked Seamus on the shoulder with the back of her hand. Seamus looked...less than enthused.

"Ye know what that means then, don't ye Shay?" Seamus' eyes grew wide, looking between us both as he stroked his beard fervently.

Shay looked down at her feet and shuffled them into the dirt, completely overcome with a realization that stole her words from her. I shook my head.

"It means, yer girl is enterin' the Triad. That must be why he brought her 'ere."

"And you think I know what a Triad is? I found *us* a way in, that should be good enough to get *her* out."

They both shook their heads in unison.

"The Triad is a series of tests of a High Fae's abilities. It's what all Moras have to do to prove their worth before being able to claim the kingdom as theirs. Once she is entered, she can't back out, or she will be stripped of her powers." He fisted his beard more and I swear he was going to yank out all the hairs along his jaw if he continued.

Stripped, like the people who were just hung. *Fuck that.* Prydia didn't strip powers, they killed the ones who asked to be stripped. After hearing of Gedeon's brutality and witnessing it for myself, there was no way he was going to let Paige be 'stripped.'

"She's like me? Like...us?" I motioned between Seamus and I, who nodded at the question. I should've put two-and-two together, but I didn't. Couldn't focus on her heritage long enough past whether she was safe or not. The desire to be there with her, to see her and to make sure she was okay grew tenfold. "What kind of tests? Is she going to be okay?" My heart rate kicked up twenty notches. Seamus looked to Shay, then away again.

His eyes raked over my arm, pure worry filling his features. "The tests 're more like...trials. They will not only test yer lass' magic but also 'er strength. The way she thinks, the way she tries to...survive." *Tries to survive?* Seamus watched as my arm braced back against the wall. "Gedeon's son entered several years ago. The lad trained his entire life, and the kingdom anticipated a victory. But then, just like that"—he snapped his fingers—"he lost, clingin' to his life in the midst of the arena. When he was pulled out, word got around that Gedeon tried to kill the boy. Next thing we knew, he was being shipped off to Sentra, meant to be purchased by 'nother Mora or High Fae, to be in servitude for life. It's the best one can hope for when they survive the loss."

Gedeon's son was entered, trained his entire life, and still lost. And Paige had a fucking brother? "So you're telling me, she has to be tested on something that she doesn't know anything about, something that her...her fae brother couldn't even do..." I paused, tugging at my bottom lip. "And he didn't *die*? So you're saying she could..." My hand raked furiously through my hair, and I began to pace. This was *not* fucking good. "And if I save her from it, if we can get her out..."

Seamus looked around, checking for anyone who may be watching or listening to us, but no one cared about three fae standing in the middle of the market. "If ye pull her out, save her as ye say, he will find her again. And she won't be saved for the trials again. He'd...well, he'd kill her. There's no question in me mind of the very fact." Shay remained silent, allowing Seamus to take the lead. "She has to finish the Triad."

Gravity shifted and I almost lost balance as I stood in front of them. I leaned back against the wall, adjusting my collar with my shaking hand again just in case it'd managed to fall. "We need to find a way into the ball. I need to see her. I need to be there, even if it's only for an hour. Any amount of time that we can have together, I need it. Please." I fought tears behind my eyes. I couldn't remember the last time I'd cried. It'd been years, but I felt the wetness slide down my cheek and cursed silently under my breath as I wiped it away.

I looked up to the sky, hoping for an answer. For a way out of this. Images of Paige and I in the woods, promising to not let go of each other, flashed through my mind. I'd go into that castle, no matter what it took to do so. Even if that made me the dumbest fucking fae alive. Because for her, I was ready to be anything, to do anything. To prove anything.

My power was sizzling under my skin, burning me up from the inside, promising to turn everything in the market to ash and bone. We needed to get out of Prydia for tonight, or it would all go up in flames. I could feel the heat licking my palms, water now rising to meet with the flames, desperately trying to break free. If Prydia didn't burn tonight, it sure as fuck would flood. I pushed off of the wall, setting my focus on the tunnel we passed through earlier. "We need to go before I turn this place into a wasteland."

"Spoken like a true fae," Shay whispered softly, finally lifting her head from the ground that held her gaze and tongue for so long.

Shay and Seamus stood beside me as we left with ease through the front arches, guards not thinking twice about anyone who was leaving. They only cared about those who entered. The guard from earlier was nowhere to be seen, yet another guard along the wall waved toward Seamus, and he inclined his head back to him, almost familiarly.

"Who was that, and how do you know so much about Gedeon?" Shay raised her brow at Seamus the moment we were far enough away from the walls, so far the guard along the wall was lost to the darkness of the night. Turns out Shay's silence was not only from my questions but also her own.

"Aye, I saw this comin'." Seamus grunted as he sat down in the grass, motioning for us to join. We weren't that far from the wall, but we were far enough to be out of view from the guards. The trees would have to provide the rest of our coverage as we tucked behind where they curved out. "I used to work for Gedeon."

"You used to work...for *him*?" Shay looked ready to fight, scream, and possibly claw his face apart. She wore her expressions so clearly on her face, and Seamus leaned back into the grass away from her.

"Yes. And it's not something I am proud of, but I was purchased at Sentra, ye know. It's not like the choice was me own, though bein' a guard was. I couldn't say no to his offer."

"You're a fucking guard?" If Shay had an elemental power, I was almost certain Seamus would be dead. I let water flow through my veins, cooling my palms as I placed my hand on her shoulder, trying to ease her anger but also ready to tug her back from Seamus. But she slapped my hand away. "You don't get it, Aeden. *We* used to be free before Vizna fell. Then tighter regulations fell upon all of us who fought alongside Vizna—but I guess Seamus had other loyalties. Gedeon is the reason my people fear coming out of Lake Kree—why merpeople there are all accounted for, monitored, and registered at birth. And Seamus used to work for him—" She spat on the ground toward him. "Something he didn't bother telling me before I put my trust in him."

That's why none of the merpeople came out of the lake when we were walking. They were scared. And Gedeon was the reason for all of it. Hanging anyone with the fire-wielding mark, putting up barriers for anyone to exist as they should in Aellethia. It was beyond wrong.

I paused, my lips coming to a thin line as I contemplated. "I'm sure Big Red can explain. It doesn't sound like he had a choice. How long ago was it that you worked for him?" It baffled me that I was standing up for Seamus, the man who tried to beat me into oblivion days ago. But he didn't deserve to lose his friends over a past mistake, and I doubted he had any remaining loyalties to the man who killed his family.

"Aye, I was loyal to Gedeon, I can't deny the very fact. But after I retired, he changed. He killed me family, Shayanna, do ye not remember?" His arms flung wide open and his eyes begged for forgiveness from Shay, who started to visibly crumble at the sight of him. They loved each other, whether that meant as friends or more was up in the air. But she couldn't stay mad at Seamus, that much was obvious.

"Why does he hate fire-wielders so much?" I deflected, allowing Shay more time to process his confession.

"Aye, that I don't know, Lad. The kingdoms were all at peace until 'bout twenty years ago. I had retired just before everything went to shit to be with me family."

I thought back to the boy being hung, and the mother crying out for her child. I never knew my parents or knew if I had parents out there who loved me as fiercely as the woman who loved Cyprian did. Sitting on the grass, the dirt and roots below us started to ripple and rise in the moonlight. Shay lifted her dress from where it fell around her knees, examining the grass at her ankles. A single stem rose from the dirt, parting the blades of grass around it. The stem produced thorns as it reached higher, a red bud unfurling once the stem settled on its length. A flower bloomed in front of us—a singular rose just as the image of the fire-wielder's grey mark settled in my mind.

I felt the strange, yet familiar sensation climbing its way across my back, this time on my right side. It settled like arms wrapping around me in a warm embrace as my magic swayed in a soothing dance beneath my skin. The fire burned with the rolling waves, parting for the new magic like the surrounding grass had. It did not compete with what already existed under my flesh and in my bones, but tried to become one, gently easing its way into the mix.

Seamus buried his face in his hands, then dragged them down over his beard. "Fuckin' a, Lad. Turn around," Seamus instructed, the moon casting a whiteness over his face. Or was his skin paling over?

I turned, ready to show whatever new mark had emerged. There was no use denying the feeling that grew within me. It belonged just as much as the others did.

I turned back around to face them. "You're an earth-wielder too, Aeden. That makes..."

"Three," Shay breathed out, finally allowing her dress to fall back down.

"I'm guessing this is worse than having two, isn't it?" My eyes were glued to the rose that grew from my sadness, not needing to hear the response that was inevitably coming. My fingertips dragged up along the stem, the thorns bending under my touch as I moved upwards toward the blossom.

Seamus' eyes fell to the rose, unable to fixate elsewhere. "Two was manageable. Three is...fuck. Three is somethin' to fear."

TWENTY-TWO

PAIGE

The night faded in and out, lucid dreams pulling on my consciousness—dreams of Aeden. He was here, and he was close. I could feel his proximity, closing the distance between us day by day as if it were another one of my senses. The only thing separating my dreams from reality was his apparent obliviousness to my existence as if I were a ghost.

He didn't respond when I reached out to him or when I shouted his name. He stayed sitting in a field of grass, next to two people I hadn't seen before. They were blurry and untouchable, but Aeden was different—he glowed vibrantly against the shadows of my dreams until there was only him. My heart thumped wildly in my chest, yearning for him, wanting to be with him. But he took no notice of me. My heart pleaded, racing to the ceaseless desire of needing him and yet, I was trapped, yelling at a wall. Shielded from him by a pane of thick, immovable glass. My power surged, hurling blasts of air at the wall to break it down. But it was no use. My power didn't work here, and I was invisible and inaudible. I pounded on the glass, crying out desperately to be noticed. Sobbing, crying out for Aeden, I fell to my knees on the grass on the other side.

He looked sad and distraught, seemingly on edge with something. He shifted to lie in the grass, a blurry figure's garbled words echoing through the panes as he slid his arms beneath his head. I watched until he fell asleep, and then listened to the pieces of conversation I could make out faintly. The other two people spoke about a woman and Vizna, the word 'died' merged the two thoughts as they glanced back over at Aeden intermittently. They looked...as if they'd seen a ghost. The black-haired woman's pale blue eyes soaked him in as he slept, a sadness lingering on both her and the man with the beard's faces. The woman tucked Aeden's fallen strands of hair behind his ear almost maternally, and my fingers ached as I remembered how my hands were through his hair not too long ago. He rolled over in his sleep and I watched through narrowed eyes as they both examined him further—his arm, his neck—

Red flashed in my vision, and there on the bottom of his neck was the edge of what looked like a mark. But that couldn't be right. I'd only seen one like it on Gedeon's back, and on the dead, painted bodies along the hallways beyond my bedroom door.

His neck shifted against the grass, dropping his collar further until it was undeniable what I was seeing.

A fire-wielder mark.

Sweating and panting for breaths that left too quickly, I sprang up into a seated position in my bed. I was panicking, anxiety clawing at my heart, squeezing tightly, and ripping the air from my lungs the moment I started to fill them. I stopped piercing the blanket with my fingertips and spread them out, opening my palms in a desperate attempt to wield. Air rushed in to fill my lungs, over and over, in and out, until I could manage my own breathing again.

It wasn't the first time I'd had a panic attack, and with the trials coming up I was sure it wouldn't be the last.

I heard Aeden's voice—*Deep breaths, count to ten slowly...*

One...

Two...

Fuck this.

I didn't have time to be weak anymore. Fight or die, those were my choices, and I was going to live. Which meant, I was going to fight. A few more days and I'd be able to breathe easier knowing I was closer to finishing the trials.

Or dead, my intrusive thoughts reminded me.

The fireplace lit the walls of my room with no light from the outside coming through the windows, only the light of the stars and moon shone over the city below in the distance. I was up earlier than usual, giving me time to read more before heading back to the training deck.

The books I'd taken from the library were sprawled out across the blanket, open, with half-finished pages waiting to be read. I flipped through one of the books, finding a folded-over page with a map on it. A bright red flourishing line like fire curled underneath the title, 'Vizna,' the name of the kingdom I was reading about before I fell asleep. *Perhaps that explained the dream I was trapped in.*

The pages were worn like someone had read through it dozens of times and had evidently marked it for their return. A few of the pages following up to the map of Vizna were crumpled and stained and a jagged seam was all that was left behind where nearly ten other pages of history were removed. The book-lover in me died seeing the destruction done to the book, and the pages, while the part of me that was hot-headed at times wanted to punch the person responsible. No doubt it was Gedeon. If the servants couldn't read, it didn't leave a lot of options for anyone with access and a means to know what they were doing. The only question was, why? Why would Gedeon remove pages from a book in *his* library that he hardly touched in the first place?

I held the book under my arm, a finger holding the place of the map as I darted out of bed. I pressed my ear to the door, and when I was sure I could hear nothing on the other side, I peeled the door open slowly by the golden handle.

The hallways were dimly lit by sconces that illuminated the wall's surface. The bloody scene of so many people—*fae*, dying on the walls, still made my stomach churn. But I held the book open from where I kept my finger tucked into the hinge of the book and looked between the map and the wallpaper.

It was undoubtedly Vizna. The castle that was drawn in the book mirrored the same one to the left of my door just a few more doors down the hall. The smaller, flat tops of the roofs and the shiny gold-like framing around each window, down to the grand doors with two large dragons breathing fire at each other that even the map spared no expense in detailing. It was as if someone spent their life perfecting a mirrored copy just for these walls as they had in the book. I flipped through to a page that was still somewhat intact, a page with the same two dragons breathing fire above a poem that read—

Our lives are bound to the ones with flames
As their hearts burn with their dragon's own—
May our kingdom forever stay alive with
The glory of the dragon heir's throne.
Their fire burns bright and holds our keep,
Our walls of flame to never be felled.
But if that light shall fail to be—
May the rightful heir bring it whence it held.

Another two dragons were drawn meticulously underneath the last line of the poem. There were no dragons on the wallpaper, save for the ones etched into the doors of the castle that only *resembled* real-life dragons—which was still unbelievable if they really did exist here—where fields of bloodied fae marked with fire along their left arms were mostly depicted. But no dragons flew above those fields or fought alongside those wounded and dying soldiers.

I walked down the hall, moving closer to the castle. The dragons drawn on the doors were fierce, with sharp claws and long tails that ended in spikes, their wings lifted with their bodies as they breathed out everlasting fire. A man stood in front of the castle, his bare back turned to the onlookers of the wallpaper. All four elements were decorating every inch of his body beneath his sleek light blonde, almost white hair. Gedeon held a bloody sword in his fist, probably sporting the same wicked grin that made shivers roll down my spine at the mere thought of it, as he faced the downfall of an entire kingdom.

"Odd choice in artwork, wouldn't you agree?" The voice was new, but already familiar as Eoghan whispered beside me. I froze in absolute terror, unsure of whether being in the hallways alone, analyzing the horror sprawled on the walls, was something that would set him off. "Relax, I'm not going to tell."

I turned to face him, turning the book around in my arms so he couldn't see the title as I squeezed it tight to my chest. "What are you doing awake?" I breathed out, trying not to raise my voice. I didn't want to alert Hector, wherever he was. Because that's exactly who'd come for me. Gedeon was always too preoccupied, it seemed.

"I could ask you the same thing, Princess."

"I'm not a princess." I dug my fingers into the book, wanting to hit Eoghan over the head with it at the mention of the twisted nickname.

"Tsk tsk, so defiant." He lifted the corner of his mouth, smirking at me.

"What do you want?"

"Oh, it isn't what *I* want that should interest you. No Princess, it's what *he* wants. Though, I suppose, maybe later my interests—"

"Then what does *he* want? Are you his lapdog too, like Hector?" I spat back at him, knowing the only man whom I should be focused on the interests of was Gedeon's. Yet he was the one I least cared about the *interests* of.

"Oh no, sweet Paige, no. You assume I am on his side. You are frightfully wrong." Eoghan raised his hand to his chest, a cat-like grin spreading across his face. "I am on my own side." *Why was he so keen on messing with my head?*

"If you aren't here of your own volition, and you aren't here of his, then why are you bothering me?" I shifted to move around him, but he stepped to the side, blocking me from moving away. "What is your problem?"

"I have news for you." He cleared his throat and his lips grew tight as he looked down at me. "Your father is putting on a show for the public, as is customary for the Triad."

"What does that even mean? What kind of show?" I was tapping my fingers on my book now, hoping Eoghan would get the hint, hurry the hell up and let me leave. Gedeon gave me little to no warning about anything and I bet he did the same for my mother when he abandoned us. Screw him and screw whatever he was planning to do.

Eoghan looked down at my hands and leaned in closer to my ear. "The kind where you get to dress up like the princess you are, dance the night away with a handsome man like myself, and show that you are ready to beat the trials with your dashing good looks."

A dance. Gedeon was hosting some kind of party for me and didn't bother to tell me. Image really was everything to him. "Like yourself? So, what? You came to ask me to go with you?" The only person who'd truly asked what I wanted to do had been Nya, aside from Eoghan's taunt of asking if I wanted to go back home. But even that had been more of a demand. *Just say the words and I'll send you on back to whatever hole you came from.*

"Would you do me the honor?" He bowed down, then lifted his head to bat his eyelashes at me.

My fingers stilled on the book. "I'll do it under two conditions."

"Oh, the princess has conditions." He propped himself against the wall and folded his arms. "Please, do continue."

"One, don't call me Princess. Two, you get one dance, and don't try anything on me like making a move. I'm taken." Although I wasn't quite clear on where Aeden and I stood in our newfound relationship change, I had to make sure Eoghan wasn't going to try anything. He was beautiful, there was no denying that, but my heart was completely shut off from anyone but Aeden. He was the only one I'd ever really wanted, the only one I lo—

"You said two conditions, Princess. That sounded more like three," he cooed. Yet his hand flew up to rest above his heart momentarily as if he had his own pain that lingered within his chest like the longing of a loved one.

I softened at the thought. Maybe his rudeness was all a facade, and underneath, he was more like me. Wounded. "I'm only going to agree because you have me cornered in a hallway and I have better things to do than contemplate who I go to a damn dance with. Do we have a deal?"

"Deal. Oh and Paige?" He looked me up and down, lifting a brow at the book I clutched onto so tightly.

"What is it, Eoghan?" My patience was wearing thin.

He reached an arm past me, stroking a finger over the hair of the man who I knew to be Gedeon. *Is he thinking of someone else? He hates Gedeon.* "You are beautiful and feisty and I like those traits, but you just aren't my type." He shook his head, peeling his fingers from the wall as he peered almost worriedly down the hallway behind him before turning back to me. I hadn't given him a look that would lead him to believe I was even remotely interested, because in all honestly, I absolutely was not. I warned him not to make a move because it felt like the right thing to do, and reading him was damn near impossible. I couldn't tell if he was a natural flirt or if it was all just him being cocky, thinking the light shone from his ass.

"Because I'm not as insane as you are?" I couldn't even feign the hurt I didn't feel at his rejection. *We're on the same page, then.*

The worry dropped from his face and was replaced by a boyish grin as he took in what I said as a compliment. The silence stretched as he took a minute to glance over the wallpaper and then again at the book in my arms. "If you want to know more about this"—he gestured at the wall—"I recommend looking for books on the Battle of Vizna."

"So this *is* Vizna?" I tried to hide how eager I was that I'd discovered something about a world I had yet to see with my own eyes beyond the windows and balconies of the castle I was trapped in. Books were magical in that sense—you could travel the world, or in my case a new world, without ever setting foot there.

Eoghan nodded and raised a finger that crooked under his bottom lip. "It is. Was." His ocean-blue eyes raked down the length of the walls. "It no longer exists. Dwindled to nothing but ashen ruins. This was the beginning of the end of the fire-wielders."

"But why? What happened?" I thought back to my dream, back to the mark I saw on Aeden. The dream was...so...*real*. But my mind was most likely toying with me, preying on my emotions. I'd passed by this bloodied wall for days now, and I also missed Aeden desperately. My subconscious was simply blending the two.

"I could tell you, but it's getting late." Eoghan lowered his hand and tried to smile, but this time it lacked the zeal of his previous attempts.

"Goodnight, Paige. I'll be on the training deck in a few hours. Leave your books hidden if you don't want him to find out you've been off learning about Aellethia and its history. He may just shit himself if he thinks you are gaining the upper hand all on your own in an effort to win the Triad." He turned and went back down the hallway, the candles casting a shadow of his exit along the walls covered in blood and fire.

Training was brutal, but my aim had improved with the lighter daggers and throwing stars. I even managed to kick Eoghan's ankle out using a swiping technique we worked on for hours. He didn't fall, but it was striking progress from being stabbed and panicking afterward. I'd be more surprised at my progress if he didn't remind me every time I managed to successfully mimic his motions that those fae who descended from Moras were stronger, more agile, and faster to learn. So, I was simply learning at a normal pace. They—I, was made for the very thing. Maybe he was just hyping me up, putting my mind in the right place to learn everything I was nearly killing myself to learn. But the strength within the power that pulsed under my flesh rang true to his words. I had, in fact, *felt* stronger since coming to Aellethia.

We were cut short at lunchtime when Hector came to retrieve me, leading me back to my room where the three maids were waiting for me. The blonde maid was holding a light purple satin gown that corsetted at the waist and loosely hanging satin sleeves that would cover maybe an inch of my arms. I choked on a gasp as I noticed the large slit up the side. Two of the maids were eagerly looking me over, not shying from the excitement they felt over the makeover that was coming. I, on the other hand, was not as enthused.

It took over an hour of scrubbing, hair pulling and curling, and dress fitting before they all stepped back to admire their work.

"You look stunning!" the blonde proclaimed, her elation almost making a smile come to my face. Almost. Only the fact that this was Gedeon's doing, parading me around like a doll so people could think I was ready for something that would most likely kill me in a few days, held me back. Resting bitch face maid and I would just have to match our expressions at the moment.

"Doesn't she look divine?" The lighter brunette led on, and the two maids squealed in delight, talking to each other about the ball. The darker-haired one continued to stare, looking displeased over some aspect of me I couldn't place, nor did I really care about whatever had caused her intense displeasure.

"Thank you both, but I need privacy now. How much time do I have before—"

"Before I come to get you?" Eoghan said, striding in through my bedroom door as if he owned the very floor he walked on.

"Right, of course. How silly of me to think I could have an ounce of privacy in this place." I sighed and sat on my bed. The slit that rode up my thigh made me hyper-aware of Eoghan's presence as I grabbed a pillow to cover myself. But it was no use, my top half only spilled over the golden embellishments at the top of the corset the more I moved to position the pillow over my legs. The maids glanced at each other and darted from the room, the blonde one blushing furiously at Eoghan before she fled last.

"You look...comfortable." Eoghan smirked at the pillow I was clutching. "I told you already, you aren't my type. Now come on, *Lord* Gedeon is waiting downstairs. Others will be arriving soon. It's time to put on a show of our own."

"Why aren't you more…I don't know, more like him?" I even questioned it myself as it came out of my mouth. However, more than one thing told me Eoghan was…different. It wasn't just the look he gave me as if he sympathized with me or how he stared at the wall as if it had disgusted him too. As odd as it seemed, Eoghan didn't give off the same vibe as my father—he wasn't a monster.

"Like Lord Dick of the century, you mean? Let's just say I have my own reasons, as do you." *So vague.*

I drew circles along the foregone pillow at my side. "I wasn't lost, you know. To Gedeon, I…*we,* weren't lost. We were *left*. Abandoned, more like," I clarified.

"Oh, you mean he lied about you being taken from him before you were even born? A mortal woman didn't just make a portal of her own and leave him?" He sat down on the bed beside me and gave a faint smile, the same one he gave me in the hallway when he spoke about Vizna. *He actually has a soul.* "Stay still, and try not to freak out."

Excuse me?

"What are you going to do?" The way I didn't recoil back told me, and possibly him, that I was starting to trust him already. A huge character flaw on my end. If I were Aeden, I would have told him to fuck right off. But me? No. I did trust Eoghan now, maybe not with my life, but to say I didn't trust him would be a lie. And if that made me naive, then so be it.

"Just, accept whatever feeling you have inside of you, and don't flood your bedroom. Understood?" His eyebrow lifted.

"Flooding my—" Eoghan slid his arm around me, and I felt a surge of water bursting like my bones were a dam holding back an entire ocean. All at once, the air beneath my skin was consumed by water, drowning in it until the two mixed. Small droplets like rain frozen in time filled every inch of the room, the light from the fire reflecting off each one like crystals. I stood up, feeling a second wave of power crawling across my back, prickling my skin. I reached behind to the edge of the gown, feeling the fine satin material skim my arm as I tried to be flexible enough to reach the spot where a familiar sensation spread.

Eoghan leaned back, watching from the bed as he beamed with excitement. He flicked his wrist, and with a flurry of wind the droplets combined and moved through the threshold of the en-suite and into the shower where they cascaded down. "Now you are ready."

"How...how did you do that? Did I just—do I have, I don't even know what to call it. I feel...wet inside, like—" I froze as Eoghan guffawed at my poor word choice.

"You can wield water now. Normally, we are let outside to be with nature and gain our powers that way, but Gedeon's tactics don't allow for that. His approach is more of a...hindrance, to what you are truly capable of."

"I don't know what to say. Thank you, Eoghan." I moved to the floor-length mirror, turning to take in the mark that resembled the one he had crawling up his arm, which wasn't ever on display unless we were training. It was hard to forget the arm that kept trying to knock you down or out over and over.

"Don't thank me just yet, I'm sure I will let you down in the future. Let's go before Hector comes looking for you." He stood up from the bed and began to move toward the door.

"Where is your guard?" I asked, and Eoghan stopped walking, dropping his hand from the door. *He had to leave his guard at home, and he doesn't like doing that.* That's what Nya had said about his guard, and it must be true because I had yet to see him.

"He's at home, contentedly. He isn't allowed here." His shoulders drooped slightly as he careened his head back over his shoulder.

"But, why?"

He winked, but the cocky gesture wasn't met with his usual grin. "That, Paige, is a question best left for daddy dearest."

TWENTY-THREE

AEDEN

I woke up to the smell of fae coffee and something that resembled a pancake. "Not that crap again, Seamus," I said groggily, rubbing the back of my head as I sat up from the grass.

Seamus chuckled and offered the food to me, which I accepted readily because it truly did look like a pancake. And if it wasn't, I didn't want to know what it really was. I was sold. "You better eat up, Lad. Today ye see yer lass. Can't be famished for that, now can ye?" His voice was hoarse and drained.

I examined Seamus as we ate and sat across from each other. "You look like shit." Another laugh rolled through him as he shook his head. He looked tired, and it appeared to be more than just a bad night of sleep. Shay was still out cold, curled up in the grass beside him. *At least someone would be well-rested.*

"How are we getting in?" I angled the pancake in the direction of the castle, the towers still visible from where we camped. It should have comforted me knowing I was so close to Paige, but seeing the walls, the castle she was in—I'd never felt more distanced from her.

A smile grew on his face, making his eyes pinch together slightly. The lines that furrowed beside his eyes were deeper, and I had to wonder if I was the cause. "Aye, don't you worry. I got us somethin' else this mornin' at the market." He raised a purple tunic in one hand, shaking some crumbs from it, and then hoisted his other arm up as it held a second one—guard's uniforms. Identical to the ones every guard in Prydia wore the day before.

"How the hell did you get that?" My mind began racing with the growing possibility that our plan was really happening. I was finally going to see her.

"I sought out an ol' colleague, told 'im I'd be needin' a uniform, or two if he could spare it. Said that I was lookin' to join the guard again. It was a bleatin' lie, but my bluff was as good as yers was yesterday, I'll 'ave ye know. Good 'nough to get us to the door."

Two uniforms. Not three.

"What about Shay? What did you get for—"

"Aye, Shay." Seamus grinned as he reached into a satchel he must've also gotten at the market, and pulled out a blue long-sleeve dress that was either ripped or purposefully bare in some spots. Gems that shined like diamonds were plastered on the front, making the dress seem less fit for a club and more fit for a castle. Which meant, to my relief, that I wouldn't have to treat Shay like a whore again, because she might actually kill me if I did. "Guards will do random checks, lookin' for yer power, but just follow me lead if anythin' happens."

"Yeah, right, like before?" I said, my tone intent on reminding him of his last failure at the entrance to Prydia, and shook my head. "We can't afford to have you clam up again. I saw what they do when they get their hands on a...well, someone like me. And if you two are caught with me, defending me, I don't think they'll hesitate in taking you too."

Seamus sat quietly for a moment, eating slowly and taking small sips of his fae coffee from a mug that looked like a stone with a large divot in the center, perhaps made by an earth-wielder who lived in Prydia, or maybe it was transported in because most of the marks along people's arms in Prydia were purple. "Ye be right Lad, but I won't let that happen to ye, or to Shay. I can do it this time, I promise ye both on me very life."

Shay yawned and sat up, snatching the remainder of Seamus' pancake from his hand. "You better not, Seamus. I forgave you for not telling me about your past, about you being a guard. But if you kill us all, I don't think I'll forgive you as easily once we are sent to the stars themselves." She took another bite and shook the pancake at him. "A coward is no friend of mine." Seamus flinched at the mention of him being a coward, something that clearly didn't sit well with him.

"Well, if Big Red here fails, I'll just burn them all down." I shrugged. "I know I can, I could feel it last night before we left. It was almost..."

I paused and looked between them both, noting the sudden uncomfortable silence. Seamus cleared his throat and began tugging on the ends of his beard. "Ye can't go burnin' down the world, Aeden. We know ye could do it if ye tried, take the whole city of Prydia with ye if ye really felt that desire in yer bones. But what would that make ye then, Boyo? Just 'nother tyrant like Gedeon." He spat in the grass and Shay nodded in agreement.

"I...I know that." I chuckled as if I were only joking. Half of me believed I was, but another part...after seeing what I saw, acknowledged that I was not joking in the least. I rubbed my knuckles along my jaw. "It's just, how can he do that to his own people? People who look up to him, who expect him to be a leader? Children, for fuck's sake, he kills *children* for having a mark. Yet, there are no armies, no hordes of enemies lining up at his gates. They all just accept it." I thought back to the mother, and her willingness to retrieve her son's body after watching him hang. She cried—wailed, even. But she didn't fight. I flung my arm toward Prydia, the sun rising beside it ominously. I sighed. "I swear to you both I won't burn anything down tonight, but if he tries to hurt Paige...if he shows even an ounce of the same hatred and neglect as he does to his own city, to *her*, I can't promise I won't turn him into a pile of ash."

"Do what it is ye need to. But don't blame the city for what ye saw, for they are all livin' in fear of their beloved *Mora*."

"What about the other Moras, are they all just as bloodthirsty?" I asked, preparing to hear that this world was full of shit leaders. Full of rulers who murdered and whose people were so weak they had no fight left within them.

Shay took the last bite of her food. "Gedeon is by far the worst, but the Mora of Buryon, Lord Leander Earthborne is...well, some say he's insane. But he stays in Buryon and doesn't tend to leave it, nor have many people actually seen him with their own eyes. It's all hearsay when it comes to him. The pixies usually have nothing to say about him either other than he killed his father after he became a Mora himself, which is honestly quite common. And Lord Eoghan Waterborne of Hydrasel is supposed to be very cunning and smart for his age, young as he is. The pixies have heard rumors about him being different from the others—more of a revolutionary of sorts. But that has yet to be proven." She shifted in the grass, her fingers tracing down the blue scales along her legs that were hardly visible under the rising sun.

"What about Vizna?" Shay and Seamus threw awkward glances at each other, but I continued. "I'm assuming the ruler is dead if there is no kingdom left. What was their Mora like before it fell?"

Shay and Seamus were quiet for a moment until Shay said, "She was...radiant. A true leader. The people loved her and her family fiercely and were loyally devoted to the kingdom so much, they say the souls of each fallen Viznian soldier remained on the field long after their bodies turned cold, unwilling to part with their true home. It is said the Mora died fighting to protect her family, but some believe a piece of her is still out there, somewhere." Shay rolled her eyes up from the blades of grass and looked over at Seamus, who patted her knee.

Seamus stood. "Stories perhaps intended for another time. We best get to Prydia now. If we can get past the guards as we did yesterday, we only need to get through 'nother wee bit o' guards to get into the castle at sundown. Those uniforms should make it easy 'nough." His cheeks flushed slightly as he held out the dress to Shay. "Shay'll be our Lady tonight—yer to be a High Fae from Hydrasel, and we are to be yer guards."

"You mean *when* we get in." My brow furrowed. "We aren't failing." I stood up, grabbed the uniform, and began dressing in the dark pants and purple tunic. He gave me a nod and grinned back at me, determination shining in his eyes as the tiredness I saw before started to slip away. He waved an arm and a circle of ice enclosed us, shielding us from view. I doubted anyone would have looked or would have even been able to see all the way from the barely visible wall, but I was thankful for it anyway. There could be loyalists anywhere this close to Prydia, this close to the madman that ruled over it. We were, after all, still within his territories. And ending the day on the fucking platform was not on my list of things to accomplish.

"But I have no marks, Seamus. They will see that." I could guess exactly what Seamus' plan was as Shay held up the dress against her and twirled, captivated by the thought of going to a ball no matter who was hosting it. No matter if she were to hide the fact she wasn't fae like we were. Not that I'd be any different in the *needing-to-hide* aspect, either. But there were things I didn't need to hide. Powers that weren't illegal along my skin.

"No, ye don't. But we do." Seamus smiled broadly, turning his back to Shay and me, and began dressing in the other uniform. "Keep those sleeves down, they won't know the difference."

The laces of my tunic were tied tighter than Seamus' to allow for the edge of my mark to be covered along my neck. I saw my reflection in the ice wall, checking my neck was fully concealed, and tested the range of motion I'd have before letting streaks of red show through the top of the collar.

It wasn't much.

Playing games against other top schools had nothing on the level of anxiety that was now building inside of me. And the magic—my magic, fed off of my emotions. It was like leeches are to flesh in a lake—hungrily devouring without sparing a single drop, plumping up horrendously in the process. And I was ready to burst from the two forces acting as one.

The turnover rate for guards was either very fucking high or there were too many for them all to know one guard from the next because we were able to enter Prydia rather easily. Not a single guard cast a glance at us, our uniforms shielding us beyond just the mark that blazed on my skin. Maybe they just saved the expense of their real job for the front door of the castle tonight.

Surely no one would dare mess with the Mora of the Aerborne line by treading into his home uninvited unless they had a death wish. That is unless they were me—a rather new-to-this-world fae driven by what could only be described as pure insanity.

In hindsight, ever since my last mark had emerged, it felt fucking empowering to know there weren't a lot of others like me. Those who were like me would be at the ball. But if I were caught tonight, I would be killed on the spot. Fuck dreading the platform. They wouldn't wait for that. *He* wouldn't wait for that.

The sad truth of it all was that my own life held little to no meaning if she wasn't in it. I felt like I breathed air for the first time when she came into my life like I found the missing piece of who I was. If the fae believed in the stars for their gods, as I'd heard Shay and Seamus both revere on more than one occasion, then I wanted to be there with her too once it was all over. Wherever she went, I'd be there. My fixation on Paige had become worse being so far away from her. I missed her laugh, her temper, the way she read books and hooked the ends of her hair between her fingers, the way her hair flowed down her back, the curves of her body, and how they felt in my hands. Among many other things.

But she needed support, not a man with his head in the gutter, and she needed to know I wanted her beyond the short, intimate time we shared before coming to Aellethia. She needed to know that, for me, it wasn't a one-time thing. Something inside of me felt like...it was fate. We were supposed to be together, had been born for each other, and existed because the other one did. I didn't have a mark to prove it, but I felt it in my blood—in my very bones—as the thought unfurled in my mind and wreaked momentary havoc on my body.

There were crowds of spectators and guests standing before the closed door of the castle as we approached, the wooden doors carved with the same air mark I'd seen before, spanning the entirety of the door. Fae proved their worth with their marks, the sheer size a notion to others of what they were capable of. And that was all without any training. It wasn't surprising that Gedeon's door echoed a solid tone of, '*If you fuck with me, you die*'—not in the least bit settling to my growing nerves.

We filed in closely behind the guests—women dressed in ball gowns with lowered collars, their marks of blue, green, or purple higher than any fae I'd seen so far that wasn't me. The men were in luxurious jackets with unique adornments that reflected one or two of the three legal elements, detailing what power they had if they weren't able to expose it beyond their clothing. It became clear to me that no one would dare flaunt the color red because no one had it on their skin. Fire-wielders were all sentenced to the same fate I'd witnessed the day before, it didn't matter if they were high fae or not, save for maybe the Moras. I'd never considered asking what kind of power they had, what made them so special compared to the rest. Was it simply a bloodline? As inconspicuously as I could, I searched for another fae with three elements along their clothing or any slight hint of red, because as much as I was sure all fire-wielders were sentenced to death, I didn't want to believe it. But the more I looked around, the more I realized I'd find none because there were none to find.

They were all dead.

All guests were escorted by men and women in purple tunics—a measure of security instead of a pleasantry, of whom the benefactor was obviously not of the fae which were flanked on either side of them. We blended in seamlessly, with Seamus on one side of Shay and me on the other. The guards were all without weapons as well, something I was skeptical about when Seamus advised me to leave the sword behind. He wasn't wrong, but I wished I had purchased a knife from the market with whatever was left of the money Seamus had given me. It was funny to think a week ago I would feel safe with just my fists and the knowledge of who I was. Yet in Aellethia, I was an unknown with an illegal power. And after seeing that platform... I pushed the thought of a blade, or noose, sliding across my throat away, rubbing the back of my neck and using my thumb to guide the collar up higher.

A brush of warmth, familiar and sweet, flooded through my veins and I followed the sensation as I looked up, being careful not to crane my neck up too far. And that's when I saw her. The world around me fell still, Shay's arm linked through mine being the only tether dragging me forward through the crowd. Paige stood against the edge of a balcony with her arms draped on the ledge, her hair cascading down in loose curls that fell just below her flawless breasts as she bent over her arms. Just being this close to her made my heart thrash while all three of my elements rode in a tailspin beneath my flesh. She was idly overlooking the guests as they were stopped and checked, one by one, before the door and I wanted to wave my arms and shout her name, shoot water or earth or fucking flames up into the air signaling I was here. But then my sanity came back as I remembered our presence was wholly unwelcome by the host, and remaining unostentatious was the only way we were getting in. I curled my arm around Shay's back and tapped Seamus on his waist. When his eyes met mine, I motioned my own up.

"I found her," I whispered. Shay and Seamus both looked up, talking about the stars in the sky as they searched inconspicuously along the balcony.

Shay's mouth hung open slightly and Seamus grinned. "Almost in, Lad. Then maybe the Stars will bless ye with a pretty girl tonight." He kept up his charade about the Stars, mentioning something about how they shined brighter when they were alone and kept quiet. I got the hint.

But I couldn't stop staring up at her, her magnificence like an arrow shooting through me, pegging me to the spot. Did she know that she commanded so much attention from me? From anyone? How could anyone be in her presence and not be in complete awe of her? Just knowing she existed was enough to make everything else fade to black.

Shayanna yanked on me again, clearing her throat as she tugged on my pants along my hip for my attention. We were next in line, and I could be captured in the next few minutes. As if she could sense danger in that moment, Paige's eyes found and locked on mine. My heart sputtered to a standstill, needing her acknowledgment to lead into a smile but she looked...really fucking scared. No. Terrified. She was terrified. Fear over her situation or mine, I couldn't tell. Before I could think more of it, before the attention fell back to us three as we tried to gain entrance next, I risked it all and winked up at her.

"Name?" A female guard requested near Seamus, not lifting her eyes from the list she held. It gave me time to reel it back, pulling my focus from the beauty on the balcony to the security detail in front of me. *If Seamus isn't ready—*

"Oh darlin' please, don't ye know who this is?" Seamus drawled on, causing the guard to glance up in sheer annoyance.

"No name, no entry." The guard tapped her feathered pen on the scrolled paper.

"Parisa Strombart of Hydrasel," Seamus said, giving the guard his own look of annoyance. But when Seamus looked annoyed, he looked more like he was ready to beat your face in. Something I would be on board with if only it didn't draw more attention our way. A few glances were already being directed our way from the rest of those in line, wondering if there was about to be a hold-up at the door.

The guard wrote the name down on her scroll and looked at Shay's arm. "And what mark, or marks, do you bare?"

"Water, obviously." Shay scoffed. The guard raised her eyebrow. And I guess because Shay was nervous, or maybe it was easier to bluff being a high fae with more than one extremely strong element, she blurted, "And earth."

The guard rolled up her scroll and folded her arms. "We require proof."

Seamus didn't hesitate. "That's a crock of shite 'nd ye know it. Ye didn't ask the lad in front of us."

"*He* is a well-known tradesman of Buryon. I have never heard of you, Lady Parisa of Hydrasel." She looked Shay up and down, raising her brow further than I thought possible. I curled my fingers in, keeping one arm around Shay's waist as the other made a tight fist. *If they're caught with me, it's the platform, or worse, for all of us.*

"Lady Parisa, if ye could, please." Shay lifted her arm and I knew it was my cue. Seamus couldn't prove both elements, but I could try. I unfurled my fingers and flicked my wrist against Shay's waist ever so slightly. A vine of white flowers grew across her rolled-up scroll, droplets of water falling gently over it. Hiding the smile I held inside was damn hard but I was sure I'd just made Seamus very proud. Shay curtsied at the guard, flashing her own glimmer of amusement, and tugged us both in closer toward her. "Do ye see 'er name on that list of yers, now?"

"It's just...odd, two guards from Prydia showing such fierce loyalty to someone not of their kingdom." Several groans and shouts from the fae waiting behind us surged forward, a few even shouting for the guard to let us through already.

"We grew up with Parisa, and yer ignorance of her wealth and power is just rude. She bleatin' staffs half the fleet of vessels for Hydrasel. Maybe we should just bring this matter to Lord Ged—"

"No, there is no need to bother the Lord with such frivolous decisions." The guard looked her over once more, pursing her lips and nodding as she wrote Shay's false powers down next to her name before she stepped to the side, making room for all three of us to enter.

Twenty-Four

AEDEN

The castle was nothing short of magnificent. As we walked through the grand foyer that was lined with statues and artwork, I kept my gaze fixed on the next set of doors that were held open for all guests to enter. Shay and Seamus continued reminding me to keep a low profile, and control my power. Everything I didn't want to do but knew I had to.

We made our way into the ballroom, where several obscenely large, golden chandeliers held flames that swirled like hurricanes rimmed with fire above each space where a candle would normally be. Pristine white walls made the golden and purple decor and adornments shine offensively as they cascaded up to the coffered ceiling about three stories or more above us. There were few sets of wooden doors that led away from the ballroom with the same air marks etched in, and perhaps one of those would be an exit strategy for us if I grabbed Paige and made a run for it.

I didn't care about his wealth or the dozens of guards that lingered within the large room we were in. I only cared about how he was treating Paige, and where the fuck he was keeping her when she wasn't on a balcony. *Where the hell is that balcony?*

"Ye won't be findin' her 'til he lets her down, Boyo, 'nd when that happens, ye'll know it." Seamus bowed his body back slightly, his breath rolling over the back of Shay's neck as he directed his words to me.

I only nodded, raking my hands through my hair as I continued to take in every part of the room. I'd need time alone with her, but how? The ballroom was full of fae either taking hors d'oeuvres from Gedeon's staff as they circled about in their white aprons or taking up space with each other along the top where the interior balcony looked down upon the rest of us. The sound of a piano being played somewhere in the expansive ballroom echoed off the walls, but it wasn't enough to cover the words of the fae next to us. I tried to focus on a few of the conversations, all of which were focused on the possibility of a new ruler for Prydia. Another Aerborne descendant, and the question of the extent of her powers because she was so new to this place, having been *saved* from the wretchedness of the mortal world.

"I hear she was with her mother in the mortal world this whole time, the poor girl. Gedeon must've been devastated to…"

"Yes, yes, her lessons with Lord…"

"Gedeon is making sure she is well-prepared, even though she…"

"She will be brilliant in her first trial in a few days, I can't wait…"

I couldn't focus on just one as more and more fae gave their input on the life of a girl they knew nothing about, acting as if her father, Lord Gedeon as he was so fondly acknowledged in his home, was her savior in getting her back home. But this wasn't her home. This was a gilded fortress, caging her in, forcing her into a fight she hadn't trained her entire life for. How did they not see that? The fire, earth, and water begged to be released, to get rid of every ill-conceived notion of my girl.

I knew there was nothing she couldn't do if she set her mind to it, but I doubted her father believed in her as much as I did. People often misjudged her, and that was before she started forming powers in a world that revolved around it. The unfairness of the test of her powers and skills was making me unravel. With the death of her mother, which I doubted anyone here cared about because she was referenced as just the mortal in the situation as I'd heard a few feet from me, and her life flipping upside down so abruptly, how could anyone throw her into a situation like this? How could anyone treat their own child like that?

A man with deeply bronzed skin and piercing eyes inclined his head at me, his jacket green and faded as if he didn't quite fit in with the rest of the fae in the room. I nodded back in acknowledgment, then turned to adjust my tunic, just in case. The piano stopped abruptly, and all heads spun to the presenter's voice. "Presenting Lord Gedeon Aerborne of Prydia, and his daughter Lady Paige Aerborne of Prydia." A loud voice boomed at the top of a staircase that connected the ground floor to the upper interior balcony. I sucked in a sharp breath and had Seamus not placed his hand on my shoulder, I would've fallen to my knees. She looked incredible.

No, incredible wasn't enough.

She looked...extraordinary.

Exquisite.

Absolutely. Fucking. Breathtaking.

Her purple dress flowed over the soft curves of her body and cupped her breasts as if it were made to be worn by her. My eyes moved up from her perfect figure and over to the air tattoo crawling up her arm, a bit of blue that mirrored my own mark along the top of her shoulder. Her skin glowed effortlessly like the stars themselves cast all their light upon her and her new marks of power. That's when it truly hit me—she's an *Aerborne*. I always knew she was strong, but her marks? I didn't need to see them to know the extent of her strength, it just proved it to everyone else. Many faces went slack around the room, jaws popping open and snapping shut like they were all fish out of water, and yet I couldn't hide the curve of my mouth as I continued to drink her in, imagining my hand sliding up the parting of her dress—

I nearly forgot Shay and Seamus were beside me until I felt Shay rub her arm against me. While I was watching Lady Paige Aerborne, Seamus and Shay were busy watching me and my own reactions, probably making sure I wouldn't give us away. But my focus shifted back to her eyes—Paige's eyes—that stayed fixed on the glass windows that lined the wall behind me, keeping her chin stiffened and upright, making her come off as intimidating to the fae below her.

That's my girl.

She hadn't lost that stubborn as fuck attitude that drove me crazy at times, and it made me smile yet again just thinking of the torture she'd been unquestionably putting her father through.

Shit. Her father.

I was so fixed on Paige that I hadn't fully registered Gedeon standing beside her, even though the guards announced him as well. Where she radiated light, he was the abysmal darkness that cast an ominous shadow in his wake and over her shoulders. Where her eyes stayed trained above the others, his eyes bore down into others. His light hair stayed in place as he walked down the steps, his piercing pale gray eyes searching the crowd hungrily, eliciting small bows and curtsies from the crowd.

I hung my head low, avoiding any possible recognition, feigning a permanent bow if his eyes ever roamed my way. If he had been watching Paige in the mortal world, then he most likely knew who I was, and I hadn't considered that possibility until I was standing under his roof. Even with the awe-struck guests, he didn't look like a proud, doting father. Actually, he looked rather annoyed that he had to hold Paige's arm at all.

The paling look of dread she showed me from the balcony flashed through my mind as I saw her glance over her shoulder at the man in black, then back out into the sea of people. Was my being here making her more afraid? And if so, was it over my presence, or was the fear I saw just an echo of the life she was forced to live in Prydia's castle?

She didn't know I possessed an illegal mark that covered my entire left arm and was the same size as her own, or that two more had come after. How scared would she be if she knew what I was? What I had become since we'd arrived here? Did she know what her father did to people, to *fae*, like me?

I hadn't thought that part through enough. I abandoned so many other thoughts aside from just seeing her, it made me wonder just how much faith Seamus and Shay had in me that made them so willing to follow me through it all. The part where Paige would ask how I got here, what happened when I got here, and if she were to see my marks...

I couldn't let her know. Not when she had so much of her own life to focus on. I couldn't have her worrying about me. It was selfish for me to want to see her in the first place. I mentally scorned myself, feeling like a downright idiot.

Paige ended her walk down the stairs and picked up another man's arm in place of Gedeon's while he made his way out of the ballroom with the man I assumed was his personal bodyguard with the way he prowled behind him. But the man holding Paige's draped arm stole my attention before I could think about who among the crowd was in her father's inner circle. He looked born of royalty too, his jacket a deep navy blue that made it quite obvious his original nature was water. He smiled down at her as he patted her hand along his arm. She smiled back up at him, and it made me want to let the fire flood from my veins and burst the two of them apart.

She was *mine*, wasn't she? My jaw clenched, watching them get closer, the piano picking up a smooth tempo that elicited movement. *Were they about to fucking dance together?* I was hers, no one else could fill the part of my heart that was solely hers and hers alone. So why did she look so damn comfortable with him?

The fae all took up a partner as if on cue and began to form a circle along the edge of the ballroom. The piano was joined by a violin in a slow beat, one that would require a dance that was more...intimate. Too fucking intimate. Paige and the man moved to the center of the room, where the slight tremor of her hand was stilled by his thumb. He removed his arm from hers and placed it low on her bare back—his fingers sprawled possessively, or maybe he was simply guiding her. Either way, he was touching things that made my irrationally jealous mind go haywire. I could feel the heat rising in me more and more. I hadn't even realized that I began to walk toward her, nearly blowing our cover until Seamus and Shay tugged me back to the edge by the back of my tunic, where the rest of us stood, waiting.

Paige moved on unsteady feet, her knee buckling a few times through the slit in her dress that now swayed between them. The man continued to press his hand against her back, forcing her to move along with his strides. Murmurs around the dance floor started, too low for me to make out but I had to assume they were about Paige and the fucker dancing with her, who I now understood was Lord Eoghan of Hydrasel—the blonde-haired, blue-eyed asshole dancing with *my girl.* I knew she felt what I did for her, had seen the way her eyes lit up after our first kiss, moments before she answered her phone. The yearning we both had for each other, nearly bursting us both to pieces in her kitchen the day we came here.

I thought I had made it quite clear then. *If we start this, I don't know how I'll ever stop.* I still hadn't found a way to make it all stop, and I didn't want to.

The Lord and Paige were whispering to each other, him dipping his head to speak against her ear. She nodded her head gently as they began to move closer, slowly edging their way while dancing. I could just reach out and take her from him if they could get a little closer and take back what was mine. They were still whispering to each other when the music changed to another song and the other fae flooded toward the center and onto the dance floor, making the entire crowd a frenzy of shuffles as they fought their way through.

The focus of everyone in the room shifted to the music, which I tuned out as I watched Eoghan release Paige, his hand finally falling from her lower back as he strode my way. A quick smirk brushed over his mouth as he walked straight past me, standing in front of Shay. He bowed low and Shay blushed over, matching the hue of her dress before taking his outstretched arm. Seamus' jaw worked as Shay left his side. Whatever was going on between them couldn't be dealt with in the castle while he was dressed as a guard, but I had my own jealousy to work through at the moment. Paige didn't meet my eyes, but her head inclined to the side toward the top of the balcony—to one of the large doors that led away from the ballroom.

"I'll be back," my voice came out gritty as I mumbled low to Seamus, who didn't peel his focus from the woman in blue on the dance floor.

Seamus dipped his head low. "Be careful, Lad. This is not the place to be gettin' discovered."

"I can handle my own." I leaned in closer to him. "So can she, you know." I left him with that and turned, picking up my pace but leaving a great enough distance between Paige and me to hopefully go unnoticed. She slipped through the door first, every inch of my body shaking as I made two laps around the balcony before following behind her.

TWENTY-FIVE

PAIGE

I saw him.

Aeden.

He was standing amongst the line of guests waiting to enter the castle for the *ball*—as I was told to call it. The florid ball was said to be in my honor, though what honor did Gedeon really want to bestow upon me that wasn't a quick death in the Triad?

My eyes must've been trying to trick me, or the dreams I'd had recently of Aeden were beginning to interfere with my waking life as well. That would explain why I was seeing him, but as for the other two, standing beside him in the crowd, well, I'd only ever seen them before in my dreams. But even that part I wasn't a hundred percent on. They looked similar to the two I saw sitting in the grass, talking about someone else while Aeden rested. They were all far from where I stood along the balcony, but as for Aeden, it would never matter how far away he was. I wouldn't ever mistake him for anyone else.

It was...it was really him.

His dark, unwavering eyes met with mine and all I could feel was an immense fear of this not being real. Of my mind playing tricks on me. Of it being some form of sick illusion. Maybe it was even Hector, shifting into the form of the person he led to this world. But if it was real—if he were in fact standing in that crowd below me and had made his way here, it only made the fear intensify.

My father would kill him.

My stomach twisted painfully at the thought of Aeden being *here*, in Prydia. *Your mortal plaything is in Costa with the fish. Most likely being thrown into a cage and cast to sea by now. I wouldn't be surprised if he were dead, like your mother.* That's what my father wanted me to believe. He wanted me to feel like I had nothing else—no one else—left in this world or the other who cared for me. Gedeon was ruthless, and I had no doubt as to what fate Aeden would meet if they crossed. I should have been elated to see him, but all I could see was red. Like the blood on the walls, like the mark on his skin in my dreams that I hoped was just that—a dream.

My breath faltered and my heartbeat hitched in my chest when he winked up at me. I continued watching him long enough to see that he was getting past the front doors, and my mind raced with how close he was, yet how stupid he was for showing his face here. Maybe he was unaware of my father's ways and had no clue what kind of danger he was walking into.

My palms were sweating—no, leaking—water droplets as I turned away from the balcony and darted to find Eoghan, who'd left me out here all alone while he talked with a few of the guards inside. He had to address their concerns about our entrance, and Gedeon was going to be reported to after their conversation had ended. Because he couldn't be bothered to cut out the middle man and talk directly to either of us.

My heart raced wildly, the storm of air and water brewing intensely inside of me. The balcony seemed longer than usual, my strides not closing the distance fast enough as I shook my hands at my sides. By the time I made my way inside and found Eoghan, both of my previously drenched hands were wrapped in balls of ice.

Eoghan examined my hands and furrowed his brow. "Nervous?"

"If I had fire, I'd be bursting with flames from the amount of anxiety I have right now." I shook out my fists, trying to will the ice away as it started to numb my fingers through to the bone.

"If you had fire, Gedeon would have killed you already." Eoghan's nonchalance sent a shiver down my spine. He flicked his wrist casually, and the balls of ice melted instantly into warm puddles of water that dripped from my fingertips and onto the floor. They felt warm—as if a lick of fire had woven through to my chilled skin.

"If I'm going to be the Mora of Prydia, then I'll be able to wield all four elements too, right? So why wait for the inevitable?" I shook the remaining bits of water from my hands, wondering if I should try to use my air magic to dry up the puddle because Eoghan certainly didn't bat a single eyelash down at the mess by my silver-heeled feet. But I decided against it, pushing the edge of my shoe into the rug and making the water go deeper into the fibers. Because to hell with Gedeon's floors.

"He doesn't plan on you ever being the Mora of Prydia, Paige. But, yes, in theory, you would have the four elements when or *if* you take his place."

"Shouldn't I be working toward getting more marks before I enter the Triad? It seems—"

"Drastic? Heinous? How about callous?" He smirked at me, but his eyes didn't match the cocky feature of his lips. "The new Moras only get to wield fire once they become that—a Mora." He shook his head as if clearing a memory he didn't want to talk about.

"What are you not saying?" I pressed on because it was quite obvious that his vague responses were more than capable of hiding a lot of information. I would consider him a friend by now only because I had no room to be picky. The more people in my corner, the better, even if they did hide things from me. He and Nya were all that I had to count on within these walls.

"A lot. There are things you don't need to know." He turned and tried to start walking away but I lurched out and flicked my wrist, sending a blast of air at the back of his knees making them buckle, but not enough to send him to the floor. He just laughed and turned back to me. "Not playing nice again, are we?"

I folded my arms across my chest. "Whoever said I was going to?"

"Fine, if you must know, the *new* law is that fire-wielding and being marked with flames is meant only for Moras. Once you win the Triad, and only then, are you able to bear the mark, because without it, you can't truly become a Mora in the first place. But if you get it before then,"—his fingers curled at his sides as he looked past my shoulder toward the training deck, a blip of a memory moving through his oceanic eyes—"well, you'd be dead."

It was a contradiction in itself. Moras wielded all four elements, that's what made them capable of ruling. But what Eoghan was saying—it defied the laws. Pass the Triad, gain the title, and *then you can claim fire?* It didn't seem right. It wasn't right.

"Who made that law? Just my father?" My fingers were turning icy now against my arms. I shook them out at my sides, closed my eyes, and took a few deep breaths in. I was pretty sure Eoghan had seen me do it before while training, so I didn't bother to hide that part of me from him. As if the balls of ice on my hands earlier hadn't indicated that enough.

His pause was brief before he continued. "My mother was in charge when the law was passed after the war you saw on those walls. She agreed with the law, and with only one other kingdom left to vote, they didn't need Buryon's insight. Nor did the Mora ever show up to give it." He mumbled some choice words under his breath. *Buryon.* Their vote wouldn't have made a difference, but surely if they disagreed they would dispute it in the least. But to completely ignore it? That was a crime on its own. "Because two out of three kingdoms left wanted to rid Aellethia of the fire-wielders, the majority had already won. And now even a future Mora is subject to the law. If you were to ask your father why you can't have the mark yet, he'd regard it as being the law and hide behind it, but I think we both know the real reason he keeps you shielded in the dark. The real reason why he wouldn't spare your life if the mark ever did show on your skin before your last trial ended. Mercy is always an option, Paige. The law didn't come from the stars. But he doesn't want to lose his position in this world, nor does he think he would be kept alive if his spawn were to ascend the throne."

He didn't need to say how undesirable my ascension would be to my father. I already saw that in his eyes every time he spoke to me. My mother was a drunk, but I couldn't quite picture her using powers, had she had any, to wield against me. Not in the ways my father had already subjected me to.

To Gedeon, there was only black and white. Fire marks meant certain death, and my throat turned dry at the image of thousands and thousands of fae sprawled along his walls covered in their own blood. If Eoghan's mother had been in charge and had been the Mora of Hydrasel at the time the law was passed that ended so many more lives after the battle, that meant he was subject to the same law during his own trials as well. Because he was the one standing in her position now. And yet, he was alive, which also meant he obeyed the law and formed the mark *after* his rise to power. The strength alone in having grown up in this world and yet denying your own power would have been astronomical. The law had been hastily formed, intended for failure after failure. Gedeon wanted to remain exactly where he was for as long as possible.

I knew Eoghan was rebellious, but if the law had been agreed upon by two out of the three Moras, one of which was no longer one of the rulers of a kingdom— "Can't it be cha—"

He held his hand up. "No. To do that, would be to side with the fallen kingdom. You'd be a traitor. It would put a target on the entire kingdom. On the *lives* within those territories of the kingdom. It would lead to more war, and having already lived through the Battle of Vizna...that kind of loss doesn't just go away."

There were many holes in the information I was reading from my father's library. Most of the books I picked up lacked anything about fire-wielding. Any mention of it was probably the reason for the many torn pages from the bindings of every book I had picked up so far.

Two guards ambled by as way too many questions flooded my brain. Questions Eoghan was finally answering in much less vague ways than I anticipated. So, all the kingdoms just went along with it because if not, it meant war? How could you go against something as natural as the two powers that formed along my skin?

The guards were well down the hall, and as they rounded the corner away from us, the last question on my mind flew from my lips. "What do you do with fire-wielders, then?" *Mercy is always an option, Paige.*

"What I have to do." Another shiver ran down my spine at his blanketed admission. Did that mean he killed them? Eoghan grabbed both of my shoulders as the same two guards circled back around and closed the distance to us from the hall. His voice lowered as he advised, "Listen to me. Do not reach out toward the flames now that your body is awakening to more powers, and try not to feel too deeply near anything on fire. Especially not fae whose original nature is fire—those able to transfer their magic to you—although most of those are dead already." His eyes darted between both of mine and for once, I could read his emotions. He was...*worried*. But that couldn't be right. "Understood?" Boots squeaked against the flooring as the guards seemed to have forgotten something and turned to go back down the hall again.

I took a step back and gave him a look of disbelief. He'd stabbed me, tried to send me home, and pointed out my inferiority almost as quickly as he reminded me of how powerful I was born to be. His demeanor changed as abruptly as a tidal wave, just like his marks insinuated. He was turbulent—a walking contradiction. Without a shred of doubt in my body, I knew he was hiding something from me. Or was it, someone? "Who else, besides you, wielded fire after this law was enacted? Surely it isn't your people that you save a big portion of your heart for." Eoghan was like a brick of ice that I was trying to crack my way through. But that wasn't the only way to get rid of ice. Ice could also be melted, and for a small beat, for a fraction of a second, I saw the ice beginning to melt at the mention of whoever in his past had been wronged by the law before. It was like the mere thought of whoever it was, made his emotions come to the forefront. He wasn't able to shield from it. It—this person—was his weakness.

"What makes you think there's someone else?" He released my shoulders, fixing his jacket sleeves and the cuffs down at the bottom along his wrists, all one thousand shades of raw emotion fleeing from his face and posture.

I grinned as another guard met up with the other two who were so obviously trying to listen in. "I may not have all the power that you have, and I may not be able to fight as well as you *yet*," —he chuckled, but I continued— "but I do pay attention. Maybe even more than you do. Also, you didn't deny it just then, either." I tossed my head over my shoulders, then focused back on Eoghan, who'd gone silent as he examined me. "It's not like you'll tell me, anyway. Thank you for the mark, and the advice."

His face lit up like I'd just served him a challenge. "I'm sure the abundance of information will prove most useful to you, then." He blatantly ignored my question, as I knew he would, and winked at me.

"Yes, and any more information about fi—" My stomach sank instantaneously as the view from the balcony ripped through my mind. I'd been so focused on getting information, I'd let it slip...

Aeden. He's here.

My palms began to freeze over again in response to the amount of heat flushing through me. Apparently, water-wielding was going to be difficult to manage. "Paige. What is it." Eoghan's cocky features fell, leaving concern in its wake.

My hands slid across each other as the ice thickened and I wished it had been any other element to be forbidden for more reasons than one. "I think I saw,"—I gulped down, wondering if I could trust him with the knowledge that my friend was alive and was here—"I think I saw the person who I came here with. But I can't let Gedeon find out." My eyes darted to where I assumed my father would be, seeing the several guards starting to line up into formation. I let loose a breath when I noticed his absence.

He shook his head slowly. "No, because if he did, he would most definitely kill that person." He paused and slid his hand through the longer tendrils of his blonde hair. "Is this person *your* person?"

I'm taken. That's what I had told Eoghan before, and although we—Aeden and I—hadn't discussed it, I felt it with every fiber of my being to be true. I was his and I was taken in every sense of the word. Whether he would still want me though was up in the air. I hated feeling so insecure about it, about us. But my world was...well it was completely different now. *I* was different. And the way that I felt about Aeden and had always felt about him was the only sure thing I had right now—the only thing that was unwavering—even if it wasn't reciprocated. It was my safe place.

"Yes, he is."

Saying that Aeden was mine aloud was almost too overwhelming and I didn't want Eoghan to see my own unease about my situation with Aeden. Although we had been through so much in such a short time, I didn't want to assume he'd come for me for reasons other than bringing his friend back home. Though how he would do that would require a well-thought-out plan, or him being here tonight was absolutely asinine. Aeden was a lot of things, but crazy wasn't one of them.

Eoghan moved his hand down to the back of his neck. "Gedeon expects us to have the first dance together. It's a tradition, of sorts, and he is too busy to fulfill that portion of the evening's plans." He completely dodged talking about Aeden further, probably because the proximity of the guards wasn't changing anymore as they stood at the other end of the room, but I welcomed the change.

I raised my voice, high enough for the echo of the large room to kick in. "I'm not surprised, honestly. My father doesn't give a damn about me and he doesn't even try to hide it." A few of the guards finally acknowledged us, and one even had the balls to cuff his sleeve higher in a threatening way. I cocked my brow at the guard before turning my attention back to Eoghan. "But thank you for offering, that was…nice…of you." I bit my tongue in taunting him. I shouldn't question Eoghan's methods any more than I could guess their true intentions. He was an enigma. He turned to observe the guards, and although I'm not sure what his face looked like, I could guess as the guard who'd raised his sleeves quickly lowered it again before straightening his back and facing the other way.

Eoghan snickered. "I'm not nice. Saying that will ruin my reputation here." That sly smile lifted again as he clasped his hands behind his back.

I shrugged. "Maybe. But I would prefer kindness over a bloody fist and a temper any day."

"For Moras, it's different." Eoghan hunched his shoulders toward me and bent down, lowering his voice as he continued. "Where Gedoen's mind is set in older, more traditional ways, mine is…well, if you continue to *pay attention*, you will know one day."

I pressed my palm to my chest and gasped. "So you might *not* have a heart of ice?"

"Oh no, it's mostly ice." Eoghan maneuvered beside me and looped his arm through mine. "Time to get going, Paige. They are going to announce you formally, and then Gedeon will leave and I will take his place. Can you dance?"

Can I *dance?* Seriously? Not in the ways the dress I was wearing would require. "No," I said flatly. I couldn't dance in the way that was expected of royalty, and shaking my hips around while jumping from place to place didn't seem like the royal thing to do, even if the thought of me pissing off my father more by doing so at the ball was rather enticing.

"I figured. Your footwork on the training deck gave that away." *Such an asshole.* I elbowed him and Eoghan smirked down at me. We made our way toward Hector, who stood impatiently waiting, his thick black boot thumping on the floor in agitation.

"I can learn. I'm a—"

"Ah yes, you learn *so* fast. I forgot, was it yesterday that I kicked your ass on the training deck or the day before?" Eoghan's lip curled up to the side.

My lips went tight and I forced a fake smile as we approached my father. "Maybe tomorrow your heart won't be the only thing encased in ice," I muttered, and I could feel the rumble of a laugh through Eoghan's jacket, but it was silent.

Gedeon and Hector looked markedly…annoyed with both of us as our slowed pace never quickened under their scrutiny and my stomach fluttered nervously as Gedeon looked me over. He shifted his gaze slowly, and then his eyes grew a fraction of an inch before narrowing and stilling at the small bit of blue along the top edge of my shoulder. "I see Lord Eoghan has proved himself useful after days of practice."

Eoghan cleared his throat and twisted his lips. "Yes, well, someone has to train the future Mora of Prydia, don't they?" He looked down and smiled at me, the sheer height of him enough to scare half the town of Jessup away, just like Aeden would have if he didn't know and actively work for half the town. Eoghan lifted his head casually back up to Gedeon and inclined his head toward the stairs. "After you, Lord Gedeon."

I swear I could see the fumes coming from Gedeon's ears as his neck flushed over in rage. His jaw ticked, but he moved to the edge of the stairs regardless, holding a stiffened arm out for me but not bothering to order me to his side. Eoghan released my arm and gave me a nudge in my father's direction, like a lamb going up to slaughter. I hesitantly stepped forward and laced my arm through his, the coldness of his emotions seeping through every delicate gold and purple thread of his dress jacket. This was the first time I had ever touched my father, and it felt nothing like I thought being in the arms of your father would feel like. It was cold, and unwelcoming, and felt...wrong. I'd sometimes wondered what it would be like to have a father in my life. Now all I wanted was to forget he existed.

He straightened his back and I lifted my chin higher in response. I didn't want him to see the amount of emotion that welled inside of me, the pain of never having him as I grew up, and the subsequent terror in my realization of the monster that he actually was and I hadn't even fully witnessed how his kingdom looked beyond my bedroom window and the training deck. I only knew the hardness of his feelings toward me. He probably dreamed of my death in the Triad with a smile on his face.

"Presenting Lord Gedeon Aerborne of Prydia, and his daughter, Lady Paige Aerborne of Prydia." The announcer rang out above the hushed crowd and I felt the heaviness of hundreds of sets of eyes glaring at me, waiting for the reveal of my marks in all their glory as they continued down to my uncovered back. It made me wonder if Gedeon's maids had assumed Eoghan had already given me the mark because they weren't able to dress me for a few days and wouldn't know if he had, or if maybe it was Gedeon's way of getting Eoghan to comply with one of the main reasons he was here for. *He will introduce you to other powers beyond air.* What I had assumed was just basic training actually went beyond that. I needed him to transfer it to me because Gedeon wasn't planning to ever let me out of the castle, and that thought sent a shiver down my spine.

Their eyes may have been piercing through me as I reached the end of the stairs and took up Eoghan's arm in place of my father's, but a quick look around as we turned to dance confirmed who I thought I had seen before on the balcony. Everyone else in the ballroom faded to nothing.

He was here. It was definitely Aeden.

My heart fell to my feet as Eoghan tried to lead us in a dance. I almost felt bad for Eoghan as he led us across the dance floor, my feet unable to grasp the concept that they had to move along with Eoghan's as I stumbled and prodded my way along.

"Ah, I think I see who your *friend* is, Paige," Eoghan spoke through a slitted grin so radiant and refined it was hard to know for sure if he'd spoken or if I'd imagined it. "You know he's staring at you, right?"

"What?" I whispered back breathlessly, the words hardly able to come out just before Eoghan pulled me in closer.

"Your. Man. Is. Staring." His eyes stayed trained on me, though his peripherals were proving to be something of value—probably learned on a battlefield, or in his court. "Stars, can you not make your lips so readable?"

I snapped my mouth shut, then mimicked the way his lips curved to hide what I was saying, but my words came out mumbled. "How...how do you know it's him?" Thank everything in Aellethia down to the very dirt that Gedeon had left the room as quickly as he'd entered it along with Hector. If Hector had seen Aeden, he would be dead. Seeing as even Eoghan knew who *my man* was, he would be more than dead. Eviscerated. Hung. Ran through with a spear. Whatever they did to people they really didn't want here, he would be that.

Eoghan whispered into my ear as we neared where Aeden was standing, confirming that he knew who I was talking about. "Because he is looking at you like you are the sun in an abysmal darkness of insignificant stars." I tried so hard not to give away who he was, not even looking his way. I never considered he would give it away for me. For us. My traitorous hands trembled at Eoghan's words. *Was he really looking at me like that?*

I slid my hands around his neck, keeping them loose to ease the tremor. "Technically, the sun is also a star so I could also be insignificant," I deadpanned nervously, trying to ignore the searing heat like I'd done so many times before—we were so close to Aeden it was sending heat waves against my skin, burning me up from the inside even though it felt like it was coming off of him at times. The dance ended, and Eoghan strode over, walking straight by Aeden and taking up the hand of the woman with black hair and doe blue eyes behind him. The same woman who I could swear was in my dream. She was strikingly beautiful, but I didn't see Aeden focusing on her. Not in the ways he was focusing on me.

I desperately needed to be anywhere but in the ballroom, where the heat was reaching uncomfortable levels but no one else seemed to be affected by it as they danced behind me.

Anywhere.

I knew the space above us led to a hallway with more rooms, somewhere away from this place where too many eyes kept falling on me. I gestured slightly to the hall above and then moved swiftly.

I could only hope he would follow.

TWENTY-SIX

PAIGE

The hallway above the ballroom held more rooms than I could count. Luckily the first one I walked into was an empty guest room not unlike my own in luxury and opulence with deep purple and golden decor, complete with a dimly lit fireplace. I cracked the door, knowing—hoping—Aeden was far enough behind me to attempt to avoid any suspicion, but close enough to know which door I'd went through. My heart thundered in my chest and my clammy fingers twirled the ends of my curled hair, waiting for him to walk through the door. Between how we left things and how messed up my current situation was, I was a bundle of TNT waiting to explode.

A beautiful tanned hand pushed against the door slowly and stole the breath from my lungs. "Paige?" His voice was broken and unsure as he whispered out into the room.

I lurched out and pulled him inside the room by his fingers, throwing my body so hard into him I thought I would break. His firm body wrapped around mine, his shoulders dipping low to bend to my height, so he could nuzzle into the crook of my neck. I felt his leg shift back to close the door and heard a faint clicking sound.

Home. This is what home felt like. He was my home.

"I'm so fucking happy to see you, you have no idea. I thought I would never see you again." His words were like a heavenly song to my ears, the heat of his breath on my neck melting my insides to goo. He squeezed me tighter, running a finger along my spine—my bare back—making me stiffen. I clasped onto his swollen forearms and pulled back, taking all of him in. The stubble along his jaw was more scruffy, a bit beyond his usual five o'clock shadow, and his hair was disheveled. His skin was tanned by the sun slightly more than it had been in Jessup from working outside more often than not. He looked like he'd gone through hell and back yet somehow came back ten times more attractive than any devil could ever leave someone. My words were frozen in my chest, my body consumed with his.

"You look downright devastating in that dress, Paige," he growled, brushing his hands along my arm that was covered in a purple air tattoo. He showed no fear or astonishment in his eyes as he looked at the tattoo but rather kept his eyes soft as if it were just another part of me. I wasn't some freak or monster to him. His fingers moved down to meet mine, twining them, and lifted my arm to his lips as he planted soft kisses along my air mark. The thing I felt so damned by at times now the spot where flushes of heat went through me with each kiss.

"You...you aren't scared of...of it?" I breathed out, the anxiety of him being afraid of what I could do seeming more insane now that I was with him. Aeden never cowered from things or people, why would he start now?

Another kiss landed on my skin as he made his way up, pulled his head back around the top of my shoulder, and chuckled before nibbling into my neck. "How could I ever be scared of something that looks so fucking hot on you?" I moaned—heat spreading between my thighs at the touch of his lips on my skin. He pulled back again and smirked down at me. I buried my face in my palm as I let out a laugh. His deep brown eyes lit up when I slid my hand down and peeked through my fingers at him. Yet all he did was pull me in closer, his arms wrapping around me while his heart beat just as madly as my own.

"I can't believe you're...you're here. I have so much to tell you. There's some kind of fight coming up, it's called a Triad. My father"—I flinched and Aeden held me closer, stroking the back of my hair as I continued—"My father is a bastard and brought me here to fight and said that you were killed. I didn't believe him." I stared up at him and his chin curled toward his chest to meet my eyes.

"Of course you didn't. You've always been too stubborn for your own good." He chuckled as I squeezed his arms and scrunched my nose up at him. His forehead dipped lower pressing into my forehead. "I've always liked that about you, you know." No questions, just acknowledgment. *My safe place.*

I nodded, biting down on my lip. *Had I known that? No, but I did now.* "I even dreamed about you. Often." I started moving my hands up along his covered arms but slid them back down when he stiffened. It was insane to think he had a mark, let alone to trust my dreams, which were *just dreams.* "Anyways, I don't have a choice in fighting or not. And these powers are supposed to help me and everyone here is like this but with smaller marks and...and did you know there's fucking trolls and centaurs here?" I was rambling but it wasn't like I'd rehearsed seeing Aeden again and telling him everything that had happened, and everything I had learned about Aellethia—it all just came tumbling out and all he did was laugh.

"Yes, Paige, I know about the trolls and centaurs, and hags are nasty as all hell. There's a lot out there that isn't like anything we could have ever imagined, and it's quite incredible." There was a level of wonder in his eyes, something I'd only seen when he talked about things he admired. He continued, "I was told about your father and the Triad." He squeezed my elbows and pulled me in even closer, his eyes locking onto mine. "Fuck him for making you do that. Fuck everything for the messed-up position you are being put into. I wish I could…I wish I could have been here for you." He pulled back and looked toward the window which was covered by heavy, purple curtains. "I wish I were with *you*, and not out there. I've been losing my fucking mind over not knowing if you were okay. I couldn't breathe"—his eyes moved back down to me, looking me over wildly—"or think straight, knowing you were, knowing you *are*, trapped in this place. I'm so sorry, but I'll do everything I can to help once I find a way to. I'm going to get you out of here. I swear it."

I nearly melted into him knowing he was out there searching for *me*. He was thinking about *me*. Obligation wasn't his driving force, and his desire wasn't to go home. It was to be with me.

"I missed you so much, you have no idea." I looked up at him in awe, the realization of him wanting me, of being here with me, clouding all my previous thoughts and concerns and shoving them far past the curtain-covered window as his hand slid down to the base of my spine. I arched into it, my breasts pushing in close to his torso. He bent down and brushed his nose and lips against the crown of my head.

"I'm here now, and you have me. All of me. Not just tonight, but all of my nights. I want all of my days to be consumed with thoughts of you, and all of my nights showing you just how fucking much I have been thinking about you, and only you." I shuddered against him, my legs melting under the heat and softness of his words. "You are it for me, Paige. And I won't let some twisted, absent father try to hurt you. I *will* get you out of here and I *will* find a way for us to be safe. Together."

I was done for, my legs felt like molten blobs and my arms became jello. For a moment I thought I'd begun to float again like I had in the bathroom just from thinking of Aeden, of his lips on mine as we crashed into each other. But I wasn't floating. And this wasn't a dream. I pinched myself, just to be sure. Aeden lowered his hand to cup under my ass before lifting me with one arm while the other cradled the back of my head. In one swift movement, he was pushing his mouth against mine. A flurry of power moved inside of me, wanting to break free, high on so many emotions and sensations it was almost overwhelming. He wasn't kissing me out of lust. His lips moved slowly, caressing and pressing gently. It was different from anything I had experienced before, more deep and tender as if he wanted nothing more than to be with me.

He deepened the kiss, parting my lips with his tongue in gentle swipes before our tongues moved harmoniously together, matching the two elements as they twisted inside of me in passionate waves. I reached around to his shoulders and dug my fingers into his guard uniform, a brilliant disguise for getting into a castle as heavily guarded as this one. He also looked really good in laced tunics, something I never pictured him wearing, but he pulled it off like they were designed for every hard ridge and line of his body. He moved us to the edge of the bed, his fingers digging into my thighs before laying me down. He bit my lip and I moaned as he took my bottom lip into his mouth.

He groaned, equally satisfied, and moved down, planting kisses along my neck, moving to the top edge of my shoulder where the two marks billowed together. My nipples peaked against his cheek as he moved lower where my thighs were spreading to grant him better access until he just stopped. I silently thanked the maids for placing a slit up so high, although earlier I had tried to shield my leg from overexposure. My breaths came heavy and uneven and I could feel Aeden's chest moving against my stomach, his rapid heart meeting the pace of my own.

I raked my fingers through his hair, pushing the ends away from his eyes before I curled up to kiss his forehead. "I've wanted you for so long and my dreams have been so crazy lately...it's hard to believe any of this is real."

I kept my voice low as I tried not to snap back into reality, fear creeping back in, prickling my skin. The light that flooded in from underneath the door was seeping into my line of vision. There were hundreds of fae beyond that door, and one of them would certainly kill Aeden for him being here, dressed as a guard, alone in a room with me. My eyes flicked between the door and Aeden, my lip trembling as I bit it back.

Aeden rested his chin on my stomach, ignoring the door entirely as he looked up at me and pushed his fingers into his hair to meet mine. He twined our fingers and pulled my hand down to his lips and I watched as my knuckles slowly grazed over his mouth. Golden flecks sparkled against the dark pools of his eyes, coming to life with the flickering light of the fireplace. If I thought I was breathless earlier, I was surely wrong. I silently opened my palm and summoned more air into my lungs.

"I'm here, Paige. I'm. Really. Here." He punctuated each word with a kiss along my stomach through the fabric of my dress, solidifying his existence more and more while my breaths slowed under his touch. "What I feel. For you. Is very. Very. Real." His kisses were moving up and up toward my breasts and with a jumble of incoherent sounds that sounded almost like his name, I rolled my head back down, pressing it deep into the pillow. He paused and drew his body up, his head level with my own.

"Even with things as fucked up as they are right now, I couldn't be more obsessed with you if I tried. I'm so in love with you, with everything you do and who you are that I would burn the world beyond these four walls down just to stay here with you a few more minutes. Because this,"—he motioned between us with his hand—"being here with you, is what is real. And that's a world I won't ever survive without—any world where you and I can't be just like this."

His reassurance sent electricity through my body. I wasn't dreaming, and he was really here. My best friend, and the man I never thought would be mine, was confessing his love. For *me*. I threw my body weight against him and flipped him onto his back, straddling him so fast I almost went flying off the bed before I put my palm out to send a blast of air out to steady me. Aeden couldn't help but release a laugh, but it quickly died down as he grasped my hips, steadying me with his palms and fingertips.

"That power comes in handy, doesn't it?" His lip curled up to one side, revealing his dimpled cheek. It was nice to know that even though we were friends for a while before turning into...whatever we were now, we were still essentially the same people we had always been around each other. And I needed something like that to never change. Ever.

"Besides throwing huge balls of air at nothing and filling my lungs when I get breathless after training, I can sometimes levitate, so there is that," I admitted.

I leaned down to kiss him more, savoring every last bit of contact before the moment was over. We would have to go back to the ball, or at least I would. The thought of hiding Aeden inside the ginormous castle crossed my mind briefly before I remembered the amount of power Gedeon had and the number of servants and guards who did whatever he told them to do. And asking for Nya's help was out of the question. Her absence from the ball told me she wasn't invited, because she wasn't a High Fae, nor was she respected. There would be no mercy shown for her if she were to aid me in hiding him.

I pushed those thoughts away, refocusing on the here and now that was Aeden and I, in this room, together at last. I sat back up and reached down to the laces on Aeden's shirt, pulling on them slightly to loosen them. I wanted his clothes gone and judging by the hardness that pressed against my spread legs, he felt the same exact way. I bent to kiss him again, moving slowly down his jaw, releasing a growl of pleasure from him as I began to rock my hips against him.

"Paige, wa—" I kissed his lips, stealing his demands from his mouth. I didn't want to wait. I didn't want him to think he needed to take his time with me and *wait* any more than I already had. Than we clearly both had. I'd been waiting so long for this moment and I wanted him with a rawness I couldn't fully comprehend or explain. It went beyond a want. I *needed* him.

I moved down to his neck, biting and sucking at his skin causing him to groan more. His fingertips dug into my hips, and I couldn't tell if he was pushing me away or pulling me closer. Maybe he didn't quite know, either. His pulse quickened as I moved down his neck, pushing the edge of his tunic down until—

I shot up and back as red flashed into my vision. A curling, fiery billow of red flames peeked out from Aeden's collar, and terror took over my body. My head spun as I reached behind me, my fingers clawing frantically, awkwardly—searching. I tuned into my power, unsure if the heat I felt along my skin was desire...or something else. But the power inside of me...it was only air and water. It remained unchanged. No fire flared in my veins. But Aeden.

He was a...

Aeden...was a...

"Fire-wielder?!" I whisper-shouted at him as anger pushed aside the fear for a split second. He hadn't told me anything about his mark, had even *flinched* when I... "How, when...where?" And then another thought, one that battled with the fondness I held for him rose. Had he known this whole time? Known about Aellethia, choosing to live next to me—I swallowed down the rising bile in my throat. "Have you been watching me this whole time, knowing *I* was from here too? Did you know about this place? Did *he* send you?!" My voice tipped, wavering like the magic was responding in my bones. I snapped back further and he sat up slowly.

When he reached for my hands, I flinched back, fearing the fire mark would spread to me like Eoghan's did.

Do not reach out toward the flames now that your body is awakening to more powers, and try not to feel too deeply near anything on fire. Especially not fae whose original nature is fire. That was the warning Eoghan bestowed upon me before the ball. And seeing the red flames along his neck, and the way he wasn't denying it at all...

I had just gone through the very emotion that drove my air magic mad, yet his fire magic didn't come to me. *I was safe.*

"Please, don't. You don't under—"

"I don't understand? Do you understand what it is to be a fire-wielder? Is that your original nature?" And then my anger turned to fear and sadness. My father wouldn't have sent a fire-wielder to retrieve me—to *watch* me. He hated them. And his mark would mean...it would mean death. He had tried to conceal it, to hide it from everyone not barring myself, by lacing up his tunic that I—

"I didn't know I was from here, just like you didn't know. When I first got here"—he shook out his head and drew his fingers through his hair—"I almost burned down an entire bar, Paige. And then...then I blasted myself into a lake with water and grew a fucking rose when I was...look, Paige, I didn't ask for any of this just like you didn't. But you don't have to be afraid." He reached for me again but this time I jumped up from the bed. He didn't deny it at all. His original nature *was* fire. But, how?

Suddenly, the door whipped open and Eoghan stepped inside, closing the door hastily behind him. Aeden got up from the bed and glared at him like he was going to set him on fire, and with that fire mark, I bet he could do it.

Eoghan looked him up and down as Aeden's fingers clenched open and closed. The golden specks in Aeden's eyes turned to sparks of embers and the room spiked in temperature. That's when it finally clicked that Aeden was the source. He had been, all along.

Eoghan cocked a brow at Aeden before he smirked wickedly at him, and then at me. I fixed the strap along my arm that had fallen out of place, which only made his expression turn more mischievous. "Ah, well. This is fun and all. But he has to go. Right now, Paige."

TWENTY-SEVEN

AEDEN

My fists grew hot and I didn't have to look down to know they were most likely on fire as I stared at the man who danced with Paige. Not only had he held her closely against him, but he was also welcome in this castle, and with that kind of closeness between them...my mind started telling me things that I didn't want to listen to. Was I just being a jealous dick about every guy who'd ever touched Paige? Probably. But now she knew how I felt about her, how much I wanted her. I'd even gone as far as telling her I was in love with her. I found the strength to pull my eyes from the royal fucker to look at her. The look of alarm she gave me when she saw my mark affected me more than the people in the bar had and it broke me apart on the inside so much that I could feel my elements all whirling in confusion. How she pulled away from me may haunt me in my dreams for the rest of my life.

She didn't want me anymore.

I looked between the two of them, the guy who I believed to be another Mora was probably hand-picked by her father to serve as a distraction—and she played right into it. Rage was coming in hot waves, heating the room so much I could see a bead of sweat move down Paige's chest, sliding between her perfect breasts. I was only making things worse, not even bothering to hide my original nature at that point.

"You need to learn to control that or the *real* guards will find you before I can help get you out of here." *The fuck?* He smirked at me, ignoring Paige's wild eyes as he leaned against the wall.

"I don't need your help." I simmered the flames to nothing in my hands and he cocked a brow at me. "I can find my own way out of here." I didn't trust him and I sure as hell wasn't going to be helped by someone like him, someone who put people like me—fae, like me—on a fucking platform. I stepped in closer to Paige as the sounds of screaming and shouting began to erupt from beyond the door.

"I'm sure you can't, actually. This place is a death trap for your kind." Eoghan examined his nails casually, then pushed his hand out toward me. "I'm Eoghan, and you must be Paige's...*person?*" He glanced over at Paige. "Or did you find another chum out there on the dance floor?" His smile was directed back at me, twisting and taunting, and I don't think I'd ever wanted to punch someone more in my life.

I tightened the strings along my neck while Eoghan stared at what I knew were the flames along the edge of my collar. I pushed down the edges of my sleeves because I watched his eyes flutter down to the edge where another flash of red poked through. He didn't even look surprised. He knew what I was. Knew exactly where my mark started and stopped.

"Stop being such an asshole, E—" Eoghan grabbed Paige by the wrist and spun her around, making her face me as his eyes dragged down her exposed back. "Paige, you didn't tell me he was a fire-wielder. You got lucky, this time."

I could see her throat work, her eyes widening as she took in whatever he meant by that.

"Get your fucking hands off of her."

"Why? Would you prefer your hands on her?" Eoghan's eyes darted up to me before he spun her back around to face him. "I don't think that's a very good idea," he said over her shoulder, which drooped inward at his words. She moved to stand beside him, eyes glued to the floor.

Why wasn't she fighting?

"Oh, so you think you know what's best for her?" I closed the distance between Paige and I, and Eoghan rolled his fucking eyes. "Please Paige, I..." I reached for her hands, my thumb managing to graze her delicate skin before she pulled away again which sent a sharp pain skittering across my chest.

"I didn't know..." she breathed out as she shuffled in toward Eoghan, and the world caved in around me.

I held up my hand, hoping her eyes were too fixed on the floor to see the slight tremor in my fingers. "It's fine. I'll go." I should've tried harder, *fought harder*, to make her see that I wasn't a threat. Whatever lies they'd been feeding her, it wasn't me. I would never hurt her. But she didn't want me here anymore. As if having a giant target on my back wasn't bad enough, I'd also managed to lose the one person I loved more than anything in the world.

Inside, the room fell silent while outside, beyond the closed door, was anything but. Paige's chest moved with her deep breaths as she glanced over her shoulder at the door, or Eoghan, I wasn't sure. She was trying to stay calm, just as I'd taught her what seemed like a lifetime ago, and I was the reason she felt compelled to do so. I was making it worse.

"Please, just...I can't...it's not...it isn't you..." she whispered, her faint gasps between her pauses—the very reason she was pausing—was making my own breath catch as her palm fluttered up to her chest. Because it *was* me. I was the issue, the *problem*. She wasn't flinching or steering clear of *Lord* Eoghan.

The prick.

"I get it." But I didn't. Not really. *This is who I am now.* I didn't want to regret the power that flourished within me, but a part of me did. Not that it mattered, really. It had become just as much a part of me as any other part of my body was. I was still me, possibly even more so now. I'd become whole, in a way, and she didn't see that. I thought what we had and what we were, that what I felt for her was at least somewhat reciprocated. But I guess I was wrong. "Your bodyguard can show me out." It didn't matter that I didn't trust him, not anymore. If I got caught, if I was discovered, what was I truly losing? My heart was already shredding to pieces.

Eoghan pushed himself off the wall and straightened his jacket, then nodded. "Paige, head on back to your room. I'll say I took you back there for safety. And your—"

"Aeden," I growled out.

"Right, excuse me." His tone turned mocking, his hands going up to either side of him as he smirked again at me. *Asshole.* Paige was right about that. "Aeden, here, will follow close behind me. When we get outside, I'll make you a portal to beyond the castle."

The pixies have heard rumors about him being different from the others, more of a revolutionary. But that has yet to be proven.

Well, fuck me. I was about to test that rumor.

"Why not make the portal here?" It was Paige who spoke up. And damn if it didn't put an arrow through my already breaking heart that she needed me gone that badly.

"Gedeon's house is warded, which means no portals for me. But the moment we get outside, beyond the walls and the gardens, we should be able to—"

"The training deck, you made a portal there. It's close by." Paige's eyebrow cocked up, questioning Eoghan while all I could think about was how this fucker was already seeming too sketchy to trust. And judging by the sounds of slamming doors, we didn't have much time left to debate it. But I was...*intrigued.*

"Yes, I did. The wards were dropped during that particular time." Eoghan's finger went under his chin, and he watched her, analyzed her. Like he was waiting for something...as if she were a toy he couldn't put down.

Paige's eyes flashed with anger. "So, that day on the deck—Gedeon *knew* you were going to try to send me home? He knew, and he did whatever he did to those wards to make them disappear, and you just played along?" Paige's words struck out like a viper about to attack her prey and I couldn't hide the curve of my lips.

That's my girl.

"Yes, well, you passed that test. Congratulations, by the way." He winked at her.

"If you weren't going to help me, if she weren't standing right next to you, I'd—"

"Simmer down, lover boy. If you want to live, I suggest we go." The shouting grew imminently, the sounds of doors being thrust open one by one inching closer and closer. If Eoghan didn't get a chance to prove the rumor from the pixies, the guards would certainly have their go with me, and with them, I'd have no chances being taken on me. They were all Gedeon's puppets, save for Seamus. "Or we could keep standing here, looking at each other. I do admit, you are rather pleasing to lo—"

"I love you." It was quick, but it would have to be enough. I didn't try to reach out to her again. Eoghan let out a sound that was close to an *awe,* then directed Paige to stay in the room and slowly peeled the door open. He flicked his wrist and a sharp crackling sound emanated from the hall, the shouts and banging of fists on doors nearly ceasing entirely. I made my way past the door to follow Eoghan, stealing one more glance at Paige over my shoulder who looked back at me with sodden eyes as she mouthed *I'm sorry*.

Me too, sweetheart. Me too.

I was met with a thick wall of ice beyond the door, forming a barrier between the part of the hallway that led to the ballroom and the other direction that had endless rooms. "That wall won't hold forever, so if you like living, I suggest you keep up," Eoghan said. "You are, after all, the one they are hunting for."

I picked up my pace alongside him, our strides even in pace as we passed ornate doors and wallpaper full of...dying fire-wielders, blood filling the ground they lay on. *Fuck, this is what Paige saw every day.* "If you're going to try to kill me, now would be a good time."

"Do you always act so unkindly to people who try to save you?" He turned at a bend in the hall. Another long hallway, a shit ton of doors, same graphic wallpaper. "I wouldn't need to try, by the way. If I wanted you dead, you'd be dead already. I could have just pushed you out through the door and locked it behind you."

"Maybe you should have, because I can just as easily burn you down where you stand."

He chuckled. "I'd like to see you try. Perhaps another day." *Can't wait.*

I halted for a brief moment in the hallway and Eoghan let out a groan. "I didn't come alone. Will they get out?"

"They should be fine *if* they don't have a fire mark, that is." He cocked his eyebrow at me, waiting for my reply.

I shouldn't have brought them up in the first place. Implicating them was not on the agenda, but then again, neither was fleeing Prydia's castle. "No. They don't."

Eoghan stopped abruptly at a door, making me take several steps back. It wasn't any different from the others, and I had to question how he even knew where he was going when he said with such certainty, "Here we are." A huge bang erupted, followed by loud thuds. The ice wall had fallen, and the rumble of the guards' boots sent a tall vase rocking in the corner.

"Get in, quick!" Eoghan hissed, and we clambered into a room.

It was large for a single room, possibly the size of my entire rental home back in Jessup. A long desk lay opposite a bed fit for a king, while atop the desk propped a single, small painting. A portrait of a man leaning on a sword, a long purple air tattoo curling up his arm and his face set in stone like he couldn't be bothered to stand for the artist who'd painted it. He looked like Gedeon, but younger, all hard ridges and stern posture forgone.

"Below the windows outside is a trellis that leads down to the gardens." Eoghan maneuvered a lock at the top with a flick of his wrist, sending a burst of air in whirls around it to force it open. "After you."

"A trellis?" I heaved myself up and over the window, finding the footholds meant for flowers to sprawl through. I lifted a hand to flick my wrist, then thought better of it and put it back down along the sill of the window. I wanted to create a rope, something to ease my way down faster than dropping several stories to the ground. But then I remembered that I shouldn't be this powerful, to begin with. I looked up, meeting his sly grin, and cursed under my breath.

"Were you planning to burn something down just now?" He pressed his fingers to his lips and looked me over. His brow furrowed, but the guards were coming closer. They'd be in that room in under a minute. So I started descending, quickly. I heard a gust of wind roll by but didn't stop moving down, closing the distance between myself and the ground. It wasn't until I felt a channel of air go up and across my back that I froze, feeling the fabric of my tunic lift. *Shit.* I turned, glancing down at the ground, and watched as Eoghan clucked his tongue up at me. "And *you* came from the mortal world?"

I let go of the trellis, falling the remaining two stories and landing in a crouch. I righted myself, adjusting my tunic once more.

"Yes," I said.

"Yes…" he reiterated, his finger tapping along his chin in contemplation.

"I didn't know we had time for an interrogation." I glanced up at the window but there was no sign anyone, including ourselves, had entered the room, the curtains were drawn and the window was closed. If the guards were checking rooms, they more than likely wouldn't think to check beyond the windows.

"My presence almost always comes with one," Eoghan clarified, tapping his left shoulder. "Comes with the title, you see."

"Does that title also grant you the in-depth knowledge of her brother's room?" It was my turn for questions.

"Why, aren't you an observant…what should we call you? High Fae? You aren't *just* a fire-wielder." Eoghan put his hands inside his golden-trimmed pockets and turned, egging for me to follow him into the garden. He glanced over his shoulder as I finished readjusting my clothing again. "We've got a few minutes before the guards give up inside and move their search elsewhere. If it were my kingdom, I'd send them to the gardens next. Judging by the loose description of you that was given, *a fire-wielding boy with brown hair*, I think it's safe for you to resume whatever it is you were doing before you came to the ball. You might want to change up your disguise though, get a jacket or something a little less likely to show the edge of that brawny neck of yours, *if* you plan to see Paige during her trials, that is. I'm going to assume you stole that"—he gestured at my guard's uniform—"and with this many fae in Prydia for the next few days, it should be easy for you to do so again."

"You know, for someone who just had their hands all over *my girl*, you sure do sound like you want me to come back. Why." Not a question, a demand. He was almost too willing to help. Although I wasn't sure where Paige and I stood now, she would always have my heart and that damn need to protect her was always rearing its head as jealousy, or maybe that was just who I really was.

Eoghan let out a laugh as we passed rows upon rows of flowers and herbs, vegetation sprawling up more trellises curved into arches, giving the illusion of peace and prosperity while the town was nothing more than dirt and people who could barely conceal their thin frames under their ragged clothing. Eoghan shrugged and then ducked under an archway. "I'm a hopeless romantic."

"Bullshit. Why," I repeated.

"You really do make quite the pair. I'll let you in on a secret. I'm not doing this for *her*."

"I saw the way you looked at her." I scoffed, wondering at that very moment why I hadn't gone through with setting him on fire yet. His face was rather...punchable.

"What you saw was me acting, yet again, as if I were interested in a woman." That was the first remark he had made toward me that hadn't sounded like a sleight of hand or a trick. He was telling the truth. "Now the way *you* looked at her, that was something of a rarity."

Silence lingered for mere seconds before the sounds of guards shouting and metal clinking outside rang through the gardens, the brief facade of peace slamming into the dirt.

Eoghan shoved me in line with several trees, their branches reaching and weaving to form a solid wall of intertwined branches and leaves with the quick movement of his hand. "Before I make the portal, tell me something," he whispered.

"You better make it quick." Guards were approaching fast, the sounds of air whipping around the castle walls were unquestionably meant to slow down the fire-wielder they planned to capture. But that fire-wielder was tucked behind a wall of fruit-bearing branches.

"What is your mother's name?" Eoghan asked, and I shook my head out, certain I had misheard him but his voice was clear, I hadn't misheard. His royal etiquette must've mandated proper annunciation since birth.

"Are you serious right now? I'm sure I wouldn't be the only one getting in trouble for being out here, me with a fire mark and—"

"You with *every* mark," he said sharply, his eyes turning to thin slits.

I could feel the air rushing in on me the second Paige kissed me back, the second her mouth met mine. It was undeniable, just as she was. But I was so caught up in the moment, in *her*, that I didn't want to think about the sensation that spread across my back—to acknowledge its existence. It felt like all of the storms and the ebbing of the power inside of me finally came to a harmonious dance. All of the missing puzzle pieces meeting and completing each other, like how I felt when I was with her.

"I don't know who my mother is or was. I was orphaned at a young age," I admitted.

"Isn't that convenient?" A grin spread across his face. "Any last words?"

"Yeah, actually." I fisted into my pocket. "Give this to Paige, tell her as long as she has this I will be there with her. I know she can handle herself, but don't let anyone hurt her or I'll come looking for you. And if it's you that hurts her, I'll fucking kill you." I pulled my hand out from my pocket and placed the bracelet bearing my name into Eoghan's hand, which closed around mine as he shook my hand firmly.

A whirling blue portal tore into the air beside us. "You've never killed a thing in your life, have you?" He clucked his tongue and shook his head.

"Have to start somewhere." There was no point in denying it, but honestly—"I'd do it. For her, I'd do whatever it takes." The hag's death wouldn't be convincing enough to boast about, not when *thing* so clearly meant *person.*

He gave me the same look he'd given Paige inside the castle as if I were his new plaything. Like this was all some fucking twisted game to him. But I didn't have time to think about that or to take back what I'd given him for Paige. I was learning, more and more, that this place was going to test my boundaries, and Eoghan was the giant fissure in the earth that I had to hurtle over.

"Good. I'll keep her safe. Beyond this garden is a wall, and beyond that is the Hollow Woods. I'll open another portal for you there near a rundown shack at sunrise on the day of her trial, in four days' time." Eoghan opened his palm, dangling the bracelet up against the faint moonlight that filtered in through the tightly woven branches. He glanced back at me, a smile tugging at his lips as he tucked it away into his pocket and patted my back.

"This doesn't mean I trust you. And I really don't fucking like you, either." I straightened up my back and faced the portal. The guards were all around us, but the branches shielded so much of where we were that we blended right into the garden.

"No, of course not. I would expect nothing less of a dragon heir." A blast of air rammed into my back, catching me off guard and hurling me through the portal.

"Well well, if it isssn't one of the faesss from the party," a slimy, snake-like voice hissed through the cool night breeze. My brain was muddled as I tried to blink my eyes but saw nothing in the darkness. It was too dark, too distorted, my vision hazy like a steep fog surrounded me.

"Looksss like a guard, he should be tasssty." A second one chortled, laughter sounding from more than one as the sounds of leaves crunching beneath heavy feet grew closer, and closer.

The fog coating my eyes and my mind lessened and I braced myself on my knees before standing, rubbing the impact of the ground from the back of my head. Portaling felt like spinning through a blender and being stretched apart by each limb before being thrust back into stillness. It seemed impossible to land on my own two feet after going through one yet again, but I'd do it again in a heartbeat if it meant seeing Paige again.

I'll open another portal for you there near a rundown shack at sunrise on the day of her trial, in four days' time.

"I can sssmell hisss blood!" Suddenly, the portal became the least of my concerns. Blood. I pulled my hand away from the back of my head. My fingers, and my palm, were coated and warmed by a thin layer of blood. Fuck, my head throbbed, the pain searing at the removal of the pressure of my hand. I peered through slitted eyes although it was nearly pitch black out, save for the moonlight and the stars that made their way through the branches of the forest I landed in. Shiny plates and yellow eyes reflected that light, in three regions of the woods—two close by, another shimmering in the distance behind them, their eyes reaching higher than my own head. Not a hag. Those were more crouched over, and the shimmer these things elicited told me they were thin and lanky. But they were also not something I wanted smelling my blood, tasting me, or coming anywhere near me. *They could smell me.*

I threw open my bloody palm and tried to summon as much rage as possible, willing my fire to come to light. But the pain from the wound on my head made it difficult to focus, my mind fading in and out of dizzying waves. Concussed, definitely a concussion. The scales and yellow eyes were coming closer, my eyes unwilling to stay trained on just one. Each one had its own distinct, breathy voice, but visually I was seeing more than three. Three turned into four, then five or more with flashes of rebounded light coming closer.

"An easssy kill, he'sss already hurt." Leaves crunched under them as they moved slowly. They were toying with me, playing with their food before indulging in the meal I'd turn into if I couldn't get my shit together. I could run, or hobble away, sure. Or I could try to fight with the little knowledge I had of my power. The fickle beast inside of me sometimes did exactly what I needed it to. But other times, it went haywire or simply did nothing at all.

"We like to play, won't you play with usss?" A taunt. But I was no coward, and I wasn't going to start being one now. The only certain way I knew to draw out my power, my flames, to coax and will it to life, was to become enraged. Like I had in the bar in Costa, and like I'd almost done to Eoghan inside the castle. *Eoghan.* Seamus tried to teach me how to wield, to control my emotions as we walked endlessly, and when I'd fought the hag, I'd managed to burst the thing into nothing but pieces of flesh and bone. But anger? Anger would come easier, would be more fluid, than trying to still my mind as another wave of dizziness roiled together with nausea.

So I thought of Eoghan, thought of his hands on Paige, thought of her father and the way he was keeping Paige within the walls of his castle. Putting her in some fucking series of trials that aimed to end her life. Anger simmered, but it wouldn't be enough to wield anything significant.

"Make it fun for usss!" one shrieked out and the whole forest quieted.

I turned against myself. *Paige can't love someone like me. I'm nothing, no one, and she's...she's a fucking princess. What good am I to her? I'm an illegal wielder, and I took too long to show her, to tell her how I felt. How much I loved her.* Anger and agony took hold, rooting my power within me. I was angry, but not at Paige. It would never be at Paige. I was the one at fault. It was all me. *All. On. Me.* And because I waited too long, because she didn't have the love for me that I did for her, she feared me and the very power I was trying to use to save my own ass. I was a fire-wielder, and I had so stupidly believed she'd see beyond that. Believed she didn't hold the same views as her father. Believed she would still want me just as badly as I wanted her. *What the fuck was I supposed to do now?* And giving her my bracelet to remember me by was damn near pathetic. The fire inside caressed my flesh and sprang to life as the sounds of hissing cut through the silenced forest like a knife.

"Ooh, it'sss been a while sssince we had one of your kind for sssupper." Their glowing yellow eyes blinked, their eyelids forming vertical slits as the fire illuminated the serpent-like men. The closest one licked its black lips. Scales. They were all covered, head to whatever kind of fucked up toes they had. Forked tongues dripped slimy green saliva in heavy drops to the dirt. One of them pointed at me with a claw—no—fangs. They had fangs for fingernails that pierced through the tips of their scaly skin, adding to the numerous fangs that another was flashing me through parted lips. Rows and rows of lethal fangs and pointed teeth glistened, the tips sharper and ready.

I thrust my palm out, guiding the fire into a whirl of flames aiming right for the one who stood too close. The force sent me back a step and I heard one of the creatures chuckling as I rooted my feet back down into the ground.

I would not become someone's dinner tonight.

The thing veered away, rolling and hissing as another lunged toward me. I threw out my hand again to block on instinct but what came out was a torrid of boiling water that left steam in its wake. The creature shrieked, a fist-sized bit of flesh and tendons shone where scales once were.

"A fighter, yesss. We like that." The last one, who stood beyond the first two, blinked its eyes as I drew more flames to my hands.

"You're all fucking dead." I wished for a weapon as another laughed at my words. I wanted to thrust something more than just power through them. I wanted to spear them through, just as I had done to the hag. Although that was incidental, I would fully intend to do it this time.

The one who took my first hit was on its feet again and prepared to barrel into me as it crouched over and picked up speed. I fell to the ground and rolled before its impact could falter my flames. I pushed my hand into the ground, redirecting the pain and urging another element to rise above the flames as I hoped—fucking prayed to the stars because I'd had no religion before coming to this place but suddenly desperately needed something to lean back on—for a vine or some kind of huge trench to swallow up the scaly things. But nothing happened. Instead, the world slowed around me as a set of fangs made their way into my thigh, the creature's other hand lifting, ready to sink into my flesh. And fuck it burned.

I lifted my fist and willed fire to spread, coating my leg in fire. I was hardly surprised when it didn't burn me. I somehow knew, had felt it like I felt the bond between Paige and me, the love I had for her, that the fire wouldn't, couldn't, hurt me. I was immune. *Fucking immune.* The thing dislodged its fang-like claws and hissed loudly as it pulled away into the shadows, the smell of burning flesh filling my nostrils and tugging a smile over my lips.

I tried standing again, but my leg was...it was going numb. *Poison.* I put more weight on the other leg, the one I'd narrowly saved with the very element that made them so hungry for my blood and lifted myself just in time to dodge another attack before falling to the ground again.

The three of them laughed in unison, drawing closer, and surrounding me. They flexed their fists, their sharp teeth on full display even as blood dripped from one of them. But then I realized it wasn't their blood. It coated their nails—*their fangs. My blood.* The numbness was spreading, filling me from the inside and turning my limbs weak. Their bodies closed in around me, slowly, predatorily. And I was the best prey they could ever hope to find in this place. My heart began to slow and my vision speckled with blackness. *This is how I die,* I thought. *This is it.*

A glint caught in the corner of my eye, followed by a scaly head rolling to meet the tips of my fingers as I fell back, the only realization that my entire body had shifted was the visual of the pieces of stars and night sky. But even my vision was beginning to fail completely and I waited. Waited for the blackness to take hold. Waited for my life to end. Hissing and slicing sounds surrounded me before the weight of my eyelids became too much. Too heavy.

And then everything faded to black.

TWENTY-EIGHT

PAIGE

"Again!" Eoghan shouted, throwing his sword down in frustration. The shimmering blue light that danced along the blade went out, leaving the sword a dull silver hue as it unbound from Eoghan's magic. We had been practicing for hours already this morning and the sun wasn't even up yet.

The way Eoghan so casually admitted to offering me a way home as a means of some sort of fucked up test still had me on edge. Not that I had time to hold grudges, but it still hurt. Besides the shit I kept dealing with when it came to Eoghan, there was a consistent thought that kept nagging in the back of my head. It was something Aeden had said to me, when we'd shared what we could in our short time of being together, knowing how few the minutes were that we'd have. He was a fire-wielder, but he described two other elements as well. Water *and* earth. The red mark I saw...he was pressed into the bed and it was hard to focus. Did he have—"Where is your head at? Where is your fight?" Eoghan barked out and I shook the thought away. He began pacing between the fallen sword and the stored dummies.

We hadn't used dummies in days—Eoghan deemed them pointless and futile and with a healer at our ready, I had to agree with him. I needed to be prepared for things that attacked back, and thanks to Nya, the fear of getting injured was fading. Not as quickly as I needed it to, but it would have to do.

"Give her a break, you've been working her like a horse." Nya came to my side, checking me over for wounds. She was kind, something Eoghan lacked most hours of the day. I dug into my pocket with my free arm, rubbing the smooth metal of the bracelet Eoghan was decent enough to give me during one of those *kind* hours.

I love you.

And all I said back, soundlessly as I couldn't even gather the strength to raise my voice, was *I'm sorry*.

It should have been more. But I was too afraid and too selfish to tell him how I'd always felt about him. I hope he knows I do love him. I will always love him. Even if my always ends tomorrow in the first trial, I will still go on loving him in whatever afterlife would come.

A book I found called *The Stars That Guide Us* taught me that here, in Aellethia, they believed we went on to live amongst the stars, shining the brightness of our souls down upon whoever we left behind. And sometimes your brightness was replaced by another, allowing you another chance at life among the living fae again. It was a nice thought, to possibly go on living in different cycles of this world. I never gave much thought to my own beliefs of the afterlife, but if my mother was a star shining down on me right now, I hoped she would be proud of me. Even though she wasn't fae, she deserved some brightness, even if it had to come after death.

"Thanks, Nya, but Eoghan's right. The trial won't be kind to me tomorrow, and I have to be ready for it. I have to win." I released Aeden's bracelet and pulled my hand from my pocket, then reached to grab another dagger, sheathed on a leather belt I now wore every second of the day. Even when we weren't on the training deck, I begged to keep my weapons close to me, allowing me more time to practice in my room. Hector didn't seem pleased about it as he grunted the first time I slung it over my hip and walked back into the castle. He stood outside my bedroom door longer now, until the sounds of my knives hitting whatever target I'd found stopped. The minutes after I stopped, I'd wait, listening for those heavy boots to move down the hall. I was sure he would be reporting it all to Gedeon, who seemed more distracted than usual but just as callous as before.

The word that a fire-wielder had escaped the castle, while not only one but two Moras were there, was not sitting well with Gedeon. And that was putting it lightly. The castle walls were thick, but not thick enough to eliminate the sounds of crashing furniture and shouts. He was downright livid.

Eoghan played his part well, stating he was protecting me from the rogue wielder who may have sought to kill me, which Gedeon most likely did not believe was true, but he had no proof otherwise, and starting a war with another kingdom was probably far from his desired agenda at the moment. I was still in shock that Eoghan had actually helped us—had helped *him*.

The day after the ball, the number of guards grew tenfold. They flanked the walls, doors, entrances, exits, windows, and balcony edges. Gedeon spared no expense at guarding his castle, and I had to admit I loved seeing him afraid of something. Afraid of Aeden—the *plaything* of mine who drowned out at sea.

If only he knew just how wrong he was.

I'm so in love with you, with everything you do and who you are that I would burn the world beyond these four walls down just to stay here with you a few more minutes. I realized later that night, after the guests had fled and the guards had ceased their search, that Aeden had tried to tell me about his power. He'd burn the world down, *for me*. It shook me to my core that he may have meant it quite literally.

"You at least need to eat something before you fall over. I can only heal so much, you know. I can't magically make you not hungry." Nya folded her arms across her chest, clearly annoyed that I was being stubborn as usual. But that was who I'd always been, she wasn't going to change that. "At least if you faint, I can bring you back as if it never happened."

"One more hour won't make me collapse. I've gone longer without food than this." That was the one benefit of being here—knowing I'd never go hungry. Not in the sense I knew hunger to be. Before Aeden came into my life, one meal a day was normal, two was a damn luxury. Here, food was guaranteed as long as I went to the dining hall.

Eoghan smirked at Nya, seemingly pleased by my response. She threw her arms down and moved to start cleaning the weapons along the wall.

"Again," Eoghan demanded, not bothering to pick up his sword. "Try to make me bleed this time unless you prefer to do the bleeding."

I may not have been terrified of being injured out on the training deck anymore, but I wasn't naive. I could see the strength that Eoghan and Gedeon had and portrayed and the trials aimed to weed out people who were unfit to rule. They wouldn't take pity on me for being a girl—not that I ever in my life had sought that out—or not having been raised to be the perfect fighter or the perfect wielder. I may have a healer at the ready, but in the trial, I doubted Nya would be anywhere in the same vicinity as me. I had to practice as if my life depended on it, because tomorrow, it would.

A wicked grin curled along my lips as he crooked his finger, directing me. I ran toward him and slid under his arm as he lunged out, allowing me the perfect opportunity to slice my dagger into the back of his knee. I had always been fast on my feet, but the powers growing inside of me didn't just give me the strength to wield the elements. It made me stronger in general. I had never felt so powerful in my life. It was hard to imagine having all the elements, having all of that raw power at my disposal. I pounced back up on my feet and turned, right in time to meet Eoghan's counterattack. His fist met with my stomach, and I was sent flying across the deck.

"Not fast enough, Paige. But better than nothing."

My jaw fell slack, not just from the pain, but from the compliment that I had just been given. Eoghan actually complimented me. Sort of.

"Again." He readied his stance and I forced myself up, holding my hand up to stop Nya from reaching out to heal me. I could take another hour of a beating if it meant I was getting better.

The food was served the minute we sat down, Eoghan to my left and Nya to my right, with me at the head, putting me front and center across from my father. His fists curled in on themselves on top of the dark wooden table on either side of his untouched plate, his knuckles flexing in shades of red and white. He was angry already. Or, rather, still angry.

I cleared my throat and took a sip from my glass while Eoghan took a bite of his food and Nya stared down at the table. She grew up with his presence, she knew his wrath and Eoghan…Eoghan, I realized quickly, simply didn't give a shit what Gedeon thought. If Eoghan wasn't the ruler of a kingdom my father seemed inclined to remain at peace with, I was almost positive he would be whipped into the air and thrown out the window. Then again, Eoghan had his own set of strengths that would make for an interesting battle between the two of them.

"The fire-wielder is still at large." Gedeon's voice was gritty, rough, as it rang through the dining hall. The whiteness of his knuckles was such a sheer contrast to the darkness of the table. I wondered, for a brief moment, whether the tips of his nails were drawing blood on his palms under the pressure. He paused a moment after, glancing between us all. Nya kept her head down, although she was brought up to speed on what had really happened that night. Eoghan told me I was a complete idiot for trusting anyone, even Nya, with the information. I knew if Aeden were here, he would have agreed with Eoghan on the necessity for such secrecy, even if he didn't like him. But I needed her to stay in my corner, and leaving her out of it felt...wrong.

Gedeon slammed his fist down on the table. All of the plates floated up above the table, Eoghan with his fork in his hand cocked an eyebrow at him. "You think *I* don't want that fucker up on your platform just as bad? He put Paige in danger, no doubt he wanted her cuffed and bagged." Gedeon's face dropped and the plates came crashing down, giving Eoghan a split second to curl his lip up at me. Nya turned red at the mention, her cheeks and neck looking warm to the touch.

Cuffed and bagged, he thought he was funny.

My father stood up and strode over to the large windows that overlooked a portion of one of his gardens as well as a portion of the city. "It's *odd* that he was able to...*escape* my grounds." He held his gaze up and out, looking beyond the glass as he clasped his fingers behind his back.

Eoghan opened his mouth to respond, but Nya whipped her wrist and a flower grew from his opened mouth before he had the chance to speak. "It is odd, sir. We should have tried to track him down ourselves, but—"

Gedeon turned, his gray eyes as sharp as knives. "But what, Nya? I took you in, gave you a home, and fed you after the death of your parents, and *this* is how you repay me?"

Her throat bobbed and Eoghan took the flower from his mouth and turned it to ash in his palm, then released the pieces to the floor. Gedeon didn't bat an eyelash in his direction, all of his rage was turned to the girl who had nothing to do with what happened that night. Eoghan folded his arms over his chest, waiting for whatever else would come from her mouth. "I was in my room, as I am supposed to be when events like that happen."

"Don't talk back to me, girl!" Gedeon's voice cracked through the air like a fine whip, making Nya flinch back in her seat. *Hell no.*

I gripped the edge of the table, my nails biting into the wood. "If you want to be an asshole to someone, let it be me. I could have done something, and seeing as I have more power than Nya and was actually at the ball, your anger should be directed at me. Not her."

Gedeon let the words sink in for a few seconds before finally twisting his lips into an evil grin. "Oh, you have power now, do you?"

Eoghan's posture remained calm and collected while his eyes darted back and forth as if he were telling me *no*. But all I could feel was, "Yes."

"Stand," he directed me, and I did. I pushed the chair back and kept my chin high. "You too." He looked to Nya, and without hesitation, she stood straight up, like a soldier waiting for a command, whereas my demeanor remained more...defiant.

Gedeon waved his wrist and everything on the table was whisked into the next room through the opened doors that shut abruptly once the items were through. "It's okay, I wasn't going to eat or anything." Eoghan rested his head on his chin, looking absolutely bored. He continued to play the part, keeping the peace between both of their kingdoms. This was more of an internal battle to be waged—between Gedeon and the two women who occupied his home.

"You say you have power, girl, then let me see. Show me what you can do to your *friend*." He chuckled darkly. He raised a finger, flicking it in Nya's direction. "And Nya, don't hold back. Show me all those years of training in my home, all those years of my hospitality, weren't a complete waste of my generous efforts." I hadn't seen Gedeon smile this much during one meal. And I wished I never had. It was something I could live without ever seeing—how happy brutality made him. My father. My own blood. If we didn't have the same exact marks on our arms, I would question it all. But after every piece of information I'd read about marks and how they formed, and the portrait of my mother in my bedroom, there was no one else who could be my father.

Unfortunately for me.

"Fight Nya? If you wanted to see me fight, all you had to do was walk out to the training deck while I was out there, as I am all damn day long, sparring and training to survive the Triad." It's the least, the very fucking least, he could do while I was still here. While I was still alive and being held within these walls. I gritted my teeth down. Hard. So hard, I thought they might break.

"Do you not think you will live? Does the desire to overthrow me not scorch through your veins as it did mine when I was your age?" He cocked his brow and Eoghan shifted uneasily in his chair.

"No," I stated simply. I didn't expect that I would come out of this alive. I would continue to hope that I would, though. But I also didn't have a burning desire to overthrow him. I didn't know what to do with a kingdom. Wouldn't know where to begin with that much power. I was struggling to adjust to the two marks I did have. At this point, I only wanted to forget this place ever existed and go back to Jessup and take Aeden safely with me, even if it was a pipe dream. It absolutely was a pipe dream. It was never going to be that simple again. But I couldn't tell him that much.

"Tsk tsk, children these days can be such a disappointment, wouldn't you agree, Eoghan?" Eoghan straightened his back in his seat, not attempting to answer him in any way. "What a shame. He could have been great, you know. But if I only have *her* left to work with, I want to see that something is coming from these training sessions." Eoghan gave me a slight nod and Gedeon released a laugh. "Begin!" *Wait, who was—*

Nya was quick to let out a burst of water, sending me off my feet and onto the rug. I looked up at her incredulously, but her eyes darted between Gedeon and me. She was going to fight.

She waited a few seconds, allowing me time to stand back up again as she spread her legs wider in a fighting stance. Her lips grew thin, her eyes staying trained on my movements. This is who she was to her core, a fighter through and through. She gave me a slight nod and I did the first thing that came to my mind. I began to run, sending a burst of air into my back to propel me into her. The wooden planks below the rug bent up and twined together to form a barricade just before I met with her body. The force of my air didn't stop and it sent me head-first into the wood. I stumbled backward while the wood fell back into place.

I let out a soft groan and saw Nya take a step toward me, her mouth dropping open an inch and worry lacing her eyes. "No," Gedeon said flatly. "Keep going." Nya rolled her shoulders back and put her fists up. I glanced at Eoghan, who met my eyes as he tilted his forehead to Nya, urging me to continue. I shot back up and charged again, this time sending air into Nya's back to force her to me. We collided, my fist curled tightly as I punched into her ribs and ducked beneath her. I flicked my wrist again, calling on the water I knew so little about but if anything was going to encourage it, this fight with my friend should do it. A sheet of ice formed under Nya's path, causing her to slip back. I waited a moment, allowing her the chance to regain her footing.

"Fight back, Nya, or I'll find another healer to replace you!" Gedeon was flushing with rage, the sharp contrast of his white blonde hair against his reddening cheeks catching my attention. The wooden planks rattled under my feet, and Nya was on top of me before I had a chance to blink. She sent punch after punch into my face and ribs, vines springing up to hold my wrists back.

Fight, you have to fight.

I struggled for gasps of air. My legs kicked under her, and I sprung them up and around her arms then up further around her neck just before she sent another punch into my jaw, catching her off guard. The vines ripped apart, setting my hands free as I shifted my body weight and pinned Nya to the floor. I released blocks of ice that crushed her hands, keeping her in place She blinked up at me as I hesitated, my fists raised. This is what Gedeon did. Gedeon put people against each other, demanding a winner. But I didn't want to win, I wanted it to be over. I got up from where I had her pinned and placed a foot on top of her chest. Flicking my wrist, I stole the air from her lungs—something I'd painfully practiced countless times doing to myself in my bedroom—and left Nya pinned, gasping for breath, and unable to move.

I looked at Gedeon, waiting for him to end it. Nya started to choke, her face turning a purplish hue. She was going to pass out any moment now.

"Kill her," he said.

Nya kicked and thrashed along the floor, trying to get out from underneath the ice, to claw at her throat, to run from what I was doing to her. Her eyes were turning red, bloody lines forming across them. She slowed, her limbs dropping and eyes lulling back. I jolted off of her, snapping out of whatever haze I was in, and sent as much air as I could summon back into her. She let out a cry, her lungs screaming out in agony and her chest heaving. I rushed to either side of her, trying to free her hands from the ice as I heard the door slam shut.

Just like that, Gedeon was gone.

I cupped Nya's face in my hands as she smiled weakly back up at me. "I'm so sorry, I didn't want to hurt you."

"I'm glad you tried. You're a lot stronger than you think." She let out a soft laugh, her breaths becoming normal. Heat surrounded the floorboards and I watched as the ice started to melt from her hands. I looked up to find Eoghan above us, his fire turning the ice into liquid pools on the floor.

"Thank you," I said.

"You're lucky he didn't kill her for you. He's always been an ass, but...the incident the other night must've set him off." Eoghan put out his hands to help us both off the floor. I flung my body into Nya, holding her tight, and she let out another soft laugh as she hugged me back lightly.

"I don't care what his reasoning was, he acted like a child." He *was* a child. A fucking child.

"And you are acting like a spoiled, insolent mutt." The door swung back open with Gedeon and Hector bursting through. Gedeon grabbed my arm and pulled me from Nya, then used his air power to hoist me against the wall. I was pinned and unable to move. I kicked the wall and tried to move my wrists but it was no use.

Gedeon walked slowly up to me like a cat stalking its prey. "If I say fight, you fight. If I say to kill, you kill. And if I fucking catch that fire-wielder, I'll make you watch as I cut him apart, piece by piece." My chest caved in. *He knows.*

"I don't know what you're talking about." I squirmed against the wall, trying to free my hands from the air that held them down, but it was no use.

"You think I'm a fool? I know he's the one who came through the portal with you!" His teeth barred, his breaths becoming faster. His fine leather boots clanked against the wood in heavy beats before he reached Hector, grabbed him by the collar, and dragged him back to me. "Hector, tell her what you saw."

"I'm sorry, sir, I—" Hector lost his words, his hand reaching up to pull the collar away from his throat. But it was no use. Gedeon's grip was firm—unyielding.

"Now!" Gedeon's patience was wearing thin.

"I saw him, the...the same boy from the night in the woods. He had a mark on his wrist, sir. It was red, sir. A fire mark." Hector was released, and he slumped to the ground.

"And, Hector, where was it you saw the boy again?" Gedeon asked, his brows raised high.

"Climbing down the castle wall, sir, after he left Ikelos' room."

"Hmm, yes, I wonder how he came across that particular room." Gedeon fixed his lethal gaze on Eoghan but only for a split-second before he whipped his head back to me. "Make no mistake, Paige. He will be caught, and he will be executed for his crimes."

"What crimes! Why do you hate them?" I shouted back, seething through my teeth.

He chuckled. "Such a naive girl. It's a pity you will die in the Triad. The people of Aellethia only just met you." Hector finished fixing himself as he returned to the perfect soldier. Gedeon turned and exited the room, and Hector followed.

Eoghan straightened himself up and attempted to leave as well, but I yanked a dagger from my boot and flung it right into the door, missing his neck intentionally by less than an inch. The dagger vibrated as it lodged into the wood. I was certain I'd never thrown so accurately before, but the adrenaline coursing through my veins was mixing with my power, making it heady and violent.

"He's going to kill him, and it's your fault! You told me he was safe!" Eoghan turned and put his hands in his pockets.

"I never promised *his* safety, Princess, only yours." He turned on his heels, my gaze not leaving his strides until they vanished when he left the room. The heavy doors closed with a loud thud behind him.

Nya rushed over to me, her bruises and scars completely healed as she examined me for any.

"Why do you have any faith in me? You *let* me pin you down. I don't stand a chance in the trial tomorrow." I tried to hold the tears back, tried to ignore my father's threats of killing Aeden and the betrayal I felt from Eoghan. Again. But it hurt. All of it. Aeden was right not to trust Eoghan. Why the hell did I always let my guard down?

Nya shook her head. "You are different, Paige. Eoghan sees it too. Don't let what Gedeon said make you believe you will fail, that you have no fight within you. If you do, well then, you've already lost."

Twenty-Nine

AEDEN

"Oh no no no. Start, damnit," a soft voice said while rough grinding and harsh snapping sounded nearby, all echoing into my throbbing head. Why was it that whenever I woke up in this place, my head had to be pounding? "Ooh yes! C'mon now, smoke up will ya!" The voice stayed low. Soft, yet high-pitched.

A girl.

Sunlight pierced into my eyes through thin slits as I sat up. My skin tugged coarsely over a rugged surface like sandpaper, and with that sensation came a quick panic as a realization that I was shirtless snapped into my thoughts.

"Don't move too fast, there. Those nagas got you pretty good." My eyelids grew heavy again, pain coursing through every part of my body, but the voice stayed calm and the snapping and grinding paused for a moment, then continued.

"Shirt...where is..." I managed to say through gritted teeth as I shrank back against...a tree, the bark scraping against my back and arms while the branches above cast shadows along my skin. *I'm still in the woods, then.*

"Here. All washed for ya. No one is dumb enough to come around these parts though, so you're safe. That's how we survive so well out here. The name is Murrie. Don't worry, you don't have to tell me your name yet. Those nagas really are a piece of work, good thing I never leave without my ax. It really is..." She went on and on, talking about nagas and dwarves and the Hollow Woods and *High Fae bastards*, as she called them. It was all too much to take in, and with the ringing in my ears, it was hard to hear most of what she said. I reached around, my palms searching, feeling the roots of the tree lacing up and cradling me. My focus narrowed in again as she continued, "...and those branches, they just came right up in the middle of the night while you were calling out for someone..."

"Paige!" I clutched onto the roots, trying to heave myself up, but I failed miserably. So much pain coursed through my body at the sudden movement, making me dizzy again. Nausea rolled over me, the overwhelming sensation of—

"Might want to turn your head if you're going to barf." So I did. The girl let out a laugh as I steadied myself, wiping my mouth with the back of my hand. "That will all go away soon."

A silence stretched between us as I lulled my head back against the tree.

"Your name is Paige? I wouldn't take you for a...Paige." She paused, drawing in a sharp breath as she looked me over. "Those nagas poisoned you with their venom, and I'm pretty sure that bump on your head isn't helping. I was just trying to start a fire, make a brew for your leg and head, but I suck at making fires. My friend back at—"

"Mm...Murrie, right?" I cut her off as I flexed my fingers over my pulsating leg, swollen and red, a clean round wound marking the place the naga dug its fang into me. "I'm Aeden. Exactly how long have I been out for?" My breath hitched and my pulse quickened as the thought of being out for longer than I had time for sent a shock wave of anxiety through me. I needed to find Seamus and Shay, make sure they were okay, and find my way back to the place where Eoghan would let me back into the castle for Paige's first trial. And the damn sun was starting to rise. There was no ti—

"Aeden, got it. I found you two nights ago. You were out for a day, which gave me time to clean you up a bit and drag you away from the dead nagas. Once they start rotting, they stink! Have you ever sm—"

"Murrie." A tinge of bile rose to my throat again at the thought of rotting corpses and their smell. I held up my hand, and she dropped her small shoulders, falling silent. She was very small, actually, with a rather giant battle ax strapped to her back. I rubbed my eyes to clear the massive brain fog that faded in and out of my vision, but her short stature of maybe three or four feet didn't change. *A child?* My eyes burned as I rubbed at them over and over, glancing at the trees and the sunlight that pierced through the dense coverage they provided as I tried to reconcile my internal clock with being out for a full fucking day. *Shit.* If I was out for a full day, that gave me only two days to get back. And Eoghan had made it very clear, the portal would be there at sunrise. And I was hardly in a position to move, every inch of my skin tight and sodden with a pain I'd never felt before.

Her eyes darted around as her mouth remained taut, probably thinking of all the things she wanted to keep talking about. Her eyes fell still on something and I followed them to find my shirt as it hung on one of the branches that cradled me. I let out a heavy sigh and reached back for it, but instead failed at that too as I winced and let out a groan. My leg was fucked and the black uniform pants were torn, exposing where the naga succeeded in filling me with poison, and it hurt to twist or turn my body.

Murrie bolted upright, leaving behind a stick and a small pile of dried grasses as she gathered my tattered purple guard's tunic for me. She ran up and placed it over my knee, patting it in place for good measure before she returned to her spot. She glanced back at me as she teetered on the balls of her feet before crouching down and moving for her stick again.

"I'm not a guard." My voice came out coarse, my throat dry. But all she did was say *mmm* like she knew that already. Of course, she did. What Prydian guard would have a fire-wielder mark?

I smoothed my hand over the flames on my arm with an uneasiness that was more from the knowledge that Murrie had seen my mark than it was from the amount of pain that I was in. The tunic lay flat across my stomach because there was no way I'd be able to tug the thing on over my head. So, I gave up. I had been shirtless and exposed for an entire day. There would be no point in trying to claim I was anything other than what was already so obvious. She knew about the marks, *and* had seen the flames crawling up my arm. *She had washed me.* Her grunts continued as she struggled and without thinking further about it, I moved my wrist, sucking in a sharp breath as my muscles writhed under the suddenness of my movements. A small flame flickered to life in the pit she was trying to light herself, causing Murrie to shriek out and clap in delight. I let out a pained laugh as relief washed over me, seeing that for once someone wasn't afraid of me and the fire tattoo sprawling up my arm. She...enjoyed it. Valued it, even.

It was...odd. It was the first time since I'd been here, since the mark formed along my skin, that I didn't feel like I didn't belong. Seamus and Shay did their best, but the way they looked at me sometimes... "All you had to do was ask, you know," I said, clutching at my ribs and the hurt that radiated there just from fucking laughing.

She blinked back at me and her brow furrowed. "My dad always said it was rude to ask for a fae's help, let alone a High Fae." That was the second time now someone told me I was *High Fae.* Like I was somehow better than others, and it felt wrong. She opened her mouth to continue, but instead, she raised a finger in the air and shot up again, taking off faster than I'd ever seen someone capable of. I wasn't even that fast, and I was trained for years on my running speed.

"Wait! Come back! I didn't mean to scare you!" I yelled but then fell back against the tree in pain. My hands turned to fists as I braced myself, trying desperately to ignore the pain coursing through my body. Leaves started to rustle, the sounds of movement growing closer and closer.

I attempted to stand again, using my earth magic to move the roots of the tree to stabilize me, something I wasn't even sure I was capable of but seeing the cradle I was in before had me casting all doubt aside as to how powerful I could be. How much control I could have over the powers that felt chaotic within me. The roots bent and lengthened, but the sensation of moving my body shot daggers into my flesh and muscles. I fought back the desire to scream out in pain, not wanting to give away my location to anything else that might've been in the woods. If they hadn't already heard my yell.

Fuck, that was dumb.

I held up my fists, ready to fight off whatever was coming, the dense trees and brush making it hard to see beyond the small area Murrie had left me in. The rustling noise intensified to a crescendo, and just before I unleashed a wall of fire, or would have tried to at least, Murrie reappeared. Behind her, she dragged along a giant branch covered in purple leaves. She wasn't straining under the weight of the branch, and my eyebrow cocked up as I watched her. She was oddly strong for her size and age. Threateningly so.

"That brew for your leg, it needs this," she said. The ground rumbled when she heaved the branch over to the fire and released it to the ground, then settled into her position in front of the pit and began to strip the branch bare of leaves. She acted as if what she'd just done, how fast she'd just run and her strength in toting along that branch, was all completely normal. I didn't know how far she actually went, so maybe I only saw her sprinting to the area right behind the trees. I could have imagined the ground shaking under the weight, the vibrations moving up to where I sat cradled in the branches. Maybe it was the poison making her appear impossibly fast through my hazy eyes.

My shoulders sagged and I fell back against the tree, releasing a shaky breath. I pushed away the thoughts, the imaginings of a poisoned, injured man. "I thought you ran from me, most people are afraid of…" I motioned at my arm, to which she gave a slight nod but continued to fix her focus on the branch as she plucked the leaves carefully and formed a pile of them beside the fire.

"Us Dwarves tend to distance ourselves from your Fae politics. It's why we live here, in the Hollow Woods. Most common Fae are too afraid to enter, and we get to live in peace. Well, mostly in peace. Without the Fae, we still have a bunch of other things to worry about but it's a lot better than worrying about which kingdom is fighting with who or where. Ever since the Battle of Vizna, that is. Well, some of the dwarves chose to side with Prydia and Hydrasel for that battle in particular, and by *some*, I mean very few, but Buryon hasn't gotten involved in years, and—"

"Prydia…" The words spewed from my lips like venom. I knew I should have focused more on my own heritage, and even hearing the name Vizna sent a shiver down my spine, something I knew I couldn't keep dodging for as long as I had been. But *fucking* Prydia. The kingdom that was forcing Paige into some twisted game that she shouldn't have to be involved in. If moving weren't damn near impossible, I'd be over that wall right now, finding a way to get back to her.

"Yeah, Prydia. Gruesome, evil man, that Gedeon, you know?" She spoke so openly as if she knew what she was saying was treason, yet didn't care. But another glance at my mark formed an agreement between us both. She knew I'd be in the same position—that our feelings toward the Lord of Prydia were mutual. If my marks weren't an indicator, then surely my tone when I said the kingdom's name was enough. "If we weren't so close to

Prydia, I would feel safer, like we all used to be. Well, it *is* peaceful here still in comparison but—"

"Do you know where I can find a shack?" I blurted out, flexing my fingers in an attempt to numb the pain. If I could just get back there...but fuck, it hurt to move. I clenched my jaw and continued. "It's run down, close to the wall of Prydia."

Her brows pinched together in thought as she plucked more and more leaves, seemingly at war within herself. "I think so. Maybe. Most *things* stay away from the wall unless you're a naga and you want to eat whatever is stupid enough to come near th—" I cleared my throat and curled the corner of my lip up in acknowledgment. It was me. *I* was stupid enough to go near the wall again. And apparently, Eoghan thought it would be a nice welcome for me to land there, a place full of nagas and death and destruction. I *knew* trusting him was a fucking mistake. Hopefully, he wasn't lying about the portal. But I would have to take my chances with that.

She finished plucking the leaves and pushed them into a black pot, liquid sloshing as she placed it over the fire.

"Aren't you afraid to have a fire burning? I mean, won't people, or *things,* come looking?" I asked, uncertain if she was just dense in the head or if her ax skills were so far advanced that she didn't give a damn about drawing things to us. Perhaps the combination of both is what made them ideal allies in the Battle of Vizna.

She guffawed and poked the pot's contents with a stick, her brown knotted-up hair bobbing with the movement and her childlike features burning bright against the fire. Her rosy, small cheeks and narrow pointed chin led me to believe that she couldn't be more than ten. A very short ten-year-old at that. "Why would I be afraid? If anything I'm proud that I tried to light it before you went all"—she wiggled her hands in the air—*"Hey look at me with my flames* on the firepit. You're lucky you have powers to help you, but we who *don't* have it still manage to light our own fires and build our own homes and move our own things with our arms and legs and—"

"I wouldn't call this luck, but I get it. We're all pretentious assholes, and you are more than capable." I smiled softly at her. She looked like a child, innocent and small. But she spoke as if she were older. Wiser, even. "Murrie, I don't mean to be rude"—I glanced at the ax on her back and my throat went dry—"how old are you?"

"Forty-six, and I know that still makes me basically a youngling but I'm well trained. Promise. I don't go anywhere without my ax." She squeezed the handle of her ax as it lay holstered across her back like she was commending a friend for doing a good deed.

My eyes widened, the light piercing through harshly before I lowered my head and rubbed the back of it carefully along the wound. "You saved my life, and I didn't wake up tied to this tree. I can't thank you enough for your kindness, regardless of your age." She was older than I was but aged just as slowly as the Fae all did. I wondered if every living being aged slowly here, with nothing but battle or being killed at the hand of someone else preventing them from living hundreds, or thousands, of years.

She nodded again and stirred the pot calmly, pressing her lips together as if her mouth didn't run five hundred miles a minute like her feet did. "You're uh, pretty fast. Is that how you saved me last night or was I just *lucky* that you were in the area?" I questioned, idly picking up a small leaf among the roots and started slowly ripping it apart, piece by piece, consciously aware that every passing minute was a minute less that I had to get to the portal, to subsequently find Seamus and Shay and get back to the castle again whenever I could, to her. But I couldn't seem too eager to leave. Murrie had saved me, and we may have held similar views, but I never trusted anyone that quickly.

"You hit your head hard there, didn't you? Dwarves are fast by nature, and we *live* here, remember? I mean, I told you that, but I'm sure they taught you all about it in the fancy schools you grew up going to. The High Fae spare no expense at teaching their children the best." She wagged her finger at me. "It's amazing that they still pit them against each other, trying to make them the next *Mora* like it's some kind of consolation prize to hate your siblings, or kill them off, or even when the parents kill their own kin. The Stars may be twisted, but—"

"Murrie, the Mora of Prydia. Gedeon. What do you know about him?" I crunched the last leaf in my palm, dropping the incinerated bits and ashes to the forest floor. And maybe because she liked the sound of her voice too much, or it was the way my tone remained unaltered as I rubbed at my concussed wound that concealed nothing from my memory by sheer fucking luck, hiding how little I actually knew—we were just sharing information, after all—she told me.

She talked of his eagerness to kill, the cruel way he enforced the law, and increasing his kill count, making a show of it as I'd seen on the platforms. For someone who negated Fae politics, she knew quite a lot. She spoke of his son, how he failed and lost his Triad and now another girl, his newly found daughter, was there to try her luck. Murrie continued on and on, naming countless ways Gedeon was proved to be a tyrant, yet no one did a damn thing about it. Populations all across Aellethia either favored him highly or hated his guts. But most of all, he was feared. Greatly.

"My family, friends, neighbors, a lot of us gathered to fight against him, knowing his proximity to our home was too close for comfort, and no one trusted his intentions anymore after we caught wind of an ensuing battle. We fought with Vizna, and Vizna fell. Now if we leave the Hollow

Woods and go anywhere near Prydia, we may get killed the same way those wielders do, the ones like you." She looked me over again, then poured the contents of the pot into a leather pouch, adding a drop of something from a small vial from her satchel she carried, and brought it over to me. "Here. Drink this. You won't hurt so bad anymore afterward. In a few hours, you should be able to move your legs more. It's an antivenom, along with a bit of healing water from my village for the wounds on your body." I looked her over, and although she looked innocent and seemed to mean well, I wasn't sure I should be trusting her. And with as many parties as I'd attended since going to college, I knew accepting drinks from people you didn't fully trust was a huge no-no. "If you don't drink it, you'll most likely die. Unless you're a healer and you don't remember being one?" She cocked her eyebrow at me, her orange eyes lighting up with the thought.

"No, I don't believe I'm a…uh…*healer.*" I was skillful in a lot of things, but none of those would pass for what I could only assume a healer could do. The one time I cut my hand open and needed tending to, Paige had been the one to help. She shrugged as I took the drink from her, gulping it down in a swift motion before I could convince myself otherwise.

Pain no longer consumed my every breath, every movement. It was going away, just as Murrie said it would, a few hours after I took the leap of faith. She gave me food— berries, and a squirrel or a rabbit. I wasn't sure because by the time she got back from hunting and I woke up again it was already skinned. My body ached when she helped me stand and move over by the fire, talking on and on, while trying to heal me with more antivenom and healing water doses. Murrie talked about her friends, hunting, and how she learned to work with her ax—because she caught me glancing at the weapon several times. I hadn't met anyone so damn talkative before but I didn't have the heart to tell her to stop and the few bits of history and knowledge of this land would more than likely end up helping me one day.

So I listened. I watched. I became the student to an unknowing teacher. Her words became the crutch to my instability. Each time I found myself slipping, my body demanding I rest, I instead shifted my focus to the words that continued from her mouth. Even if they were nonsense at times or made absolutely no sense to me.

Murrie made a paste from the same leaves she used in the antivenom, working it into a purple mush and mixing in a fine powder, similar visually to what the fae at the caravans had been using to get high, from a small bag she carried over her shoulder. Before she applied it, she suggested I bite down on a stick, to which I declined.

I couldn't have been more wrong.

Whatever she put on me burned hotter than anything I'd ever felt. I was seething through my teeth and trying hard not to yell, but a biting cold spread through my veins as my body tried to combat the unwelcomed heat and a moment later a flurry of snow fell around us, dampening the fire I had lit before in the pit.

"Didn't they teach you how to control all of that from day one?" She lifted her arm above her head to block the swirling snow as she finished applying the remainder of the paste.

"No." I sucked in a sharp breath through my teeth, trying to keep my focus on slowing the storm and not the agony that was tearing through my skin. I wasn't ready to let her know what should have been obvious had I not gotten a head wound that did nothing to my memory. The concussion

I suffered was slight. I'd had worse happen to me when I first started to play football well before I moved to Jessup. Not that Murrie knew how unaffected I was.

Aellethia was as new to me as I was to her. I wasn't raised here, and my teachings so far were more on how to use my power. We barely touched on history unless I pressed, and even those few times were centered on telling me just how unwanted *my kind* were in this place. Control was a part of what I was learning, but I wasn't great at it yet. Actually, I really fucking sucked at it.

I could hear Seamus' rough voice and accent as I recalled a few of the things he did focus on as we walked for hours on end—*hide your fire lad, learn to show only the rest in small bits. Don't kill us all Boyo. Here's a sword, let's see you try to hit me with it.* I didn't expect him to be the best teacher, but he was all I had. And he was trying, which was something I couldn't say about anyone who signed up to try to raise me before. They wanted me for the money that came along with taking in a foster. But, Seamus? He hadn't asked for anything, and he clearly had his own money.

She finished bandaging my leg, weaving it through the tear I assumed she made instead of stripping me bare. I sat and tried to get rid of all the snow, regaining composure slowly as I waded through the magic that resided inside of me, looking for an answer. But I continuously failed, knowing the only thing I could confidently do was melt the snow faster by possibly setting everything on fire. I did, however, light another small fire for her as she pushed the snow away from us, and every bit of elation I felt before as I lit the first fire for her died with my inability to turn solid water into liquid and send it deep into the earth before it melted and drenched the soil around us. "See? I'm plenty capable without your powers," she said, straining to move the piles of snow away from us toward a slope that led into a small stream. I wanted to move, to help her, but the paste she applied was...it was fucking brutal. When I did push through the pain that spiked with the ointment, trying to move from the cradling branches, she held up her hand to stop me.

I grunted as I chuckled. "I can see that." Then I added, "More capable than me it would appear." Surprised would be a bad word to describe how I felt about her capabilities. It was inspiring because beyond how capable she was, she was also...kind. That was what stood out to me. For all the times Aellethia spat in my face, it did keep leading me into the hands of people who were kind.

It wasn't long ago that I didn't have magic to try to make my day-to-day life any easier. But my life hadn't been nearly as complicated as it was now—in hindsight, that is—and even the notion of shoveling fucking snow made me reach for the very thing I was very unacquainted with, making me feel damned useless when it didn't work the way I needed it to. In such a short time, it had become a crutch. "If you live *here*, how do you know so much about what goes on out *there*?" I asked as she wiped the snow and dirt from her hands.

"Stars, you know we *can* leave the forest. We just have to be careful around Prydia, is all. There are places we can go beyond Prydia that aren't so vile to us. You, of all Fae, should know that. We were friends with Vizna, most of us at least, but we weren't the only ones who stood by their side. Lots of dwarves, centaurs, and of course they had their dragons. The Mora did—have dragons that is—and her few family members that were left. Don't you remember it? Surely you were in the fight, what are you? Probably hundreds of years old, no doubt..." She looked me over, then crossed her arms across her chest, "you *are* from Vizna, aren't you? One of the territories? I don't remember the names of the High Fae families, but there were quite a few. I don't know how you lived this long, running from Prydia but, hey, we have lasted a long time out here too." She pushed more snow away, needing only a small inhale to continue. "I've heard there were camps but I hadn't ever seen any. Places for them to keep hidden, lay low, and re—" She stopped again, my leg stretched out and my elbow bent back into the snowy dirt. I waited, unsure how much I needed her to know but also not entirely sure of how much she knew just from looking at me. "How old are you?" Her eyebrow cocked just over her shoulder, snow cascading over the edges of her palms as they rested. They were so red from the cold, sending a wave of uselessness through me that I hadn't felt since...since Paige's mother died. The uselessness I felt when I left her back at the castle was another beast entirely of its own.

I rubbed the back of my head, pretending to wince at the head injury that was mostly just a small bump now. "I don't know...I lost count," I lied, knowing damn well I hadn't lost any portion of my memories and feeling slightly guilty for keeping up that lie. I'd only hoped she wouldn't question me further about whether I fought in the battle or not.

She raked her hands through the snow and continued working it over the edge of the slope down toward the small stream, putting out her arm and not glancing away from her work when I attempted to move near her to help again. She was damn persistent. I was still hurt, but I could help, if only she weren't so prideful, so...headstrong.

Paige would like her.

"Your head will get better soon, maybe then you will remember that number for me? It isn't polite to ask a lady her age and not answer her back when she asks, but you Fae are so predictable. After the first hundred years, you all simply forget your age. You all need to learn to appreciate life more! It drives Dwarves crazy. We all party every year on our day of birth—you should see the..." Birthday. It would be Paige's birthday, soon. She continued talking and pushing snow, hauling more efficiently than most would have, but I tuned a lot of it out. My thoughts kept drifting back to where they always did, only now I knew what she tasted like, what parts of her body felt like in my hands.

Murrie mentioned Gedeon yet again and pulled me from my thoughts faster than the snow had fallen around us. She *believed* me, believed the lies, even of omission, as I sat there listening to her words. The shine of her broad ax glistened against her back and reminded me that she could take me out if she wanted to. I would need to be careful with anymore lies around her. Very fucking careful. She did, after all, take out three nagas *and* take my limp body back to safety.

And she didn't have a single scratch on her.

The next day, my leg was usable. It could take the brunt of the weight I put on it, and movement wasn't nearly as painful.

Murrie slept by the fire while I laid, cradled, and suspended in the roots I'd woven together that first night. I didn't sleep much. I could swear I felt Paige near me in the few moments I did sleep, but every single time the feeling came, I awoke, panting and drenched in sweat. There was no use in trying to sleep. So I listened to the things around me and hoped more nagas wouldn't find us in the area of the woods we were in. Seeing how fast Murrie could move and the weight of the ax she toted without swaying, and knowing she alone moved my limp body to this place, there was no telling how far we were from where I was portaled to. The only sounds were the trickling of water from the stream, the crackling flames, and the snores that escaped Murrie as she dozed, oddly peacefully, tucked up against a tree opposite me.

Guided only by the faint slivers of silvery moonlight, I slumped out from the branches and limped down to the stream. I was trapped and dependent, yet again, on someone else. Feelings of helplessness returned, similar to how I frequently felt as a child—trapped in the endless cycle of families not wanting me, of them never caring for me or about me.

I was *a pathetic excuse for a child,* the remark something I'd often heard right before I was shifted into a new home, a new environment of a family with children of their own. The homes, schools, and peers may have changed, but the situation never did. Being wanted was foreign to me, that is until I moved far away and became my own person. I quickly became wanted by everyone once my football career took off, but they only wanted a piece of me. Women wanted my body, coaches wanted my ability. But Paige? She wanted all of me. At least, I thought she did.

A hand holding a stick reached just over my shoulder and on instinct I crooked my arm back, lifting the person in the air and flinging the body down in front of me. It was Murrie. She coughed, putting a hand to her chest but giggling slightly. "It seems you did have *some* training, then. I'm not going to hurt you, though, so can you release me? Please?" I didn't realize I'd kept my forearm pinned down against her chest as she spoke. As I withdrew, she grunted, then rose up from the ground and brushed off her knees.

"I'm sorry, I thought you were...something else." A naga, or something entirely else that lived in the woods. Possibly the Mora who'd sent me to the woods, hoping I'd be worm food right about now. I blinked back the haze of what it, or who, it could have been. "I figured you would be asleep for a while," I said, shrugging my shoulders as she situated herself next to me.

"The sun will be up soon, so it's better that I'm up now." She smiled. "I see you're feeling better," she added, then she crouched beside me and began to draw in the dirt.

I followed the lines, the triangular shapes and circles—"A map?" I asked.

"Yeah, you don't seem like you know where you are still, and I guess I can't really blame you." Her tone, the way she was eyeing my face—she was unconvinced, at best. "If you fought years ago with us, maybe you just forgot or maybe…" she stopped, ostensibly questioning her own thought process before I cut in.

"I don't travel this far from where I live, normally." I tried to play it off, but I had a feeling she could see through my bullshit lies. No, I knew she could, because her eyes were narrowing into thin slits, and yet there was no sun to wince from. I could bluff my way past guards in Prydia because putting on a personality facade was something I grew used to. But talking about Aellethia and acting like I knew a damn thing was proving to be much harder.

"Yeah, no. Of course." She shook out her head and pointed at the sand, choosing to ignore it. "This is the Hollow Woods. And this"—she drew a circle—"is where we are about now in relation to Prydia, which is somewhere you do seem familiar enough with." Another glance up at me with a lifted brow, checking for understanding or for me to reveal more about myself. I nodded, remaining silent while she continued. "Your shack should be somewhere here, I think. I'm not a hundred percent sure of that, but that's my guess. We don't go that way much because of the, well, the nagas. They love that area. How did you get here anyway?"

I looked down at her map, trying to memorize as much as I could. She had drawn Costa and Lake Kree, another kingdom far from where we were on an island far off into the ocean I saw from Costa, and other places I'd heard of from Seamus and Shay. It wasn't intricate, but it was enough detail to further my understanding of where I was, with quickly labeled scribbles for each place. The area south from here was rather vague, and I wondered if that was all barren lands or if she didn't know that area well, or maybe she was just finished drawing.

"I was traveling, and lost track of how far I'd gone. I think I confused the woods for...another one." Another lie. I couldn't trust she would be okay with being portaled, or that she wouldn't try to kill me if I had anything to do with a kingdom she described as siding with Prydia in the battle against where I supposedly came from. A battle she fought in and lost.

"Right. Traveling. In a guard's uniform, but you aren't a guard." She glazed over the purple tunic I finally managed to shrug on. Maybe she was used to sketchy crap like that, people in disguise, staying hidden in a false uniform. She had been in battle before, after all. She sat down beside me and released a heavy sigh. "You're not going to make it easily down to the shack, but I know a better healer than myself. He lives in my village, not far from here. We can go there and you can get fixed up," Murrie suggested, but I shook my head.

"No, I don't have time. I will be fine." I pointed at the map, flinching as I bent over my thigh. The swelling had gone down tremendously, but the bandage dipped where the fang had dug into my flesh. It was a wonder as to how I didn't bleed out from it. My finger fell to the spot that marked the shack. "How long will it take to get there?"

"We can get there by tomorrow, assuming we will be walking and not running. I would try to carry you again but I digress, I'm a bit too short to carry someone like yourself, and I...I *may have* dragged you here. You probably hit your head a few more times than I want to admit, and had your wound not been cauterized internally I wouldn't have attempted the haul. But, sure enough, you managed to cauterize yourself at some point. Must be that *luck* of yours, eh?" Her shoulder nudged mine, but she quickly cleared her throat, unsure of how I would respond to everything she'd said.

Murrie hadn't caused the wound on the back of my head. She hadn't caused any of the pain I felt. "It's okay, I can't blame you for trying." I studied the map further, taking note of how long it took to walk from Costa to Prydia and the distance between where we were in the forest to the shack. It was an utter wonder how I didn't see anyone on horseback in Costa, but perhaps their main methods of travel were small boats or ships, and they stuck to moving out west rather than going east toward Prydia. Oddly, I hadn't seen many people traveling at all, just the caravans of fae, but they probably remained in that area with their wagons and drugs and alcohol. And yet, I had traveled and apparently ended up walking aimlessly into the wrong woods? There was no way my story was believable. It was so terrible, it was fucking laughable. I would've laughed, too, had I not realized how fucked we might be on time if I couldn't move as well as we both hoped I could.

Murrie snapped her fingers together and her face lit up. "Actually, I have a better plan." She went to work fast, denying my help when she began twisting vines. She worked fast, her fingers weaving as her legs wound around the branches she gathered. The night sky had turned to day above us by the time she finished. "This should do it. We can leave before dawn tomorrow. Any earlier, and we might get caught by naga, or worse. It's best to travel in daylight when it comes to nagas, and with this"—she gestured at the stretcher—"we should only take about an hour or so. When did you need to be there, again?"

I couldn't hide the grin that spread across my face as I stared between her and the stretcher she created from branches and woven vines, a bed of moss covering the center. Hope filled me at the sight, the realization of what she was suggesting dawned on me well before the stretcher was completed.

"Sunrise."

Thirty

PAIGE

I laced my boots over and over, uncertain if they were too tight or too loose for the first trial, even though they had never bothered me before. The leather of my clothing was constricting, making it hard to breathe. Refraining from loosening it all, I bent my head over my bed, a book opened to a page that described one of the previous trials from hundreds of years ago. The book was composed of every kingdom's failed attempts, mostly ending in the death of a nameless would-be ruler. Very rarely did a fae make it out with their life once they failed, and if they did, they were either executed for their methods of living through the failed trial—seen as cheating and no one accepted a ruler who would cheat—or sent to Sentra, the training place of all guards, to become just that. Going to Sentra was like jumping from the top straight to the bottom of the hierarchy, living most of your life, or a chunk of it, in servitude to a Mora. For someone raised to be in a position of power, it was worse than a death sentence. The very reality of the Triad was evidence of a void of any compassion that a parent should have for their child, but it was a part of who the Fae were and who they had been for over a thousand years. Gedeon was no exception, and it made my heart twinge with sympathy for a moment because he, too, had gone through the same process. But then I remembered the grotesque way in which he almost craved pain and torture like it was deeper than how he was raised.

It was in his blood.

My blood.

I shook my head and pulled my eyes from the book, closing it and hiding it away beneath the bed. I moved to the dresser, where I had been storing small daggers and throwing stars, and tucked them discreetly away into my boots and pockets, just in case. Though weapons were given when the trial started, I didn't know what weapons the Stars would provide, and I knew my best bet was with the ones I'd been practicing with the most. After all, my precision and aim had increased tenfold since I'd arrived, hitting dead-center more often than not and taking Nya and Eoghan by surprise more than once.

Yet the trials were more than just a simple fight, and where others had failed, it was clear they lacked some important facets in their teachings. The trials were known as a test of each individual part that made up a Mora on the outside, and that was what training had looked like for the majority. *Learn to strike fast and hard, kill everything*—techniques were always aimed at the offensive side. Future leaders were strong in their fighting abilities, and powers of their original nature and not. Each trial in the Triad also tested your knowledge, endurance, willpower, and would potentially play with your morals—if you had any. Most went in cocky, arrogant, and certain their strength would get them through to the end. But I'd grown up under different circumstances than someone who had no daily struggles beyond the ones we all fought internally, and I had to learn how to survive essentially on my own from an early age.

The trials were no different in that aspect.

Where so many were keen on destroying everything in the arena, I knew the end-all would need more than something that would require *just* brawn. I could only hope the Stars kept that much intact for my trials.

Gedeon may have been right in thinking I wouldn't be strong enough, but he would be damned wrong in thinking I wouldn't find out how to play by their rules.

No one knew what the trial would be today, only that it would aim to test my strength in fighting without powers. Use any powers or gifts—if you had one as it was a rarity on its own—and you were pulled, unable to complete the Triad. It meant death or servitude, or as I was told, *stripping my powers* and being banned. It was whatever the Mora saw fit to do, and my father was no savior.

I reached into the dresser once more, the edges of the metal frame that held my mother's portrait scraping against my fingers as I shuffled to the bottom. I stilled, contemplating on indulging in the pain that thoughts of my mother always led to. I bunched up a tunic and smothered the frame, sending it to the bottom of the dresser, and pulled Aeden's bracelet up instead. I looped it around my wrist and pushed my tunic sleeve down quickly to cover it. I'd been keeping it completely hidden since Eoghan had given it to me, holding it close in any pocket or flap of clothing that wouldn't expose it. But something told me to wear it—if not for the fear of dying and leaving behind any evidence of him, then for the desire to be close to Aeden during the trial. He wanted me to have it, so I would feel like he was with me even when he couldn't be. A wash of calm rolled over me as the cold metal slid down my wrist and fell into place.

I will live to see him again.

A knock sounded, followed by the soft taps of boots on the wooden floor as the door swung open. I turned to see Eoghan and Nya, their frames outlined in dark shadows and firelight.

"You ready, Princess?" Eoghan asked, a wry smile spreading across his face. I hated the nickname and wanted to reach into my boot and fling one of the daggers I had tucked away right into his pristine teeth, but that would reveal my hidden stash.

"What difference does it make to you?" I urged my breathing to remain calm, reminding myself that he wasn't worth the effort. His allegiance hung in the air, and with the way that he skewed the truth or eliminated facts, his presence wasn't sitting well with me. I couldn't take him for his word when he'd told me that Aeden had escaped the grounds with his life. There was something he wasn't telling me, and I was tired of receiving half-truths and information that had holes in it. But I still dreamt about Aeden every night and felt him close. He was still alive, but whether he was safe or not was unknown, and it made me crazy.

Nya approached me, grabbing my forearms and looking me over. She could heal wounds and any scars, but as far as I could tell, she could not eliminate anxiety, although it looked as if she were trying to. "Stay focused in the arena. Don't let fear take over, and don't get distracted by the audience. They love a good show, but you aren't there to give them a show. You are there to win."

Her eyes darted around me as I rolled my lips inward and nodded, and then she fell back into step with Eoghan, who cleared his throat and motioned for her to exit the room. She pursed her lips, keeping in whatever thoughts she had on the matter before I inclined my head, prompting her to leave the room. When the door closed behind her, Eoghan strode closer, his boots mere pinpricks against the floor. Seconds passed, then a few more before I spoke, desperation seeping from my words as I asked, "Is he going to make it to the arena?"

Eoghan clasped his hands behind his back, then shrugged his shoulders. "I don't know." His jaw clenched as his gaze fell to the window that overlooked the darkened city, covered in nothing but moonlight and the dim flickering of candlelight. He grazed his hand across his stubble and relented. "I think that wherever he is, he will try everything in his power to be there."

"Just where *exactly* did you take him? How do I know you didn't get him killed, or do it yourself?" I choked on the words, holding back tears and aggravation, trying desperately not to flick out some of my power at him, even though it was futile. I stood no chance against him.

His eyes flicked to meet mine, the red light of the fire dancing across his blue eyes like a storm cloud floating across the sky. "What good is he to me if he's dead? Do you really think I am that cruel?" Eoghan asked, sounding as if I actually did unleash some of the air from my fingertips into his gut.

"What use would you have of him if he's alive?" I countered, my power swirling in a fury under my flesh, wishing it had been the real reason he looked so pained.

Unclasping his hands and taking another step forward, his eyes fell to mine, searching for something there until he blinked. His voice came in a whisper, inches from my face as he dipped low. "Don't play games with me, Paige. You know his life has great value. Not only to you but to me as well."

I flexed my fingers as they itched to slap across his face for getting that close to me, but his words were spreading into my thoughts like ink seeping into paper, the sincerity of his voice sending shivers down my spine as he looked me over and cocked his brow.

"Ah, so you do know, don't you?" he purred, a smirk pulling at the corner of his mouth. "Tell me, since it couldn't possibly be found in any book you've found in the library, was it Hector who unknowingly gave you the missing piece of information? Or did I walk in on you two *after* you'd seen him fully naked?" I blushed at the thought before I tamped it down and rage unfurled from me. I wasn't sure before if Eoghan had taken notice of when Hector stated he'd seen flames on Aeden's wrist, until now. We'd both seen the fiery mark on his neck, there was no denying I figured out that his entire arm was covered in a fire-wielder's mark. And when I asked Aeden about it, he didn't agree, nor did he deny it. And that was answer enough in itself. But Eoghan wasn't there for that part of our conversation, and I didn't need to share my insights with him. I couldn't trust what he'd do with what I knew. Even though that was all pointless in trying to conceal. He was piecing things together, just as I had.

"He must've been so thrown when he saw you, if he didn't have that final air mark before the party, I'm sure you were the cause." His smile grew cat-like as my breathing stopped. "Oh, you didn't know?" He rubbed at his jawline, playing with the coy smile on his face as he took in my shock. Aeden was like us, only he'd formed every mark without entering the Triad.

My gut sank to the floor, thinking what the information could mean to Eoghan. To anyone who wasn't so blindingly in love with him to conceal anything that may hurt him. What he was...it was a death sentence. But what it could mean for the world? *This* world? I could only imagine. "He isn't a pawn you can use whenever you please," I gritted out through my teeth.

"A pawn? No. He isn't a pawn, Princess. He's the whole damn board." Eoghan grinned ear to ear, sending more chills throughout my body.

"This goes nowhere. No one can know. Please..." I pleaded, and Eoghan drew his pinched fingers across his lips, throwing away the proverbial key.

A knock sounded, shattering my thoughts and Nya rasped through the door, "Company is coming any minute now." Her footsteps faded down the hallway as she abandoned the door, possibly avoiding a repeat of what had happened the last time she was caught treating me with any decency.

Eoghan straightened himself, losing the grin that held the secret of the only person I had left to love. "Now that we are seeing eye-to-eye, I came here to warn you. This trial is going to be difficult for you. I won't act like it isn't going to possibly claim your life." He examined me, his brow furrowing. "Do you have the bracelet?"

I moved my hands to the back pockets of my pants. "Why would I—"

Eoghan cut in hurriedly. "Listen to me. I know you don't trust me, and you have damn good reasons to not. I told you before that I would let you down, remember? But this isn't one of those times." He glanced back at the door then reached behind me for my wrist, yanking my hand from my pocket and pulling at the sleeve. Aeden's bracelet glinted in the orangey light, a shining beacon of hope for the trial I was about to enter. He looked back up at me and nodded, pulling my sleeve back down swiftly to conceal it. "Good. Keep it on until the trial is over."

I yanked my arm free. "Why should I trust anything you say?" I huffed out, growing more impatient with him as he stepped back toward the door.

"If I flat-out said, 'trust me,' you would do the opposite, wouldn't you?" I expected him to be grinning or smirking or doing some kind of asshole expression that would make me hate and distrust him more. But if I wasn't mistaken, he looked more concerned than anything as his brows crinkled together. The doorknob rattled open and Hector stepped through the threshold, looking ready to toss me over his shoulder. Eoghan turned on his heels, his head just above Hector's and said, "Just wishing her the best, Hector. No need to be so"—he wagged a finger up and down—"*you*." Hector's lip curled into a snarl that he righted almost immediately, remembering that Eoghan was a Mora in his own right even if he wasn't *his* Mora.

"I can walk myself there." I stalked past the two of them, reaching for my sleeve to tug it down further. I had no idea whether I should rip the bracelet off, or trust Eoghan this one last time until Gedeon came into view at the end of the hallway, eliminating my option to take the bracelet off unless I wanted him to see it.

Gedeon's lip curved up wickedly as I approached him. The three ladies who had been tending to me rushed out frantically from behind him, coming to a standstill when he put his arm up. "The time for preparation is over. Paige doesn't need your untimely support. It appears she was ready before you three had the decency to wake up and do your job." The blonde looked ready to cry as the brunette grabbed hold of their arms and dragged them back down another hall, escaping Gedeon's wrath.

I flinched at the thought of the women getting in trouble over me waking up early and evading their help. Just as I reached my hand out toward them, wanting to apologize, I was slammed into the wall by a surge of wind. My daggers pinched against my thigh and I bit my tongue from yelping out when a set of hands fell across my shoulders and eased me onto my feet, catching me off guard. "Don't you think the trial is enough for her to endure today?" Eoghan whipped back at Gedeon.

"You can't coddle them all, it only weakens them." His words were like a snake bite as he spoke not only to me but to Eoghan as well. He adjusted his sleeves, then calmly turned as Hector approached, taking up space by Gedeon's side. Without hesitation, both descended the stairs to where Nya and a large purple portal were waiting.

Eoghan's concern for my well-being was starting to edge me shamefully into his favor again, but then I remembered just how shady and secretive he was and shot it right down. "I'm fine." I grunted as I elbowed him away, brushing my braided hair back down into place and righting myself and one of the hidden blades before walking to meet them below. I heard Eoghan's soft steps follow distinctly behind me until the whooshing of the portal took me back to the forest, before Aeden and I ever made the mistake of walking through and listening to the calling that was no longer there. I felt no urge, no desire to walk through and find my place anymore, and the knowledge that a portal could either whisper sweet bliss into your ear or be entirely lifeless was…unnerving. Beyond the portal, I could hear the faint sounds of shouts and cheers as the trial drew out an audience that Nya had told me to ignore. The Triad was a spectacle that all were invited to witness and enjoy, though the thought of Fae wanting to watch as potential Moras fought to their own death made me shudder as my own mortality hung in the air.

Gedeon and Hector walked through first, the sounds of cheering growing astronomically. Eoghan adjusted his posture and sleeves, sliding into his role with ease and dipping his head at me one final time, then followed behind them. The crowd cheered more, the sounds vibrating the paintings hanging on Gedeon's walls. Nya squeezed me tight, giving me one final hug.

"I can do this," I said, hugging her back a little tighter.

"I know you can, Paige. I'll be rooting for you in the stands. I wish I could be of use to you during the trial, but any aid by a healer in the arena is forbidden." Her shoulders dropped as she pulled away. "Don't die, okay?" Her eyes locked with mine, and I squeezed her forearms before letting her go.

"Now, there are three rules, and only three." She straightened her back and raised a finger. "One, absolutely no use of any powers, or gifts, for this trial. This is the only rule that changes with each trial."

"Got it." I nodded and she continued.

Another finger lifted beside the first. "Second, absolutely no aid is to be accepted by anyone in the arena at the commencement of the trial."

"Okay."

Three ominous fingers floated in front of my face, and for a brief moment, I'd forgotten the first two rules as anxiety began to gnaw at my insides. "Third, and most important of all, you can only complete each trial by going through the final door. If any door, including the final, is not open, your task is not complete."

I cocked my head. Even though I'd read the three rules, that one was the only peculiar one. "How will I know what task I missed?"

"If a task is missed, you usually can not progress to the next door to begin with. But, in those cases, you will have to backtrack and think of anything you may have missed righting."

I nodded again, flexing my fingers by my side. "I'm ready."

"Good luck, Paige." I knew she wanted to say more, but the guards surrounding the portal made our encounter less private than any further declarations of faith would allow. She examined me thoroughly, her eyes beginning to well with tears that she stifled as quickly as they'd formed. She turned and walked into the portal as the crowd grew silent with anticipation.

I took a deep breath, threw back my shoulders, and walked through.

The crowd roared, feet slamming in the stands resembling the sounds of thunder crashing in the sky. My fingernails bit into the dirt, my mind trying to stabilize from the rapid movement inside the portal. Something was being shouted in unison and a ticking sound began. I looked up, the sun had not yet replaced the moon, but the stars had started to fade.

"27, 26, 25," the crowd counted on.

I stood up, the dizziness stilling. I scanned the crowd, unable to make out individual faces amongst the tens of thousands that had come to watch.

Instantly I hoped Aeden hadn't made it to the arena. He needed to keep a low profile, and this was not the place to be, being who he was.

I ceased the thought from taking over, instead narrowing my mind on the trial, taking in every bit of my surroundings before it began.

This is not how I will die. I can do this.

"19, 18, 17."

There were high walls made of stone covered in vines on all sides from where I stood, and two openings that looked no different from each other. Along one of the walls were weapons and a few supplies. I took up the lightest sword, knowing I may need to run and any added weight would only slow me down.

"9, 8, 7."

From the supplies, I grabbed the rope and tied it quickly around my waist.

"3, 2, 1." A loud buzzer rang out with the roar of the audience.

The trial had begun.

A chain rattled and heavy metal doors started closing at each opening. If this were a maze, which had been used before in previous trials, then going to the right and staying to the right as much as I could would be my best bet. And if it wasn't, then picking the right may end in my death. I had seconds to choose a door, and I glanced at the audience for just a moment, their eyes fixed on me and my surroundings as I silently cursed at myself for allowing their distraction to take hold, before sliding under the door to my right.

The heavy metal door sliced into the dirt, and the crowd went silent. I pushed up from the floor just before a large, wooden mace came crashing down where I'd been moments ago, a fist larger than half my body attached to it.

Screams of enjoyment rang through my ears, hands and feet stomping wildly throughout the arena as I raised my head just enough to see what had almost claimed my life.

A troll.

Fearsome, violent, and large creatures, trolls are mostly found in the Tilvey Mountains or Highland Mountains or put to work mining in the Tilvey Mines.

The books I'd read that described the different beings that lived in Aellethia flashed in my mind before another slam of the mace came down to my left, nearly smashing me before I rolled to evade it.

The magic inside of me was pushing against my flesh, begging to be unleashed, but I flexed my fingers around the sword instead, reminding myself that trying to use any of my powers would be the quickest way to end me. I wanted to create a flank of ice, to make it fall. But it was forbidden. The mace lifted from the ground again and I stole a quick look at the face of the troll that was summoned by the Stars to be in my trial. Its eyes were wide, red, and sharp, veins pulsing like its anger demanded to be unleashed in the cruelest of ways.

Trolls are one of the most violent and angry beings in all of Aellethia, often fighting and killing without provocation.

The troll was definitely angry, probably forced into this just as I had been, and certainly seemed provoked even if it didn't need to be, to be ready to kill me.

It released a snarl as I ran around the ring of the room, noticing another door that led elsewhere but was sealed off, encased in ice.

Rule three.

I looked at the troll, who turned to meet where I stood, and froze. I needed to break the ice, but I didn't have a weapon that would be able to break through *that* much ice. The troll lifted the mace with fury and just before it met the ground, I took off, sprinting for the door.

The troll let out a loud growl, stomping its feet so much that the ground shook beneath my boots. The crowd let out a roar of laughter as I fell to the ground, my elbows biting into the dirt as I tried to flee backward. The troll stomped its towering feet, coming closer and closer as I neared the door. Just before the troll came within feet of me, it swung the mace down and I tucked my sword in and rolled to the side, the sounds of ice shards falling silencing the crowd. I bolted to get to the other end of the circular room, aiming to turn the troll around before I made my way toward the icy door again.

The size of the trolls is their downfall as they are more clumsy than not, and are prone to falling over or becoming easily confused with fast movement.

Reaching the wall opposite the doors, I called out for the troll, urging its massive body to turn toward me. Whipping its head in my direction, the troll started to turn its feet, nearly stumbling over one foot as it moved to cross the other. I darted for the space between the separated feet and slid against the dirt. Racing toward the door, I began waving my arms and shouting for the troll's attention. A thick bead of drool sloshed free from its gaping mouth, confusion taking hold of the creature.

"Over here!" I shouted, getting as close to the door as I could before the mace was lifted sloppily up into the air, and right before it started to fall again, I braced against the wall and pushed off in a fervent run to the other side. The sounds of the ice cracking and shattering as the mace smashed into the door echoed in the arena. The door was free of the thick ice, but not opening in the slightest. The arena demanded a fight, and even though I'd found a way to eliminate the ice, I hadn't rightfully fought the troll.

The troll shook its head, looking left and right and slamming the mace down again over the chunks of fallen ice, looking for the fae that had tricked it. I reached for the rope on my waist and quickly untied the loose knot that held it in place, then bolted back toward the troll's feet. I made a loop around one ankle before the earth rattled under me—the mace continuously crushing the ice to pieces, ice shards spewing in all directions. I held onto the rope and moved around the other foot, looping around the other ankle. The troll let out another ragged growl, the drooping gut of the troll making it unable to reach toward its own feet. I kept my hold on the rope, walking backward and hoping, against all odds, that my plan would work.

I waved my sword and shouted again, drawing as much attention to myself as I could. "Hey, big guy! Over here! Where's that big mace of yours?" I frantically goaded the troll until the mace swung in a circle, crashing into the wall of the room and sending chunks of stone and rock tumbling around me.

Shit.

A heavy shard of rock skimmed across my leg as I tried to dodge the cascading pieces, drawing a large gash into my leg, blood dripping onto the dirt shortly after. The troll's mace stiffened at its side as it sniffed the air, its red eyes landing on me. Another growl belted from the belly of the monster, rumbling the stones on the ground.

Pushing myself to ignore the burning pain in my leg, I clutched the rope in one hand and the sword in the other and ran along the wall, using the surface to steady myself as my blood continued to color the dirt. The troll's side came into view and the rope became taut, ready. Drool oozed from the mouth of the troll as it became rabid, the smell of the blood working in my favor even though it made me slower. I dropped my sword and reached into my boot, pulling a dagger out and flinging it as hard as I could. A wailing cry sounded throughout the arena as my dagger pierced the flesh of the troll right behind its knee, piercing the tendon. Fumbling for the dagger lodged behind its knee, the troll threw its leg forward, tripping and sending the troll backward as the ropes took hold. The beast fell on its back and shook the earth beneath my feet so much that I stumbled to the ground.

The beast was reaching for the dagger unsuccessfully as I regained my footing and my sword and raced toward the other leg, using the sword to slice through the backside of the other knee. The troll kicked out reflexively and sent me flying backward, knocking me into the door and taking the breath from my lungs.

And the crowd remained silent.

Struggling, gasping for air, and becoming dizzy from blood loss, I fell, crouching down to the dirt on bent knees. The troll was furiously trying to stand, to use its legs by bending them and trying to push up. But the sheer weight of its body on the severed and pierced tendons only hurt it more, sending its head back into the dirt, arms tucked under its body reaching for the dagger and crying out in pain.

This is it, I can do this.

Panting, the floor uneven in front of me as I clutched my sword to my side, I picked myself back up again using the sword as if it were a cane and stumbled to the head of the troll knowing I could end its life quickly if I could make it there before it regained its focus on me. But as I approached its neck and heaved my sword up, the troll stopped and stared at me. Not at my face, but at the arm that held the sword. The place where my sleeve, now bunched up near my elbow, no longer held the secret of Aeden's bracelet, and instead glinted against the morning sun that had started to come above the arena as if a spotlight had come down from the Stars before they disappeared completely for the day. My breath hitched, the troll's eyes darting between my eyes and my arm while its body stilled and eyebrows furrowed, as if confused.

I peeled my eyes away from the troll and swung my sword down, a black-red pool covering the dirt as I severed through the thick flesh and pulsing artery. The troll's eyes flitted, then closed, releasing a sigh that sent a gust of wind into the sky before its head flopped to the side and the metal door cranked open. I fell to my knees, unable to hear the reactions of the crowd over the thumping in my ears as I tried to stand, falling over and over again until I came close enough to the door. With only a few feet left to go, I collapsed to the ground and forced myself to crawl through.

THIRTY-ONE

AEDEN

Moonlight shone against the lightening night sky, slits of silvery light penetrating through the trees as Murrie tried to keep her pace. She'd been running on and off for over an hour, stopping only to catch her breath and adjust her satchel. I aided where I could, using my air magic to lift the stretcher off the ground, but I could only do so much without direction on using my newfound power. And it was starting to feel less reachable as if my inability to sleep soundly lately was playing a part.

All of the power in me was so new, so strange yet so familiar. Like I'd been meant for this, meant to wield such a force, meant to be more powerful than I'd ever imagined. Perhaps that was just something that lingered in the back of my head and should stay there. I knew I was powerful or could be once trained, and I knew I descended from people who lived in Vizna or one of Vizna's territories. Where else would I get the sprawling fire mark to begin with?

Yet I couldn't get the look of Eoghan's face out of my mind, right before the bastard pushed me into the portal. What he said had bothered me, eating away at the denial that I pushed through my mind over and over, telling me I was as worthless in Aellethia as I had always been in the mortal world. I wasn't special, had never been special, and never accepted that feeling before. Even being recruited to play football in college didn't feel like an accomplishment I'd earned or deserved. But what he said about a dragon heir and that smug grin on his face when he saw my bracelet told me something entirely different.

Murrie ceased once more, grunting as she came to a halt against a tree. "We are...almost...there...just a few...more minutes and..." She wiped the sweat from her brow, continuing, "I'm sorry for all...the breaks...I just need...to breathe and drink some...water maybe." She sat down and started drinking from her pouch. Straining from using so much of my air magic—the power that was so new it was hard to differentiate between the others at times—I relinquished the hold I had over the stretcher, sending my ass rapidly to the ground.

"Maybe I could walk the rest of the way, we can't be that far, right?" I asked, glancing around the trees. It was hard to tell, but the trees weren't the same anymore as they were before. They were becoming thicker, more dense at the tops like they had been around much longer than the trees where we camped at. There weren't as many hills either, the ground seeming to level out into flatter land, and more boulders dotted the area. Like the boulder I hit my head on. I reached my hand back and rubbed the area, the pain entirely gone now unlike the memory.

Murrie peered around through slitted eyes as she drank from her pouch. "It's about another hour if you were to walk it, or less than half that if I run it. I don't think you have the time to waste, but that's up to you," she said as she held the pouch up to me, offering what she had.

I grabbed it on impulse, then paused as I held it in my hands. I remembered Seamus using his own power to drink, and though he taught me how, I was still utter shit at it and I wanted to continue to try. Concentrating on the sensation of the water, I tried to distinguish it from the others. I held my hand above the top of the pouch, feeling its lightness as it was nearly empty, deciding it would be best to possibly ruin a container of water than blast my face with any one of the elements that were fighting to be released. I held onto what bit of water power I could find in me, trying hard not to focus on the fire that raged along every inch of my flesh, or the earth that settled below it. I twisted my wrist slightly and a few drops of water drained into the pouch. Nothing like the stream of fluidity that Seamus produced, but at least I didn't set the pouch on fire or drench myself like I had before. I heard Murrie giggling as I looked up and cocked my brow at her.

"So tell me something, Aeden," she said as she stood, dusting the leaves from her pants. "When you train your entire life to be one of the best wielders Aellethia has, do they not teach you how to make your own source of water?" Her question hung in the air as I contemplated my next statements. I could either keep lying my way through it, acting like the head wound really did hinder my memory, or I could ask the questions that have been on my mind. The ones that I was afraid to voice allowed. The ones that could confirm my suspicions. The ones that could end my life faster than just having the fire mark. Obliviousness was sometimes blissful, but in Aellethia, it probably ended your life more often than not.

But we were alone in the woods. No leaves rustled, no lurking noises in the distance. Nothing and no one. If Murrie truly had been a part of the battle that took down the kingdom where I was believed to be from, then surely she knew something. And I was still alive. That had to count for something.

I shook my head, deciding on putting my fucking guard down to get some answers. "Murrie"—I handed the pouch back to her as she leaned into my lowered voice— "I haven't been here long. This is all new to me, and I don't know where I fit into all of this." I let the words fall around us as she cocked her head to the side, rubbing her jawline with her fingers, her childlike features lighting up with whatever she was thinking.

I continued, standing up from the twisted vines. "Let me reintroduce myself. My name is Aeden Flynn, and I just got here. I didn't…" I hesitated, knowing it could very well be the end of the line for us if she responded wrongly, *acted* wrongly, to what I was about to say. "I didn't grow up here. I'm twenty-two years old, and I came here through a portal with the girl I'm in love with. The girl I'm trying to go be with right now. I don't know why I have these marks, and…" I looked up, noticing for the first time since I'd met Murrie, she was utterly silent while I rambled on.

Desperately needing an answer, I continued. "What is a dragon heir?"

Murrie fell to her knees at the mention of a dragon heir and dropped her head as her arms grazed across the dirt and leaves, bending in a way that took me a moment to realize she was, in fact, bowing down to me. As if I were royalty. I didn't know how to react, so I fell down in front of her, readying myself to hold out for her to either give me the answers I needed whenever she came back up or to use this as a sort of distraction to attack me. The flames sizzled along the edges of my skin, preparing for the latter.

She lifted her head, her eyebrows creasing as she noticed I was down on the ground as well. "I never thought the rumors were true. Couldn't imagine what it would be like to…to hide an infant. Not until I rescued you did I start to believe…." She looked me up and down, then shook herself and bowed her head again.

Frustration took over, and my words came out more gruff than I would normally speak as I pressed, "Please, Murrie. I need answers. I can't ask just anyone, and the friends I was traveling with, well, I don't know if I will ever find them again." I let out a shudder as I thought about never being able to find them, to at least thank them. I should have tried to make my way back to them instead of running. But the chance of being caught around all those guards in Prydia was too high. It was too much of a risk.

Silence, more eyebrows folding together in deep thought as her eyes darted around my face. "Please," I begged.

"You, you look just like her, too. You know? The resemblance is almost uncanny, other than the fact that she was a woman, and you are, well definitely *not* that. Has no one told you who you are? I mean it's obvious just from the length of your mark, and the fact that you have—"

"Please, Murrie. Just, just tell me." I needed to hear the words. Needed the validation that I felt deep within me. The feeling that I belonged here wasn't enough. It was like I was *made* for this place. Beyond the explanation that I was a fae or a high fae, or just had all of this power. I knew the words she was going to speak before she spoke—I could feel it in my soul.

She seized my hand, curling her small fingers around mine as she said, "You're a Fireborne, Aeden. And to my knowledge, you are the last one. The son of Lady Savaria Fireborne. She was rumored in our village to have escaped, many of the people who fought in the war for her never saw a body, and taking Gedeon's word was...well, it wasn't easy for anyone who sided with Vizna to believe she died at his hand."

"Fireborne," I breathed out as Murrie released her grip. I spread my fingers wide and closed them again as if testing the name on my skin and deep in my bones. Everything Murrie said about who I was didn't feel real, yet at the same time, I knew it was.

I was a Fireborne.

I am a Fireborne.

"But, dragon heir? What did—"

"The fact that someone else told you that you were a dragon heir means that person knows exactly who you are, and that is bad. Very, very bad. Tell me, do you trust this person?" Murrie asked.

Did I trust him? Lord Fucker that sent me too close to the wall, knowing damn well that nagas thrived there? "Fuck no," I said. The fact that I was still holding on to the grim chance that he would keep his word about the portal by a shed was idiocy in itself. Was I an idiot for trying to make my way to a portal that most likely wasn't there? Yes. But was I an idiot in love who'd do anything, believe anyone, to get back to her? Also, yes.

"Yeah, the fae I know of would use that information to do whatever they want with. And if you don't trust them, then that really isn't good, Lord Aeden," she said, and the hairs on my skin stood up at the mention of being a Lord. I didn't know if I liked the sound of that since the two Lords I'd seen so far in Aellethia were the biggest dicks in existence. I didn't want to be thrown into that mix.

"Stick to Aeden. I'm just Aeden, Murrie." I groaned, drawing my hand down the length of my face and over the grown-out stubble. "I don't trust his intentions with a lot of things, but the fact that I am still standing right now has to count for something. No guards are chasing me down right now." I shrugged, ignoring the fact that I kept evaluating whether I was still living or not and using that as an indicator of trusting someone or not. *Times have definitely fucking changed.* "So, does a dragon heir mean I get a dragon now?" I let out a laugh and flicked my wrist to lift the stretcher again.

Murrie stood up, righting herself again and grabbing hold of the floating stretcher. She was silent for a moment as she fidgeted, moving strands of vines up and down along the sturdy branches that were on either side of the stretcher. "Actually, yeah. That's kind of what made Vizna so powerful, to begin with. Only the Moras of Vizna and their descendants inherit a dragon when they are born to call their own, one that is born to them as well. If your parents kept the tradition strong, yours is probably somewhere waiting for you, although most that were bound before the war were killed. But we don't have much time before the sun comes up, as much as I would love to keep talking about Vizna and your heritage. Can I ask, why are you so set on this shack?"

"Wait, a real dragon? I've never owned a pet in my life and now you're telling me I might own a fucking dragon?" My hands started to shake as I swung myself into the stretcher. If only I knew how to propel us once I lifted this then maybe Murrie could keep talking and give me more information. The fact that I could lift the damn thing was a miracle in itself. I tried to focus on her question and ended up explaining that I believed a portal would be there, leading me to the arena to watch the girl I loved, Gedeon's daughter, and make sure she made it out of her first trial alive.

Murrie made soppy eyes and grinned before she took off, the gusts of air whizzing by, masking my shakiness. I was something, someone. My parents weren't junkies or degenerates like I'd been told by many foster parents throughout my life. And I probably had a dragon somewhere in Aellethia, waiting for me to return home.

The shack was further than Murrie had predicted, and the sun was already peeking through the trees when we arrived. Not even the few boards that were left standing from decimated walls could conceal the fact that there was no portal waiting for me.

"Over here!" Murrie cried out. I made my way around the side to where she stood on a small porch in front of the remnants of a door, its splintered pieces hanging on a single hinge. An iced-over scroll was unrolled and plastered to it, as she read:

Dragon Boy,

So sorry about the portal, but glad you made it here alive. Nagas are nasty little things, aren't they?

I had to let you know I would be a complete fool to let you come back—something I'm not too keen on ever explaining for myself if it were discovered you stepped through one of my portals. As for you, you'd be better off staying away from any portal, especially if they are purple. For fuck's sake, any one of us could send you into a grave and you wouldn't know until it was too late.

Anyway, I have it on good authority to let you know that she will live past her first trial, all thanks to your shiny little gift.

Stay hidden, and for the love of the Stars, don't find your way back into Prydia. They kill boys like you, don't you know?

P.S. Try looking for some dwarves, I hear they are privy to protecting your kind.

I could hear the sarcastic, mocking tone of Eoghan's voice as I reread the note alongside Murrie, and then the ice around the scroll turned to liquid, breaking the paper up piece by piece as it deteriorated and fell to the wooden planks below our feet.

I balled my hands at my sides, feeling my temperature start to rise, and noticed Murrie taking a few steps back and away from me. "I'm going to fucking kill him." I seethed as flames began to flicker up along my arms, the singe of the heat against my skin a welcomed sensation. A twig snapped behind me and I twisted my head and lifted my arms, ready to take down anything Eoghan may have sent through before closing up the portal he'd used to get to where I stood now. The same one he refused to leave open for me. But there was only Murrie, her own hands lifted in defense as her weapon lay strapped across her back.

I immediately dispersed the fire and fixed the sleeves of my tunic nervously, pulling at the tattered cloth and fixating on it as I found myself unable to meet her eyes. A wave of mortification washed over me. "I'm sorry, it's just…it's hard sometimes. To control—to separate my fucking emotions from the shit happening inside of me." And by shit, I meant power. But it didn't feel like a *power* when all I kept doing was losing control of it. In fact, for someone with so much proclaimed power, I had never felt more powerless in my life. "I shouldn't have trusted him. I knew it, but I did it anyway. And now…now how am I supposed to get back to her?"

Murrie's hands fell to her sides but her shoulders remained tense like she was unsure if my temper would come back out of its hidey-hole. She stepped closer to me, making her chin shoot skyward as the height difference between us became eccentric. "He's right, you know," she said as she placed a settling hand against my side while she stood on her tip-toes just to reach that far. "Us dwarves will definitely try to keep you safe. Although I don't think *safe* is your thing."

"No, definitely not. I'll be fine, but her…I worry about her all the time." I hung my head low and patted her hand, smiling down at her as I struggled to stay calm and not flare the fire back up. Out of all of the elements inside of me, I could feel the strength of the fire above all. The urge to set it free was harder to fight, and now that I held air power as well, it was almost consuming everything I had to not lash out. My body was becoming a bomb with a detonation switch that I couldn't find, nor was I sure if I *should* find it, yet I held onto the tiniest sliver of hope knowing that I wasn't alone in this. She was like this too, or would be soon if she kept passing trials.

As if Murrie could sense that my thoughts had turned to Paige again, she pulled her hand from my leg and said, "She passed her first trial, hot shot. I think she deserves more credit than what you are giving her." I let out a sigh, not knowing how far I should go into explaining but trying anyway. It wasn't that I didn't believe in her ability. It was quite the opposite, actually. I knew she could handle anything, but it didn't mean I had to eat it up and love that she was being put into a pit of death, or whatever it was the Triad had in store. It also went beyond that, like a pull that I had to her, tethering her to me. I needed to keep her safe like I needed to breathe. It was as simple as that.

The twisted face Murrie gave me after I put so much of my feelings on display for yet another near stranger since I'd arrived here had me grinning back at her. Maybe I wouldn't have to have my walls so high all the time. Maybe some people just allowed you to exist, to be you. But then I remembered I was hiding out in a fucking forest because most of this world didn't want me to exist and my happiness crashed to the ground again.

"Look, maybe going to her isn't in the cards just yet. You really shouldn't be exposing yourself. Keeping a low profile is what will keep you alive. Unless you have a death wish and want to show everyone who you truly are?" She cocked her small brow at me, folding her arms and taking a stance that made her seem larger than she actually was as I shook my head fervently. Her huge ax glinted in the faint sunlight and I had to wonder what the other dwarves must be like. Were they all as badass as her, or did I just get extremely lucky when she found me near death mere days before?

"What good am I if I'm not there with her?" I asked, and even as the word vomit escaped my mouth, I knew I was in for a long talk about just how important I really was. Sure enough, Murrie went on about being the son of a Mora, the future leader of a fallen kingdom that still had people who were hiding out somewhere. People were relying on the hope that my existence would give to them, fae that despised the laws that were put into place out of fear. The rush I felt wasn't like what playing a game on a football field and winning felt like. In fact, comparing anything in Aellethia to football seemed to minimize the very core of who I knew I was now, and I wasn't about to backtrack. Not when Paige was fighting her way through trials because she knew there was no other way out of her situation. She had embraced who she was, and now it was time I did the same.

Murrie and I sat near the decomposing structure, discussing and formulating ways that I could turn this shithole of a situation around. Her mouth ran a mile a minute and I tried to soak in every bit of detail that she lay out before me—from geographical regions that went beyond my knowledge of Costa and Prydia to weapons and the advancements of magic that I had yet to unfold. She knew people, was well-versed in many things I'd never considered or heard of before, and knew how to stay hidden, and I knew damn well that she could fight alongside me and hold her own.

Before the sun started its downward descent, we made our way back to the camp we'd been at before, opting to ditch the stretcher and walk. There was only one final thing weighing on my mind, and I knew we had to settle it before any of what we had discussed could come to fruition.

"We need to find Seamus and Shay first, and then I'll be fucking ready."

Thirty-Two

PAIGE

I awoke to the sounds of my own screams and racing heart, followed by what was unmistakably Eoghan's voice.

"Paige! Paige! Stop fighting me, fuck!" His fingers wrapped tightly around my arms, barring me in as I tried desperately to fight him off while he pressed me deeper into the cloud-like mattress. I squeezed my eyes shut and focused on my breathing, willing a sense of calm to come over me that took every last bit of effort I had.

Eoghan cleared his throat and let out a low whistle. "That injury took Nya hours to work on, and here I thought you were about to make more." I forced my eyes open and saw him staring back at me, his hands still bracing my body into the mattress in the room deemed mine as I jerked my shoulders to get him off of me. "Careful, Princess. You've been out for the entire day."

"Let go of me," I demanded, my voice coming out hoarse like it hadn't just been used to yell and goad a troll toward me earlier in the trial. *Shit, the trial.* "Did I pass?"

Eoghan's tongue poked into his cheek and then he released my arms before he stood, moving to the foot of my bed and leaning forward against it with his arms crossed. "Uh, yeah. You passed."

A small smile formed on my lips. "Were you hoping I'd fail, then?" I reached under the blanket slowly and rubbed my leg, taking immediate notice of the lack of pain. The pain I should've been in. The pain that seemed capable of ending me in the arena. But it wasn't there.

He chuckled. "No, quite the contrary." The crackle of the fire across the room filled the void of sound between us as I squinted at him. "You should see how your father is fairing. He looks ready to blow the entire castle to pieces."

The amount of lightness and triumph that statement gave me was enough to bring a faint bristly laugh from my lips, burning my throat slightly. But then I remembered how much of an untrustworthy dick Eoghan was and I fought it back down quickly. But it was too late. Eoghan had heard my reaction and a slight quirk fell upon the corner of his mouth.

"Ah, *there's* the girl from just before the ball. For a moment, I thought you hated me."

"Who's to say I don't?" I bit back, sitting up more in my bed and crossing my arms. Shock took over as I realized the bracelet was no longer on my arm. I flicked my wrist frantically, and Eoghan took a step back, allowing the blanket to soar off of me and across the room. I'd practiced with flimsy clothing so many times before, there was nothing but confidence in the movement. Confidence and the fear of having lost my last connection to Aeden.

"Looking for this?" he questioned, pulling Aeden's bracelet from the inside of his jacket, dangling the fine chain, and making it glint beautifully against the dancing firelight.

I stood abruptly, stomping up to him and holding my hand out. "That belongs to me," I seethed. "Give it back. Now."

"Relax," he said softly as he let the chain fall into my open hand. "There's fae and beasts out there that will *kill* for the very knowledge held in the palm of your hand. You are fortunate I took this from you before Gedeon stormed in, wondering just what the hell caused that poor, misguided troll to hesitate." Eoghan leaned in. "I'm not the enemy, Paige." His face softened when he pulled back and it took every ounce of willpower I had to stop the twitch in my fingers. Because they wanted to slap him. My own power seemed to hum at the very thought.

"How can I believe a word you say when everything you let out of your mouth is laced with half-truths and hidden secrets?" Eoghan took a step back, then turned and walked toward the fireplace, leaning his crooked arm against the mantle as it braced his weight. I retreated to the other half of the room, remembering to keep my distance from the flames unless I preferred to be put to death before the remaining trials could test my worth further. My emotions were too all over the place, and I couldn't risk it. Just like if I'd known what Aeden was before touching him...well, even that I wasn't sure about. I was scared, but the desire to be with him went beyond the feelings I'd had for him for so long. They evolved, just like we were both doing in this fucking world.

"We all have roles to fill, Paige." He looked over his shoulder at me, then asked, "Have you wondered what's beyond this castle?"

"What good is it to think about a city that is ruled by a madman when I can't even be sure if the people in front of me, inside this castle, aren't just like him?"

He frowned, then dipped his head down toward the fire, lifting his idle hand and forming a small ball of flames that floated perfectly above his open palm. I took another few steps back until I hit the wall, balling the fist that held Aeden's bracelet down by my side.

He dropped his voice low, the proximity of the flames in his hand casting a brighter glow on his face than the fireplace could even try to as he held his gaze on the hovering fire. "Fire-wielders shouldn't be feared, hunted down, or tortured and put to death. In these walls, and even beyond them, it's hard to imagine that others could think differently." He flipped his palm over and the flame followed, moving gently over his knuckles as he moved his fingers one-by-one. "That they *do* think differently. It wasn't long ago that fire-wielding was just as normal and accepted as any other. It wasn't until," the ball of fire split into two, then formed shapes that were almost human. But they were fae, and when one approached the other with violent intentions, it engulfed it entirely, growing twice the size as it had been before. "Gedeon got greedy, and Hydra—*my*—kingdom followed suit under false pretenses. Now we all suffer the consequences of the betrayal that fell upon Vizna and the poor souls who were born with fire under their flesh."

He curled his fingers in and extinguished the ball, then lifted himself from the mantle and turned toward me. I moved back to the bed, sitting on the edge of it as I waged a silent war in my mind. *Should I trust Eoghan again? Or just say fuck it and force him out of my room?* I looked down at the bracelet, feeling the warmth of Aeden's presence even if he wasn't with me. I couldn't remain closed off and bitter about things that I simply couldn't justify knowing Aeden's people, and people beyond these walls, needed someone with the mindset that Eoghan just laid before me. If he were lying, then he deserved an award for how utterly convincing he'd been, so much so that I almost had the urge to cross the room and throw my arms around him as he wore sorrow on his face like a second skin.

I mentally thanked Nya for healing and changing me, not wanting to think for a second that Eoghan had a hand in aiding the recovery process or getting me out of my leather corset and bloodied clothing. I let out a sigh and tucked the bracelet away safely in the pocket of my pants.

"Tell me one thing," I said.

"Only one?"

"One is all I need to see you answer; to know that you aren't lying right now."

He rubbed his smooth jaw. "Okay."

"Do you value Aeden's life as you value the rest of the fire-wielders? Do you *want* him to live?"

"Oh Princess, but that's two things, and you unmistakably said one." He smirked and I was reminded of the time I'd given him rules to abide by before he'd asked me to the ball. I rested my head on my hand, propping it on my bouncing leg.

"You know, I think I liked it better when we only talked on the training deck."

He cocked his head to the side. "You mean for the first day or so I was here and tried to coerce you through a portal back to your hometown?"

"No, more like when I yelled and charged my way into your side and nearly got my knife into you."

"So when we aren't talking. You mean, when we are fighting."

"Yes. That." I laid back on my bed and he chuckled. "So, Eoghan. Do you value the life of the man I love?"

He approached the bed and took up space beside me, his elbow grazing mine as he laid back. "Truthfully? Yes."

He turned his head at the same moment as I did mine, our eyes locking to show he wasn't lying. He needed me to see the sincerity, to not only hear it laced in his words but also to know that his were the eyes of the one Mora I could trust. I could almost envision how his kingdom was run—fae that didn't fear their leader, but greatly respected him. I so desperately wanted to believe it, but never having seen it, his kingdom or territories, left the debate up in the air. I hadn't focused my reading on Hydrasel, but perhaps I needed to.

Aeden would never take someone for their word without seeing it first through his own eyes. He always felt people out, using their actions and their words in his favor. He also went with his gut instinct, which seemed to bode well for him more often than not. I don't know what fully transpired between the two, and I probably never would, but the dreams I was deep into just before I awoke led me to believe, in my heart, that he was alive. That was my gut instinct. It was silly to admit, but something told me I'd feel it if he weren't...if he did...if he died.

As if Eoghan could read my thoughts, he lifted his index finger and placed it between my eyes, asking, "My turn for a question, What's in that head of yours when you go to sleep? I've never seen someone so violent before when they weren't conscious."

I shrugged my shoulders against the sheet. "I don't know. Bad dreams lately." It was the truth, in a sense. He didn't need to know I'd seen Aeden's mark in my dreams before seeing them in person, and that I'd seen his companions before, or believed I had.

"Mmm." He smacked his hand against the bed and shot up. "I know what would be fun. You want to piss off your father?"

"Hell yes, I do." I sat up alongside him, not caring what exactly would do the trick to get Gedeon riled up, though my existence seemed to be enough most of the time.

"Want to see Prydia?" He wiggled his eyebrows.

My jaw fell slack, then I rolled my lips in and nodded firmly. "I'd love that, actually."

"Good, let's sneak out before anyone knows you woke up."

"Oh, for the Star's sake, Paige, we really need to work on your air magic," Eoghan grunted as a gust of wind lifted me up and then lowered me down a few floors from the training deck. Oddly enough, the deck was vacant from any guard except for one, who fled to the other side of the deck as soon as he witnessed a few dummies becoming engulfed in flames by a lit wall sconce whose flame swayed rather fiercely in the nighttime breeze—or rather by Eoghan, who had to hold back a laugh as if he were a child pulling the biggest prank of his life. It was quite fun to watch the guard, who seemed to have little grasp of his magic when panic set in. In seconds, he was in the corner blowing the flames with his air magic, rolling the dummy further along toward the other side of the deck.

"One day, I'll be able to blow you away. Literally. Then you won't be laughing at my downfalls. Just wait."

"Yeah, you can try, Princess, but all I'm seeing right now is someone in desperate need of some training. You know the bastard moved up the timetable for your next trial, right?"

I gulped audibly, feeling a sudden burst of fear climb across my body. "Really? H...how?"

"Yes. You've got about...three days? That's the shortest amount of time I've seen yet from trial to trial. Your birthday is soon, but they could've pushed the second trial closer to the third instead of the first. The Stars must've agreed with your father because the arena is already being set, timer and all."

"Fuck." My birthday *was* coming up. I'd be twenty soon. I crossed my arms and shivered as I stood on a mound of dirt. We made it to the city without catching any guards' attention, but knowing I could hardly wield water, the only other element I had to use in the next trial, made me uneasy. "Is three days enough to train?"

"No, but it will have to be." He shrugged just one shoulder. "I've done more with less."

We walked in silence as I fisted my pocket to hold on to the bracelet that brought me more comfort than any jewelry had before, and Eoghan strolled idly beside me, one hand in his pocket as well. The lack of guards was starting to concern me, not for my own well-being, but knowing without a shred of doubt that Gedeon would have flanked his city in guards with how dictatorial he was if he had the guards to spare.

"Where is everyone?" I asked, only seeing a few people scattered around in between buildings, ducking in alleyways in their rags and bare feet. I should've been surprised at the way people were living in the city, but I wasn't.

"The guards are spreading out more to search for the missing fire-wielder. It's an all-hands-on-deck situation. I'm half inclined to believe he will ask for assistance from other kingdoms soon, as the days go on with no wielder found matching his description."

"What about the people that live here? Where are they?"

"Curfew was enacted that night. No one is allowed outside after dark."

I cocked my eyebrow at him. "But who is here to enact that rule?"

"Me, and now you." He nudged into me, letting out a chuckle. "Or so they think. I'm sure Hector stomps around during the day, keeping people in line with a few of the castle guards at his feet."

"It isn't funny, Eoghan. These people, living like this. Is this how Aellethia is? Is everyone holed up in shacks with nothing to their name?"

He bit at his cheek, contemplating. "No. This city was once more lively, fae had more rights and could claim small fortunes from their endeavors. But the High Fae, the ones with more power, became more greedy after the battle, leaving less and less for those who worked beneath them. It's something that I've been watching dwindle over the years—a fae's ability to provide for themselves much less their families, struggling and dying off from things we hadn't seen before. Starvation and illness were known, but now...." He let out a sigh as we turned a corner, leading into a much more open space full of shops with few items in their windows. I wondered silently if they lived with so little for so long, or if they were recently taken for everything they had. "Now we hear more and more reports of it killing us." *Us.* He included himself with the Fae, not just the High Fae. All of them. If I didn't believe a word he said before about doing things for his people because of his tendency to bend the truth, that singular word had just spoken volumes in his favor. He really *did* care for them.

"So, before my father turned into a power-hungry mogul and Vizna went to ruin, what was all of this like?" I gestured at a line of shops that stretched out before us, a few small children running inside an abandoned building across the street from it, no parents in the vicinity.

"It was beautiful." He ran his fingers through his hair, leaning against one of the buildings and making the wood groan out under his weight. The shops hadn't been repaired or maintained, and I had to imagine that feeding the shop owners' families was thankfully higher on the priority ladder before maintenance could be a factor. "Fae would come from other towns and kingdoms just to walk the streets here. Traveling was a pleasant pastime, spending time with your loved ones and having the coin to spend on a good time was normal."

"And now it's a ghost town at night, and no one can afford to feed their children?"

He nodded, lifting himself from the wood as it groaned more violently. Eoghan flicked his wrist and a wash of water lifted the thickly caked mud from the street, shifting it into a line on the edges of the street rather than covering it. "We have a task force in Hydrasel that goes out into our kingdom and territories—feeding the underprivileged, providing clothing—helping where we can. We are seeing a positive turn-around, but the High Fae, ones like you saw at the ball that night, are getting more and more greedy. Just like him."

"I would ask if Prydia has something like your kingdom does, but I think I know my answer." I waved my arm at the rundown shacks, the dirt and bits of shredded clothing along the streets, and a few wagons on their last leg with rotting handles that were hard to imagine as any passable means of transport. With as much power as Gedeon toted around and the lavishness of his castle, one should expect a great city beneath him. Yet, seeing this city made every part of him so clear to me. And it was sickening.

He was a tyrant, through and through.

Eoghan began leading the way through the streets as I followed closely behind. He was silent as I took in as much of my surroundings as I could. There was an occasional house that was kept up and relatively clean, and as we neared a larger street even more full of shops, the plague of Gedeon seemed to lessen, but not enough to warrant applause for him. The city was, overall, in ruins.

We stopped walking when we came across a platform, ropes hanging with nooses tied at the ends, and if I wasn't mistaken, a pile of bodies in the distance beyond the platform. Tears rolled down my cheeks at the sight of what a true monster could do to people. Fae were dying, starving, rotting in the damn streets. The marks on their skin were clear even as the moonlight waned above us. They were faded, gray. But even without seeing the mark, it was so painfully evident as to which element marked their flesh. The very reason they were where they were now.

Fire-wielders. Dead. All of them.

"Is this what he does to them?" I stifled a cry through my already rough throat and wiped at my tears. A hand slipped over my shoulder, and where there had been so many times I'd used that against him and flung him down on the deck or tried to, I didn't fight it this time. Because this wasn't training. This was all real.

"Yes. This is what is done to keep the fire-wielder population from ever growing again."

"But these are kids!" I pointed at the two bodies, who even in the distance were undeniably smaller than the rest. I felt bile rise in my throat and I covered my mouth to keep from vomiting all over my boots.

"Keep your voice down, Paige." Eoghan darted his eyes toward a window, where the heads of several small children were peering out at us. Another stood alone, looking through a window from another building, meeting my eyes moments before another tear rolled down my cheek. "You don't want to implicate them."

"Would that be punishable by death, too?" I choked out as he squeezed my shoulder. He whistled low at the children, making their heads duck back down. "I'm sorry, I just, he can't. He can't be like this. This isn't right."

"No," he stated simply. "No, it isn't."

He turned me around and tugged me toward him and I let my body fall into his as he held me, letting me sob against him until I could steady them from falling anymore.

"We should get back, I'm sure someone by now has noticed you aren't in your room, possibly reporting it as we speak." He pushed me from him by both of my shoulders and smiled down at me, but it didn't meet his eyes. His eyes were...full of sorrow, and if the moonlight weren't being covered by clouds, I could've sworn I saw his own tears welling to the surface.

"Thank you for taking me here. I...I needed to see this." Even if it was horrific and would probably haunt me further in my already occurring nightmares, it had opened my eyes. It gave me a further purpose in defeating the trials. If winning the Triad brought Gedeon down, then I'd make damn sure to try doing just that. Because it was no longer about me, and whether I could get to Aeden afterwards.

Fuck, I'd been so selfish before. No wonder Eoghan treated me like I was a brat at times. I needed to win the Triad for *them*, for everyone who was so mistreated by my father. And I was the only person who could make that happen.

THIRTY-THREE

PAIGE

My knees slammed into something solid and my arms were outstretched, thankfully, catching my face before it knocked to the ground. I clenched my jaw tight and flung my eyes open. Wooden boards filled the floor space and moved up along the sides, almost like...

A ship.

The hull swayed as if acknowledging my presence, and the dreaded sounds of even ticking and muffled chanting rang above my head, beyond the roof of the inside of the ship.

I stood up shakily, having never been on a boat before and feeling that deep in the pit of my stomach as the contents of dinner from the night before threatened to burst through my mouth. But as the chanting continued, I knew I needed to find whatever it was that this trial would be demanding of me. I had to fight through.

There were bits of light flooding through where the above floorboards were separating, and I used it to my advantage as I tried to find any tools or weapons that were granted by the Stars themselves. Yet, the only things I could find were the very same devices I'd used in the first trial, hanging on the wall and swinging with the movement. I hadn't read about the same weapons being the only choices for the second trial from what I'd chosen in the first, but they would have to do.

The chanting and ticking stopped, creating a void that was soon filled with the sounds of rushing water. I pulled my arm away from my waist as I finished knotting the rope and discovered two holes the size of my head rapidly allowing water into the vessel. I rushed over to one of the holes, looking around for anything that could stifle the amount of water, to plug it up or fix it. Putting my hands above my head, I reached up for the ceiling, hoping there was a way to the top deck. When I realized none of the boards above me were moving, my stomach sank with the dipping of the ship under a crashing wave.

A whimper, followed by pleading cries came from a dark corner shielded from the light and I fixated on the darkness. "Hello?" The whooshing of water continued and filled the floor of the cabin and my boots lapped in a small pool that almost covered my soles. I estimated the amount of time before it reached my head, and it wasn't good. Not at all. Fear clawed at my throat as another cry pierced through the thick, salty air.

"I want to help, but I need you to come into the light. Please!" But there was no answer, only more cries and whimpers intermingled with prayers to the Stars. The voice was soft and delicate, like a child's. "I won't hurt you, please come out. Please...I..."

Water crept into my boots through the eyelets and I flicked my wrist haphazardly, creating a layer of ice over my boots to stop the water from flooding in.

Ice.

I didn't hesitate using the same methods over the holes in the walls, creating a thick, uneven layer of ice that sealed them like bandages over a wound. It wouldn't hold for long, but it would hopefully give me the time I needed to find my way to the top deck and find out where the hell I was.

Just as the water ceased its onslaught, the crying was stifled as well and was replaced with sounds of clinking. Sharp clinking. Metal on metal, then turning rough like metal against wood. A small foot peeked into the ray of light that came through one of the floorboards and I gasped loudly at the sight. The cavernous void echoed with laughter as a spindly, long set of fingers covered in mangled gray skin reached out into the light.

"Foolish girl."

The hairs on my back raised as the only voice I heard changed from childlike to monstrous. It was the sound of murder—of flesh-eating, terrorizing, death. The words wormed their way across my flesh and demanded I use my power again before setting my sights on the entirety of whatever lay beyond the dark corner.

But another cry escaped, *the child?* Followed by a smack and a sharp yelp that made ripples form in the water at my feet.

There were two things beyond the darkness, and one of them was absolute evil.

"Shut up, powerless one!" More crying and sobbing. "Come into the dark, girl. I want to taste you!"

Powerless? The only ones without power in this kingdom were those that were too young to have them, or ones that were stripped, although I hadn't seen the latter. The other thing beyond the darkness was surely a child, and that tore into my gut and drove anger into my lungs. "Let the child go," I yelled as my hand clutched the sword, raising it above my head in a fighting stance.

"I have no use for this *child*, but you," it drawled, and the slippery sounds coming from the corner thrust an image into my mind of a tongue sliding over lips. "You, I would love a taste of. Come closer!"

Chains rattled more while the boat rocked and tilted violently, forcing my balance to slip, sending my fingers and sword into the dark and I screamed out in pain as the thing attacked instantly. I shot myself backward, sliding my body along the slick floorboards with a blast of water that propelled me away. The boat righted itself again, washing away the trail of blood on the wooden planks left by my hand while the water from the leaks became level.

"Are you hurt?" I cried out to the child, whose muffled sobs continued. "I need you to stay strong," I said to the child, but I also stated it to myself as I pushed up from the floor, ignoring the bleeding wound as much as I could.

"Silence!" Another slapping sound echoed in the space as the agitation of the creature intensified. "You smell like *him.* Like the one who killed my sister!"

I didn't want to hear more, but I needed to edge it from the dark as much as the chains would allow. That was the only reason I could think of as to why it hadn't come out.

"Who?" I inched a bit closer, holding my sword tightly to my side as blood dripped down the hilt and onto the blade.

"The boy. *So much power!*"

Another inch closer, a drop of blood formed a small ripple in the water. The chains rattled and a gnarled hand shot out again. But I didn't hesitate. I jerked my wrist and willed the water from below to form a pole of ice, directing the stream upwards and encasing the hand, then anchoring it to the floor and ceiling. Lifting my sword, I froze. I couldn't risk cutting its arm off and enraging it to the point where the child was hurt. No. I needed to keep it away, so I could get to them. *Save them,* if I could.

The water rippled again as it cried out in frustration. "I *will* kill you, just as he killed my sister! If the child is what you want, then I shall eat it first!" The child let out a scream as ripping cloth began to echo in the small space.

"No!" The ripping sounds ceased and a cackle, sharp and rancorous, filled the air. So much malice seeped from those words, yet I hadn't done a thing to deserve whatever it was they were convinced I'd done. That whoever the *he* was, had done. Who the hell did I smell like? Gedeon?

"Give me a taste, girl, and I won't need to eat this pointless creature." The beast's tone shifted, edging toward an absolutely sickening sweetness.

"If I give you something to"—I gulped—"to satiate you, will you free the child?"

"I can not, but I can tell you *how.*" Another cackle and the slippery tongue sounds sent a shiver down my spine.

Knowing was better than not, and I was 1 already losing blood. Decidedly, I chose to gain knowledge from it rather than not. I hovered my bleeding hand, which gripped the sword, just over the beast's hand that was encased in ice as a memory of a page I read flitted across my thoughts.

This was a hag.

The hands, the want for power-laced blood. I'd read that its need to feed was constant, like bloodlust, and it consumed them.

I allowed a few drops of blood to pool onto the ice and a sharp tongue darted out to lapse at it, making me flinch back just as it poked out quickly from the dark.

"Mmm, yes. Your gift is delicious!"

My gift? I don't have a gift.

I ignored it, knowing we were short on time, and so was the kid. "Tell me how to free the child."

Chains rattled along with the cackling as the beast moaned and laughed in pleasure from my blood, making bile rise in my throat once more.

"You must break the chain."

But I couldn't see the chain. A popping sound drew my attention to the walls, where the ice began to crack under the pressure of the water that tried to fight its way in. I tried to cast more ice over it, to reseal it, but the cracking continued even through the new layer.

I peered around the space again, searching for a way out, needing a door to allow more light in. But there was nothing.

A scraping sound screeched out followed by another shrieking cackle. This damn hag loved to mock me, and I wondered if the audience had some way to view what was going on inside the boat, if *they* were all mocking me as well.

"Looking for this?" Another scraping sound like nails on a chalkboard crashed into my ears.

The Stars placed the door right by a chained hag and a child, and I didn't have to question what had to happen for me to get to the top deck. But I don't think the Stars imagined the route I would take. I wouldn't charge my weapons into the darkness without being able to see that I wouldn't hurt the child, but other ruthless leaders would. They wouldn't think twice about killing a child to free themselves.

But I refused to be like them. Like *him*.

The ice ruptured, freeing the flow of water from one of the holes and creating a larger hole in its place as the water ripped its way through. I lunged my hand over the ice once more, forcing the hag to move its tongue out again. Instantly, I froze it to the block still encasing their hand, drawing a deep bellow from the hag. I focused my efforts on moving the ice up along its tongue and another hand with a chain lashed out, nearly striking my shoulder as it attempted to claw me away. But my focus held firm. Ignoring the rushing water that reached higher and higher, now up to my calf, I created another pole of ice that anchored its chained hand to the floorboards. Eventually, the bellowing became muffled as my ice reached higher and higher. I could feel my magic sliding up and into the hag's mouth, or maybe I had imagined it. Either way, the hag grew silent, and I heard the child gasp.

"C-c-cold," the child said.

"Are you alright?" I slammed my sword over the bit of chain hanging out from the ice, hoping that I was right to assume the Stars would be twisted enough to chain the two together. The chain broke and splashed into the rising water. "Are you free?"

"I c-c-can move my arms, but my legs are stuck!"

And I can't swim.

The water was almost up to my waist.

"Help!" *My thoughts exactly, kid.*

The door began to open, allowing light into the space that was once dark. The hag was almost entirely covered in ice, but as I got closer to the child, I realized I'd encased the child's legs as well, anchoring the girl, who couldn't be more than eight years old, to the floor. And the water was rising faster as the other hole burst open. Creating another layer of ice over it would be useless.

"Take deep breaths, okay? I'm going to get you out."

"Help me! Please!" The child had its chin tilted up, evading the rising water levels as the light continued to flood in just feet above our heads. I loosened one end of the rope from my waist, dropping the sword to wrap the rope around the child's waist below the water and binding us together. I didn't miss the irony on behalf of the Stars, who'd bound the child to a monster while I, in turn, bound the child to me.

I'd been taught over the past few days how to wield my water magic more proficiently, but I hadn't learned how to turn the ice back into liquid water. It was a difficult thing to comprehend, the undoing of a solid. Forming one was much easier. "Hold on to this rope, okay?" The child's tears stayed level on their cheeks as her green eyes glinted up against the shining sun above. "I'm going to get you out of here, I promise."

Fear clawed into my throat as I watched the child's face become consumed with water. I tried to feel a connection to the ice as I did with the water, trying desperately to turn it back, to free her.

"Help!" Water spit from her mouth as she cried out, and I silently cursed the Stars for not allowing the use of my original nature.

There has to be another way.

I reached into my boot and freed a dagger, then took a deep breath and worked my way down into the water. I wedged my blade between the ice and the floorboards as hard as I could, freeing one of her feet from the icy connection. I shot up above the water, seeing the child was completely submerged now and bubbles were escaping to the surface. Taking another deep breath, I sank down and went to work on the other just as something lunged upward and into me with such force I was shot up into the air before the rope went taut around my waist and yanked me back into the water.

The hag isn't dead.

I clenched my jaw and formed spears of ice, propelling them through the water to where the hag was still anchored by the ice to the floor by its hands. The hag began to kick out feverishly as I pierced its flesh, over and over. Blood pooled around the water that was becoming too high, sloshing against my chest while the bubbles from the child's mouth were becoming less. Screaming out in fury as the reality of the child dying in front of me became all too real, I summoned a blast of ice down the throat of the hag as its mouth hung open, ending its life for good.

The blood in the water made it difficult to see just where the girl was, but I took a deep breath and submerged myself once more, holding onto the rope to draw me closer to her. Because she was still immovable, and soon, we both would be if my feet no longer could touch the floor. I went to work, chiseling the second I found her foot. Her body grew limp in the water, and her eyes…from what I could see through the water, her eyes were as lifeless as her limbs had become. I tugged her close to me and thrust my feet through the water, my boots scraping against the floor as I leveled our heads with the spot where the light was pooling in. The water was too high, and panic set in as my own body began to sink.

I closed my eyes, and for a fleeting moment, I stilled with the thought that my life could end. *This is how I die.* My air magic contended with me, trying to be freed, to fight, to allow more air into my lungs. To give me more time. A reddened glint caught my eyes through the dissipating blood as I forced them open, and Aeden's bracelet pulled me back from a darkness that I didn't want to be consumed by.

I clutched the girl tighter and looked up, forcing as much water magic as I could behind us and propelling us up and through the entrance to the deck. We shot into the air and landed forcefully on the deck, our bodies rolling together as the ropes kept us bound to each other.

I rolled onto my side, coughing up water and taking in air. Salty, thick air that burned as it slid down my throat through my gaping mouth. My eyes flared open as I turned to my other side, seeing a stilled girl. *No, no, no.* Forcing myself up onto my knees, I pressed my ear to her chest and listened, trying to ease my own thumping heart. Then, a smaller, gentler flutter brushed my ear through her ragged clothing.

She's alive.

I pressed and pressed against her ribs, then tilted her chin up and forced air into her lifeless mouth. But after a few rounds, water began to lap at my knees and the girl's heart was weakening more and more.

I let out a ragged exhale and settled my palms over her chest, taking in deep breaths and trying to feel the water beneath her flesh and in her lungs. But deciphering between blood and water was a challenge. Eoghan had tried and tried to teach me over the past few days, probably thinking I'd use it to attack something, but working with another element was more difficult than I'd imagined. He did point out that my emotions would be a big factor, and that drowning in them would wreak havoc on my ability to wield while I was still learning how to cast. Right now, my emotions were so scattered it was dizzying. And the reminder that we were sinking into an ocean with no land in sight only made it worse.

A swell of liquid rested just under my palms beneath her skin, and if I tried to pull it out and ended up bursting an artery, I would cause the girl's death faster than drowning would. But I had no choice. If I couldn't use my air magic, then it would be my only chance to bring her back.

I flexed my fingers and focused entirely on the liquid. I pushed away any conflicts and muted out anything that wasn't her and the water. When I finally grasped it, I drew what I felt out from her lips and cast it to the floor. She choked and her chest heaved like the life had just been punched back into her. For once, I was relieved to see the water around my knees. And the fact that it wasn't a shade of crimson made it all the better.

I pulled her to me, embracing her as she continued to heave up more water. Tears were welling in my eyes at the feeling of her heart beating more heavily through her clothes, and it made my own swell.

"I've got you. I'm here," I whispered, thinking back to the moment I first heard the news about my mother. The air had left my lungs under different circumstances, but having Aeden there with me had made all the difference in bringing me back. Just as I hoped I was doing now for the little girl. I smiled down at her, brushing her hair from her face and looking her over again. *She's alive.* "Can you stand?"

The girl nodded against me and we stood together, my arms taking the brunt of her weight to steady her until she was able to stand on her own.

And then she rushed back into my arms. "We're sinking!" She shivered against me while I fell silent as I looked around. In the distance, a sealed metal door floated above the water with no land beneath it. I didn't know if the Stars somehow knew I couldn't swim, or if it was just a terrible coincidence. Either way, we might as well have been below deck because drowning seemed inevitable.

"Can you swim?" I asked the girl, and to my relief, she nodded again.

The boat rocked again, but the water around us was still. The girl seemed to notice where my eyes were darting, and she whimpered in fear. I gripped the girl's hand and moved us up a set of stairs to the highest part of the deck, positioning us at the very front where water had yet to claim. The boat was rather large and sank too quickly to be from the two holes below. Somewhere else was damaged. Whatever was below the ship cast a large, ominous shadow as it knocked into the boat again, making my legs buckle with the loss of balance. The girl wrapped her arms around my waist, shivering in fear.

I searched both sides of the boat, looking for something to float on, but found nothing. "The water is filling up, Miss. Are we...are we going to die?" The sadness in her eyes pulled on my heart, and then the thought hit me. If I could draw water from the girl, maybe I could draw it from the boat, too.

"I need you to stay here, and hold onto the railing." I got down on my knees while she raced to the railing, just as the thing in the water raked its body against the boat again. Even if she could swim, neither of us would survive whatever beast lay in the water, waiting for us to go overboard.

I braced my hands against the floorboards, feeling the swell of water that filled the vessel and matching its immensity to my own power. The water magic inside of me was weakening, straining under the use I'd put it through, and my limbs were growing tired from exertion. I'd been warned before about becoming drained, knowing it could very well kill me. But I couldn't let that deter me from giving everything I had to lift the sinking ship from the water. The metal door gleamed like a trophy in the distance, and I screamed out as I released as much power as I could feel. Water poured out around the edges of the boat and my arms started to shake with the intensity of the power, consuming every piece of me that I offered to it. I pushed more and more, watching the water recede from the deck and the distance increasing between us and the beast below.

Blackened dots speckled my vision, but I kept pushing until the water was completely drained, then for good measure, I used the last of what I could feel inside of me and encased the bow of the ship with ice, sealing any holes from the outside. I collapsed forward, feeling small hands catch my head just as the sounds of the metal door began to grate open.

"I've got you, Miss."

That was the last thing I heard before the light faded from view, and darkness ate into my vision completely.

THIRTY-FOUR

PAIGE

"**Y**ou really need to stop making this a habit, Princess." I opened my eyes and shot up in my bed, surrounding Eoghan in an embrace as tears rolled down my face. "Easy now, you lost consciousness again. You nearly depleted yourself." He patted my back while I let every emotion from the last trial consume me. I was terrified and felt death closer than I had in the last trial. Closer than I'd ever felt it before. The knowledge that it wasn't over yet crashed into me, and I blinked in confusion as I tried to remember just how I'd gotten out of the second trial.

"How did I—"

"Get out?" Eoghan cut in. He gripped my shoulders and pulled me from him. "Gedeon is furious. He thinks you cheated."

"I didn't use any air magic." *Rule 1.* My thoughts were hazy, but on that one aspect, I was quite certain. I hadn't cheated.

Eoghan shook his head. "Not that. He thinks you accepted aid, breaking rule two."

"But I—" I chewed on my bottom lip. "Who helped?"

"That girl you saved was the daughter of a fisherman. She steered the boat to the door, and dragged you through it, effectively aiding you in completing the trial."

Fuck.

"I didn't ask for her help." I may have blacked out, but I knew I would never ask a child for help in a situation like that. If anything, I'd tell her to swim to safety and leave me behind. I had actually considered it for a few minutes before...before I nearly drained myself. It was all coming back to me now.

A smirk formed on Eoghan's lips and his eyes lit with mischief. "Exactly, Princess. You did not *accept aid,* as is stated in the rules. But Gedeon swears that you broke the rules."

"So, what now?" I looked down at the purple mark swirling along my arm as my chest caved at the thought of everything I'd worked toward being absolutely pointless. Gedeon was ruthless, and if he thought I cheated, then I had no hope of changing his mind. I might as well have the words *guilty* stamped along my marks as well.

"Now, we wait." It was Nya who spoke, stepping in through the door. I raced into her, hugging her like the world would end if I didn't. "You probably shouldn't be standing right now." Nya gave a faint laugh as she hugged me to her tighter than I had. "He will need permission from the other Mora's to label you a cheat in a circumstance like this one. Half of Aellethia thinks you are a hero for saving the girl when it would have been much easier to leave her behind."

The girl's dark green eyes flashed into my mind, and a small smile spread across my face. I wasn't trying to gain approval from anyone in the crowd, but maybe it would help in the final decision. I looked to Eoghan over my shoulder as I let go of Nya, the world around me went hazy for a moment, but I forced it back before I'd get scolded again on standing and scrunched my brows together. "Have you already put in your two cents, then?"

"Oh, yes. I said you're guilty. A cheat, through and through." A wicked grin flashed on his face before I used my air magic to send him backward against the bed, causing a roaring laugh to escape Eoghan. "You really shouldn't be doing that, Princess. Draining yourself is serious. But I'm in your corner as far as the trial goes. You didn't ask for help, and it isn't your fault the girl you saved felt the need to repay you for your efforts."

"Everything will be fine, Paige." Nya wrapped her fingers around my shoulders, sending healing magic throughout my body. "You did deplete yourself quite a bit though, it's amazing that you're already awake after only a few hours. And that move with the ship? That was incredible."

"Your teacher must really know their shit," Eoghan said.

"He's a dick, but he knows a little about water-wielding, I guess." A stream of water poured over my face and I yelped out, laughing and chucking a soggy boot at him with my air magic that he dodged easily as it flew over his shoulder.

I fell into the plush purple chair and Nya stood at the foot of my bed as the laughter died down. Maybe it was the brush with death or the trip out to Prydia that had opened my eyes. But I was finally starting to forgive Eoghan. I couldn't think too much about it, though, because then I'd find another thing about him that would still piss me off.

"Leander Earthborne, that's his name, right? The other Mora?" I asked.

Eoghan and Nya glanced at each other, then nodded in unison. But the grimness spread around the room like a plague as Eoghan spoke up. "He's a bit...off, I've heard. I'm not sure how he will handle the news because I've never actually met him, but I do know one thing."

"What's that?" I asked, pulling my legs to my chest and hugging them there.

"That little girl's mother is from one of the Buryon territories, and she has made it quite clear that you should not be labeled a cheat."

"Really?"

"Well, she fashioned a rather large sign out of vines that read *Save Paige* and spread it over the side of a mountain. Apparently, the whole town helped her. If it were me, I wouldn't be able to ignore that." Eoghan smiled and rubbed at the back of his neck. "He may be a madman, who really knows. But if you had saved my people without knowing where they were from, I would extend the same kindness to you even without knowing who you were."

Nya nodded. "We can only hope to the Stars that Leander has no vendetta against you, as your fa—"

The door burst opened, stealing the words from Nya's lips as my father and Hector stepped into the room. Eoghan sat up on my bed and thrust his shoulders back just as Gedeon raked his eyes over him.

"Lord Eoghan, it would appear that you have a talent for finding your way into the beds of my children."

My eyes flared wide as I released my legs to the floor.

Children? Did he just say—

Eoghan didn't blink, didn't bat a single lash as he stood and adjusted his jacket casually. "Do you have a ruling, then?" The comment had no effect on him. He pushed his hands into his pockets as my mind swirled at the thought of having a sibling to the point where I couldn't care less about the ruling even though it would determine whether I lived or died.

Did I have a brother, or a sister? Were they alive? Were they like him? Did they look like me?

The words dried in my throat as Nya kept her gaze on me while Eoghan refrained from acknowledging my existence. The bastard kept the information from me, and what the fuck was that about being *in bed* with them?

Gedeon's face heated, the redness spreading on his neck making the purple mark that resided there spring to life even more than it usually did against his pale skin.

My father turned to look at me, my jaw falling slack as I gaped at the knowledge that was just put in front of me. He smirked cruelly, knowing he'd just hit a soft spot. "Lord Leander believes that Paige deserves to continue the Triad, seeing as"—he dropped his voice and grumbled under his breath—"she did not explicitly *ask* for aid, as his guard so flatly relayed for him." His reaction to Leander's verdict given by his guard must've been worse until he saw my own reaction to the realization that I'd been lied to. Again. It also must've been enough not to warrant thrusting me against the wall again with his air magic. He'd wounded me enough with what I was just now finding out. *I had a sibling.* I might still have a sibling. Gedeon was sadistic, and hiding everything from me was expected. But when it came to Eoghan, I thought we were past the lies and the hiding.

I guess I was wrong.

A matching smirk tugged at Eoghan's mouth as mine shut, my teeth grinding painfully as I imagined ripping into Eoghan the moment the door slammed shut again. He didn't direct one glance at me, not even as Gedeon pulled him from the room with *business to attend to.* Nya and I were left alone, and it dawned on me—Nya had lived here most of her life.

She cleared her throat and took a seat on the bed, patting the spot beside her and turning a hue that matched the shade of her hair.

"You knew." A statement, not a question.

"Paige, I—"

"You *knew.* You knew I had someone else. I'd been alone most of my life, and it wasn't until"—I peered at the closed door, not wanting to bring up Aeden in the castle knowing Gedeon could be right outside—"I grew up *alone.* And you couldn't mention that I had a sibling with all the time we've spent together? Do I really deserve so little?" I flexed my fingers, digging my nails into the armchair. I was livid. "Oh, and to hear that Eoghan was fucking them? Or is that an ongoing thing? Are they even alive?"

Her cheeks reddened more while she reached up to rub her hand down her face. "Your brother, he um, well, you see..." she bit down on her lip, unsure of what to say next as she stuttered on her words.

Brother.

I let the word sink in as if I were adding it to the swirling power beneath my skin, but it didn't feel quite right.

"What's his name? Can you at least tell me that?"

Some color drained from her face as she softened her look, forming a small smile as she said, "Ikelos."

"Where is *Ikelos?*"

Nya shook her head, and I didn't know if that meant he wasn't alive anymore or if she didn't know, or if she simply couldn't tell me. Either way, it made me even more angry than I thought possible.

"Listen, Nya. If I win this Triad and become your new Mora, do you want me on your bad side?" I glared at her as she thought about it for a moment before shaking her head again.

"Good. Now tell me." I blinked back the rage, subduing my own redness from my eyes as I added, "Please."

"He lives in Hydrasel, with—"

Eoghan sauntered back into the room, patting down the sleeves of his jacket as if he hadn't left on the biggest cliffhanger of my life. He leaned up against the wall across from where I sat and folded a leg over the other like a completely relaxed douche bag.

"Are you kidding me?" I yelled, storming up to him, standing on my toes to give me more height which did nothing in comparison to the vast size difference between us.

"Paige, he—" Nya began, but Eoghan held up his hand to her.

"Wait, let's hear what the princess thinks."

If I were a fire-wielder, Eoghan would be a ball of flames, just like Aeden wanted to do to him the night of the ball. Aeden was trying to protect me it seemed, but I just wanted to blast Eoghan to pieces. I didn't need protection from him, I craved revenge. "You kept *my own brother* a secret from me. How could you?" I slapped him, turning his head a fraction of an inch.

He reached up to rub at his cheek. "Is that all you've got, then?" He was mocking me. Humiliating me. Taking it in and soaking in the fact that he, yet again, held all the cards, and I was a mere player in his game. Another piece to his ever-expanding puzzle.

"Paige, wait!" Nya cried out just as I raised my icy fist. I should've slammed it into his balls, but I angled my fist and held it there, inches from where it could send Eoghan buckling. He had no plans to move. *He was going to let me wail on him.*

I dropped my fist and Nya flicked her wrist, releasing a sigh as the ice turned to liquid and fell to the floor. I made a mental note to ask her how the hell she did that, seeing the value of it from the second trial as a life-or-death necessity.

"Which of you is going to tell me *why* he isn't here?"

"He isn't allowed here. *My guard* isn't allowed back." The words echoed in my brain as I remembered Eoghan letting this information out before, on the night I'd asked him where his guard was. Eoghan's jaw flexed as he looked beyond the room and out through the window.

"So, what then, he just lives with you? And you, you..."

His eyes darted back to meet mine. "I love him." His voice didn't waver, his gaze never shifted. In fact, they lit up at the mention of him. *He really did love him.* I felt the familiar tightness in my chest as I thought about the word, and let it roll through my thoughts. He loved him, like I so blindingly loved Aeden.

Eoghan crossed his arms and the storm that brewed in his dark blue eyes was the same from each of the moments he'd spoken nothing but the truth to me. *My brother was alive. My brother was...is* loved. *My brother. Ikelos.* "If he could be here, he would." He reached down and took my cold hand into his own, then added, "He wants to meet you, but Gedeon won't let him come back."

"Then take me to him. Take me to Hydrasel." A flutter of hope swelled in my chest before it came crashing down as Eoghan shook his head, and then ran his fingers through his golden-blonde hair.

"No can do, Princess. You can't leave. Not until your Triad is over."

I looked over at Nya, who shook her head as well. Seconds passed that felt like minutes. I walked backward, falling into the chair, feeling wholly defeated. I rested my head in my hands, taking in deep breaths.

"So that's it, then? I have more family than that monster out there, but if I can't survive the last trial, I will never know what he's like?" Tears began to form a thin pool over my eyes. I'd lost so much so fast recently and the knowledge that I'd missed out on having a brother was adding a heavier weight to my shoulders that was almost too much to bear.

"He's kind. Selfless. And entirely too smart for his own good." Eoghan released a sigh as a small smile grew. The smile of someone clearly smitten. "He's a bit like you, in that sense."

"Then why did he fail? Why isn't he here right now, ruling in place of Gedeon? I've read about hundreds of Triads and failed attempts. Most end up dead, but you said he was your guard." And I'd just gotten off too easily in the eyes of Gedeon, and even by the man himself as he didn't push me across the room with any of the powers he wielded, and it was placing my suspicions on high alert as my anxiety continued to climb.

"I think he would prefer to tell you about that, after your last trial." More secrets, more things that I wasn't privy to. I rolled my eyes, but knowing my brother was indeed alive and knew about me was enough information for one night. Maybe I didn't need to know the *how* part just yet, and I'd have to accept that and move on from it if I wanted Eoghan to keep talking about him.

Which I did.

THIRTY-FIVE

AEDEN

"Wake your arse up, Lad, ye've got trainin' to do!" Never in a hundred years would I have thought I'd be happy to wake up to a man's voice, but to hear Seamus', I was fucking elated.

Nearly a week had gone by since we'd found Shay and Seamus. We started with backtracking to the places I'd been with them, leaving out the castle for obvious reasons, and starting with the makeshift campground outside of Prydia. Murrie poked around the cold ash from the fire pit Seamus and I made the day of the ball and found a familiarly dark bottle hidden under layers of soot—more soot than we could've made for the short time that it had existed for. That bottle, which couldn't have been there before from when we last used it, led us to the caravan of partying fae, who were going on possibly three weeks, or more, of dancing and drinking and fucking that it almost made me envious of them.

But that wasn't what I was there for. I had someone worth fighting for, and a kingdom of people hiding out that were praying to the Stars for someone like me to exist, as Murrie put it. I wasn't cocky about it—if anything, it scared the shit out of me. But seeing just how inspired Murrie was made my heart swell and gave me a greater sense of purpose than I'd ever could have hoped for.

"Seamus, let the boy sleep. You kept him up all night talking about your glory days. He deserves to be commended." I stretched out and turned over to see Shay and Seamus on the bed of grass and vines I'd made for each of us to sleep on. My earth magic wasn't going to help me much in a fight at this point, not unless the enemy needed to be made comfortable. I could only make things grow so far, and couldn't grasp the concept of using them in any offensive way. Snoring sounds cut short as Murrie leapt up from her deep sleep and grabbed hold of her ax, her chest heaving and eyes wild as she glanced around our rocky campsite.

"Easy lass, no one 'ere will touch a hair on yer little head." Seamus was adjusting his tunic, not even flinching as Murrie's clutch tightened around her ax. He'd be a fool not to fear her, and if I had to pick between the two of them as to who would win in a fight, my bets were solidly on Murrie. Something told me that I might actually see the day, too. They'd been butting heads since we found him and Shay at the revelry, dancing half-naked and drunk off their asses. Seamus coped with alcohol, and Shay liked to get lost in the moment. I knew they were worried about me by the way their faces lit up when we found them, but Murrie gave them the same look she did me when I continuously lied to her in the woods. She was unconvinced.

Her eyes narrowed at Seamus. "Little? Why I—"

"Stop." I sat up from my bed and rubbed at my temples. "Please, just, stop."

"I'm with Aeden. You both are insufferable," Shay said, standing from her spot before she began to undress. It was so common for her ass to be on display that I didn't bother shielding my eyes anymore. She needed to be in the water the moment she woke up, and if she didn't get the chance, she would be cranky. Which explained several days of our previous travel, now that I knew. Seamus explained it to me before, I just didn't fully listen in the cave because everything was so new to me. *She needs to swim. It's in her blood like the fire is in yers and water is in mine. Keeping it in only makes ye go mad.* Shay needed water like I needed to release the fire that continued to build up inside of me. It was as simple as that.

"I'll show him how insufferable I can really be," Murrie mumbled. I threw her a dark look over my shoulder, making her drop the ax to the ground. She folded her arms across her chest while Seamus remained nescient. He still acted blissfully unaware of how mad she became at the mention of her being little, much less hearing Seamus' insistence that I needed to work on how to wield my power every waking hour of the day. Because Murrie found little fault with anything I did or said, and she praised me a bit too much even when I did something that turned out to be a complete disaster. The other day, I'd formed a huge fireball that I accidentally threw too hard into the side of the mountain, sending rocks tumbling down toward us and almost pummeling Shay, had she not jumped from the cliff and dove into the water below. Murrie had clapped and cheered behind me, causing Seamus to tug at his beard furiously as he scowled at her.

Water splashed in the chasm of space below the cliff we were camping on and our horses whinnied from the sound of Shay jumping in, her tail beating hard against the cresting waves. The horses were borrowed, more or less, from unsuspecting fae at an inn on the border of the mountains where The Highlands began. They were discussing Paige's triumph over her second trial, which distracted me momentarily before we walked away with their horses as they remained piss drunk and none the wiser to what we were getting away with.

I'd grown accustomed to walking everywhere in Aellethia, having not seen or heard of any horses, and Seamus relented the reason for it was because the cost for a single horse wasn't obtainable for the average fae anymore, and instead of riding them, people had taken to eating them instead, having minimal to no use for traveling as that was a luxury of its own. Even the wagons I saw in Costa that first full day of being here, I wondered if they ever moved. Now I understood they usually didn't unless someone toted the wagons themselves.

Needless to say, when we found only two horses, I knew I'd be riding bitch on one of them. I may be powerful, or meant to be, and I might even have remnants of a kingdom to put back together, but I also had no prior experience riding a horse. Yet, of course, the former guard did. I had to put up with having Seamus' arms on either side of my waist while my balls...well, they fucking hurt as I adjusted to the bouncing that went along with the movements of the horse.

We'd been trekking through The Highlands and on toward The Fields of Araros like that for days on horseback in search of a dragon that may or may not exist, and at times, it was hard to imagine how my life had come to this.

A *fucking* dragon. As if I knew what to do when, or if, we ever found it.

Murrie began sharpening her blade behind me while Seamus stretched by the cliff's edge, waiting for Shay to let him know to use his water magic to shoot her back up to solid ground. I didn't hesitate in filling them in on where I'd been and what I'd discovered when we found them at the revelry, yet the looks on Shay and Seamus' faces when we discussed my heritage and the possibility of me being a dragon heir was less dramatic than I'd pictured. In fact, they'd assumed who I was when I started accumulating more power, yet hadn't thought to let me in on it. Was I angry? Yes. Abso-fucking-lutely. But I had more important things to focus on than holding a grudge against the few people I could rely on.

"Boyo, give Shay a hand, will ye?" Seamus motioned for me to stand beside him and I joined, happy to use a power that I wasn't completely worthless in. He guided me through how to cup her with the water instead of drowning her in it, which was more complex than I'd imagined. Shay waited below patiently as her chest bobbed in the water, watching me practice on the few fish she'd caught with her net while she took her morning swim. After the fourth fish, Seamus gave me the clear to practice on Shay, but the face she was giving him had me questioning if there were more fish I should practice on. "Don't doubt yerself now. How do ye expect to ride a dragon if ye don't have the balls to lift a mermaid from the water?" He smirked at me, his words intentionally taunting the magic that flowed inside of me just as easily as my lungs took in air.

"Fuck you," I said, and he let out a belly laugh that eased both Shay and I before I attempted it on her.

"You can do it, Aeden! Show that orange-haired troll what you can do!" It was Murrie, the cheerleader, a rock in one hand and her ax in the other, both lifted above her head as she shook them to cheer me on.

Seamus mumbled something under his breath, but as my eyes flicked back to him, he simply pointed at Shay down below. I drew in a deep breath as I glanced at the fish that lay at my feet. I'd attempted something like this before when my magic developed, only I ended up sinking into Lake Kree more before Seamus lifted me out of the water. He'd done it with ease, and I'd almost killed myself.

Seamus cleared his throat while Shay shouted encouragement from the water. I narrowed in on the water magic that rested at the top of my flesh and sent it below in a fish-sized capsule. Seamus covered his mouth with his hand as his cheeks grew red and I could hear Shay's distant voice growing louder as she came up. Her arm was encased in a bubble of water, the rest of her body refusing to dangle as she wrapped her limbs around the encased one like a koala bear to a tree. Seamus burst into laughter as I brought her onto solid ground, and then Shay walked up to him and punched him on the shoulder.

"You could've helped him!" she shouted at Seamus, calling him all sorts of derogatory names that related to his fiery red hair and Murrie burst into laughter behind us, clapping for Shay and for myself as well, although I could've dropped her to her death.

"Sorry, Shay." Perhaps if I hadn't pictured her as a small fish, I would've made a bigger bubble for her entire body.

She softened her features after throwing her last fist at Seamus. "It's not your fault, Aeden." She scowled at Seamus, his cheeks and neck red from laughter that he tried to stifle with his fist.

"I only have a day. *One fucking day* to find this dragon and try to make our plan work. And I can't even wield my power correctly."

The laughter died down and everyone's face grew dim, the red draining from Seamus' face as he spoke. "Aye. True. But ye have us, Aeden." He spread his arms wide, encompassing the campsite. "We won't let ye fail in gettin' yer lass."

"It isn't just about her anymore." My gaze roamed from beyond the chasm to just above the mountains we had yet to traverse. "People survived the Battle of Vizna. *My* people. What will they do if I can't even find my dragon? What if I can't make it to them because it lit me on fire? What do I do then?" Honestly, I had no clue what a dragon could do here, but in the mortal world, fictional dragons breathed fire. And when Murrie dragged her hand down her face, I figured I'd said something wrong.

"Oh, Aeden." Shay walked closer to me and took my hands in hers. "The Mora's of Vizna were *bound* to their dragons from birth. If you do have a dragon out here, it can probably already sense you. You shouldn't be afraid of something that is a part of you."

Seamus nodded behind her, moving to pick up the fish around me and position it above the fire as Murrie, astonishingly, aided him without so much as a glower of disapproval toward him.

Shay's vibrantly blue eyes glistened as she continued. "It's been so long since any of us have seen that type of bond, but I promise you, there is nothing to be afraid of."

Was it really fear that was taking over me? Not in the sense they believed it was. I wasn't *afraid* of a dragon, I was afraid of *failing*. Afraid of never seeing Paige again. Afraid of being the reason for more death and destruction because I couldn't do my part in this world. The burden was growing heavier on my shoulders with each passing day, the weight of two worlds crashing down on me as I struggled to breathe beneath it all.

"What if I don't have a dragon bound to me and we are wasting time looking for something that doesn't exist?"

"It's not a waste to try. It's a waste to never try and fail knowing you could have tried harder." It was Murrie who came up behind me, placing her small hand on my leg. She looked up at me, then pointed to a peak topped with green grass. "That's where dragons have been spotted by my people since the fall of Vizna. *That's* where your dragon will be." She was so certain my mother had upheld the traditions passed through thousands of years of bonding a baby to a dragon, there was no inflection or wavering in her tone as she spoke. She was certain, and it eased the tight knot inside of my chest that twisted with the thoughts of being wrong. Yet the devil on my shoulder spoke louder to confront it.

"What if she dies?" I'd moved on from the dragon, and buried my mind in graphic details of Paige competing in her last trial. She'd be in the arena before the sun could fully rise tomorrow, and it was tearing at me not knowing how she was doing.

"The lass will be fine." Seamus kept his eyes locked on the fish, turning the sticks that speared through them over and over. The fire cast a light against his face that drew out the darkness of his thoughts. He'd known loss, possibly more than the rest of us, yet here he was. Still moving forward, persevering past his loneliness I knew ate at him more than he dared to show. Shay walked over to him and sat beside him, stroking his back while silently allowing him to feel even if he didn't want to.

Even Murrie put aside their differences and didn't call him any names or fight him on belittling my fears as she shuffled in her spot next to the fire. I'd told her about his wife and daughter, trying to edge her on the path of sympathy which only seemed to work at times like this before she was back to bickering with him again. Maybe that was the way she showed him she acknowledged his past, but wouldn't let it hinder his future, just as she did for me.

The Fields of Araros that stretched out below the Araros Peaks were beautiful, the sun casting it in golden hues as it shone directly above us. It was midday, and the field had dozens of horses, thousands of flowers, a few centaurs, and no fucking dragons. I'd felt tingling in my arms and along my marks since entering the field but chalked it up to riding for hours on the back of a horse. Seamus set the horse to a canter, then trotted when we neared taller grass.

"Should we go further?" Shay yelled from the back of the horse she shared with Murrie.

"Ask the li—" Seamus started to yell behind me and I shoved my elbow into his gut for Murrie's sake. "Ask *Murrie*!" Seamus corrected, drawing out her name as he spoke as if he were trying to get used to the feel of it against his mouth.

"Better," I said, and Seamus' chest expanded behind me as he chuckled at my remark. But dammit if Murrie hadn't proven herself more than worthy to have no backlash to her name or who she was. I'd be dead by now if it weren't for her, and he was made well aware of that fact.

"A bit further, I think!" Murries head bobbed as the trotting horse took off into a gallop, leading us through more fields and rolling hills. The peaks were fading behind us until they were hardly visible, then another one grew closer in front of us.

Their horse fell to a trot again, steadying our own, and the tingling grew to an agonizing throb that felt like ropes being tied around every inch of my skin. "Stop!" I shouted, mostly talking to the invisible ropes but halting both the horses swiftly enough that I was flung forward onto the neck of the horse, making it rear up while I held tightly to its mane.

Seamus jumped off before the horse's front hooves hit the ground again. "What in the bleatin' hell is wrong with ye, Aeden? Ye scared poor Misty."

Murrie and Shay slid from the back of their horse as well, but the pain in my arms was like my mark was trying to burn its way through my body, and kept me from following them as I stayed on the horse. "You named the horse?" I asked incredulously, wincing and rubbing at my forearms. Murrie rushed to Misty's side and tugged on my leg, urging me to slide off. I swung my leg over and slid off as Seamus clucked his tongue at me for mistreating his new pet.

"What do you feel, Aeden?" Murrie started to search me over, tugging on my legs until I fell on my knees to the ground, allowing her to look over where the pain was emanating from. "Do you feel it?"

"Feel like I'm being burned from the inside out by some magical rug burn? Yeah." I summoned water over my arms but it slid right off, even as I tried to ice it over.

"Ye okay, Lad?" Seamus patted Misty on the ass, sending her galloping into the taller grass ahead of us. He held his hand out to help me up, but Murrie swatted his arm away.

"Don't touch him," she spat, then her eyes started to search the patchy skies above us. A large shadow cast itself over a stream of thick clouds and Murrie shouted, "Run!"

She whipped her ax from her back and ran into the grasses, and Seamus held a large shield of ice above him and Shay as they ran. But I couldn't move. I felt glued in place, but it wasn't fear that held me down. It was the ropes, spreading to each part of my body before nothing was left to feel other than the sharp burn and tug of them as I fought to get up from the ground.

The shadow raced above me again, and a sharp ringing vibrated in my ears. I could hear the others shouting for me, but the voices of my friends began to die down until all that was left was the high-pitched noise that droned everything else out. My chest started to burn, the growing, darkening shadow narrowing in, closing the distance between myself and whatever was about to attack me. I tried looking up, but my neck and head were being pulled down by the invisible force spreading throughout my body. Seamus ran back out from the grass and started to pull me across the ground, but a loud growl escaped from the sky above, and without knowing what I was doing, I kicked at him until he released me and fell back into the grass. I had no reason to want to stay other than the notion that I should like it was embedded in the very weaving of my veins.

Then, everything fell still. The heat in my chest simmered and fell, the tethers relinquished their hold, and the burning subsided on my arms. I lifted my chin just as the ground shook beneath my knees, the huge shadow shielding my eyes from the sun with its body. Its...very large body, with wings that tucked in against a slick, scaly, red, and golden body, and as the ringing in my ears fell silent, a bold, yet soothing voice replaced it.

I've been waiting for you, Aeden Fireborne.

THIRTY-SIX

PAIGE

G etting Eoghan to talk about my brother was harder than learning how to fight had ever been. With fighting, I could actually gain *something* with the more effort I gave. While questioning Eoghan usually ended in grunts and more wielding lessons, I found that biting my tongue was the only way I would learn about Ikelos. Eoghan would occasionally slip, calling out a similarity between my brother and me, and if I pushed for more, he would shut down. I discovered that Ikelos liked the ocean, preferred a bow and arrow on horseback, and best of all, he despised our father. And that was enough for me to instantly like him.

Nya and Eoghan worked long hours with me, teaching me how to wield air to the best of my ability. To no one's surprise, my father never pitched in his knowledge, even though he was undeniably the best air-wielder alive in all of Aellethia. Eoghan was great, but he couldn't do everything that Gedeon could as well as he could do it. The same went for Eoghan with his water power. Wielding with your original nature would always be the best, and the strongest, choice. Unless, of course, you were stuck to using anything but—like I had been in the last trial.

It would take years for me to be able to wield the kind of power I would need to get rid of Gedeon. If I became Mora, I would have no choice but to let him live in the castle, untouched, as Eoghan had allowed his mother, the previous Mora of Hydrasel. Eoghan kept his mother as an advisor, which told me he either feared her greatly or loved her just as equally. Yet, I couldn't imagine letting Gedeon live if I did win the Triad. I hadn't thought much about it before because my goal had been so centered on merely surviving the Triad and then getting Aeden to go back to the mortal world with me when it was all over.

That had all changed when Eoghan took me to the city, and then later when I discovered I had a sibling in Aellethia. There was no way in hell I'd go back to Jessup now. Aellethia was where I belonged, and the more I passed by the grim wallpaper of dead fire-wielders, the more I believed it was where Aeden belonged, too.

A pawn? No. He isn't a pawn, Princess. He's the whole damn board.

Eoghan snapped his fingers in my face, and as I batted my eyes to clear the thoughts I was having about Aeden, yet again, a cold stream of water fell over my body.

"You're a prick."

"Yeah, I know." He let a cool smile slide across his face.

We practiced for four days and five nights, each time ending the day with only a few hours to allow for rest. Nya and Eoghan were as determined as I was for a new Mora to take over Prydia, and Gedeon was nowhere to be found. It wasn't until the last night before my last trial that Gedeon requested that I, and I alone, would go to the dining hall for breakfast before the last trial began. It ran my anxiety into a frenzy as I wondered why he would need to see me again at all. Certainly letting the arena have its go at me was enough.

Hector didn't dare try to lift me over his shoulder anymore as he retrieved me from the training deck to bring me back to my bedroom. Instead, he communicated with head jerks and grunts, motioning for me to follow him, and I obliged him, but not without a look that told him I could throw him over the ledge or across the room if I wanted to.

I may have put on a good front as the distance he gave me was becoming greater as the days went on, but I knew better. Hector was a guard, which meant he'd proven himself powerful at Sentra and was chosen by a Mora for protection. Hector could easily kill me with brute strength, and the fact that he was a shifter as well gave him the element of surprise if he ever needed it.

I was bone tired every night by the time I made it to my room for the few hours of rest I should've used to do that—rest. And this night was no different. The door closed behind me as Hector left me to my own devices, the slamming of the door ripping through my mind until it settled on what haunted me every time I was alone with my thoughts since the last trial and led me to search the library and all the books I could find about gifts.

Mmm, yes. Your gift is delicious!

It had evaded my thoughts out of necessity during the trial as easily as the water filled the boat before we nearly drowned. But once I was in my room and the rest of the shit happening around me fell by the wayside, I became consumed with the idea of it.

The hag tasted my blood and loved it. Not only because of my power, as I'd learned they searched for the most powerful fae to eat, but because of a gift. A gift I didn't know about, nor had anyone told me about. The only gifts I'd heard of were those of healers, like Nya, and shifters, like Hector.

I wasn't like either of them. But the hag was sure of the taste of a gift within my blood. Perhaps it was lying. Perhaps it was only trying to distract me from winning the trial. But what good would that serve a hag who was chained to a sinking ship?

None.

There were almost a hundred gifts documented and not one of them resonated with anything I had or could do. Maybe my gift was resilience because at this point I was shocked to still be alive, even if that wasn't a gift I'd read about yet.

I laid in bed, fighting my eyes which continued to get heavier and heavier as the minutes went by. One minute, I was holding a book, watching the fire die beneath the blackness of my eyelids. The next minute, I was standing in a large chamber made up of gray stone walls and a faint glowing light that flickered further down, illuminating the furthest parts of the cavernous room. I put my hands out, feeling nothing but warm, humid air. I looked down at my feet and started to inch them forward, not understanding why I was so focused on my movements. But then a figure rushed past me, clad in black from head to toe.

Hector.

And he didn't take notice of me as I stood quite plainly in the middle of the room.

I sucked in a breath, unsure if perhaps he was in too much of a frenzy to notice me, or if maybe I'd become that unimportant to him. Surely, he believed I was going to be dead soon, anyway. Yet, as I inched closer to him, I became certain that he could not see me, even as I waved my arms in front of his face.

Was I dead?

I pinched the skin of my arm, letting out a soft *ouch* as I stood watching what Hector was doing while he fumbled in his pockets.

Nope. Not dead.

Yet.

But if whatever made me invisible to him changed or altered in any way, I would be.

Hector withdrew something small from his pocket, staring at the object for a second as I wedged myself closer, trying not to touch him. Just as I got close enough, he let out a sigh and wiped his brow, then put it back in his pocket. Something fell on the floor behind us and we both jumped at the sound.

"Fuckin' rats," Hector mumbled under his breath as his chest heaved in and out rapidly. I'd never seen him like this, much less hearing him speak so informally that I had to question if Hector had a twin.

Terrified. *Hector...is definitely scared.*

Hector shifted into a childlike form, and as he turned to unknowingly face me, I stared at what he'd become, unable to blink.

He'd turned into a child. But not just any child. It was one of the children from the city that Eoghan and I saw as we stood in front of the place where they killed fire-wielders. I couldn't be quite certain, but the hair, and the eyes...were so...familiar. I reached my hand up to my chest, trying to calm the storm that was begging to be released, and just as he started to walk away from the room and up the stairs, a bright, blinding light came from the same spot I stood, sending Hector backward down the stairs.

"What the fuck!" He shouted, rebounding from the floor to stand as he held a hand to his forehead, scanning the room for the source of the light. I looked around with him but focused on my body as it hummed in satisfaction like a power had just been released. But there was no new mark, and as I continued to scan my body that was shaking uncontrollably, a pair of hands that I felt but didn't see fell on the tops of my shoulders and shook me so hard that the world went black before a faint light and the softness of my bed became a reality again.

"Paige, wake up!" Nya shouted and my eyes flew open wide. She searched my eyes with pure concern, then wiped the hair from my forehead before saying, "Eoghan sent me, he needed to...to tell you..." Her throat bobbed as my own constricted from the dream I was having before. *Was it a dream?* They were starting to become so...real.

My body was still vibrating from the strange glow that erupted before I was jolted back, the one I could have sworn came from *me*. How long could I have been asleep for? I sat upright and rushed to the drapes, drawing them open and shuddering as I saw it was still dark out. If I hadn't missed breakfast with Gedeon, then what was so important?

"He wanted to warn you," she repeated.

"Warn me about what?" I made my way back to the bed, sitting beside her as we turned to face each other. My hands were shaking as I braced them on either side of me, pressing them deep into the cloud-like bed.

She shook her head. "He wasn't clear, but he um..."

"Spit it out, Nya."

"Gedeon is planning something, Paige." She paused, reaching for my hands and taking them into her own. "Something *not* good. Eoghan says Gedeon wants you dead."

I held back an agitated eye-roll. "That isn't exactly *news,* Nya."

"The breakfast, tomorrow"—she chewed at her cheek and checked the door over with her eyes before turning back to me—"He didn't say what, but he'd heard them talking after he left, and..." The sounds of feet approaching down the hall made Nya quiet, but I nodded, taking in my bottom lip and considering what she was saying. He couldn't outright kill me before the trial had a chance to, *could he?*

"Does anyone know you're here?" I whispered, and she nodded, pushing her hair back behind her ear and replacing her stern features with more calm ones. A soft smile conflicted with terror-filled eyes as the door opened and Hector stepped in.

I could feel the blood rushing from my face as I stared back at the guard, a false show of calm as I searched over the man who did not resemble a child at all. Not like he had minutes before in my dream.

It was, after all, just a dream. Wasn't it? Maybe I was still dreaming, even if that pinch seemed real enough.

My fingers dug into the bedsheet as Nya stood up, placed a hand on my shoulder, and lightly kissed the top of my head. "I came to wish you the best of luck, dearest Paige," she whispered as Hector stared her down from across the room. He let out a grunt, prompting Nya to follow him back out, and the room fell into silence once more before I threw my head back against my pillow.

I didn't know whether I should give my trust to Eoghan again or not, but the look on Nya's face was pleading with me to push aside our differences, although vast and full of betrayal on his end, and allow him to help me. To save my life. If one thing was certain though, it was that I trusted him far more than I could ever trust my father. Eoghan was keen on withholding the full truth but did so with the belief that he was helping more than hurting. Yet Gedeon used the truth and weaponized it, aiming to hurt others more than not.

I wasn't surprised he hadn't told Nya what he'd learned, but I didn't have long before I would be sitting in a room with my father again, and with the sounds of feet now pacing beyond my door, I knew sneaking out and finding Eoghan was out of the question.

I took a deep inhale, easing the panic as it ebbed throughout my body, and exhaled it with finality. I had no choice but to trust him again. If I wanted to live or had any hope of doing so, my trust would lie firmly with him.

My fingers were ice-cold as I flexed them against my leather pants. Red tunic sleeves, dyed by using leftover beets I'd taken from one of the meals provided by my father's staff nights ago, hung idly in my vision as I stared down at my feet. The same color that covered Aeden's arm now rested on my own, easing some of the anxiety I had for the day ahead of me.

Nya and one of Gedeon's guards came back a few hours later to escort me, oddly silent as they kept their distance and walked firmly ten paces in front of me, leaving me in near solitude. Hector must have scolded her about the way she came to my room earlier, or maybe it was Gedeon directly. She didn't speak once, or look back in my direction as I dragged my fingertips against the wallpaper, touching body after body after blood-soaked body. Bloodshed. So much of it, as was their fate from that day on. My fate hung in the balance as I edged closer and closer, each step another toward the spine-tingling chill of death as I approached the dining hall.

Anxiety swelled within me, making the room spin at times, but I kept pushing against it until the room stilled again, taking in deep breaths and forcing it back out. I could hear a group of guards murmuring, one of them blatantly taking bets against me as we turned down another hall. I glowered at them even though they didn't report to me and therefore held no allegiance to me.

Yet.

I had to keep my hopes high, or risk failing the last trial due to my own fucking thoughts. I knew I could wield air well enough to win, and my fighting skills were almost on par with Nya as long as a throwing ax or stars or daggers, like the ones stashed in my boots or hidden by my hip, were in at least one of my fists. *Twelve.* That's how many daggers I'd been able to stash away since I first began taking them slowly from the training deck.

I'd have twelve chances at throwing a blade if it were needed. I was terrible with other weapons in comparison.

Nya and the guard made another turn ahead and as I neared the turn as well, I was pulled back by a force of air and thrown into a body. A hand wrapped around to cover my mouth before I could let out a cry, and as I looked up, a knot of tension unraveled from me.

Eoghan.

"Shhh," he whispered as he held a finger to his lips.

"What the hell?" I mouthed, my eyes darting ahead to find the two walking on without me.

"No time to explain. Find Ikelos." He turned me to face him, and just as he did, my eyes fell on his throat as his Adam's apple bobbed hesitantly. In a blur, Eoghan tilted my chin up and pressed a kiss to my lips so fast and hard that I grabbed onto his forearms in retaliation to push him away.

"Gedeon won't be pleased to hear about this, Lord Eoghan." The bold guard had left Nya and returned for me. I took a step back as Eoghan released me, my forehead crinkled in confusion as I stared back at him.

"I was simply stricken by her beauty and wanted her to *remember* me. You may leave." He swatted his hand toward the guard as if he were nothing more than a fly on the wall. His lip curled up as the guard scowled back, and then I was tugged in the other direction as the guard grabbed and pulled on my wrist, moving us both toward the dining hall.

I wiped at my lips as I turned my head over my shoulder and watched Eoghan fade into the darkness of the hall, feeling a tingling sensation where his mouth had touched mine. He bowed slightly, dipping his head, and then tilted it up at the last moment. His glances moved just over the edge of my shoulder and his blue eyes were full of...fear and sadness and...something I couldn't understand before we grew too far apart and his entire frame was engulfed by blackness.

Find Ikelos?

Whatever he meant by that, it was an odd time to bring up, seeing as he'd just *kissed me* and I was about to enter the last trial of the Triad. But Eoghan couldn't have wanted to kiss me. He had declared his love for my brother and something about him told me that he didn't share himself, or my brother, with anyone else.

So why kiss *me* and send me to find my *brother*?

The guard let go of my wrist, his fingers unknowingly so close to Aeden's bracelet that it made my heart leap as he threw me toward Nya, who stood waiting by the entrance to the dining hall.

She kept her eyes low, her auburn hair covering most of her features as she reached for my hand, taking it in both of hers. "Paige, it isn't safe this time to wear the bracelet. Let me hold onto it for you. I promise to keep it safe." Her words scraped a shiver down my back, but as the guard kept his back to us and allowed us privacy, I unclasped the bracelet slowly while she kept her grip on my hand. Her hands were cold and harsh, much like her demeanor had been since she'd come to gather me for the moment that could be our last. I held it out to her, and she paused for a moment before snatching it and stowing it into her pocket and I could've sworn I saw the glimmer of a smirk behind her hair as she lifted her face to meet mine. She jerked her head and motioned for me to enter the room as nerves and unease spread throughout me.

Something is wrong.

I walked with jaded steps into the room where Gedeon sat, waiting for me in the chair that no one else dared to touch. My gaze peeled from Nya over my shoulder as she kept her hand and my bracelet in her pocket, and roamed over the spread of fruits and cheeses, ending on the glass decanter of wine in front of a place setting meant for me.

I gulped and slid into the seat as my anxiety toiled viciously within my stomach. Gedeon had not once offered alcohol of any kind, nor had he ever smiled at me the way that he was right now. His teeth were so startlingly white they were blinding as his fingers steepled under his chin.

The doors clunked shut behind me, and between the smile and the sound, I jolted in my seat. I glanced back and noticed Nya was absent from the room now. I pinched myself under the guise of the table, wincing as my nails dug into my forearm.

Shit. This is real.

The kiss, the coolness of Nya's hands, and the fucking spread of wine and food like a classy meal fit for a princess. It was all making my stomach churn harder and harder.

"Paige, my daughter." My father's grin widened and my eyes turned to slits as his teeth burned into my irises. Or maybe it was the disbelief of his soothing tone that made my gaze turn vicious as if we'd traded places and it was me that was always so wicked. I stared into his gray, lifeless eyes searching for clues, yet he was oblivious to it or ignored it, and continued anyway. "I wanted to raise my glass to you, on this day. The day the Triad comes to a close is a most glorious moment for not only the kingdoms but for history itself." He'd demolished half the history of Vizna from his library, ripping out pages of information. He didn't give a *damn* about history, or the other kingdoms unless it was his own.

I wanted to yell at him, pierce his hand to the table with the small forks laid out near the plate of grapes, or stab his stone-cold eyes out. He didn't care about congratulating me for getting this far. This was a show, but for whom and why, I couldn't put my finger on it.

"Why now?" I questioned as he moved his hand to cup his goblet of wine, which he pulled away from as he mulled over my words.

"You know, you are more like me than you care to acknowledge." His fake, plastered smile turned wicked and revolting, then flushed with anger as he took in the color of my tunic sleeves—red—for the man I loved. For the kingdom he annihilated. For the blood I wouldn't let him see if I lost and died today.

I can't die today. I won't give him that satisfaction.

"That's a lie, I'm nothing like you," I bit back as he pushed his spine into his chair. Rigid, and cold. That's all he ever could be.

"Perhaps." He tapped on his glass with his finger and leaned forward again, trying and failing to ignore the new color of my sleeves. "But it is tradition to entertain the Mora before overthrowing him."

"Is it also tradition to send your own child to grow up in another world and then push them into the Triad without proper training? I don't believe Ikelos endured the same treatment."

His eyebrow lifted. "If your training wasn't *proper*, I suggest you take that up with Eoghan."

Hector entered the room and strutted over to where Gedeon sat. He bent down to whisper into his ear, then slipped something to him under the table. When he was done, Hector winked at me with his dark, obsidian, and soulless eyes while Gedeon locked his eyes on mine. "It would seem your training was enough to warrant a kiss, was it not?"

I assumed the guard alerted Hector, and my hand fell to the spot where a dagger rested against my hip. I wanted to throw it into Hector's chest and end his life, but being that he was Gedeon's right-hand man, that wouldn't do me much good until *after* the trial.

My cheeks heated, but not because of the mention of when Eoghan kissed me, which left nothing for me to feel other than confusion and a severe lack of butterflies and the weird tingling sensation that still buzzed against my lips. Honestly, it had felt as if I'd just kissed my brother, which was sickening in its own right. Instead, the warmth on my face was caused by pure, unfiltered rage at the man who claimed to be my father and his loyal hound. A small storm of wine swirled in our goblets while my mouth turned sour at his implications. Gedeon motioned for Hector to take his leave, and he slipped out of the room after bowing before his Lord.

"Save it for the trial, daughter." He lifted his glass, and I followed suit—whatever was needed to get me the hell out of this room and into the arena. I needed to rip into something, and if it couldn't be him then it would have to be whatever awaited me in the last trial.

I let half the contents of the wineglass slide down my throat and then put the glass back down just as Gedeon did. He looked me over like he had when my air mark formed, the first time I sat in this room, and his jaw twitched.

Now that that's settled.

"I will send my regards to your *not-so-mortal* boy." His grin spread in a twisted fashion like he'd just successfully won another battle as he opened his palm, revealing the shining, golden bracelet. Aeden's.

My stomach hit the floor and I felt like throwing up. *This can't be happening.* Nothing good could come of him knowing about who Aeden was, and that bracelet had just given him what he needed to know. He already knew he was a fire-wielder, but *this?* This meant so much more.

My mind raced as I thought about the odd way that Nya walked ahead of me, keeping her eyes hidden. I should've known it wasn't her. *I'd been tricked by the fucking shifter.*

"All the luck, *dearest Paige.*" His voice warped with the room around us and my head began to throb, but before I could try to stand, or fight with him, or reach for the damn bracelet, a portal formed below my feet and sucked me into the arena.

THIRTY-SEVEN

AEDEN

*V*arasyn.

My dragon's name is Varasyn.

My fucking *dragon.*

Red wings like blood, with a thin, golden overlay flexed out on either side of her and spread just beyond me as I sat in front of the fire I'd cast for us in the open field. There weren't any straggling fae, looming castles with dickhead Moras, or anything that would try to kill us, in sight. I found it peaceful, but I could see why there was nothing around except for fields of greenery and flowers.

Dragons. Dragons had claimed this area for themselves, or maybe just Varasyn herself. She didn't say. She was the only dragon we'd seen so far since she found her way to me, but if any more were to show up, I firmly believed Seamus would shit himself.

He sat hunched and curled up near the fire, or as close as he could safely get before the tremor of his hand that he was trying to mask under his tunic sleeves would become more evident to Murrie and Shay. I was keenly aware of it, mostly because a distinctively female voice came into my mind and tittered as she pointed it out.

"The red-haired one is shaking, do you think he's cold?"

We both knew he wasn't cold. In fact, it was a warm, late summer night, even with the elevation we'd gained. I nearly spit up the water I was drinking but chanced a look at Seamus over my canteen as I covered up another laugh, making Shay lift an eyebrow curiously in my direction. Varasyn spoke through some sort of bond that we had, and her voice crept into my thoughts as if they were my own.

Over the last few hours before nightfall, Murrie had been kind, boisterous, and enthused enough to tell me about the connection we had. Varasyn was using that time to stand her ground, letting loose several snarls toward Seamus and Shay whenever they got too close to me. Shay wasn't nearly as afraid of Varasyn as Seamus was, or she put up a better front than he did. Murrie, on the other hand, gained Varasyn's trust the minute she bowed down to her—just like she did to me back in the forest.

I was told that our bond was set through a sacred ritual that the Moras of Vizna had done traditionally for thousands of years. Once a baby was born to a Mora, an egg would be given to the parents and then the ritual would begin to unite the two before the dragon hatched. Once the dragon did hatch, the bond was sealed for eternity. She would always be mine, and from the moment I met her, I knew I never wanted it any other way. Having her close filled a void in my chest that I never knew existed. The only person who ever filled an emptiness similar was...

"Paige."

Varasyn said her name to me as if she could feel the pain and suffering it caused me even with Varasyn and I reunited.

I nodded my head and tipped the canteen back again, and Varasyn responded by cocking her head to the side and bending her neck down toward me. She was huge, although I had no other experiences with dragons before. It was hard to imagine one more massive than her, but Murrie assured me she may get bigger with age seeing as she was just as old as I was. The way Seamus' eyes grew at the mention of her getting any bigger made Murrie more agitated with him. She was knowledgeable about many niches of history that would help us, whereas Seamus was more lackadaisical toward history and knew more about women, and power. But Murrie couldn't train me to wield better, and Seamus and Shay had become the only other friends I had. I needed all of them, and I didn't try to hide that I *wanted* all of them with me as well. It was more than the way they'd proven their loyalty to me—they were my family, something I'd never had before.

"It's her birthday tomorrow," I said to Varasyn without the use of our bond. I was adjusting to the concept that I could direct my thoughts toward her, allowing more private conversations to remain just that. But I also didn't care if the others heard me.

Seamus' head lifted and his hand stilled briefly before I heard a low snarl escape Varasyn. He gulped audibly, his eyes darting between the two of us before he tamped down his fear again to respond to me. "What's that, Lad? Whose birth—ow!"

"Shut up, you big, bearded lug! Whose birthday do you think?" Shay motioned toward the path we walked from, beyond the mountains, and I knew she was gesturing toward Prydia as well. Even without me swooning so fucking hard every time we discussed her, it was pretty obvious who the *she* was, seeing as how the Triad had to conclude on the contender's twentieth birthday. I doubted even Paige knew that when I saw her last, and when Seamus finally told me that, I wanted to tackle him to the ground. If I'd known that before the ball, I would've...I don't know what I would've done differently.

"Ah. Right." Seamus rubbed the back of his neck as he looked down toward the ground, then peeled his eyes away and landed them back on me. "She'll win it, Lad. If she's like ye, I know in me heart she'll make it out ali—"

Shay smacked him again on his arm and Varasyn huffed a steamy cloud out through her nostrils, evidently not as entertained by all of this as I was. It was like Seamus had gone completely blank with fear and had forgotten everything we'd been working toward over these past few days. If Seamus weren't being directed to stay behind, I'd be concerned that he would be the downfall of the plan. How he was once a guard for Gedeon made me question the sanity of the Mora of Prydia even more.

My lips curved up as I looked up and over to my dragon by my side, having her to thank for everything that we were about to do the next day. And she was more than up to the challenge.

"We will get her. Together."

Murrie dug into her satchel, the handle of her ax bobbing against her head as she rummaged deeper, then let out a sigh of relief as she pulled out several bottles, roots, and leaves. One of those bottles held the clear liquid she had added to a mix before, and that potion had healed me so well, it would put the hospitals of the mortal world out of business. If Murrie were fae, she would probably have the gift to heal others, something Seamus said was rare and well sought-after. Fae that had the gift to heal used their magic and was therefore faster than waiting on mixes and brews. It was also more effective in keeping someone alive who was on the brink of death.

"What are you making?" I asked, mostly curious but also trying to keep my mind from racing as we prepared for what tomorrow would bring.

Murrie looked up at me slowly, pulling her eyes away from her hands as she shuffled the bottles around, seeming to take inventory before I interrupted her train of thought. "Things to heal, stop the poison from spreading, maybe one for sleep? Although, I would hate for you to get that one confused with, oh wait—" She scratched at her head for a moment, then muttered nonsense to herself and let it trail until nothing made much sense that came from her mouth. Seamus and Shay looked at each other worriedly, then both flashed fake grins back at me.

"We are so fucked," I said more to myself, but I didn't know how to stop my thoughts from being heard by Varasyn yet.

Varasyn nudged into my back. *"Let them sort it out. You need to practice before we run out of time."*

I dragged my knuckles across my jaw, looking up at the thousands of stars in the sky. It was easy to see why the fae believed the stars were behind every choice as they shone their mockery down onto us. The Stars knew what was waiting for Paige in the last trial as the entire arena was crafted by the Stars themselves. Whether they held all the cards in their hands was another question entirely.

Varasyn nudged into my back again, more forcefully this time, and I used the push she gave to roll up onto my feet. Despite having three sets of eyes on me and an eerie silence falling over us all, I moved to where Varasyn guided me through our bond. Without saying a word, I got into position, holding onto her with everything I could as we set off to fly among the divine stars.

PAIGE

The arena took my breath away as I slammed into its compact dirt. My back stayed plastered to the ground as if I were frozen to the spot, set in place by the pain ricocheting throughout my body. The dim light of the growing sun blurred my vision. Or so I thought.

The crowd roared to life as I pushed hard against the ground until I was able to sit up. I continued to rub my eyes, waiting for the blur of gray globs all around me to form more distinctive shapes. But it was more than my vision. Something was off, and the remnants of sweet floral wine turned sour in my throat.

A clattering sound like chains and metal and something rough crashed nearby and I stumbled up onto my feet just as my vision started to settle on the objects around me. Dozens of men made of stone, frozen in place and wielding a variety of weapons, surrounded me, coming within mere feet from me as they started moving. Inch by inch, they all began reaching for the weapons strapped to their backs or sides as if they were all puppets tied to the same string with one goal.

My first instinct was to reach for a blade, or several, and start throwing them. But these men were stone. The only weapon of value I could use was my air magic.

I braced my leg back as one of the statues edged their stone elbow back enough to grab their metal sword, and within seconds the blade flared to life in a red glow.

Bonded swords?

I looked around, using the slowness of the stone men to my advantage to take note of each of their weapons, coming to life with the same glowing color and something in my heart twinged but I couldn't make out for the life of me *why*. A ring of fire blazed around the formation of men, caging us in a circle and forcing me to call on my magic, quickly.

I held up my palms toward the nearest man, forming a ball of air the size of his body and unleashing it with another gust of wind behind it. The launched orb took out a row of five or six men, their bodies crumbling under the force of my power. I continued in a circle, forming large orbs and sending them hurdling into more and more stone men. But as I moved with my back to the first set I'd knocked down, an ominous rattling sound filled my ears.

I whipped around, my jaw falling slack as the men were mending themselves back together as if the strings of the puppeteer were being tightened to solidify them again.

Fuck.

A stone foot stomped to my side before a sword crashed down to the dirt in front of me. I stumbled back, falling into the newly made pile of broken stone men, and the circle of fire that kept me from darting away doubled in height as if in response to my use of power.

The voice of fae screaming and cheering rang out throughout the arena, and before I could stand, most of the men had reformed and gained a hold on their weapons except for the line I'd last taken down. But the bits of stone wriggling under my fingers as they bit into the dirt told me that it wouldn't be much longer until they were whole again as well.

My eyes flashed to the sealed door beyond the rising wall of fire, my mind screaming that I should avoid the inferno at all costs but something else lingered there as well. I felt like I was reaching for a thought, a memory, that kept slipping from me. I ignored the feeling in my chest and ran toward the flames, avoiding the reconstructed stone men as they slammed their weapons into the dirt, trying to knock me to the ground.

A flail swung rigidly with a force I didn't want to collide with my head as I came closer and closer before I fell and slid across the dirt, sending up a cloud of dust. I lifted my forearm to shield myself, simultaneously reaching for the only power I could use in the last trial. Horror struck me as it felt absent, dormant. Like it hadn't ever existed, feeling only water swirling violently and consuming every part of me.

What the—

A pair of small axes swung down, crossing over my throat, holding me in place against the ground I was sliding on as another weapon aimed for my legs. I curled up my hips, kicking up at the arms of the stone man holding the sword. The fire-bonded sword knocked to the ground and the red glow faded into the dust as a pair of stone arms cracked from the force of my kick. My hands shot up to yank on one of the axes, shimmying it to free it from the ground and taking it up in my hands as I got to my feet again. I took off sprinting, dodging more burning weapons as mine remained a metallic hue, the sun, and fire from the ring glinting off of it as I got closer and closer to the flames blocking me from the stone bodies.

I turned and tried my magic again, but reaching for it was impossible, as if a shield were placed over it entirely and left no access for me. My father...

I took one second to look over my shoulder, scanning the crowd in the arena for the man who sired me, my eyes landing on him as he sat in a secluded section laden with gold, elevated like the king he was. He smirked at me, lifting a glass of wine to his lips, then raising it out toward me as he winked.

The wine.

He drugged the wine.

I froze, giving just enough time for a dagger to rip through the air. The blade landed firmly in the front of my shoulder, inches away from being fatal. Inches from my heart and arteries. *Fuck.* The crowd went wild as I screamed out in pain. *If you pull it out, only more blood will come.* Eoghan's words from the training deck flashed in my head, urging me to keep the blade in place to avoid possible blood loss. I covered my shoulder, applying pressure with my hand as I took off running until I was closer to the side where my father sat.

The flames danced in front of my face as my eyes settled on Eoghan a few seats down from him and the fae in the stands jumped up from their seats and leaned in, loving the close distance I was putting between myself and them, but taking no notice as to whom I was staring at. His eyes were wide with fear, darting up to the sky before landing on me again. His clasped hands separated and his index finger pointed to the sky.

But the stars had put me here, so why, in all of Aellethia, would I ever begin to *pray* that *they* would save *me*?

Another sword slashed down, narrowly missing the backside of my leg before I took off running again, using the fire as a guide as I stayed dangerously close to it. I wanted to chance one last look away from the men trying to kill me, their feet lifting and slamming into the dirt. They'd proven to be lethal enough with the sheer force they exerted and the number of them, and taking that risk, moving my eyes from them again could end my life.

I pressed harder against my skin where the dagger jutted out from, trying to ease the stream of blood that was seeping into my tunic and pooling against the inside of my corset, the warm liquid a terrifying indicator of what I was starting to feel.

I was going to die.

I couldn't get beyond the fire without my air magic to separate it while I crossed, and I couldn't use another element without being labeled a cheat, allowing Gedeon the pleasure of ending my life rather than these stone men and the stars above who'd sent them. I fell to my knees, taking the hilt of two daggers into my palms. I was put here to fight, and fuck if I wasn't going to fight until my last dying breath.

THIRTY-NINE

AEDEN

We were flying as fast as we could, the mountains far behind us and the grass and trees far below us. The sun was lifting parallel to where we were in the sky and my heart started to sink, along with the dipping sensation in my stomach every time Varasyn changed our elevation.

"We aren't going to make it," I said as my thoughts hung on only one thing. Her. It was always her, and it would always *be* her.

"Nonsense." Her wings beat faster, then she tucked them in and tilted her long neck down. My ass lifted from the saddle I'd made from vines and my stomach rose to my throat, pulling a yell from me as Varasyn laughed. *"Don't question my speed again, Aeden."*

The vines tugged at my feet and legs, holding them in place until she spread her wings wide again and leveled us out.

"Noted."

In the distance, the terrain turned from lush to barren desert with shadows of mounded sand casting darkness as the sun continued to rise. *"How does she know where we are supposed to go?"* It was more of a thought but turned into me questioning my dragon, yet again, as I struggled to keep my thoughts from her over our bond.

She huffed as if she were annoyed and I braced myself for another steep descent that didn't come. Thankfully. If I thought it was hard adjusting to riding a horse, riding a dragon was another thing entirely. *"I wasn't always secluded to the fields, just as you weren't always stuck in the mortal realm."*

Fair enough. I didn't want to aggravate her more or question her further until after we'd successfully rescued Paige. If I managed to piss off the only means of escape we had, who knows if she'd come back for me. Taking Paige from the arena wasn't going to be a walk in the park. I knew it, Seamus and Shay and Murrie, who'd all stayed behind on my orders, knew it, and Varasyn abhorrently rejected the idea altogether. It didn't take long to turn her to see it from my side, and I had the bond to thank for that.

"You are risking your life for this girl. She better be wor—"

"She is." Everything inside of me told me this was a good plan, it was the *only* plan, but as the view of a giant stone oval came into view in the middle of a fucking desert, even I had to question my sanity. Briefly. *"Without her, I won't become the leader you all need me to be."* Without her, I am nothing. She is everything.

"You were born *to lead, Aeden. But if you insist."* Varasyn tucked her wings in again, and the lack of notice she gave me as my ass rose above the saddle while she dove down told me she wasn't happy about my motives.

But I was.

The arena was left open to the sky by design, allowing the stars to view the spectacle for themselves, and would be instrumental in rescuing Paige from finishing her Triad. After all, she may believe she could claim Prydia by beating what the Stars had laid out for her, as she rightfully should inherit. But I knew by the look on her father's face at the ball that night that nothing she did would ever give her the title she deserved. He'd find some way to end her life the moment she came out of the trial, of that, I was certain. And until we could find a way to beat him together, Paige would have no chance at turning it all around.

She may be angry at me for taking her chances from her and might see it as me not trusting in her abilities, which wasn't the case at all. She could probably take me down with all the training she'd gone through to be able to fight her way through two trials so far, one of which explicitly did not allow the use of magic. But fuck if I was going to let her die at the hands of her father, let alone anyone.

I was doing this for love, and to give her a *real* chance to take Prydia.

She would understand.

Varasyn huffed, her neck vibrating as she growled. Individual bodies of fae were coming into view, and even the gusts of wind that were whooshing by as we descended more couldn't block out the roar from the crowd as they stood and cheered, eyes fixed on the center of the arena and the ground.

The time for hesitating, for turning back, was long over. We were so close, yet all eyes stayed trained on the figures in the arena. The pit in my stomach started to knot as I saw a figure I knew right away was Paige running along a ring of fire, and nearly a hundred other figures holding red, glowing weapons I'd assumed were on fire, in their hands as they approached her. But they couldn't be fire-wielders, *could they?*

The center came into view as I stood up from my saddle, not giving a fuck to brace for impact as I saw Paige fall to her knees. I flicked my wrist and undid the vines that kept me leashed to the saddle.

"Paige!" I yelled as Varasyn's wings bowed out, and I jumped from her back, landing in the middle of Paige's trial.

Fae were shouting and screaming from their places in the stands, but all I could focus on was her, clutching onto two daggers while the hilt of one stuck out from her fucking shoulder.

No. She can't be dying.

"I'll fend them off!" Varasyn shouted through our bond, whipping her tail out furiously at the statues of men who were moving through some force of magic I couldn't comprehend. I ducked my head as her tail whipped above where I landed, taking out so many of the stone soldiers that pieces of rubble went flying all around me and dust filled the air. I forced myself up, not feeling anything but the desperate need to get to Paige, to get her back to Varasyn and fly us far away from here.

The dust settled and her head craned to look toward me. A deep groove formed between her brows while she held onto her shoulder and the dagger that stayed in place. The pain in her face tore at me, making me run faster toward her. Varasyn slammed her tail down again, and more shouts and screams filled the arena. I slid against the ground before a mace could smash my head in, and turned back to find Varasyn.

"I need more coverage over here!" I shouted to Varasyn, who lifted into the air and charged down on more of them in response.

"I'm doing what I can! Get her and let's go!"

I was paces from her, closing the distance as fast as I could move and dodging the weapons that were cutting into the air to stop me, but she held my eyes like she was...confused. She raised her daggers toward me. "Stop!" she cried out over the mayhem that was happening behind me, the fire blazing high behind her. I looked over my shoulder, then turned my head back to her, searching over the place where the dagger was lodged and to her lips that trembled in fear. *She was still here, still fighting.*

"I'm here for you, Paige. We need to go!" I yelled, holding my hand out for her and closing the distance as much as I could before she shouted again, stopping me in my tracks.

There were hardly any stone men left that weren't in pieces scattered along the dirt. Varasyn had continued smashing them down until they were nothing but a layer of gray dust, which took out portions of the wall of fire, smothering the flames. Yet Paige was shouting for something, *someone* to stop.

Her fucking father's eyes drew my attention as a gust of wind lifted my chin to him. His cocky grin spread faster than the stone men were falling, but he didn't bother using his power to fight me from where he stood above. I formed a ball of flames, not giving a shit who saw what I was capable of because the dragon had certainly given all of that away anyway, and threw it toward him in the stands, which took out a few seats and a chunk of stone wall, but not him or the guard standing beside him.

Paige recoiled in the dirt, scooting herself backward, closer to the wall of fire, and holding up her hands.

"Come any closer, and this goes right to your throat." She snarled, switching from holding onto the hilt and moving to pinch the tip of the blade.

"Paige, I—" I tried to get out, then darted my eyes back to where her father stood, finding it empty. Most of the arena had vacated the premises, and if they were still here, they were running and toppling over one another in absolute fear.

"Hurry!" Varasyn began approaching from behind, and I tossed my head over my shoulder, then back to Paige.

Of course, she's scared of the dragon.

"Listen, Paige, we have to—" I held my arms out to her again just as a dagger flew by, seemingly aimed for my neck, before I ducked to dodge it. The tip ended close to Varasyn, who let out a loud growl and snapped her teeth. I didn't need to hear through our bond that she was not going to get along well with Paige after that threat.

"How do you know my name?" Paige questioned, not paying any attention to the dragon behind me anymore. Varasyn would have to forgive her.

"Of course, I know your name, Paige!" My palm flared across my chest. "I'm Aeden. You *know* me. Remember?" I let a faint smile spread over my face, waiting for her to drop the act or remember who I was. Perhaps she hit her head? I knew my stubble had turned into more of a short beard, and perhaps I looked more worn and rugged, but surely she knew who I was. It hadn't been that long ago since she'd seen me. This was beyond her wanting or not wanting me. It was like her memory...

She didn't appear to have a head wound. No. This was much worse than that. "What did he do to you?" I curled my fingers into fists which she noticed and threatened another dagger my way after moving it to her uninjured arm. She lifted it, but before she had the chance to try to kill me again, I whipped my wrist to form vines around her hands and legs. She wriggled and pulled, wincing each time she strained where her injury was.

"Untie me!" A blast of ice knocked me to the ground as she managed to maneuver her wrist beyond her ties, forcing me to bind her further as I stood up again, covering her hands with vines until nothing but the tips of her fingers were visible.

A huff of hot air rolled down my spine as Varasyn stopped to stand behind me. *"This is the girl?"* she asked incredulously, snapping her teeth at her and releasing a snarl.

"Relax," I said aloud so Paige could hear me, and Varasyn's lips stopped curling, but not by much.

"If you plan to kill me, then just do it!" Paige snapped at me, and my heart shattered as her face went from confusion and fear to downright hatred.

She fucking *hates me.*

"Whatever he did to you, Paige, I'll fix it." I ran my fingers through my hair, then leaned down to scoop her into my arms. She fought back as much as she could, but her small frame fell still as she watched Varasyn lower her neck. "I'm *not* getting on," she grumbled under her breath as she started to flail again, her back bowing in a way that made it difficult to hold on to her.

"Cut it out. I'm trying to *help* you." I paused at the tip of Varasyn's wings, looking down at Paige as she writhed in my arms. The color of her tunic reminded me of the fire on my arms and a lick of pride ran through my veins as I took in the patchy dye with areas where the red was more light, almost pink, that spread from her sleeves to just beneath her corset as she kept writhing in my hands. It was a complete contrast to the purple that was customary for Prydia, or the white the tunic must've been before. She'd done this herself. *For me?*

"You are going to hurt yourself more than you are hurting me." Physically, that was true. That dagger in her shoulder had to fucking hurt and she was making it bleed more and more by moving so much, although the red covered the blood in some areas, it wasn't deep enough to make it unnoticeable this close-up. Emotionally, however, I was destroyed. She froze, her eyes flaring as she looked at something behind us and before I could turn, arrows started flying into the arena.

Fucking guards. It wasn't enough making her forget me, he had to send guards to end us both.

"Now!" Varasyn cried out, and I took advantage of the distraction, rushing up to Varasyn's neck and securing both of us with vines. We were up and flying above the stadium in seconds. The guard's magic was whipping through the air in an almost annoying way, sending small bursts of air magic at us and trying to deter our path. But they were up against a fucking dragon. They had no chance with what small amount of power they held against us as we flew further and further away.

"Can you let go of me already?" She was trying to disguise the amount of pain she was in by trying to pick a fight with me, and I had to wonder what *he'd done* to her to make her look at me like that. The most beautiful, striking girl I'd ever seen, the same remarkable emerald eyes jaded over with her newfound loathing of me. I cocked my head over the edge of Varasyn, raising my brow at her as I held her tightly in my hands and over my lap.

"You sure about that?" I said, trying not to sound like a total dick, but fuck it. She already hated me somehow, how much worse could it be? I silently hoped for a cure, something Murrie could make us back at camp, but Varasyn shook her head as she careened around a small valley.

"I hope for your sake, she comes back. If she doesn't and she tries to hurl another dagger at yo—"

"She will remember me, Varasyn. She just needs time."

She huffed and her neck expanded before she banked to our right, curving above a stream. *"You put too much faith in her."*

"You don't know her," I gritted through my teeth, and Paige nudged against me trying to loosen my grip again.

"You don't know *me* either," Paige mumbled in response.

My fingers curled around the edges of her thigh and her upper arm gently as I bent down to whisper in her ear, "I *love* you. And I believe *you* love *me* too."

I lifted my shoulders and drew back from her as she scoffed, glancing around at the empty valleys and the mountains that we were about to fly over. I squeezed onto her but didn't meet her eyes, not wanting to see the hate that filled them and the tension that she held onto as she continued to turn her head to look down, probably calculating how she could get away from me the second we landed if she would wait that long. She was fucking brave, and I wouldn't put it past her to try to jump from the back of a dragon and try her powers again if she got the chance, even with her hands and ankles bound.

I took in a deep breath, knowing whatever lay ahead of this day, we would be fighting for the future of our kingdoms, and *I* would be fighting for *her*.

"*I won't let her forget how much she means to me. Not ever.*"

ACKNOWLEDGEMENTS

I want to start off by saying thank you to my family—there's a lot of you, but you have all been so kind and thoughtful and supportive during my whim of an adventure that has been writing. With more books down the road, it will *eventually* seem less chaotic, I hope.

To my beta readers, thank you for your feedback and your love for each of my characters and my writing. It truly helps to have people in your corner, but even more so when those people can be critical of you at times and push you to grow. I will forever be grateful for you all dealing with my over-bearing questions—the what-ifs, and whether or not you found the magical time in your already busy lives to read the chapters I sent over. Thank you so much for finding that time and for not yelling at me every day I'd call asking for an update. You are the real MVP's.

To my ARC readers, thank you so so so much for signing up to join me on this writing journey. I am amazed at the amount of love this book has already garnered, and can not wait to expand on that throughout the series.

Finally, to you all. The readers. I know your endless TBR's are already bursting at the seams, but somehow you managed to pull this book out and start reading it and I am SO GLAD you did. Like, truly madly deeply GLAD and happy and elated and...all the words. You are magnificent. And you are so appreciated.

About the Author

Elsa lives with her family in Florida, where it's usually too hot to do anything other than stay inside and read or write. Born in Iceland, the land of fire and ice and way too many tall descendants of Vikings, Elsa loves the idea of strong lead characters who fight (sometimes in more ways than one) for who they are or who they want to be (or be with).

Though never an avid reader until she hit her motherhood era, Elsa took to writing just as quickly as she did to reading, with genres heavily favored in romance/fantasy and contemporary romance.

You can find more from E.S. Portman here:

Author's Website:
https://www.authoresportman.com/
Instagram:
https://www.instagram.com/esportman.author/

Leave a review, if you can! Reviews help indie authors so much!
Goodreads:
https://www.goodreads.com/esportmanauthor